NIKKI COPLESTON is the author of four previou
detective Jeff Lincoln. Her stories have won a
Literary Festival and Frome Festival Short Story (
active member of Frome Writers' Collective.

After a career in local government in Lond
in 2012 to write full time.

A keen photographer, Nikki takes her inspiration from the landscape
of the West Country, although her novels reveal the darker side of life in
rural towns and the countryside. She lives in Wells with husband John and
Harvey the cat.

For more information, go to her website at www.nikkicopleston.com.

ALSO BY NIKKI COPLESTON

THE DI JEFF LINCOLN SERIES

The Price of Silence
A Saintly Grave Disturbed
The Shame of Innocence
The Promise of Salvation

NIKKI COPLESTON

A STRANGE AND MURDEROUS AIR

A JEFF LINCOLN NOVEL

SilverWood

Published in 2023 by SilverWood Books
for Silver Crow (www.silvercrowbooks.co.uk)

SilverWood Books Ltd
14 Small Street, Bristol, BS1 1DE, United Kingdom
www.silverwoodbooks.co.uk

ISBN 978-1-80042-265-0 (paperback)
Also available as an ebook

British Library Cataloguing in Publication Data
A CIP catalogue record for this book is available from the British Library

Page design and typesetting by SilverWood Books

To Catharine Lake, wherever you are

CHAPTER 1

'Come on Kate, where are you? You're not usually late.'

From the bay window of her terraced house, Jill Fortune checked the street one more time. The pavement was empty. Where had Kate got to? If she'd been held up, she'd have phoned, surely? No, it didn't look as if she was coming for her lesson today.

A black Vauxhall Astra sat across from the house, driver at the wheel, something vaguely familiar about his face but – no, Kate always arrived on foot, straight from school.

Jill let the heavy curtain drop back. She wasn't surprised that Kate had skipped today's piano lesson. The way she'd stumbled through the Mozart last time, her fingers moving clumsily across the keys, it was obvious she hadn't been practising. At nearly fifteen, she'd reached the age when so many students gave up, when GCSEs or falling in love took priority. Jill's own daughter, Annika, had been just the same.

She rang Kate's mobile, but it went to voicemail.

'It's Mrs Fortune,' she said, trying to keep her tone light. 'Just wondering where you are. Call me when you get this message, Kate, or text me.'

Once the summer term ended in a week or two, Kate Amos would probably cast away her Mozart and Bach for ever. Which would be a shame.

Jill returned to the kitchen, where afternoon sun streamed in over the big pine table.

'Oh Finzi, you can't lie there.' She gave the tabby cat a gentle push, but he stayed where he was, stretched out across a corner of the table, toasting himself.

She glanced at the clock. Twenty past four. Kate was twenty minutes late. Should she phone Trish, the girl's mother? She'd still be at work at the library though, so what was the point? Instead, she went on sorting through the pile of papers she'd brought downstairs from the box room.

Why had she still got all this stuff? Out-of-date exam timetables, concert programmes, brochures for holidays she never took, evening classes for which she never enrolled. All of it could be thrown away.

But there – *that* was what she was looking for! A scuffed folder with *Ministry of Defence* printed on the front. Inside was a short report with a letter stapled to it. Ramsay would be so pleased to see this.

Since Kate hadn't turned up, she could go and see her old friend Ramsay Keiller now, show him what she'd found. She slipped the report and letter into an envelope, grabbed her bright purple purse – a jokey present from Annika – and locked up. It wouldn't take long to cycle up to his farm shop, Keiller's Yard.

One last look up and down the street. An Openreach van was parked by the junction box on the corner with an engineer squatting on a camp stool in front of a cat's cradle of wires. Across the street, outside number seventeen, the black Astra still sat with the window wound down, although she couldn't really see the driver's face.

She set off on her bike for Keiller's Yard, a mile or so away, where the town of Barbury met the countryside on the edge of the sweeping Wiltshire downs. As she cycled past the unfamiliar black car, the driver's window slid silently closed.

CHAPTER 2

TUESDAY 4 JULY 2017

At Barley Lane police station, Detective Inspector Jeff Lincoln made himself a mug of sweet black coffee and took it back to his desk. He needed caffeine to kickstart his brain in the mornings, especially when he'd got paperwork to finish. As soon as DCI Claire Connors had taken over as his line manager in April, he'd tried to clear his backlog. Not to impress her – Connors wasn't the impressionable type – but because he was tired of playing catch-up, of never being able to find what he was looking for in any of his in trays.

But, of course, the road to hell is paved with good intentions.

At the next desk, his sergeant, DS Mike Woods, was already halfway through his first cup of tea. DC Graham Dilke was sorting out a paper jam in the printer.

'No Breezy?' Lincoln nodded across to the chair usually occupied by DC Dennis Breeze. It was conspicuously empty, although his desk was its familiar muddle of unread memos and at least one back issue of the *Daily Mail*.

'Reckon he's still recovering from the weekend. He was going to his cousin's wedding, wasn't he? Some posh hotel near Devizes? He'll probably roll in a bit later.'

'Don't they say the bigger the wedding, the shorter the marriage?'

Woody looked hurt. 'That doesn't always follow. Suki and I had a big wedding and we're still going strong.'

'He's had Monday to recover, so where is he today?'

The door opened and Pam Smyth raced in, unbuckling her cycle helmet on the way. She ruffled her hair back into shape.

'Morning, boss. Morning, Sarge. No Breezy?'

They all looked towards the empty chair, canted backwards on its pedestal through being continually tilted by the bulky Breeze.

'He had a wedding,' Lincoln reminded her. 'Somewhere near Devizes.'

'Oh yes, his cousin got married again. Third time lucky, he said.' As she pulled her chair out and switched her screen on, the phone rang and she picked it up. 'Barley Lane police station. How can we help? A car abandoned where? When?'

'We don't do abandoned cars,' Lincoln muttered at his screen. 'That's the council's job.'

'Right, thanks for letting us know.' She put the phone down. 'A Land Rover's been found abandoned in a field gate on Hangman's Lane off the A345, near Turnpike Corner Airfield.'

'We don't do abandoned cars,' Lincoln said again.

She ran her hands through her short blonde hair, her eyes bright. 'This one's got a dead body in it.'

'So what do we know?' Woody asked as he and Lincoln left Barley Lane. 'And why are *we* dealing with it, and not Park Street?'

'Don't look a gift horse in the mouth. If DCI Connors wants me to be Senior Investigator instead of someone from her Park Street team, I'm not going to argue.'

'If Barley Lane's going to close…'

'It's closing, Woody. There's no *if* about it. The building's already up for sale.'

'We won't all fit into Park Street, though, will we?'

'Let's not worry about that now. Come on, we've got a suspicious death to investigate.'

They drove north out of Barbury, through the trailing ribbon of prestigious 1930s houses that had once looked out across open fields. Now, those houses enjoyed the view of yet another private estate sprawling over the undulating landscape of Barbury Down. The whole valley would be filled with houses before long.

As they drove, Lincoln relayed what little Connors had told him.

'A farm worker found a Land Rover blocking his field gate this morning when he went to feed his pigs. Thought it was a drunk driver sleeping it off, then realised the bloke was dead. When the paramedics arrived, they saw he'd been shot.'

Woody snorted. 'Reckon between them they'll have messed up our crime scene.'

By the time they arrived at Hangman's Lane, a cordon was in place to keep the gawpers out and to prevent further contamination of the scene. Lincoln and Woody parked at the edge of the cordon and climbed into the obligatory coveralls, then tramped to the field entrance where the well-worn Land Rover Defender had come to rest. Beyond the wide metal gate, acres of baked mud stretched away, dotted with pig arks.

'Morning, Jeff. Morning, Mike.' Pathologist Ken Burges's balding head popped up from the other side of the vehicle. 'I was expecting someone from Park Street to be in charge.'

Lincoln snorted. 'Thanks for the vote of confidence, Ken. I'd convinced myself the DCI chose me because I was the best man for the job. Best *person*,' he amended hastily.

Ken chuckled. 'Good to see you both. Shame we never meet in more cheerful circumstances.'

Lincoln peered in through the open window on the driver's side. The dead man was slumped across the steering wheel, head turned away, arms hanging down. His hair was grey and wavy, curling where it touched his collar. He wasn't wearing a jacket. From this angle, there was no evidence of the wound that had killed him, although the metallic smell of drying blood was discernible.

'You need to come round here,' said Ken, stepping back so Lincoln could take a look at the body from the passenger side.

The man's face was squashed against the steering wheel, his spectacles pushed up on his forehead and digging into the waxy flesh. Bushy eyebrows overshadowed hooded lids. Pressed awkwardly against the wheel, his mouth had assumed an expression close to a sneer. The fabric of his check shirt, on the lower left side, was dark with blood.

'Can't be sure yet, of course,' said Ken, 'but I don't think he was shot through the car window – the angle's all wrong. Probably shot elsewhere, then got behind the wheel without realising how badly hurt he was. Made it to here before he lost consciousness.'

Lincoln shook his head sadly. 'But why was he driving along this lane? It doesn't go anywhere except the pig farm.' He turned to the constable stationed nearby. 'Got a name for him?'

'The vehicle is registered to a Mr Ramsay Keiller, sir. Date of birth, twenty-ninth of April 1946.'

Woody gasped. 'Ramsay Keiller? He's got that smallholding at Turnpike Corner, and the farm shop next to it. Keiller's Yard. Ted, my father-in-law, knows him. He and Ramsay used to have allotments next to each other.'

'Small world.' Lincoln turned back to the constable. 'Was the window down when he was found?'

'Must've been, sir. The guy from the farm says he reached in to give him a shake, wake him up, then realised he was dead.'

'Reckon he's been here a few hours,' said Woody. 'The inside of the car's damp from the night air.'

Ken nodded. 'At a rough estimate – and you know that's all I ever give you at this stage – I'd say he's been dead at least twelve hours but no more than twenty.'

11

'So he was shot sometime yesterday afternoon, early evening. Any idea of the calibre of the bullet?'

Ken rolled his eyes at Lincoln's question. 'I'm flattered by the powers of deduction you think I have, Jeff. He hasn't been blasted by a shotgun, but beyond that, I really can't say. The sooner I get him back to the mortuary...'

Lincoln could take a hint. 'Come on, Woody. Let's leave the experts to it and get out of the way.'

They walked a few yards back along the lane, the sun already starting to feel hot.

'Armed robbery gone wrong?' Woody wondered.

'A farm shop isn't an obvious target.'

They surveyed the scene one more time before the body was removed and the Land Rover taken away for forensic examination. It was a beautiful morning, the hedgerows noisy with birdsong, traffic on the A345 no more than a quiet drone.

The sound of a different type of engine made them both look up. A light aircraft was circling in the bright blue sky, the sun catching its wings and cockpit as the plane wheeled and soared.

'Turnpike Corner's still busy then,' said Lincoln. 'Thought they were running the airfield down.'

'Only private planes now, and not for much longer, according to *The Messenger*.'

'If you can believe anything you read in that rag!' Lincoln started to head back to where they'd parked the car. 'Has he got family, this Ramsay Keiller? We'll need someone to ID him.'

'A couple of grown-up sons. He lost his wife a while back. Another reason him and Ted got on – both widowers.'

'But why did he drive along here? If he was shot at the farm shop, he'd have driven *towards* town to get help, surely, not away from it. Where does he live?'

'His bungalow's next to the farm shop.'

'Let's go over there then. See what more we can find out.'

CHAPTER 3

Keiller's Yard seemed like the last outpost of Barbury's agricultural past, caught between the creep of new housing estates from the edge of town and the gradual redevelopment of Turnpike Corner Airfield beyond. It wasn't large, but it was isolated enough to feel as if it was in the countryside, rather than being perched on its last remaining scrap.

On one side of the cobbled forecourt was the log cabin that housed the farm shop, with crates of produce propped outside on benches, displaying seasonal fruit and vegetables. On the other side stood Keiller's home, a small bungalow the colour of a banana milkshake. It didn't look a lot bigger than an old-fashioned chalet at a holiday camp, and it even had a little verandah and wooden railings to complete the picture. Vegetable beds, bushes of soft fruit and a few apple trees surrounded it on three sides.

Security cameras stared down over both buildings. With farms so often targeted by thieves, even a small enterprise like Keiller's needed CCTV coverage.

'Doesn't look as if there's anyone here,' said Lincoln as they got out of the car. He could still hear the traffic on the main road half a mile away, and a light aircraft – perhaps the same one they'd watched earlier – was whining above them.

Between the shop and the bungalow, a parched-looking paddock sloped away towards a stand of trees, with a chicken run in their shade. The aroma of grain, manure and hot straw filled the air.

At first glance, though, there was nothing to suggest Keiller had been shot here: no blood; no shell casings; no signs of a disturbance inside the dim shop, where the only sound was the steady thrumming of a freezer against the back wall. Nothing looked amiss – apart from the absence of the shopkeeper.

On the desk in the tiny office, a diary lay open. Lincoln flipped through it, searching for a list of contacts. The first two names were Adam and Jamie.

'The sons,' said Woody, peering over his shoulder.

Lincoln rang Adam's number but got voicemail, so he left a message asking him to call back urgently. He tried Jamie's number, but it was unanswered, with no voicemail option before the ringing cut out.

'He's left his laptop on.' Woody pointed to the glowing power light, although the screen had gone blank. A scribbled list was propped beside the screen. 'Reckon he was doing an order to the dairy,' he said, perusing it, 'but got interrupted.'

Peering under the desk, Lincoln located a small safe, but it was locked, with no keys in sight.

'Doesn't look as if they found the safe,' he said, knees creaking as he stood up again, 'but I bet they've emptied the till.'

But the till drawer was still full of loose change and notes – at least a couple of hundred pounds' worth.

Woody shook his head, puzzled. 'Why hold up a shop and leave the cash behind?'

Lincoln didn't have an answer. 'Maybe the motive wasn't robbery after all.' As he slammed the till shut, he spotted a purple plastic purse lying on the counter.

'Must belong to someone musical,' said Woody, following his gaze. He pointed to the treble clef motif attached to the tab of the zip. 'Kate's got one like that on her phone case. Haven't you noticed? Trish bought it for her from that little music shop in the Half Moon Centre.'

Lincoln hadn't noticed, even though Kate was poring over her phone whenever he saw her. Not that he'd seen her recently, or her mother. When had he and Trish last spent any time together? No time to think about that now.

He picked the purse up and opened it. No name inside, no cards, only a ten-pound note and a few coins. 'A customer must've left it behind.'

As Lincoln dropped the purse back on the counter, a shiver of apprehension chilled him. What had happened here yesterday afternoon? Had Keiller left his desk to serve a customer, to be confronted by someone, maybe several people, with a gun? Had he foiled a robbery, only to get shot as he got away?

'What kind of bastard turns a gun on a man in his seventies?' Woody put into words what Lincoln was thinking.

'Let's check the bungalow, make sure there's no one lying hurt in there.'

Hurt – or dead.

But there was nothing untoward in the bungalow, where a collection of balsa wood model aeroplanes dangled from the ceiling of the spare room, and photos of aircraft were dotted over the walls.

'Bit of an aircraft enthusiast, was he?' Lincoln nodded towards a poster for Yeovilton Air Day 2016, last July. Keiller certainly wouldn't be going to it this year!

On the bedside cabinet sat a pair of powerful Barr & Stroud binoculars and a digital camera – a Canon EOS 6D with a long lens – alongside an airband scanner.

Woody let out a low whistle. 'Reckon whoever came to rob the shop would've made more out of nicking this lot.'

'So why didn't they? The front door wasn't locked. We need to make sure it's locked now, though. We don't want anything disappearing before the crime scene investigators get here.'

Back outside, they turned towards the assortment of sheds and shelters on one side of the paddock, fierce sunshine glancing off the galvanised steel roofs. Hens scuffled noisily in their pen, the cockerel strutting back and forth on the other side of the netting.

Lincoln wondered aloud if they needed feeding.

Woody, who usually knew about such things, wasn't sure. 'Probably as long as they've got fresh water they'll be okay for a bit. Hey, look at that!' A big fence panel had been smashed, then roughly repaired with some wooden boards.

'And there.' Lincoln pointed at graffiti daubed on the side of the stable, an indecipherable tag in luminous spray paint. Fresh-looking chipboard was tacked over a window that must have been broken at some point, and across the bottom panel of the door where someone had kicked it in.

His phone rang as he was peeling off his sweaty gloves.

'Adam Keiller here,' said a gruff voice. 'You left a message to call you.'

A minute later, Lincoln was putting his phone away. 'That was Adam. He'll do the formal ID. He'll meet us at the hospital. His brother's away on holiday, but he'll let him know what's happened.'

'I don't envy him, having to break that sort of news.'

Lincoln gazed across the smallholding, a place in which Keiller must have taken a great deal of pride. 'I'll call Park Street,' he said. 'Update Connors and get a forensic team over here.'

With Keiller's Yard sealed off and the CSIs – crime scene investigators – on their way, they drove over to the mortuary at Presford General.

'Tell me about Ramsay Keiller,' said Lincoln as they joined the inevitable traffic queue approaching the roundabout by the railway bridge. 'Retired teacher like your father-in-law?'

'No,' said Woody. 'He worked for the Ministry of Defence. A bit of a boffin according to Ted.'

Plenty of boffins around Barbury, with all the military establishments on Salisbury Plain. The secret biological warfare place, for instance, although they didn't call it that.

'Not germ warfare?'

'No,' said Woody. 'Aeronautics.'

'That would explain his interest in model aeroplanes.'

'Ted's going to be upset when he hears what's happened. Suki was only saying to him the other day how he and Ramsay should get together sometime. Will you say anything to Trish?'

Lincoln took his time answering. He and Trish were close but had been closer. And they'd lived together for a while. Now, though, their relationship seemed to be drifting. Job pressures, working hours that too rarely coincided, Trish's understandable concern to put Kate first... all these had pushed them apart. Should he tell her about Ramsay before Ted, her father, heard it on the news?

'We need to keep it to ourselves as long as possible, Woody. Ted will find out soon enough.'

As they went through the automatic doors into Presford General, a man marched towards them. He was stocky, carrying a bit too much weight for his height, and wore an expensive-looking suit over a navy polo shirt. Wiry dark hair. A five o'clock shadow.

'Adam Keiller,' he said grimly, and strode ahead of them towards the mortuary. Once they reached the darkened room though, his brusque efficiency deserted him and he reeled back at the sight of his father's body on the gurney.

'I can't believe someone would shoot him,' he gasped. 'Why would anyone do that?'

'We're assuming someone came to rob the shop and he tried to stop them. Although we can't rule out some other motive. Had he fallen out with anyone?'

Adam shook his head emphatically, unable to take his gaze off his father's face. 'He got on with most people. Not everyone agreed with his politics, but...'

'His politics?'

'You'd probably call him a trendy lefty. He was a student in the sixties. Anti-war, anti-apartheid. Only a couple of years ago he was protesting against the developers building on the allotments in the Nether Valley.'

A campaign that Woody's father-in-law, Ted Whittington, had organised – and won.

'What did he do before he retired?' asked Lincoln.

'He was a draughtsman. Ministry of Defence. Aircraft design.'

Woody grinned. 'We saw the models he made. You're in the same line of work?'

'Good God, no! I'm a doctor.' Adam looked towards the door. 'Can we go somewhere else? I need to get out of here.'

They walked to the far side of the hospital grounds where a row of benches faced the open fields, although, instead of sitting down, they leant on the fence.

'Takes me back to when my mother was in hospital here,' Adam confessed, staring out across the valley. The sun was at its most fierce, but he seemed not to care. 'Long time ago now. She died in 2005.'

'Your dad never remarried?'

'No. Never saw the need. He learnt to look after himself when Mum got sick.'

'It's not just the practical stuff, though, is it?' said Lincoln. 'It's the companionship you miss when you're on your own.' As he knew from his own experience.

They watched horses cropping grass in the field below them. A stumpy Shetland pony sought the shade of the trees, shaking its mane and flicking its tail, irritated by flies.

'Couldn't get hold of Jamie,' said Adam, 'but I've left him a message. He's on his way back from touring the Highlands. He's due back tomorrow.'

'Are you close?'

'Not really. I'm eight years older, so there's a bit of a gap. He's always been closer to Dad. Similar interests.' He turned away from the fields and began to walk slowly back towards the main building. 'So, when's the autopsy?'

'Later today or first thing tomorrow,' said Lincoln. 'You work here at the hospital?'

'Only from time to time. I'm in private practice, much to Dad's disgust.' After taking a few more paces, Adam stopped again. 'Why was he driving along Hangman's Lane? It doesn't go anywhere. Why wasn't he heading for here?'

'We don't know,' said Lincoln. 'He'd lost a lot of blood, may not have been thinking clearly.' They had yet to call at the farm to find out if Keiller knew the owners. He might have been trying to reach them before it was too late. 'No one's threatened him, as far as you know?'

Adam shook his head. 'Unless you count the vandalism.'

'Vandalism?'

'Oh, just kids messing about. It'd been going on for a while, so it was getting on his nerves. I've been trying to persuade him to sell up, take things easy, but...' He spread his hands, as if admitting his failure. He took a deep breath. 'I need to go over there, to the yard.'

'I'm sorry, Adam,' said Lincoln, 'you can't yet. We're treating the whole site as a crime scene.'

'But what about Eunice?'

'Eunice?'

'Eunice Peel. She helps Dad out. She's there most days.'

Woody took his notebook out. 'Have you got a number for her?'

'No, but it'll be in his phone. You found that, didn't you?'

'It must be with your father's things.' Lincoln hadn't had a chance to check, but assumed Keiller's mobile had been in his pocket or in the Land Rover. 'We'll find the number. If Eunice has turned up there already, the officers on duty will have told her what's happened.'

'I should warn you,' said Adam, 'she's a bit... odd. You have to take a lot of what Eunice says with a pinch of salt.'

CHAPTER 4

Lincoln and Woody got back to Barley Lane to find that Breeze had arrived while they'd been out.

'How was the wedding?' Woody asked him, taking a Tupperware box out of his drawer and prising the lid off.

The aroma of cheese and tomato sandwiches made Lincoln's mouth water, reminding him he'd skipped breakfast – again – and could do with a coffee. He went across to the filing cabinet where a tray of mugs, coffee jars and tea tins sat beside the kettle. He supposed that Park Street would have a proper staff room, with a coffee maker or one of those gadgets with pods that he could never get the hang of. Assuming a move to Park Street was on the cards.

'The wedding?' Breeze turned away from his keyboard. 'Don't remember much about it, to be honest, Sarge. Overdid the booze a bit.' His bright red Meat Loaf T-shirt strained across his belly as he folded his arms and leant back. 'I'm getting too old for that sort of thing.'

Pam rolled her eyes. Lincoln had little sympathy for him either. The forty-something detective constable always overdid it, spending too long with his mates in the pub, then eating too much in the Indian restaurant afterwards. He'd certainly overdone it on his recent holiday in Ibiza, partying so hard he fell asleep by the pool next day and got sunstroke.

But now Breeze seemed keen to get down to work. 'Gray says we've got a murder.'

Lincoln dumped his coffee mug on his desk. 'We've got a dead man at the wheel of his car, and he'd been shot. We won't know much more until after the autopsy.'

'Gang related?'

'Unlikely. The victim's in his seventies.'

Breeze looked mildly disappointed. 'Who is he, then?'

Woody had printed off a photo he'd found on the farm shop's website and now he stuck it on the whiteboard in pride of place. 'Ramsay Keiller, seventy-one, widower with two grown-up sons, Adam and Jamie. Adam did the ID.'

They all stared at Keiller's long, angular face, bushy eyebrows, greying hair. From beneath hooded lids, his dark eyes gazed fiercely out.

Pam gasped. 'Ramsay Keiller? I was only in his shop last week. I often pop in if I cycle round that way. And he's the guy in the Land Rover?'

'Afraid so,' said Lincoln. 'Ken Burges put the time of death at sometime late yesterday afternoon, early evening. Keiller must have left the shop before it shut at six. The display stands were still out front when we arrived this morning and he hadn't locked up. No evidence of a shooting there, but the CSIs are going over the place now. They might find something we missed earlier.'

'A robbery?' asked Graham Dilke.

'Looked more like the *Marie Celeste*,' said Woody. 'Everything just as he'd left it yesterday afternoon. Money in the till, camera and stuff in his bungalow, things you'd expect a thief to nick. We reckon he tried to send the thieves packing and got shot in the process.'

'We always had a chat when I went in there,' Pam said, 'unless Eunice was on the till.'

'His son warned us about Eunice,' said Lincoln. 'What's she like?'

'Pint-sized, bad-tempered, rushes everywhere. Makes it obvious she'd rather look after the animals than deal with the customers.'

Lincoln wrote Eunice's name on the whiteboard, and then the names of Keiller's two sons.

'Adam is a doctor in town. Jamie's away on holiday, but we need to speak to him as soon as possible.'

Breeze leaned back in his chair. 'No Mrs Keiller?'

Lincoln shook his head. 'She died in 2005 and it looks as if he's been living on his own. We can't rule out a lover or partner, obviously, but Adam wasn't aware of anyone. We'll know more when we've taken a look at his phone and his laptop.'

If the motive wasn't robbery, the next most likely motives were jealousy – a relationship that had turned out badly – or revenge for some real or imagined transgression.

'He worked for the Ministry of Defence, didn't he?' said Pam. 'Aircraft design? He told me all about it one day.'

'He's been retired for a long time,' said Lincoln. 'I doubt if anything he worked on for the MoD has any relevance now.'

'CCTV?' asked Dilke.

'A couple of cameras. Let's hope they were switched on and working.'

When the desk phone rang, Pam picked it up. Apparently, Eunice Peel had arrived at the yard and was refusing to leave until she'd checked on the livestock.

Lincoln abandoned his coffee and picked up his jacket. 'Pam, let's go and talk to her. Woody, check with the people at the pig farm, see if there was any reason for Keiller to be heading their way. Graham, Dennis, see what else you can find out about him. Come on Pam, let's see what Eunice can tell us.'

CHAPTER 5

Annika Fortune left her desk at Barbury Life and Travel and slipped outside to smokers' corner. The only other sinner there this lunchtime was Lee from marketing, and his cigarette was almost finished. He was studying his phone, scrolling away without even glancing across at her.

With her cigarette lit, she took her phone out and rang her mother's mobile. No answer. She tried the landline.

Lee threw his cigarette butt down and walked away. Annika watched it smoulder on the ground while she listened to her mother's landline ringing and ringing until the machine came on.

'Can you call me back when you get this message, Mum?' she said, trying to keep the irritation out of her voice. 'I've got some good news.'

She hung up, stubbing out her cigarette half-smoked, watching it buckle against the brickwork. She'd have to give up smoking soon. But not yet.

CHAPTER 6

As Lincoln parked outside the cordon at Keiller's Yard, he saw a uniformed officer being harangued by a short woman of sixty-something. She was dressed in khaki dungarees and a camouflage jacket and was angrily giving the young officer a piece of her mind.

'Yep, that's Eunice,' said Pam as they got out of the car. 'Looks as if that poor guy's catching the sharp edge of her tongue.'

'I need to get in there to feed those birds,' Eunice was berating the constable. 'What harm can I do? You'll do a sight more harm to those animals by keeping me out!'

'What's the problem?' Lincoln asked, towering over her.

Hands on hips, she turned her face up to his. Her skin was leathery, as if she spent most of her time out of doors. Her tightly curled hair was the colour of apricots, although close to her scalp it was white.

'I need to get into the paddock. Why won't they let me in?'

'This whole area is still a crime scene,' he told her. 'You're aware of what's happened to Mr Keiller, aren't you?'

'Of course I'm aware, but I still need to see to my girls.'

'Your girls?'

'My hens.' She suddenly dived to the left, taking Lincoln, Pam and the uniform by surprise as she nipped past them, heading for the chicken run. The uniform swiftly caught up with her, though, blocking her path until she turned around and stomped back to where Lincoln and Pam still stood.

'This won't take long,' said Lincoln. 'By the time we've had a talk, you should be able to go into the paddock.'

Stuffing her hands into the pockets of her dungarees, Eunice walked ahead with a swagger and dumped herself down at a picnic table outside the shop. Lincoln and Pam sat opposite her.

'What happened exactly?' she asked, still fierce. 'Nobody's told me anything except Ramsay's dead.'

'He was found in his Land Rover,' said Lincoln. 'He'd been shot, possibly giving chase to someone who tried to rob the shop. When did you last see him?'

'Sunday.' She looked away towards the entrance gate, where two or three people – would-be customers or possibly reporters – were being turned away. 'I was here to feed the animals. Monday's my day off.'

'So he's on his own on a Monday?' Pam asked.

'Monday's always quiet. He does the orders to the wholesaler and the dairy. He can manage on his own on a Monday.'

'You weren't here first thing this morning?' Lincoln wondered what time she normally started work and why she didn't seem more upset. Maybe it hadn't sunk in yet.

'I'm usually here by nine, but this morning my mother…' She tutted. 'She wouldn't let me leave the house. Shouting, chucking things around. Dementia. She's ninety. I should get someone in, a nurse or something, but I wouldn't want to leave her with a stranger.'

'So, today…'

'I phoned Ramsay to say I'd be late. Left a message.' She nodded in the direction of the office. 'It'll be on the machine.'

'We'll go into the shop in a minute,' said Lincoln. 'See if you can tell us if anything's missing. You must know the place as well as anybody.'

She gave him a dirty look, as if she thought he was accusing her of something. 'The shop's Ramsay's territory unless he needs me to go on the till. My area of expertise is the animals and my girls.'

'Your hens.' Pam said it with a smile, trying to put her at ease. 'What other animals are here now?'

'Two goats and a donkey. He had some Jacob sheep too, but he sold them, end of last year.'

'Why was that?' Lincoln asked. 'Finances tight?'

She nodded, although her apricot curls scarcely quivered. 'It's never easy, running a place like this, at the mercy of the weather all year round.'

'And you're the only employee?'

'He takes on one or two casuals in the summer to help with getting the vegetables in, but that's all, and that won't be until the schools break up. He uses kids to do it.'

Alarm bells rang in Lincoln's head. He didn't want to hear them, but he'd come across too many instances of youngsters being exploited by older men – and not only by being paid too little for the work they did. He made a mental note to check there'd been no allegations against Keiller in the past, nothing to suggest he'd ever been suspected of sexual abuse or any other kind of assault.

'Eunice, can you show us round the shop and the office, see if there's anything that seems out of place, anything missing?'

24

'I told you, indoors is Ramsay's territory, not mine.'

'Let's take a look anyway.'

Back in the shop, Lincoln and Pam watched while she checked cupboards and shelves, and the drawers behind the counter. She did so in a cursory way, though, pretending, as if she really didn't know what she was looking for. When they took her into the office, she cast her gaze around it as a stranger might.

'Can you access the security camera footage?' asked Pam. 'Is it recording to a box or onto Mr Keiller's laptop?'

'There's a box, yes, but the cameras are buggered. Some kids took pot shots at them with air rifles a week or so ago. He hasn't replaced them yet.'

A coincidence? Or had someone disabled the security cameras on purpose? Were these the same kids who'd worked for Keiller in the past? Those alarm bells rang again.

'They shot out the windows in the tool shed, too,' she went on, 'and they keep busting the fence panels. Ramsay takes it all in his stride, gets some chipboard out and hammers it across the broken bits. Me, I'd kill the little bastards if I ever got my hands on them.'

'Violence isn't the answer though, is it?' said Pam.

'Neither's being soft on them. They've gotta be taught a lesson.'

'Right now,' said Lincoln, 'we're only interested in what's happened to Mr Keiller. We'll take a look at the security footage anyway, and we'll need to take the laptop, too.'

'Take it. I never use the bloody thing.' She shrugged one shoulder like a disgruntled teenager.

Lincoln pointed to the purple purse still lying on the counter. 'Is that yours?'

She snorted. 'Do I look like the sort of person who'd have a purse that vile colour, with dingle-dangles on it? Someone must've left it behind. He should've put it away in the safe until they came back for it.' She reached out to pick it up, but Pam stopped her.

'We'll look after it,' she said gently, and Eunice pulled her hand back.

They went outside again, and she busied herself in the paddock, topping up water bowls and making a fuss of the animals as she fed them.

Lincoln squinted up at the two security cameras trained on the yard. 'Let's hope she's wrong about the cameras being buggered.'

'You think they were broken deliberately before the robbery?' Pam wondered.

'It'd be quicker and quieter to cut the wires, wouldn't it? And didn't she say they were broken a week ago? If you're going to sabotage security cameras before you rob a place, you do it when there's no time to get them fixed.'

Eunice strode back towards them, covering the distance as quickly as someone with much longer legs. 'So what happens now?' she asked.

'We'll be keeping an eye on the place overnight,' said Lincoln.

'But then what?'

'I expect Mr Keiller's sons will sort it all out,' said Pam. 'Do you need a lift home?'

Eunice shook her head. 'My scooter's outside.' She barrelled past the cordon to an orange Lambretta, a peaked crash helmet slung across the handlebars. 'Mother will wonder where I've got to.'

They watched her don her grubby white helmet, start up the scooter and shoot off.

'Bag that purse as well as the laptop,' said Lincoln. 'Even if it's nothing to do with what's happened, we shouldn't leave it lying around.'

They went back into the shop and collected up the laptop, the security system hard drive and the purse. As they headed back to the car, Lincoln's phone rang. DCI Connors told him the autopsy was scheduled for five-thirty and she wanted him to be there.

It was going to be a long day.

CHAPTER 7

Annika Fortune rapped on the front door of her mother's house until her knuckles stung. When she got no answer there, she went along the footpath behind the terrace and up through the long, narrow back garden.

Where could Jill be? She always put the landline phone on silent when she had piano pupils, of course, but she turned the ringer back on when they'd gone. After trying in vain to reach her all day, Annika had come round to Arundel Terrace as soon as she'd finished work, to make sure her mother was okay.

She found the spare keys in the peg bag behind the shed door, where they'd always been kept. So much for security!

And why didn't Annika have her own keys to her mother's house? That was all down to Matt, her boyfriend for most of last year. He'd borrowed her keys while she was out at work and let himself into Jill's house several times while she, too, was out. He'd stolen food and drink, small amounts of cash, even helped himself to toiletries from the bathroom.

He was only rumbled when Jill came home one day and found him in her study.

'And he was trying to get into my computer, I'm sure of it,' Jill had declared, angrier than Annika had seen her in a long time. 'It all makes sense now, the odds and ends that have been disappearing, things being moved around. I thought I was imagining it, but I was right. How long's he been doing this, Annika?'

'I don't know. He certainly hasn't been bringing the food and drink home to share with me.'

When she'd confronted him, he'd given her some lame excuse about wanting to see where she'd grown up.

'And I've never lived in a proper house,' he'd said, as if that excused his intrusions. 'I wanted to know what it felt like to have a whole house to myself.'

'Now I'll have to get all the bloody locks changed,' Jill had snapped at her. 'I can't be sure he won't try it again.'

Annika had stopped seeing him, hurt that he'd betrayed her trust, hurt that her mother thought she'd been in on it. Matt was long gone, but Jill still didn't seem to trust her to keep her keys to herself, refusing to risk another ill-chosen boyfriend taking advantage of them both.

Now their roles were reversed and Annika's usual impatience with her mother was held in check by anxiety about her.

She let herself into the kitchen, nearly tripping over Finzi, who shot past her and into the garden.

'Too bloody lazy to use the cat flap, are you?' She watched the fluffy tabby as it disappeared down the path.

The kitchen table was heaped with books and papers. Where had they all come from? Was Jill decluttering? She wasn't thinking of moving, was she? Downsizing. Selling the house at last. Whatever her mother had been doing, she'd left the house in the middle of it. No note saying where she was going. Nothing.

Annika tried Jill's mobile one more time. At least it was ringing. *Come on, Mum, answer it!*

Then she realised the ringing was so loud it must be close by. She shoved the piles of books apart and there, under a battered old folder, was her mother's phone, ringing and ringing.

CHAPTER 8

Lincoln didn't enjoy watching autopsies, even though he knew it was important for him to be there. It was the least he could do for the victim, showing up at the hospital, watching pathologist Ken Burges practise his skills.

'Pretty straightforward one, this,' said Ken as he finished up. He dried his hands and strolled across to the workbench. 'The bullet entered his left side but penetrated as far as his liver, making a bit of a mess on the way. However, I was able to retrieve it.' He swiped the screen of his tablet to reveal an image of the bullet. 'A nine millimetre round. It's gone off to Ballistics.'

'How was he able to drive after he'd been shot like that?'

'If it had hit his hepatic artery, he'd have died where he was shot. However, it went into his liver a bit higher up. He made it to the Land Rover, grabbed a towel from the footwell by the looks of it – not very clean, but better than nothing – and managed to staunch the entry wound. Probably had no idea how badly hurt he was. But I doubt if he was able to drive more than a few minutes before he lost consciousness.'

'How many minutes?'

'Five or six.'

Roughly the time it would take to drive from Keiller's Yard to Hangman's Lane.

'Shot from how far away?'

'No way of knowing, Jeff, except it wasn't point blank. No gunshot residue on his clothing. Odd thing is, if his attacker intended to kill him, you'd expect him to be shot in the head or the chest. Maybe our victim was turning away, flinching?' Ken twisted himself round to demonstrate. 'You wouldn't normally expect to shoot someone in the side if you wanted to be sure of killing them.'

'Any other injuries?'

'Nothing obvious, no defensive wounds. I've got a few more tests to run, but he was in remarkably good health for a man in his early seventies. The outdoor life must have kept him fit.'

'He took over the smallholding when he retired.'

'Good for him. Too many men let themselves go to seed when they stop work.' Ken's fingers combed a few wisps of hair over his crown. 'I met him once, a few years ago, at a conference on biological warfare.'

'Really? His son told us he was a draughtsman who worked on aircraft design. What was he doing at a conference on biological warfare?'

'He was speaking *against* it. Against biological weapons. He was a harsh critic of what goes on at the research establishment on the Plain.'

'I don't like to think about what they're working on there, or how they test the stuff they come up with, but a lot of it's for vaccines, isn't it? New medicines? It's not all bad.'

Ken shrugged. 'Ramsay felt the risks were too high a price to pay. A lot of service personnel were used as guinea pigs during the Cold War, without being warned of the dangers. Quite a few of them died.'

Lincoln didn't want to get into an argument, especially one that seemed irrelevant to Keiller's death. 'How long ago was this conference?'

'Late nineties? He'd left the MoD by then, I think, and was teaching at the Community College.' Ken leant against the workbench, arms folded. 'I'm packing up soon myself. My wife's not well.'

'Oh Lord, Ken! Sorry to hear that.'

'Motor neurone disease. She's going to need my help a lot more now, so it seems like a good time to go.'

'I'll miss your expertise.'

'You're staying on?' A note of surprise in Ken's voice. 'Thought you'd be pushing off when Barley Lane closes down. Still, a move to Park Street could be exactly what you need – a change of scene, a fresh start.'

As he drove back towards Barley Lane, Lincoln mulled over what Ken had said. He might need a change of scene, but did he *want* one? He'd had enough disruption in his life over the last few years: marriage break-up; his purchase of the Old Vicarage that was taking an age – and a small fortune – to restore; a few bumps in his career. He'd had three different line managers in the space of two years, and now a fourth, Claire Connors, one of the small number of black DCIs in the county, was in post. Would she be his *last* DCI?

And, of course, he needed to make more time for Trish.

He forced himself to concentrate on what he'd learnt from Ramsay Keiller's autopsy. Within minutes of being shot, Keiller was dead, but in those few minutes he'd managed to drive from the smallholding to Hangman's Lane, where he'd managed to bring the Land Rover to a halt before he lost consciousness.

Woody rang. He'd spoken to the pig farmer who'd discovered the body. He knew Keiller slightly, but he'd never had any dealings with him. The lane wasn't used by anyone much, apart from feed lorries and the workers at the pig farm.

'He said there's a dirt track that branches off the lane to the farm, but it comes to a dead end where it meets the perimeter fence of the airfield, so Keiller couldn't have been going there. Reckon he pulled off the main road into Hangman's Lane because he could feel himself passing out. If he hadn't done that, there could've been a nasty accident.'

With the chemical smell of the mortuary still in his nostrils, Lincoln swung his car into the yard behind Barley Lane nick, desperate for coffee.

Keiller had been shot, but why? If someone had set out to kill him, why not shoot him in the head or the chest? Why not finish him off with a second bullet? No, most likely, someone came to rob the shop, bringing a gun to instil fear in whoever they found there. It went off when Keiller challenged them and they fled empty-handed, thinking he was only wounded. The bullet had been sent off to Ballistics, but would there be a match on the database? Lincoln hoped so.

'Gray and I didn't find much on Keiller,' Breeze said, as Lincoln picked up a mug and headed for the kettle. 'No criminal record, although he was involved in lots of protests over the years.'

'Protests against what?'

'Footpath closures, nuclear weapons, experiments on animals – you name it.'

'No allegations made by any of the youngsters who worked for him in the school holidays, then? I was afraid...'

'Doesn't mean he never did anything. Just means he never got caught.'

Lincoln sighed. 'Why was that the first thing I thought of? What's made us all so suspicious of older men being around young people?'

Breeze chortled. 'Jimmy Savile, for a start. Rolf Harris. Gary Glitter. And they're just the ones who got found out.'

'So who wanted Ramsay Keiller dead?'

'Pam took a look at Keiller's CCTV recordings before she went home,' said Woody. 'The earliest footage is from June first, but it doesn't show any intruders until the evening of the twenty-sixth, when a couple of kids on bikes turn up and knock the cameras out.'

'Only you can't see their faces,' said Breeze. 'They were wearing hoodies. Not exactly crack shots, either. It took 'em several goes before they hit the cameras.'

Eunice Peel had been right about the cameras being buggered then. Another disappointment. 'Print out anything that might help us identify them, anyway.'

'You're thinking the vandals came back and attacked Keiller himself?'

Lincoln made himself a coffee. 'I doubt it, Dennis. That smallholding's an easy target for kids up to a bit of mischief with an air rifle, with the nearest building half a mile away. But kids using a handgun? That's very different territory.'

'The CSIs found a shell casing,' Woody put in. 'Nine millimetre. Looks as if he was shot on the forecourt where the Land Rover would've been parked. Reckon we missed it this morning because we'd parked right on top of it.'

A stupid, elementary mistake to make. Lincoln hoped he and Woody hadn't committed any other *faux pas*.

The whiteboard had begun to fill with more photos: of Keiller; of the smallholding; of Adam. According to the website of Baddesley Grange, a private healthcare clinic a few miles out of Barbury, Adam was a doctor there, specialising in orthopaedics. He was pictured with a glamorous wife and two young children.

'Have we heard anything from Jamie Keiller?' asked Lincoln.

Woody shook his head. 'Reckon it'll take him a good few hours to drive down here from Scotland, even assuming Adam has managed to get hold of him.'

'I never answer my phone when I'm on holiday,' said Breeze with pride. 'Never.'

Woody looked concerned. 'Supposing there was a family emergency?'

'Cuh, who's gonna want to get hold of *me* in an emergency?'

'You've got family, haven't you?'

'Not so's you'd notice.'

'Keiller's Yard,' said Lincoln, getting back to the point. 'Here are some photos of it, but they don't help much. Apart from the damaged fence panels, everything looked pretty normal.'

'Whose bike's that?' Woody jabbed his pen at a photo of the front of the shop. 'There, that's a handlebar sticking out. There must be a bike leaning against the end wall.'

Lincoln peered at it: a handlebar and the edge of a bicycle basket. 'Maybe Eunice uses it for deliveries? More environmentally friendly than her Lambretta.' He made a note to check with her in the morning.

Breeze sighed. 'At least we can assume we're not looking at a love triangle, eh? Not at his age.'

'Don't be so sure,' Lincoln said. 'Keiller was a very fit seventy-something. But no, there was nothing in his bungalow to suggest he was involved with anyone. We brought his laptop back with us, but his phone must be with the rest of his things.'

'You think the CSIs have sent it to Park Street?' said Woody.

Lincoln sighed. 'I'd better chase it up.'

As he reached for the phone, it rang. Somehow he knew it was bad news – call it sixth sense or simply pessimism.

'Jeff, DCI Connors here, Park Street. I know you won't be too happy about this, but DCS Youngman feels the Keiller investigation is best handled from here.'

CHAPTER 9

When it turned eight o'clock, Annika called the police and said her mother was missing. As soon as she'd said it, she knew she'd made a mistake. The call handler seemed to think so too.

'How old is she?'

She had to work it out. 'Sixty-eight.'

'And is she vulnerable? On medication?'

'She's not vulnerable, no, and she doesn't take anything that I know of.' Not these days, anyway, although when Annika was small, Jill had taken every herbal remedy under the sun, not all of them legal.

The call handler suggested Annika check the house again, and the garden. 'She may have had a fall.'

'I've done all that. She's definitely not here.'

'Does your mum drive? Is her car there?'

Jill didn't drive any more. For some reason, she'd suddenly got rid of her car after Easter. Parking in Arundel Terrace was always a nightmare, and the elderly diesel-guzzling VW Polo didn't do much for her green credentials, but Annika had still been surprised that her mother had made up her mind to ditch the car so quickly.

'She cycles everywhere these days,' she told the woman on the phone. Even as she said it, Annika realised she hadn't checked to see if Jill's bike was there. She hurried through the kitchen and out to the shed.

No bike.

'So she's probably gone off somewhere to see friends, perhaps?' the woman suggested, not unkindly. 'Give it a few more hours.'

Annika gave up, even though she knew Jill wouldn't have gone off and left Finzi to fend for himself.

She hadn't been alone in this house for years. She'd grown up here and had loved the place when she was small. Once she'd reached her teens, though, she could hardly wait to get away from its suffocating atmosphere. A narrow house squeezed between two other narrow houses, with chintzy curtains at the windows and clumpy furniture that had mostly belonged to her grandparents, it was too often full of shadows. From the front rooms, the only view was of similar houses across the street, a mirror image of this terrace, but sunnier.

She wandered into the front room and stood staring at the piano, remembering all those hateful hours of other children's playing. The good ones were nearly as irritating as the bad, reminding her how close she'd come to playing well, if only she'd tried harder, had stuck at it instead of giving up.

Supposing Jill had been knocked off her bike again? She'd had a bad accident years ago, which had left her with chronic back pain and a dodgy hip. Drivers were so cavalier about cyclists. And she never wore a helmet. Supposing she'd been admitted, unconscious, to Presford General, or was lying in a ditch somewhere?

As she crossed the hall, she saw that the light on the telephone was blinking. She hadn't thought to check the answering machine for messages.

The earliest was from some company selling loft insulation, the second from Annika herself at lunchtime today. She sounded petulant, she thought, annoyed that her mother wasn't picking up. She deleted it.

The third and final message had been left this afternoon at five-eighteen, a woman with a Scottish accent.

'Mrs Fraser here, Flora's mother. She went to your house, but you weren't there so she had a wasted journey. Could you not have sent her a text, Mrs Fortune, if you knew you were going to be out? Please call me back.'

Jill's timetable lay open on the piano keys. Only two pupils on Monday, Bradley Owen at three and Kate Amos at four. Today, only one, Flora Fraser, who presumably had turned up at four-thirty to find her piano teacher out.

What would happen to tomorrow's pupils if Jill wasn't back by then?

Annika threw up the sash window to let some air into the bedroom that had once been hers. She leant out, gazing at the dreary view beyond the long back garden. The old bus garages on the main road had been ugly enough, but now they'd been replaced by an even uglier block of retirement flats, Fremantle House.

'Are you going to get one of those new flats?' she'd asked Jill when a flyer came through the door last year, announcing an open day.

'Are you serious? They're for old people.'

'Over fifty-fives, it says here. And you're way over fifty-five.'

Should she have lied just now and told the police her mother *was* vulnerable? They might have sent somebody round tonight instead of making her wait until tomorrow.

But Jill was a very young sixty-eight, compared to how Grandma had been at the same age.

Annika's mobile rang, sounding strangely echoey in this high-ceilinged bedroom. It was Roz, wondering where she'd got to.

'I was expecting you hours ago, Annie. We were eating out, remember?'

'Sorry, Roz, my mum's... Well, she's not here and that's a bit strange.'

But Roz, whose own mother was a world away in Australia, laughed. 'She's entitled to a life of her own, isn't she, your mum? A private life? Wouldn't you be mad if she expected you to check in with her all the time?'

'This is different. She wouldn't go away without telling me.'

'So you haven't told her about the baby yet?'

Annika stared at the narrow bed that had been hers until she left home. The thought of having a child, of bringing a baby into this world... She and Roz had agreed to start a family, but that's as far as they'd got. Maybe that's as far as they'd ever get.

'Of course I haven't told her. I couldn't get hold of her on the phone.'

'So, are we still eating out?'

'Let's eat out tomorrow instead. Sorry, Roz, I'm not really in the mood now.'

'But there's nothing in the fridge. I'll have to order take-out.'

'Don't order anything for me, then. I'll stay here a bit longer to make sure she's okay.'

'Suit yourself.' And Roz hung up, leaving Annika feeling guilty.

The light was fading, the shadows deepening. Birdsong filled the garden. How often had she sat here in this bedroom, trying to do her homework despite the distractions beyond the window?

The phone rang in the hall and she hurried down to answer it, getting there just as the machine kicked in.

'Hi Jill, this is Christine from the Local History Group. We were expecting you at the meeting tonight and it's not like you to miss it. Hope you're not poorly. If you need anything, you know where I am.'

No point phoning Christine back. Whoever she was, she sounded as puzzled about Jill's whereabouts as Annika was.

She thought about going home, sharing a Chinese takeaway or a pizza with Roz, but then dismissed the idea. Something terrible had happened, she knew it had. She couldn't leave now.

She phoned the local hospital, waiting an age to be put through. Standing in the hall, the handset tucked between her shoulder and her chin, she noticed her mother's patchwork shoulder bag on the shelf of the hall stand.

She hung up abruptly, opened the bag and flipped through it. Jill's wallet was there, her bank cards zipped up inside it. Where would she have gone overnight without even her bank cards?

Oh God, had she done something stupid?

Now the police would have to take her seriously. Annika picked up the phone again and dialled 999.

CHAPTER 10

Lincoln poured himself a glass of Jameson's and took it out onto the verandah at the back of the Old Vicarage. A party was in full swing at Fountains, the house that backed onto his – albeit some distance away at the top of its own pristine lawns. Raucous laughter and the clink of glass on glass, the drone of conversation punctuated by drunken shouts. And was that a barbecue he could smell?

The partygoers sounded predominantly male. As darkness began to fall, the music started, garage or something equally monotonous. He couldn't settle. He was jealous of his privacy, glad that the beech hedge he and Ted, Trish's dad, had planted in March would eventually grow tall enough to obscure his view of Fountains.

He reviewed his conversation with DCI Claire Connors about DCS Youngman wanting him to lead the investigation into Ramsay Keiller's murder, but from Park Street.

'And the rest of my team? Do they sit twiddling their thumbs at Barley Lane?'

'Of course not, Jeff,' Connors had said. 'You delegate, same as you've always done. From what I've heard of your DS's abilities, he'll manage your team fine on the ground, even if you're over here at Park Street.'

Yes, Woody was more than capable of managing the team, but somehow...

'So we'll see you here Thursday. Eight o'clock. Okay? I'll get security sorted out, find you a desk and a parking space, though it's pretty much first come, first served – for desks as well as parking.'

Now, the relentless bash and bang of his neighbour's music drove him back indoors. The house smelt dusty after being shut up all day, but he'd never tire of the Old Vicarage, even though he knew he'd been mad to buy it, with all that needed doing to it.

Too late now.

He meant to phone Trish to forewarn her about Ramsay Keiller's death. Her father was bound to be upset when he heard the news. And yet he hesitated, nervous. He hadn't phoned, or even texted her, for nearly two weeks, was no longer sure about the state of their relationship. Lovers? Friends? No longer an item?

He rang the landline, knowing she often turned her mobile off once she got home from the library, but it was Kate who answered.

'Mum's not back yet,' she said. 'She's got a meeting. Local History Group or something, at the library. You want me to give her a message?'

'I'll try her later. How's your music going?'

'Why d'you ask?' She sounded defensive. Did she think he was checking up on her?

'No special reason. You'll be finishing your piano lessons for the summer soon, I suppose.'

'The last one's next Monday. We break up the end of that week.'

'Off anywhere in the holidays? Going to your dad's?' Vic Amos had remarried since he and Trish had divorced, but Kate often went to stay with him and Gail, his second wife.

'Only for, like, a long weekend. It's difficult now.'

'Why's that?'

'You know my dad and Gail had a little girl? Well, they're having another baby and it'll feel kind of awkward. Don't say anything, though, I'm not supposed to know. Only I overheard Gail and Dad talking about it when I was there last. I haven't told Mum.'

'Better let your dad be the one to tell her.'

'I suppose. What d'you want Mum for?'

'Nothing special. I'll phone again later.'

He hung up, wondering how Trish would take the news that Vic was to be a father again. She always insisted she didn't miss him, that they couldn't have stayed together, but she must feel at least a little resentment towards the woman who'd replaced her in Vic's life.

No matter how hard you tried, it was difficult to get over a first love, even when that love had turned sour.

He finished his drink, thought about having another. Decided against it. Changed his mind. Was this how he'd spend the next few years? On his own, yet craving company? Wanting Trish to move in with him, and yet always unsure about taking that crucial step?

He put some music on, some John Martyn he hadn't played in a while because it made him feel mournful. Tonight, though, he wanted to feel mournful.

He wondered how soon Ted would hear about his old friend's death. Word would get around, the police presence at the smallholding, Adam Keiller going through his father's address book, phoning with the bad news...

Switch off, he told himself. Enjoy your drink, the music, being at home at the end of a long day. The day after tomorrow, you'll be at Park Street by

39

eight o'clock, probably having to drive around looking for a parking space. Probably having to hunt around for a spare desk.

It would be like starting at school or college, the new boy who doesn't know the rules.

He'd finish this drink and then make himself a sandwich.

He leant back in his chair and shut his eyes.

CHAPTER 11

Lincoln arrived at Barley Lane just after eight-fifteen.

'There's an elderly lady gone missing, boss.' DC Graham Dilke watched him hang his jacket over the back of his chair and pick up his empty mug. 'From Arundel Terrace. Park Street are following it up.'

'How elderly?' Lincoln inspected the inside of the mug and decided it needed a quick rinse, although that was unlikely to rid it of its mahogany patina.

'Sixty-eight.'

Woody looked up from his keyboard. 'That's not elderly, Graham. A lot of people are still working at sixty-eight. Ramsay Keiller was seventy-something, still running a smallholding and his farm shop.'

By the time Lincoln returned from cleaning his mug in the cloakroom sink, Pam had arrived. She wasn't alone.

'This is Jamie Keiller,' she said. 'He was waiting out front, so I brought him round.'

Jamie was a taller, younger version of his father, much slimmer than his older brother and with none of Adam's assertiveness.

'I-I couldn't get in,' he said. 'Adam said to come to the police station, but I couldn't find a door bell that worked.'

'Apologies for that.' Lincoln signalled for him to sit down. 'This station isn't public access any more. But you're here now. Just got back from Scotland?'

'We stopped overnight with some friends in Hertford.' Jamie glanced nervously round the CID room as if seeking an escape route. 'We were just leaving when Adam phoned. He said Dad had been shot. What happened?'

Lincoln put him in the picture as far as he could. 'Nothing appears to have been stolen, but we're guessing your dad was shot foiling an armed robbery.'

Woody put a cup of tea on the desk for Jamie. 'We heard he'd had some bother with vandals.'

'Yeah, since April, May.' Jamie stared at his tea without picking it up. 'It was getting to him. He talked about selling up.'

'It was that bad?'

'It built up. He'd get a fence panel fixed and they'd be back within a week to kick it out again. Last time they came back, they were taking pot shots at the livestock, frightening the goats.'

'Did the security cameras ever pick them up?'

'Not well enough to identify them. Kids. Kids with air rifles.'

'Did your dad report them to the police?'

'Yeah, but you didn't bother sending anyone out, did you?' His tone was bitter. 'All you said was that he should increase his security. Like it was *his* fault.'

'He must have been put through to Park Street station,' said Lincoln. 'I'm sorry it wasn't followed up. Your dad employed casual workers sometimes?'

'Not since last summer. He wasn't going to take any on this year. Too much trouble.'

Those alarm bells rang again in Lincoln's head. 'Trouble? What kind of trouble?'

'All the forms, all the bureaucracy. I said I'd help him this year, and my boys would help out too. I've got two sons, ten and twelve. They were looking forward to helping their grandad in the holidays.' He hung his head for a moment, then lifted it as if determined not to let his grief get the better of him. 'So you think it was a robbery gone wrong?'

'That seems the most obvious explanation. No other reason someone would come after him with a gun, is there? No disputes with anyone?'

'Disputes? Dad?' Jamie brushed the suggestion aside, sweeping his cup and saucer across the desk as he did so. Tea slopped out, spreading fast towards the piles of paperwork stacked there. Woody leapt up and grabbed the cloth they used to clean the whiteboard, dropping it on the lake of spilt tea.

Lincoln ignored the distraction. 'Yes, disputes. Fallings out.'

'Dad got on with everybody. Well, except his bosses. He didn't always get on with them.' Jamie edged back from the desk so Woody could finish blotting up the tea. 'But his bosses aren't going to come after him with a gun, are they? Not all this time later.'

'Was he in a relationship?'

'He never said. There was a woman he met through the U3A, but that was a few years ago. Heather something or other. She was at the bungalow once when I dropped in on him. But I didn't get the impression it was anything *romantic*. And what's that got to do with what's happened now?'

'Nothing at all,' said Lincoln, although it crossed his mind that if Keiller had been involved with a woman a couple of years ago, he might have had other relationships since. As Ken Burges had remarked at the autopsy, Keiller was a fit man for his age.

'Those model planes are quite something,' Woody said. 'Did your dad make them all himself?'

'He loved his planes. That's one of the reasons he bought that land, because it's close enough to the airfield to do a bit of plane spotting. Not that Turnpike Corner's anything like as busy as it was. They've sold half of it off for housing.'

'He worked on aircraft design at the MoD?' Lincoln asked.

'Yeah, but he could never talk about it. Official Secrets Act and all that. And then they sacked him.'

'Sacked him?' Lincoln exchanged a look with Woody. 'Why?'

Jamie's face hardened. 'He spoke out against what was going on at the scientific research place. His bosses told him he'd better look for a career outside the Civil Service.'

'And?' Woody sat down again.

'He got a job at Barbury Tech, teaching engineering drawing. Loved it – until they took it off the curriculum. No demand, they said. It's all CAD now. Computer-aided design. He'd learnt all that himself, used CAD at the MoD, but it was manual drawing he enjoyed.'

Lincoln nodded, sympathising with the late Ramsay Keiller, his conscience forcing him out of one job, computers forcing him out of another.

'He'd had an allotment for years,' Jamie went on. 'Then he thought he'd like to keep poultry. Approached one or two local smallholders for advice and one of them was Eunice Peel. She was struggling on her own so she agreed to sell him her plot, livestock and all – on condition that she could still work there. Dad couldn't believe his luck. The last few years, I've never seen him happier. He was living the dream.'

Until vandals started to target the place. Lincoln was still wondering about the youngsters that Keiller had employed over previous summers. Might there be a connection, kids with a grudge seeking revenge? Could acts of vandalism escalate to *murder*? Surely the most obvious explanation was a hold-up by inept thieves.

'And where do *you* work?' asked Woody.

'Barbury Electronics, on Southampton Road.' He shoved his chair back and stood up. 'I should get going. I need to see Adam. Begin to make the funeral arrangements.'

'I'm sorry,' said Lincoln, 'but we can't release Mr Keiller's body yet.'

'Okay, but there's still stuff we need to sort out.'

As soon as Woody returned from showing the young man out, Lincoln called a team briefing, although someone was missing. 'Where's Breezy?'

'Another late night, knowing him,' said Pam.

Dilke was quick to defend his colleague, 'He could be ill.'

'Then he should've called in sick.'

Lincoln held up his hand to shush them so he could make his announcement. 'From tomorrow, I'll be based at Park Street. Not my choice, but DCS Youngman might've taken us off the case altogether if I'd said no.'

No one spoke. Dilke's mobile pinged, but he ignored it. Woody stared at the whiteboard. Pam stared at Lincoln.

'As it is,' Lincoln went on, 'splitting the investigation between here and Park Street's going to be messy, but anything you can action from here, I'll make sure you get it.'

Pam was the first to respond, reaching across to her desk to retrieve a sheet of paper. 'I printed off an aerial view of the smallholding,' she said, passing the photo around.

'That land must be worth a lot, given its position,' Dilke remarked. 'Look, nearly everywhere around it's been built on already.'

Lincoln stuck the photo on the whiteboard. 'Then why didn't Eunice Peel offer it to developers when she had the chance? I bet they'd have paid her much more for it than Ramsay Keiller did.'

'The airfield was a lot busier then,' Woody pointed out. 'Reckon no developer would've wanted land that close to it. Since then, of course, things have changed. They've moved most of the military operations to other bases elsewhere on the Plain.'

'What about his private life?' Pam asked.

'There was a woman called Heather a few years ago,' said Lincoln, 'but it doesn't sound as if she's around now. When we can take a look at his phone records…'

'I suppose the tech team at Park Street's doing that?' Dilke's resentment was audible. That was the sort of task *he* usually undertook.

'As long as it gets done, Graham, don't quibble about who actually does it. Let's take a look at what we know so far.' Lincoln took them through a possible scenario. 'Keiller's in his office. Breaks off what he's doing and goes out to the front of the shop. Let's assume one or more people have come to rob the shop. Why haven't they barged straight in? Why did they wait for Keiller to go out onto the forecourt?'

Pam frowned at the whiteboard. 'Maybe they didn't want him to know what they'd come for? Wanted to take a casual look around to see who else was there before they threatened him?'

44

'Did they steal anything?' asked Dilke. 'Anything at all?'

'Not as far as we can tell. The safe was shut and locked, the till was full of cash.'

'Maybe the gun went off accidentally and they panicked,' Dilke suggested. 'When they saw they'd hit Keiller, they left without even going into the shop.'

Lincoln nodded. 'That seems the most likely explanation. A bungled raid.'

Pam pointed to the photo that showed the front of the farm shop. 'Whose bike is that? Look, you can see the handlebars and the edge of a wicker basket. It's leaning against the end wall of the log cabin.'

'Woody noticed that earlier. Maybe Eunice uses it for deliveries. A gunman's not going to turn up on a pushbike, is he?' Lincoln studied the photo of Ramsay Keiller. 'Do we think Keiller was still campaigning, still an activist? Apart from backing your father-in-law's Save Our Allotments campaign, Woody.'

Woody grinned. 'There was no paperwork in his bungalow to suggest anything like that, but then, I reckon when you downsize from a house to a bungalow that small, something has to go.'

'Adam described him as a trendy lefty,' Lincoln continued, 'but why would that make him a target now? He was obliged to leave his job at the MoD because he objected to what was going on at Porton Down, but that was years ago. More likely, we're looking at a ham-fisted robbery that...' He broke off as Breeze barged in and flopped down at his desk. 'Morning, Dennis. Good to see you. Another rough night?'

Breeze did indeed look unwell, a grey tinge to his usually florid complexion, a day's worth of stubble on his chin. Lincoln noticed that he was wearing the same scarlet Meat Loaf T-shirt he'd worn yesterday – he recognised the stains down the front.

'Sorry, boss,' Breeze mumbled, standing up to shed his leather jacket. 'Haven't felt right since the weekend, but I'm getting over it.' He sat down again, cranking his chair round so he could see the whiteboard. 'What's new?'

'We've spoken to Jamie, Keiller's younger son,' said Lincoln, 'but he couldn't add much.'

'And a woman's gone missing,' Dilke chipped in.

Breeze unwrapped some nicotine gum and lobbed it into his mouth. He'd given up smoking some time ago, but still seemed reliant on his gum. 'Who's that, then?'

'A piano teacher,' Pam told him. 'From Arundel Terrace. A Mrs Jill Fortune. Her daughter reported it.'

'Jill Fortune?' Lincoln and Woody exclaimed together.

Pam's eyebrows went up. 'You know her?'

'My niece goes to her for piano lessons,' said Woody.

'Kate,' Lincoln added. 'Trish's daughter.'

Pam gaped. 'What, *your* Trish?' The colour rose in her cheeks.

'Yes,' said Lincoln. '*My* Trish. Kate has a lesson with Jill every Monday. So why's the daughter so concerned? Jill can't have been missing for long.'

'She hasn't taken her phone with her, or her bank cards. Locked the house up and went off somewhere on her bike.'

Lincoln and Woody looked at each other.

Woody's eyes lit up. 'That purple purse on the counter, with the treble clef wotsit on it. Someone musical, I said, didn't I?'

Lincoln nodded. 'That bike at the farm shop.'

'How far to Keiller's Yard from Arundel Terrace?' asked Dilke, studying the route on his phone.

'About a mile, just over,' said Pam.

Lincoln turned back to the whiteboard. Should he be adding Jill Fortune's name to Ramsay Keiller's?

'So she cycles up to Keiller's Yard to get some fruit and veg,' he said, trying out his theory. 'She's got cash in her purse so she doesn't need her bank cards. Doesn't need her phone, so she leaves that at home too. And gets caught up in the shooting.'

'Collateral damage,' said Breeze.

'Kate's piano lesson would've finished at five on Monday,' Lincoln went on, 'so Jill must've gone up to Keiller's Yard after that. She'd have arrived around the time we think Keiller was shot.'

Woody nodded, his face grim. 'Reckon she saw what happened, so the thief, or thieves, have taken her with them.'

Breeze leant back in his chair. The springs protested. 'I don't fancy her chances, then, do you?'

'I need to speak to DCI Connors,' said Lincoln, striding across to his desk. 'Not sure if she'll see this as good news or bad.'

CHAPTER 12

Jamie Keiller drove up the sweeping gravel drive to his brother's house. Every time he came here, which wasn't often, he asked himself how Adam could afford a place like this. Private medicine obviously paid well. He'd never have been able to buy anywhere so grand if he'd gone into general practice.

But Jamie had more important issues on his mind right now. He sprang up the wide front steps two at a time and slammed his hand against the doorbell. Instantly, the door opened and there was Adam, in dark polo shirt and slacks, not a hair out of place, as if the violent death of their father had left him quite unruffled. He'd put on weight since Jamie had seen him last – three months ago? Six? – but he still had the air of a man without an iota of self-doubt.

Jamie had only one question for him. 'Fucking hell, Adam, what have you done?'

CHAPTER 13

Jill Fortune opened her eyes. No, not another day in this awful place! She felt nauseous, her head thumped, her shoulders ached from having her hands tied behind her and her lower back was killing her. She was hungry and a taste like diesel fumes coated the inside of her mouth.

She'd lost track of the hours, of how many times the man had brought her water and some sort of foul, chewy biscuit thing. For the second time, the second dawn, she'd stared at the crooked gap between the bottom of the door and the concrete floor as darkness thinned into daylight.

Monday. What had happened? She remembered swinging into Keiller's Yard, leaning her bike against the end wall of the farm shop, going inside the quiet, dim shop, seeing Ramsay leaving off what he was doing in his office, coming out to the counter and smiling when he saw it was her.

'Jill! What a nice surprise!'

'I've found something I think you've been looking for. I didn't even realise I had it. It's that report you were talking about, only there's more to it...'

She'd broken off when she heard the shop door open behind her. She'd glanced round at the tall, heavily built man who'd come in. Late thirties or early forties, dark curly hair. Something unwholesome about him. Grubby jacket with lots of pockets, a dirty T-shirt...

She'd turned back to Ramsay, but the new arrival hadn't given her a chance to finish what she'd been saying.

'I hit your bike when I pulled in,' he'd said. 'Better take a look at it.'

'Oh no!' She'd dumped her purse on the counter and rushed out of the shop.

The man had lumbered towards his car and gone round to the driver's side. 'It's over here.'

She'd expected to see her bike crushed beneath its wheels, but... 'Where is it?'

Out of the corner of her eye, she'd seen Ramsay coming outside after her.

'Back there.' The driver had put one hand on her shoulder and pointed across the yard. She'd spun around, angry and confused...

A blow, and then darkness descending like a heavy cloak, taking everything with it. A sense of falling and then nothing until sometime yesterday morning. Opening her eyes and finding herself on the rough, unforgiving floor of this garage or workshop. Daylight slipping under the door to illuminate the ridges and grooves of bare concrete. Her arm ached and she guessed he'd injected her with something to keep her quiet. But the worst indignity? Having to pee in a bucket.

Three times he'd come with water and a snack bar he'd unwrapped for her. She'd eaten it greedily once he'd untied her hands, even though it was sickly sweet and tasted vile. She'd guzzled the water without caring that it ran down her chin and onto her shirt. Could she have hit out at him? Yes, but she'd never have overpowered him.

Without a word, he'd watched her eat and drink. She'd thought about shouting for help after he'd gone the first time, but then she'd heard the whine and squeal of a helicopter and knew no one would hear her, no matter how loudly she called out. She was somewhere too remote to be heard. That's why he hadn't bothered to gag her.

Where was she? How far from Barbury? She knew Ramsay would have raised the alarm as soon as he could, so wherever she was, it must be out of the way.

Who was he, this man, and what did he want from her? Did he think she had money, a family who'd pay a big ransom to get her back?

She thought of that newspaper woman in the sixties, Muriel Mackay, kidnapped when her abductors mistook her for the wife of Rupert Murdoch, her husband's boss. Her body was never found. Her family never knew what had happened to her, but how the media had delighted in suggesting her kidnappers had fed her to the pigs!

Don't think like that! Ramsay's got CCTV. The police will be able to see exactly what happened when they check it. They'll see the registration number of the car.

It can only be a matter of time.

Her stomach groaning with hunger, Jill let herself slip away, back into sleep, hoping that, when she woke up again, she'd find this was all simply the most outrageous nightmare.

CHAPTER 14

DCI Claire Connors shunted her chair back from her desk and stood up, not tall but solidly built, top heavy.

'Okay, Jeff. So, based on a bicycle and a purse that happen to have been left at the farm shop, you think this missing woman's been caught up in the attack on Keiller?'

'I'm sure of it, ma'am. We need her daughter to confirm the purse is Jill's, of course, and we need to get the bike brought in, but...'

'Why didn't the shooter kill her too?'

'Because he didn't want to shoot a woman? Because she was just an innocent bystander? Because shooting Keiller was an accident?' He shrugged. 'I don't know. The important thing, surely, is to find her.'

'Do we know if Jill Fortune had access to a firearm?' Before he could answer, she went on, 'Because we'll look bloody silly if this was some sort of lovers' tiff and we're still looking for an armed robber.'

'Some lovers' tiff! But no, you're right, ma'am, we have to make sure we don't...'

'And he's a farmer. Farmers have shotguns, don't they?'

'He wasn't shot with a shotgun, and anyway, Keiller's Yard isn't *that* sort of farm. And as for Mrs Fortune having a gun...'

Connors fixed him with a look. 'White, middle class and female. Does that rule her out as a perpetrator? Don't jump to conclusions, Jeff. That way, danger lies.'

As if he needed to be told.

She came out from behind her desk and crossed to the window, adjusting the blinds to dim her office a little. 'You know DS Orla Cook?'

It was Orla who'd taken Lincoln's statement in February after Connors' predecessor, DCI Dale Jacobs, had screwed up an arrest – a screw-up that resulted in a woman being shot dead in front of Lincoln. In the immediate aftermath, with Jacobs all too ready to blame him for what happened, he'd needed moral support as much as anything. Orla Cook had been the best he could have hoped for, taking his statement without judgement, making sure everything was done by the book.

'Yes,' he told Connors now. 'I know DS Cook.'

'I want you to work together. If we can establish for certain that the Fortune woman's disappearance is linked to Keiller's murder, we'll be using all the resources we have, here and at Barley Lane. Get together with Orla now and bring her up to speed.'

'And the rest of my team?'

'There'll be more than enough for them to do, Jeff, the way this case is unfolding.' She returned to her desk, signalling that the meeting was over. 'Now, I've got to get something drafted for Media Relations. You should find Orla in the conference room.'

Out in the corridor, he met dark-haired Orla striding towards him, a folder tucked under her arm. She led him into the conference room.

'Christ, it's hot in here!' She slid the folder and her tablet onto the polished table and went over to the window, wrestling with the blind until it shot upwards with a clatter. She cranked the window open as far as it would go – a meagre three or four inches – before taking a seat at the head of the table. 'We're meant to rely on the air con,' she said, 'but it's stopped working.'

'Isn't Park Street nick supposed to be state of the art?'

She raised a cynical eyebrow. 'Supposed to be, yes. Sit round here,' she said, as he was about to sit across from her. She waved him into a seat at right angles to her own. 'We don't need any reminders of the last time we met, boss: you one side of the interview desk and me on the other.'

'Thanks. I never want to go through that again.'

'It was Dale Jacobs who should have had his knuckles rapped over that fucked-up arrest, not you.' She flipped her folder open. 'So, you're working here from tomorrow?'

'Only temporarily. The DCI wants us to work together on this case. You've heard the shooting and Jill Fortune's disappearance could be linked?'

'From what the DCI's told me, it's a bit of a stretch, isn't it? A purse and a pushbike we don't even know are Jill's?'

'The purse belongs to someone musical. Jill's a piano teacher. She cycles everywhere and her bike's missing. The purse is here, but we need to get the bike brought in from Keiller's Yard so her daughter can take a look at it, confirm it's Jill's – or not. If we could lift Jill's prints from the purse, match them to something in the house…'

'Worth a try. Annika, the daughter, hasn't been much help so far. She and her mum don't seem very close.'

'She lives a long way away?'

'Amberstone. Three miles, give or take.'

Lincoln snorted. 'Amberstone to Arundel Terrace can be an hour's drive in the rush hour.'

'Yes, but less than fifteen otherwise.' Orla pulled a photograph from her folder. 'Here's your music teacher.'

It was Jill's smile that struck him first. Something mischievous about it, something rueful, as if the camera had caught her unawares and she planned to get her own back on the photographer as soon as the picture was taken.

Her fair hair was loose and long, and her brightly coloured earrings, three beads on top of one another, dangled down through her curls. The hand that cupped her chin was laden with rings, a cascade of bangles on her wrist.

'This is Jill?' Whenever Trish had mentioned Kate's piano teacher, he'd envisaged someone like his own music mistress at school – a bird-like woman with grey hair cropped like a man's, her usual attire a navy-blue trouser suit, white shirt and tie.

'That photo's a few years old, obviously, but Annika couldn't come up with anything more recent.'

'So Jill probably looks nothing like this now.'

'The description she gave us isn't too far out,' said Orla. 'Long grey hair tied back in a ponytail, usually wears lots of rings and bangles. Jeans and T-shirts, or long skirts. Ageing hippy.'

'What's wrong with that? Better than giving in to everyone else's idea of a senior citizen.'

'If you say so, boss. You're closer to that age group than I am.'

'Not *that* close!' He caught her eye in time to see she was teasing him. At least, he hoped she was. 'Do we know when she left home?'

'She had pupils on Monday afternoon, but she wasn't answering her phone when Annika tried to ring her yesterday lunchtime. A kid turned up for a lesson yesterday afternoon and there was no one home, and Jill missed some meeting at the library yesterday evening.'

Was that the same meeting Trish was attending when Lincoln phoned and spoke to Kate?

'One bit of good news,' Orla went on. 'We've narrowed the window down a bit. The guy who supplies the farm shop called here earlier, said Keiller rang him at half four Monday afternoon, sounding perfectly fine, no hint of trouble.'

'So Keiller must've been shot between half four and six, before he had a chance to pack up the display outside the shop and lock up. Which fits the estimated time of death.' He paused, thinking about Kate's piano lesson. 'Jill couldn't have left home until after five. She had a pupil from four o'clock to five.'

'Which narrows the window even more, assuming the Fortune woman was caught up in all this. How long would it take her to cycle from Arundel Terrace to Keiller's Yard, minimum?'

'Ten minutes? Fifteen? It's just over a mile, slightly uphill most of the way.'

'So we're saying the shooting took place between five-fifteen and six o'clock?'

Lincoln nodded. Why did Jill cycle up to Keiller's Yard at a time of day when traffic was at its heaviest? He wondered again if he'd got it all wrong and that Jill's disappearance and the purple purse on the farm shop counter were no more than a coincidence. They needed to get that bike brought in and hope that Annika recognised it.

Orla sat back. 'So, what's the most likely motive for Keiller's shooting? A robbery gone wrong? A farm shop's only going to be slim pickings, isn't it? And an *armed* robbery?'

'There is another possibility. Last summer, Keiller employed school leavers to help out on the smallholding. Risky sort of set-up, unsupervised teenagers spending time with an older man. Supposing there was some sort of inappropriate behaviour?'

'Sexual assault? He came on to one of them?'

'No, no!' Lincoln held his hands up, not wanting her to run away with that idea. 'I'm only speculating, thinking of other motives apart from robbery.'

'And there's the vandalism.'

'That could just be kids running wild, having a bit of fun at a remote site, with little fear of getting caught. It needn't be personal.'

Orla looked thoughtful, gazing across towards the window. 'If Keiller came onto one of those kids last summer, or there'd been some sort of dispute with them, you'd think they'd have had a go at him last year. You know what kids are like: can't wait for anything and a year's an eternity to them.' She tapped her tablet screen, making notes as she spoke. 'I'll check for any allegations against him, anyway. Was he in financial trouble?'

'Things were tight, apparently, but it was the vandalism that was getting to him, according to his son.'

'Could Jill Fortune be the perpetrator?'

Lincoln hadn't seriously considered it, despite Connors' warning about not dismissing the possibility simply because Jill was white, female and middle class. 'It seems unlikely. I can't see her pedalling up to Turnpike Corner with a gun in her basket, confronting Keiller outside his shop and shooting him. How did she get away? Her bike's still there. Assuming that *is* her bike. And what's her motive?'

'Love? Jealousy?'

He picked up Jill's photo again and stared into her face. 'What else do we know about her? Is Annika her only family?'

'Her marriage ended some years ago, no other children. No close friends, no other relatives she might have gone to, according to Annika. What kind of life is that? No friends, no family?'

A life a lot like his own, Lincoln realised. 'I don't suppose Annika's made the connection between the shooting and her mum going missing.'

'*Nobody* made the connection, boss, until you guys found that purse.'

'If Annika's at her mother's house now, we should go over there, kill two birds with one stone: show her a picture of the purse and find something with Jill's prints on.'

CHAPTER 15

Arundel Terrace was a street of Edwardian houses with bay windows and deep, Minton-tiled porches. In the summer heat, with the sun almost overhead, it was quiet and still.

Annika led them down the dark hallway into the kitchen, where they sat across from her at a big pine table. Piles of papers, folders and old magazines were stacked to one side.

'Have you found her?' The young woman's voice was pleading.

Lincoln searched for some resemblance to Jill in her daughter, but Annika, somewhere in her early thirties, was sharper and neater in every way, her dark chestnut hair straightened and sleek, her dress style business-like.

'Does your mum shop at Keiller's Yard?' he asked.

The question clearly puzzled her. 'Yes, sometimes. Why?' She looked from his face to Orla's. 'What's this about?'

'There was an incident there,' said Orla, 'a shooting...'

'Oh God! That was at Ramsay's? There was something on the local news this morning, but I didn't realise it was...' She gripped the edge of the table. 'Has Mum been shot?'

She'd said *Ramsay's*, Lincoln noted, as if she knew Keiller herself.

'First, we need you to look at this.' He showed her a photograph of the purple purse. 'Do you recognise it?'

She studied it warily. 'That's Mum's, yes. The treble clef thing – I bought her that as a joke, to stick on the zip, because of her music. Where did you find it?'

'It was left on the counter in the farm shop. We think your mum saw what happened there on Monday afternoon.'

'And she may have been taken hostage,' Orla added.

Annika's eyes widened in horror. 'Oh God! She's already dead, then, isn't she? If she saw what happened, they'll kill her, won't they, so she can't identify them?'

'We don't know that,' said Lincoln. 'It's more likely they've taken her with them as insurance.'

She reared up in her chair. 'Insurance? Don't talk to me about *insurance*! I earn my living selling bloody insurance.'

'Was she friends with Mr Keiller?'

She nodded. 'Mum was at school with his wife, Maggie. We used to go over to their house a lot when I was small, and me and their son, Jamie, played together. Maggie died a few years ago, but Mum kept in touch with Ramsay.' She sighed. 'So now Jamie's lost his dad too.'

'Your mum and Mr Keiller,' Orla asked. 'Were they *good* friends?'

'They've always got on, yes, but... Oh, no, not like that! They weren't *sleeping* together.' Annika's hair shimmered in the sunlight as she shook her head. 'But none of that's relevant, is it, if she walked in on a robbery? Where could they have taken her? Who are they? There must be cameras at the farm shop. Have you checked the cameras?'

'The cameras are damaged,' said Lincoln, 'and there's no other CCTV coverage in the area.'

'Wouldn't they be demanding a ransom if they'd taken her hostage?'

'That may be their next move,' said Orla. 'You've had no messages? No phone calls to the landline or your mum's mobile?'

'No. I keep checking her phone but no, nothing.'

'We have to ask,' said Lincoln carefully. 'Does your mum have access to a gun?'

'A *gun*? Where would my mum get hold of a *gun*? And why the hell would she want one? You're not saying... Don't tell me you think Mum shot Ramsay! Is that what you're saying?'

'We needed to ask the question,' Lincoln said.

'Okay, so now you've got that out of the way...' Fury blazed in the young woman's eyes.

'And you've no reason to think she's troubled in any way? That she might have gone off somewhere?' Another necessary question. It would be foolish to dismiss the possibility that Jill was depressed or had experienced some sort of breakdown.

Annika shook her head. 'No, she's fine. She's fine.' She sounded deflated, her anger replaced by despair. 'But why would anyone want to hurt her? She's never done anything to hurt anyone.'

Lincoln and Orla looked the house over together, not conducting a search as such, but simply trying to gain an impression of the missing woman.

'So where's the cat?' Orla nodded her head towards a wicker basket in the corner of the kitchen. Several cat toys lay nearby, cloth mice and ping pong balls.

'Annika said something about the woman next door keeping an eye on it. And look, there's a cat flap.'

'Hmm, I'm not a big fan of cats.'

'I won't invite you over to my house, then. Although Tux...'

'Invite me over? Why would you invite me over?'

'Forget it, I just meant... I've got a cat, that's all I meant.' He'd need to be more careful what he said. Orla seemed quick to take offence.

One whole wall of Jill's dining room was taken up with shelves of vinyl records. Lincoln was surprised to see she favoured blues music as well as the classics she taught. Her music system was top of the range, and he paused to read the label on the record she'd left on the turntable: *Dan's Swannsong 1974*. Funny way to spell swansong...

Orla interrupted his train of thought. 'Are we done down here, boss?' Without waiting for an answer, she tramped up the stairs and he followed.

They edged past a mahogany chest of drawers on the landing.

'All this heavy furniture,' she scoffed, keeping her voice low so Annika, waiting downstairs, wouldn't overhear her. 'My granny had hulking great pieces like this. Better to clear it all out, let some light in.'

He agreed. On a hot day like today, the house felt quite devoid of fresh air.

After scanning the main bedroom and the spare room – more looming furniture – they reached the box room, which Jill used as a study, with shelves and a small desk. A poster on the pinboard advertised a gig at the Full Moon pub in March 2012: the Plain Janes, Barbury's own blues duo. Lincoln peered at the photo of the two women. Was the keyboard player Jill? She rose even higher in his estimation and he wished he could have spent longer perusing her record collection.

'She didn't like the suggestion that her mum had shot Keiller, did she?' said Orla.

'No, but we had to ask. We'd look stupid if they'd had a thing going on and we didn't even consider it.'

'But there could still be somebody in her life, couldn't there? Even at her age? Wow! Look at all these books!'

One whole bookcase was crammed with titles on aircraft, warfare and military history. Lincoln opened a volume on Wiltshire through the war years and found an inscription on the fly leaf: *To Daddy from Jill with lots of love. Xmas 1962*

'Must be her dad's books.' he said.

'Christ, can't get rid of his furniture, can't get rid of his books...'

'It's not always easy to part with stuff when someone dies.' He recalled how long it had taken him to decide what to do with the few possessions of Cathy's that he'd held onto. He'd been unable to part with anything for a long time, putting it into storage, revisiting it from time to time, sitting among stacked-up furniture and cartons of crockery and ornaments. Eventually, after a lot of soul-searching, he'd got rid of most of it, but it had been a wrench.

Several piles of typescript sat on shelves above Jill's desk. 'Why's she got all this stuff?' Orla lifted up a bundle tied with pink legal tape. 'Did she write all this herself?'

Lincoln peered at the top sheet. *'Barbury Abbey: an exploration of its mystical origins* by Stephen P Quilter, whoever he is.'

Orla picked up another bundle. *'Moses Thatcher, Wiltshire's tragic farmer poet* by Marie Williamson. Sounds a laugh a minute.'

'Maybe Jill's interested in local history. My friend Trish…' He stopped himself. 'A friend of mine, Trish Whittington, is in charge of the local history collection at Barbury Library. This is the sort of material that's on the shelves there.'

Orla rolled her eyes. 'Haven't been inside a library since I was a student. Bedroom next?'

The double bed was unmade, the sheets shoved back, one pillow turned ninety degrees as if Jill had sat propped up in bed to read the paperback that now lay, face down, on the bedside cabinet. *Strange Fruit*, about Billie Holiday and the civil rights movement.

More heavy furniture, figured walnut from the 1930s perhaps, not even antique. For someone who looked so much like a free spirit – in her youth, at least – Jill seemed to have weighed herself down with her parents' possessions.

'Water glass, boss, for her prints.' Orla slid the empty tumbler into an evidence bag.

'Not sure we can do much more here,' Lincoln decided. 'Let's get back.'

Traffic had built up. Lincoln eased the car forward a few feet and pulled the handbrake on. Why build a ring road when you could have built a bypass?

'You really believe she's been taken hostage, boss?' Orla uncapped her water flask and took a swig.

'Let's believe it until we know otherwise. But no, it's more likely they've dumped her somewhere. Dead or alive.'

'Why didn't they shoot her there and then?'

'They probably didn't expect anyone else to be there. They went to rob the farm shop or to kill Keiller or both, and Jill got in the way, upset their plans. Let's hope we get the ballistics report back soon, see if the gun's already on record.'

The traffic eased a little and they were moving again. He could see that photo of Jill in his mind's eye, the smile, the tumble of thick fair hair. What had she stumbled into when she went up to Keiller's Yard for a few vegetables? This is what always got to him, charting a victim's unwitting journey from a normal day through to disaster and, sadly all too often, death.

At Park Street, Orla let him double-park behind her own car, since there were no free spaces, then led him inside.

'Let's go to the incident room, find you somewhere you can sit tomorrow.'

His heart sank at the prospect of turning up here every morning instead of at Barley Lane.

The incident room was large and square, with big windows on two sides, the blinds down, the atmosphere stuffy. Desks were arranged in rows, with little privacy, little separation. Like a call centre, he thought. How can anyone concentrate in a space like this?

'We can squeeze you in over here, boss.' Orla headed for an empty desk in the corner, next to the photocopier and the water cooler. He followed her, calculating the valuable minutes he was wasting when he could be back at Barley Lane working out how to find the missing woman. 'You'll need to grab yourself a chair, but at least you've got a desk. You want something to eat?'

His stomach growled at the mention of food.

'There's a machine in the corridor,' she went on before he'd had a chance to reply. 'You'll need pound coins and fifties.'

He had just enough change for an egg mayo sandwich, and ate it, far too quickly, standing in the corridor, giving himself heartburn.

He returned to the incident room, found an empty chair and skated it across to his desk, expecting it to be reclaimed any minute. No one was paying him any attention though. The team members were intent on answering constantly ringing phones. He wasn't sure he could put a name to any of the Park Street crowd, it had been so long since the last training session he'd attended here.

When the phone at his elbow buzzed, he picked it up. 'Barley Lane – er, sorry, Park Street...'

'I saw him,' a woman was saying, agitated. 'Outside Keiller's Yard. The man you're looking for. In a black car. I saw him.'

CHAPTER 16

'I didn't think about it at the time,' the caller was saying, breathless in her excitement, 'but then I saw the appeal on the telly, and I realised that must have been him, the gunman.'

Lincoln desperately scanned the desk for something to write with, something to write on, ending up with a stubby bit of pencil and the remains of a jotter pad.

'Tell me what you saw exactly,' he said, 'Miss...'

'Mrs Pope. Linda Pope. I was driving past the farm shop, Keiller's Yard, and this black car *flew* out of the entrance, *flew* out, and he was going so fast he couldn't corner, and he went right over to my side of the road. Clipped my wing mirror. I've got a horrible bruise from the seat belt where I had to do an emergency stop. He drove off towards the main road.'

'Did you get a good look at him?'

'Thirties, early forties. Scruffy. Big chap. Sort of hunched over the wheel.'

'Was there anyone else in the car, as far as you could see?'

'Not in the front, no, but I don't know about the back. I was that shocked, the way he flew out.'

'Did you notice the registration number?' Lincoln crossed his fingers.

'No, but I looked on the dashcam when I got home and made a note.'

A little later, Lincoln stood up in front of his Park Street colleagues, relaying the gist of Linda Pope's phone call.

'Mrs Pope checked her dashcam when she got home and wrote down the index number of the car that pulled out of Keiller's Yard right in front of her.' He turned to the whiteboard – exactly the same as at Barley Lane, but with fancier marker pens – and wrote the number on it. 'It's a 2007 black Vauxhall Astra. Registered owner, Elinor Morton.'

'It was a *woman* who shot Keiller?' Orla looked shocked.

'No, it was definitely a man driving. Mrs Pope's sending the dashcam footage over so we can see for ourselves. She described a white male, late thirties or early forties. Scruffy. She thought he might be wearing a khaki jacket, army surplus type of thing. No sign of a passenger, but Jill could've been in the boot, or lying on the back seat.'

'How can we be sure it's the shooter she saw?' The question came from DI Rick Nevin, unhealthily overweight and visibly suffering in the heat. Lincoln had worked with him years ago, but their outlooks were very different. Nevin was coasting towards retirement, as if he'd put himself into neutral and taken the handbrake off.

'We *can't* be sure, Rick, but he came tearing out of the yard so fast his car fishtailed, and then he drove off at speed.'

'And what time was this, boss?' Orla again.

'Mrs Pope says it was quarter to five, but we know that can't be right as Jill was teaching until five, so she couldn't have got to the yard until twenty past five at the earliest.'

'The exact time should be on the dashcam footage,' said Orla. 'We can check that when we get it.' She nodded at the name Lincoln had scrawled on the whiteboard. 'So who else drives Elinor Morton's car? What do we know about her?'

Lincoln checked the information he'd got from the DVLA. 'Elinor Morton is sixty-five, lives in Amesbury, no criminal record. The car could've been stolen, although she hasn't reported it. We need to send someone over to talk to her.'

Nevin frowned. 'We could phone her, couldn't we?'

'No, because if she's in on this, we'd be alerting her. She could hide evidence before we got there. What are we waiting for?' he asked when nobody moved.

'We'll need to run it past the DCI.' Nevin shifted in his seat but didn't get up. 'Or *you* will. She'll want to know what's going on.'

The DCI wasn't in her office, so Lincoln hung around in the corridor for a few minutes, feeling like a schoolboy who's been sent to see the head teacher. While he waited, his mobile rang: Trish, sounding angry.

'Why didn't you tell me about Ramsay? It's been such a shock for Dad. They've been friends for ages.'

'I tried to call you, Trish, but you were out at some meeting or other. Didn't Kate tell you I'd rung?'

'No.' She breathed out, her anger defused. He hadn't meant to land Kate in it. 'And now Jill Fortune's missing. What's happened, Jeff? It's awful.'

'We need to speak to Kate.'

'Why?'

'Because she's the last person who saw Jill before she went to Keiller's Yard. The last person we know of, I mean.'

'But what can Kate tell you that you don't already know?'

61

'Jill may have said something about going up there. Kate may remember what Jill was wearing that afternoon. We can't *not* talk to her. And she'd want to help, wouldn't she, if she thought she could add anything? She does know Jill's missing, doesn't she?'

'Of course she knows. It's all over the news.'

'Listen, I'll get someone to speak to Kate at home – with you there, naturally. Is that okay?'

'When? Today? I don't finish work till six.'

'Can you be home by half six?'

'I'll try. Will you be there?'

He wished he could say yes, but it should be someone impartial. 'I'll send Pam Smyth over.'

The double doors along the corridor opened, and DCI Connors appeared, a bottle of water in one hand, a Snickers bar in the other. He quickly pocketed his phone.

'Waiting to see me, Jeff? Or trying to catch me out?' She waved the Snickers bar at him. 'Not very healthy, I know, but a woman's got to eat.'

He held the door open and followed her into her office. 'Late lunch, ma'am?'

'No time for lunch. But I can always make time for chocolate.' She sat down, signalled for him to take a seat too. 'What's the latest?'

He told her about the Astra seen leaving Keiller's Yard with a man at the wheel. 'Either Elinor Morton lets someone else drive her car or else it's been stolen and she hasn't got around to reporting it. Someone needs to go over to Amesbury to talk to her.'

'What are you waiting for? We need to move fast on this case.' Connors unscrewed the cap of her water bottle. 'Send someone over there.'

Back at his corner desk, having detailed a couple of uniforms to call at Elinor Morton's house, Lincoln prepared for his temporary transfer to Park Street. He got himself fixed up with a laptop, security codes and the right level of access. He wasn't sure he'd remember everyone's name, but he could probably bluff his way through tomorrow.

When the dashcam footage arrived in Orla's inbox, she called him and Rick Nevin over. 'Not brilliant resolution, but like Linda Pope told you, boss, the driver's a white male, around forty, a bit unkempt. No sign of a passenger.'

'Look at the time stamp.' Nevin leant forward, although the size of his belly prevented him getting very close. 'Sixteen forty-four. Nearly quarter to five. Same as she told you on the phone, Jeff.'

'The time on the dashcam must be wrong,' said Lincoln. 'Jill couldn't have left her house till after five.'

'Or the dashcam and Mrs Pope are both right,' said Orla. 'Keiller was shot around quarter to five, but Jill wasn't there.'

'Which means we're back at square one.' Nevin sat down on the nearest chair. Sweat beaded his upper lip and, beneath thinning hair, his scalp shone damply. He folded his arms and grinned as if being back at square one was what he'd wanted all along.

Lincoln watched as Orla replayed the dashcam footage, noting the reckless way the Astra pulled out of the yard, colliding with the wing mirror of Linda Pope's Yaris. But why would the man come back nearly an hour later to kidnap Jill? She'd have been no threat to him if she hadn't seen the shooting. Something didn't add up.

'We should hear back soon from the guys who've gone over to Amesbury,' Orla said, glancing at her watch. 'See if the Morton woman can tell us who was driving her car.'

'We still don't know for sure that Mrs Fortune went to the farm shop that afternoon, do we?' Nevin pushed himself up from the chair and lumbered back to his own desk. 'She could've left her purse there anytime, couldn't she? And are we a hundred per cent sure the bike is hers?'

'We need to get the bike brought in,' Lincoln said. 'Can someone do that?' He glanced across to Orla.

'I'll get that sorted,' she said, 'though Annika may not be able to say for certain it's Jill's.'

'We've got to start somewhere.'

A few minutes later, she came over to his desk with two cardboard mugs of coffee. He'd been hoping for something a little more authentic than the usual vending machine offering, but he wasn't complaining.

'Thanks.'

'One-fifty,' she grinned, 'but this one's on me. The guys are back from Amesbury. Elinor Morton was out, no sign of the car, no sign of anyone else there. According to the neighbours, she lives on her own, rarely has visitors, bit of a recluse. They've had issues with her for a long time, something to do with an old camper van she keeps in the front garden. They aren't exactly on speaking terms.'

'When did they see her last?'

'Sunday morning. She was driving off somewhere. Hasn't been back since.'

'She was on her own?'

'Sounds like it. Apparently there's a son, Ezra, about forty, but he and Elinor had a big falling-out two or three years back and he left. Neighbours haven't seen him since. They'll call us as soon as she comes back to the house.'

'So who was driving the Astra on Monday afternoon?'

Orla shrugged. 'I'll check Ezra out, but it doesn't sound as if it was him.'

The whiteboard drew Lincoln's gaze again, but the timeline wasn't going to re-configure itself no matter how long he stared at it. When the Astra tore out of Keiller's Yard at quarter to five, Jill was still in her front room at Arundel Terrace, listening to Kate playing the piano.

Was it possible that the shooting and Jill's disappearance were unrelated? Was Rick Nevin right? She could have left her purse on the counter any time before Monday afternoon. Supposing the bike left there wasn't hers after all? Had he wasted time trying to connect the cases when there was no connection at all?

He felt as if he was wading through treacle, trying to make sense of such contradictory evidence. If only he was back at Barley Lane, with his familiar team…

'Ezra Morton,' Orla called across to him. 'Date of birth, eleventh of August 1977. He's been done for drunk and disorderly, petty theft, threatening behaviour, obstructing a police officer, taking and driving away. Jailed in 2012 for common assault. Got eighteen months, out after six.'

Lincoln went over to look at the mugshot on her screen. It showed an unhappy young man, scowling, dishevelled.

'He'd fit the description Linda Pope gave us of the driver.'

'Yes, boss, but so would a lot of men. This photo's five years old. And why would he go after Ramsay Keiller?'

'He's a petty thief. Maybe he thought the farm shop was an easy target.'

'If it was so easy, why take a gun?'

Lincoln didn't have an answer. 'Let's get the bike brought in, confirm one way or the other whether it's Jill's. And I know,' he put in, before either Orla or Nevin could say anything, 'it won't tell us *when* she left it there, but it'll be one less question mark on the board. That common assault charge in 2012 – who was Ezra Morton's victim?'

Orla turned from her screen. 'Bloody hell, it was Elinor Morton! The bastard attacked his own mother!'

CHAPTER 17

Pam had never been to Trish Whittington's house before. It was much smaller than she'd imagined, tall and narrow, a flight of steps up to the front door. The tiny front yard under the bay window looked messy, with weeds sprouting between the paving slabs, and wheelie bins taking up a lot of the space.

At one end of the terrace was the busy road leading west out of Barbury; at the other was the railway line between London Waterloo and the West Country, Bristol and beyond. She knew Lincoln had actually lived here with Trish and her daughter for a bit while the Old Vicarage was being done up, but she could understand why he'd moved out again, even though his house still needed loads doing to it.

Trish came to the door looking flustered, as if she'd only just got back from work and hadn't had time to prepare herself. She wasn't especially pretty, though she had nice eyes. Her hair was sort of ash blonde, not quite long enough to be tied up the way she'd got it, a messy little topknot. What did the boss see in her? If they were so close, why were she and Kate still living here, while he was on his own in the Old Vicarage?

'I'll fetch Kate,' said Trish, leading her into the house. 'Won't be a sec.'

Pam waited in the room with the bay window while Trish called up the stairs to her daughter. After several minutes, Kate stomped down the stairs and into the front room. She slumped onto the sofa, making no secret of her irritation.

Pam smoothed out a fresh page in her notebook, smiling hopefully at the teenager. 'You know about Mrs Fortune, don't you, Kate? That she's been reported missing?'

Kate shifted in her seat and glanced up at her mother, who was perched on the arm of the sofa. 'Mum told me, yes. And it's on the news.'

'We think you were the last person to see her before she left her house on Monday. Did she say anything about her plans for the rest of that day?'

'Why would she? She's a teacher. She wouldn't have talked to me about something like that.'

'Okay, then… Do you remember what she was wearing?'

'Didn't really notice.'

'Have a think, love,' said Trish, putting on a bright smile. 'You were sitting next to her for an hour. You must have noticed something.'

'Not that I can remember.'

Pam had another go. 'What does she usually wear when she teaches you? Jeans or a skirt? Shorts?'

'Shorts?' Kate snorted. 'Mrs Fortune would never wear *shorts*.'

'Not even in weather like this?'

'She just never would!' As if she realised she was being rude, she said, more politely, 'I've never seen her in shorts, anyway.'

'But on Monday, she was wearing…' Her mother tried once again to prompt her.

'A skirt, probably. She usually wears a skirt.'

'How did she do her hair on Monday?' asked Pam. 'Was it loose or tied up?'

Another blank look. 'Didn't really notice. I was looking at my music, not at Mrs Fortune's hair.' And with that, Kate leapt off the sofa and fled upstairs. Her bedroom door slammed.

'Sorry.' Trish, embarrassed, fiddled with a strand of hair that had slipped loose from her topknot. 'This must have hit her harder than I realised. She's not usually difficult like that. Please don't take it personally.'

Pam brushed the apology away. 'That's okay. It must be hard for her, knowing Jill went missing so soon after she left her. She'd have finished her lesson at five – is that right?'

'Yes. She gets out of school at quarter to four and walks round to Arundel Terrace for four o'clock. Next week's lesson would've been her last before they break up for the summer.' Trish looked at her imploringly. 'You haven't heard anything?'

'I can't really say. No news is good news.' Except in this instance, Pam thought, it isn't, not really.

CHAPTER 18

The bicycle left outside the farm shop did indeed belong to Jill Fortune. A security number stencilled on the frame confirmed it.

'She'd registered it?' Orla sounded as surprised as Lincoln was. 'Bet that daughter of hers did it for her, wearing her insurance-selling hat.'

'At least we know Jill went to the farm shop, even if the timing isn't right.' He was still troubled by the Astra's speedy departure from Keiller's Yard at quarter to five and Jill's arrival at least half an hour later. It didn't add up, although an uncomfortable idea was forming in his mind: had Kate skipped her lesson? But surely she wouldn't have lied about something like that? 'Now we need to find Elinor Morton and ask her who's been driving her car.'

'If it's been stolen, she still hasn't reported it.'

'Let's go back and talk to the neighbours.'

'What, now? But boss, it's after seven.' Orla looked as if she was about to go home. 'And supposing the Astra's there? The guy driving it is armed, remember?'

'If the car's there, which is unlikely, we'll back off and call for the armed response unit. We need to get inside that house, find something that'll help us track Elinor down – a diary, calendar, whatever. If we can find out where she was heading on Sunday, we'll be able to establish when and where the car was stolen. She could be lying hurt somewhere if the bloke took the car by force.'

The light was beginning to fade by the time they reached the Amesbury house, a weary-looking semi at the end of a row of much smarter homes. The render was flaking off its walls, and tiles were missing from its roof. A camper van took up most of the front garden, tyres flat, windows spattered with bird shit, algae on the sides, moss on the roof. Clearly, the neighbour's complaints about it had been both justified and ineffective.

No sign of the Astra.

Lincoln pushed through knee-high grass and weeds to reach the camper van's door. Locked. And it didn't look as if anyone had tried opening it in a while.

At the side of the house, a wilderness of brambles and ivy engulfed a garage that would have collapsed if the greenery hadn't been holding it up.

Beyond it lay a paddock and the edge of the estate, and, beyond that, traffic rumbled incessantly along the A303.

One of the constables, PC Parks, knocked hard on the front door. As expected, no answer.

'Let's try the back.' Orla led the way down a path cluttered with recycling crates and broken boxes.

The back door wasn't locked and, when she opened it, several cats streamed out through the gap, vanishing into the overgrown garden. She stepped inside, Parks and Lincoln following.

'Oh Christ!' She held her hand over her nose as she went indoors. The smell of tomcat piss was overwhelming, and flies circled plates of cat food that had been left on the floor. 'No wonder she doesn't get many visitors.'

They proceeded cautiously through the rooms on the ground floor, more cats scattering ahead of them. The windows were shut, so the place was suffocatingly hot and airless. The living room and front room were a muddle of bulging black bin liners, stacked newspapers and plastic crates.

A hoarder's home, Lincoln thought sadly. Kitchen worktops littered with food cartons, unwashed milk bottles with mould gathering in them and foil trays of congealing, half-eaten meals. Somewhere under all the mess was a cooker heaped with wrappers and packaging, junk mail and bills.

'How do people live like this?' Orla took her hand away from her nose.

'God knows!' Not much hope of finding a handy list of contact numbers stuck to the fridge. Lincoln noticed that the phone jack had been ripped out of the wall and none of the ceiling lights had bulbs in them.

He traipsed up the stairs behind Parks, squeezing past stacks of mouldering newspapers and magazines. The bathroom hadn't been cleaned in a long time, grimy towels flung down on the ruckled mat, the cabinet mirror fogged by dust and dirt.

Only one bedroom had a bed in it – the sheets grey and tired, a greasy dent in the single pillow. Leggings, jumpers, T-shirts and underwear were draped over a chair and, by the look and smell of them, were rarely laundered. The other two bedrooms were so crammed with black bin bags of stuff the doors could only be opened a crack. No point searching them.

He'd been fearful of finding evidence that Elinor had been driven away under duress on Sunday morning, or had been hurt by whoever took her car, but there was nothing to suggest anyone else had set foot inside this house for a very long time. They'd found nothing more disturbing than a home, a life, in chaos.

'Anything like a diary, notebook, papers?'

Orla shook her head. 'Maybe check the kitchen again?'

All they found was an old cardboard box – resting on what appeared to be desiccated cat turds – in the bottom of a cupboard next to the cooker. It was crammed full of correspondence going back several years, application forms, out-of-date timetables, mail order catalogues and a thick folder, so tatty it was falling apart, with "Danny Swann" printed carefully in biro on the front.

Lincoln opened it gingerly, the name ringing so faint a bell he couldn't even be sure he'd heard it.

Orla peered over his shoulder. 'Who the fuck's Danny Swann?'

'No idea.'

Whoever he was, Swann must once have aspired to teenage stardom. The folder was full of copies of his glossy black and white portrait, with his signature printed on them. In some shots he clutched a microphone so close to his mouth, he seemed in danger of damaging his teeth. In others, he lounged in a leather armchair or leant against a graffiti-daubed brick wall. In most photos he wore skin-tight jeans, baggy jumpers and a scowl. The look screamed early sixties.

Orla plucked one of the photos from Lincoln's hand. 'Good-looking chap,' she said, although she didn't sound as if she meant it. 'Look at that hairstyle. What was he? One of the Beatles?'

'Before my time. You really think I'm that old? I wasn't even born when the Beatles were around.' He took the photo back.

She snorted. 'Perhaps he had a band called the Cygnets.'

'That's not as far-fetched as you think.'

A couple of programmes slipped out of the folder: Swann topping the bill at Barbury Playhouse, December 1965; *Swoon to Danny Swann and his band!* at the Civil Service Club, New Year 1966; local pop sensation Danny Swann at the ABC bingo hall a month later.

'Not exactly Hammersmith Odeon or the Finsbury Park Astoria.'

Orla looked up, puzzled. 'The Finsbury Park what?'

'Never mind. Elinor must've been a big fan, back in the day.' He shoved the box aside. No address book or even a scribbled list of contacts. 'We're wasting time. There's nothing here. Let's try next door, see what they can tell us.'

No one answered their knock on the neighbouring front door, but then a woman came round the side of the house, cigarette and can of lager in one hand, mobile in the other. She was as tall as Lincoln and could have topped his weight by several stone.

'We're looking for Elinor Morton.' He showed her his ID and she strained to read his name in the failing light.

'Gemma Dickinson,' she said, drawing on her cigarette and screwing up her eyes against the smoke. 'You found her yet? You found Elinor?'

'We were hoping you could help us get in touch with her. Has she got family round here?'

'Not sure she's got any family apart from Ezra and, like I told the coppers who were round here earlier, they're what you'd call *estranged*.' She put heavy emphasis on the word.

'What about friends, visitors?'

'Who's gonna visit, the state of that place? I've told her, I'll get the council round if she doesn't sort herself out. She should be in a home.' She flicked ash from her cigarette. 'Or the loony bin. The woman's mental. Okay, she's had a hard life, single mum bringing up that lout of a son on her own, but she's not the only one.'

'Do you know where Ezra's living?' asked Orla.

'No idea. He's long gone. Sleeping rough for all I know. Sort of thing he'd do. He lived in the camper van for nearly a year after he got out of prison, wouldn't go indoors. Used to do his business round the back of the garage. Can you imagine the stink? And he didn't wash. She was afraid of him, that's what it was. Big lad like that. And she's only small.'

'So you can't think where she was driving off to on Sunday?'

Gemma shook her head. 'Nah. She never goes out much these days, only to do her shopping down One Stop. What's this about? Not in any danger, am I? She's not gone off her nut or something?'

'We think her car's been used in the commission of a crime,' said Orla. 'You need to let us know if she comes back, or if you see the car here.'

Gemma jammed her cigarette in the corner of her mouth. 'Frankly,' she said, the cigarette waggling, 'I wouldn't care if I never saw her or that son of hers ever again. They should be locked up, the pair of them.'

CHAPTER 19

When Lincoln got home to the Old Vicarage, he headed for the shower even before he'd poured himself a drink. What a day! The smell of Elinor Morton's house still lingered in his nostrils, and he thanked God he didn't have her as a neighbour. Irritating as the residents of the Fountains could be, all was quiet over there tonight so, after he'd showered and dressed, he took his drink out to the veranda at the back.

The bushes beside him rustled and Tux stepped languidly onto the lawn. The fur on top of its head was ruffled and as Lincoln reached out to smooth the tufts back into place, the cat pushed a hot, dry muzzle up into his palm. It had taken a while to win the trust of the little black and white cat, and Tux never deigned to curl up on his lap, but they got on well enough.

Lincoln thought back to the stench of tomcat pee in Elinor's house. How did a woman get into that situation? Never throwing anything away, having to manoeuvre around barriers of old newspapers, walls of bin bags, the impenetrable clutter of the dirty kitchen. He tended to agree with her neighbour Gemma: Elinor had a mental health problem and needed professional help. So why had neither she nor her son apparently sought that help?

Who had driven Elinor's car to Keiller's Yard on Monday, shot Keiller and driven off at speed? Where was Elinor now?

And where was Jill Fortune?

Tux rubbed round his legs, then sprang up the stone steps to the kitchen door.

'Okay,' said Lincoln, 'I can take a hint. You're starving.' He knocked back his drink and followed the cat indoors.

Trish rang as he was getting himself some supper, although he was almost past hunger. Still, she'd approve of his food choices: cherry tomatoes, mozzarella, celery, cucumber. He wouldn't mention the mound of salted peanuts he was adding to make it more palatable.

'I'm sorry about the way Kate behaved,' she said in a rush. 'You know yourself, she's not normally rude.'

'Hey, rewind a bit! Have I missed something?' He set his plate aside and dipped a stalk of celery into the salt.

'Pam Smyth came round to talk to Kate. I thought she'd have reported back by now.'

'I've been at Park Street all afternoon, only just got in.' He crunched on the celery. 'What happened with Kate?'

'What are you eating?'

'Celery. I haven't eaten all day. What happened with Pam and Kate?'

'Kate got a bit upset, that's all. I think it suddenly hit her, Jill going missing, maybe something bad happening to her.'

'Understandable. Jill's been her piano teacher for a while now. Are they talking about it at school, the other girls?'

'Of course. She didn't want to go to school this morning. She's taking it really hard.'

'Listen,' he said carefully, 'there's no chance Kate finished her lesson early on Monday, is there? Or didn't go to it?'

'Of course she went! I was here when she got home. She told me how well Mrs Fortune said she'd played. Why?'

'Just trying to work something out.' And failing. 'How well do *you* know Jill?'

'Me? I don't really know her. I met her when Kate first started going to her for piano lessons, but otherwise we only meet at Local History Society meetings. Of course, now I know why she wasn't at the meeting last night.'

'Did she ever mention Ramsay? Were they friends?'

'Ramsay and Jill?' Trish went quiet for a while, making Lincoln check his phone screen in case she'd been cut off. Then, 'Sorry, I just realised she's the same age as my mum would be now. They were probably at the grammar school together.'

'With Ramsay's wife, too, then. Jill and Maggie Keiller were schoolfriends, according to the daughter.'

She sighed. 'And now Jill's the only one left.'

Lincoln felt sad for her. He knew that Mrs Whittington, Eva, had died suddenly when Trish was in her twenties, not long before Kate was born. And now someone who might have remembered her from their schooldays was missing.

'And you're not aware of a partner or a close friend she's involved with?'

'The Local History Society meets to discuss local history, Jeff, not our respective love lives.' She laughed as she said it. 'But no, I've never heard her mention anyone.'

He thought back to the piles of typescript in the box room at Arundel Terrace. 'Is Jill an expert on Barbury Abbey?'

'Not that I know of.'

'Or Moses Thatcher?'

'The farmer bard? Someone in the Local History Society has been writing about him. Why?'

'Marie Williams?'

'Marie Williamson. Okay, Jeff, why the sudden interest in local history?'

'Why would Jill have the manuscript of Marie's Moses Thatcher book?'

'She's probably doing the index for it.'

'The index?'

'You know, that thing at the back of a book that takes you to the right page. Jill does indexes as a sideline.'

'No need to be sarcastic,' he said. 'I never really thought about how indexes get there. So, if you don't want to do it yourself, you can pay someone else to do it for you?'

'A professional indexer like Jill can charge quite a lot. It's hours and hours of work. But those books aren't why she's gone missing, are they? Isn't it because she saw what happened to Ramsay?'

Except she *couldn't* have seen what happened to Ramsay, Lincoln thought ruefully. When that gun went off, Jill was still listening to Kate running through her scales or whatever she did.

Or was she? Doubt was niggling at him ever more insistently.

'I can't talk about it, Trish. And we really don't know.'

She sighed. 'Why ever didn't I think of it before?'

'What?'

'That Jill and Mum were at school together. I'll have to ask her what Mum was like. Wouldn't it be funny if they'd been friends?'

CHAPTER 20

Late in the afternoon, the man brought Jill a cup of water and, bizarrely, a few grapes. She noticed he had a dirty bandage wrapped around his thumb, a smudge of blood showing through. He untied her hands and watched her drink, waiting while she savoured every grape, even though they were wrinkled, the skins tough. Then he tied up her hands again, the bandaged thumb making him clumsy, and yanked her to her feet. Her legs were like rubber, and she'd have dropped to the floor again if he hadn't been holding her up.

'Please let me go,' she begged. 'Whatever you want from me, it isn't worth the trouble you'll be in when they find you.'

He grunted. He wasn't going to waste words on her. Instead, he spun her round, blindfolded her and pulled her outside. The sun warmed her face for a few seconds before he swept her up and dumped her, like a sack of laundry, into the boot of his car.

The car bumped noisily over concrete for minutes on end. She thought of the airfield with its cracked and pitted surface. Was that where he'd been holding her, in one of those outbuildings at Turnpike Corner? No wonder he hadn't bothered to gag her. No one would have heard her.

How ridiculous to think that all this time, she'd been less than half a mile from Keiller's Yard.

The road surface was quieter now and she heard traffic. Then the car cornered suddenly, slamming her up against the side panel of the boot. Fresh pain roared up her neck and over the back of her head and, despite trying to hold on, she slipped back into unconsciousness.

When she opened her eyes again, she thought for a brief, delicious moment that she was in her own bed, waking from a nightmare. But no. Another concrete space but without a crack of light under the door. A concrete coffin. Buried alive.

Her heart raced. She couldn't breathe. No, no, no, not that! A childhood terror so real she'd been afraid to fall asleep at night, convinced she'd die and wake up underground, six feet of soil on top of her, no one to hear her...

Jill screamed – and her scream echoed. Not a concrete coffin then, but a big concrete box. Could she move? She tested each limb in turn. Her arms were free, and one leg, but her left leg was weighed down by a chain around her ankle. Her arms and legs worked, but they ached with that cold burning she hadn't felt for years. Ever since she'd been knocked off her bike and nearly killed, she'd suffered with chronic back pain. Her recovery had begun with a series of exercises she'd done every day. She still had good days and bad. Still sometimes got out of bed and could hardly stand upright, but that mix of yoga and Pilates had been crucial.

And now all of that was being undone.

A heavy door grated against the floor and a shaft of pale light ran across her body. She caught a glimpse of leaves beyond the man's silhouette. Leaves and a darkening sky. She was above ground, at least.

'What do you want from me?' she cried out. 'Do you need money? I'm not rich. There's no point holding me to ransom. Just tell me what…'

He clapped his hand over her mouth. 'Stop talking at me! Shut the fuck up!'

She obeyed, stunned by the sound of his voice. A sound she recognised. The man who'd plagued her for weeks on the phone. She thought he'd given up, but she'd been wrong.

He took his hand away. 'Don't scream. No one can hear you.'

Yes, it was him. She recognised the voice, a certain note in it, a tone she could almost see on the page as a minor chord, quite low.

She knew now who this rough stranger must be. She'd have laughed if she'd had the strength, but she was weak and her stomach groaned with hunger. She could hardly move for the agony of cramped muscles.

'You're Daniel's son,' she managed to say. 'You're Ezra.'

CHAPTER 21

Lincoln arrived at Park Street soon after eight next morning. He'd woken at five and, unable to get back to sleep, had got up and showered, made coffee and checked his emails, trying to put his thoughts in order before he had to leave for work.

As he expected, the chair he'd commandeered yesterday had been restored to the desk from which he'd nicked it, and it was now occupied. He sighed, hunting around for one that looked spare. The incident room was already busy, but apparently there'd been no updates on Jill Fortune's disappearance or the Keiller shooting.

Orla hurried in, coffee shop beaker in hand, her dark hair still wet from the shower. She must have noticed him looking at her hair, because she pushed her damp curls back from her face and said, almost defiantly, 'I've come straight from the gym.'

'Wish I had your energy.'

'Use it or lose it, boss.'

He gave her a weak smile. 'Any news?'

She shook her head as she dumped the beaker down. 'The Astra's gone off the radar completely. As you know, we've got patrols out looking for it, but it hasn't shown up yet.'

'Whoever he is, he must be sticking to minor roads, or he's holed up somewhere. Have we dug up anything else about Mrs Morton?'

'For a start, it's *Miss* Morton. She never married. No father's name on Ezra's birth certificate. Like the neighbour said, she brought him up on her own.'

'In that house.'

'It may not always have been that bad,' Orla supposed. 'She probably started out trying to do the best for them both, but things went downhill.'

'Not helped by having a son who'd rather crap in the garden than come indoors.'

'That too.' She took a sip of her coffee. 'I looked up Danny Swann last night when I got home, by the way. Surprised you've never heard of him, boss. He was a big star in the sixties.'

'I told you, that was before my time.'

'Yeah, but his band was still around in the eighties, when you'd have been a teenager. The Barbury Blues Band?'

Lincoln shook his head. 'I was certainly into blues music, but I didn't live round here then, and if they were local...'

'They started out as a local band, but they toured the country, went abroad. They were big in the States for a while.'

'So what happened to them?'

'Danny Swann left in the seventies,' Orla said, 'but the band carried on for another ten years or so before folding. Swann went on a trip and never came back.'

'A trip? To where?'

She rolled her eyes. 'An *acid* trip. According to Wikipedia, he took a particularly powerful dose of LSD when they were in LA and it messed with his head. Permanently.'

'Another casualty of the music scene. Like Peter Green.'

'Who?'

She wouldn't have heard of John Mayall's Bluesbreakers, Lincoln guessed. Might have heard of Fleetwood Mac since they were still around, but... 'You're not saying it's *Danny* we should be looking for?'

'Hardly! He died in April. Although that might explain why we can't find him.' She fluttered her hands in the air. 'He's nothing more than a ghostly apparition.'

Lincoln sat back in his chair. 'But what's Swann got to do with either Ramsay Keiller or Jill Fortune?'

'Nothing, apart from Elinor Morton having all that stuff about him. I was just checking him out in case it led anywhere.'

They sat in silence for a few more minutes until Lincoln decided some coffee might help his thought processes.

'Jill's into blues music,' he said, jingling the change in his trouser pocket, hoping he'd got the right coins. 'Hey, that would explain the title of the disc on her turntable.'

Orla looked up, puzzled. 'What disc?'

'There was an album on her turntable, *Dan's Swannsong 1974*. Jill must have been a fan back in the day.'

'And that's relevant how?'

'Didn't say it was. Just saying.' He loped across to the drinks machine, intent on charming it into dispensing a black coffee, with sugar.

'Elinor must've been a fan from way back,' Orla said, 'keeping all those signed photos and programmes all these years.'

'In the bottom of a cupboard, on top of a pile of cat doodah. Probably kept it because she never throws anything away.'

'Maybe Jill and Elinor know each other. They're the same sort of age, give or take a year or two.'

'How old would Swann have been now?'

She did a quick calculation. 'Seventy, seventy-one. Born in 1946.'

'Same age as Keiller.'

'And thousands of other men in Barbury.'

Lincoln inserted the right money into the machine. A cardboard cup dropped down and a brackish liquid dribbled miserably into it. His heart sank.

'There isn't a kettle here anywhere?' he enquired hopefully as he carried the cup back to his desk. It didn't even *smell* like coffee.

'Not allowed,' said Orla. 'Health and safety.'

The whiteboard drew him once more. 'Someone driving Elinor's car shoots Keiller and speeds away from the scene. But why come back?' He asked the question with little hope of an answer. 'By the time Jill arrived, someone could've found Keiller and raised the alarm. The place would've been heaving with emergency services. And how did he know Jill would be there? It doesn't make sense.'

The board glared back at him with all the silent defiance of the whiteboard at Barley Lane.

'Unless,' said Orla, 'the kid is lying about going to her piano lesson.'

She was voicing what he hadn't wanted to. He looked round at her. 'Lying?'

'Think about it, boss. How else does the timing work out? If Jill left home at *four* fifteen, say, instead of *five* fifteen, she'd have been at the farm shop when Keiller was shot.'

He recalled how defensive Kate had been on the phone when he'd asked her about her music lessons, as if she thought he was checking up on her. Was a guilty conscience making her jumpy?

He needed to act now, or else the investigation would run aground on this irreconcilable timeline. And he needed to deal with it in person, not over the phone.

'I've got to slip out for an hour or so,' he said. 'Can you dig a bit more on Elinor Morton? We need to find out where she might be and who could be driving her car. Give the neighbour a ring, check no one's come back to the house.'

'Okay, boss. When will you be back? In case the DCI asks.'

'Lunchtime.' Then, remembering that the DCI didn't do lunch, he corrected himself. 'By midday.'

He hurried from the central car park to the library, unsure whether Trish was even working today. He'd lost track of her regular schedule. The young woman on the front desk told him Ms Whittington was in the Local Studies section but had somebody with her.

'This is urgent,' he said, flashing his ID.

'I'll take you up then.'

Trish wasn't with a customer, as he'd assumed. The man she was talking to wore a council lanyard. He was also in jeans and an open neck shirt, sleeves rolled up to reveal bony wrists and sinewy forearms.

When she saw Lincoln, her face filled with dread. She must have thought he'd come to give her bad news about Jill, he guessed. He should have sent her a text first, except she probably wouldn't have seen it.

The man with the lanyard looked round at him, clearly put out by the intrusion. 'We're in the middle of a meeting here,' he said. 'Do you mind waiting?'

'I do,' said Lincoln, flashing his own ID badge. 'This is a police matter and I need to speak to Ms Whittington now.'

'I'm sorry, Steve.' Trish spread her hands in apology as her colleague rose resentfully to his feet.

'We'll pick this up again later.' Steve scooped up his notepad and pen and barged past Lincoln on his way out. The library assistant trotted after him.

Trish turned anxious eyes on Lincoln. 'What's happened? Have you found her?' She took a deep breath, bracing herself for bad news.

'Not yet, but I need to ask you something. Can you be *absolutely* sure that Kate went along to her piano lesson on Monday afternoon?'

'Of course she did! Why?'

'Because we're pretty sure Jill was on her way to Keiller's Yard long before Kate's lesson would have finished.'

'Are you calling my daughter a liar?'

'I'm saying Kate didn't go to Arundel Terrace that afternoon, and she's too afraid or too embarrassed to say so.'

Trish turned away, her gaze raking the shelves of books that took up three walls of her tiny office. 'No!' she said, sounding as if she was trying to convince herself as much as Lincoln. 'Kate wouldn't lie about a thing like that.'

'Please, Trish, ask her again. I'm guessing she's told a little white lie, never thinking for a minute that she'd be caught out, and now she doesn't know how to admit it.'

Her silence told him he was probably right.

'Please, Trish.'

Her desk phone rang and she reached for it – an enquiry about census records from the sound of it. She covered the mouthpiece. 'I'll speak to her,' she promised him. 'But if you're wrong…'

He didn't wait to hear the consequences.

CHAPTER 22

Trish couldn't wait until Kate came home from school, so she asked Briony to hold the fort for an hour.

Her assistant wasn't happy. 'But we've got those researchers coming in at eleven thirty. They'll want things from the basement. I can't go down there *and* keep an eye on things up here.'

'Ask Selina to go on the desk. She's perfectly capable of answering the phone and showing people where things are. I need to leave now, Briony. It's a family emergency.'

Family emergencies didn't cut much ice with Briony, but she could hardly stop her boss from leaving the library if she needed to.

Fifteen minutes later, Trish was striding down the broad drive to the office at Kate's school.

'I need to speak to my daughter, Kate Amos,' she told Gilda, the school secretary. 'Urgently. It's nothing awful,' she added hastily, in case Gilda assumed there'd been a death in the family, 'but it *is* really important.'

Within minutes Kate had been summoned from her classroom and shown into the school library, where Gilda promised they wouldn't be disturbed. It was a sunny room, familiar to Trish from her own schooldays here. Now, though, the view from the picture windows was of the redbrick backs of new teaching blocks instead of the sweep of the daisy-strewn playing field that she remembered.

As soon as she saw her face, Trish could tell Kate knew she was in trouble.

'Sit down, Kate,' she said, taking a seat at one of the study tables. Someone had gouged I LUV JAKE into the wood, probably with the point of a compass. Nothing changes, she thought. 'Kate, you need to tell me the truth about Monday afternoon. Did you go to your lesson at Mrs Fortune's?'

Behind the glasses she had to wear most of the time now, Kate's eyes widened. 'Of course I did! I told you. I told that Pam woman.'

'Did the lesson finish early? Were you there right up until five?'

Kate chewed the tip of her thumb. 'Actually, we did finish a bit early. Why?'

'How early?'

'Um...'

'How early, Kate? Come on, you must remember. It was only three days ago.'

'Stop going on at me! First it was that detective and now it's you. Don't you believe me?'

Trish sat back in the uncomfortable chair and studied I LUV JAKE. It could have been there for years, decades, since she'd been a pupil here. 'I want to believe you, Katy, really I do, but the police are pretty sure...'

'The *police*? Jeff, you mean. I suppose it's *Jeff* who's told you I'm lying.' She would've flounced off if they'd been at home, but it wasn't an option here.

'And *are* you lying? Look, I'll understand if you tell me now. The longer you insist that you were at your lesson on Monday, the harder it'll be to find Mrs Fortune. You're not a child any more, Kate. You're nearly fifteen. Take some responsibility for your actions and tell me the truth.'

Her daughter folded her arms on the table and lowered her head onto them. Her glasses fell off and her hair slid out of its headband. Her shoulders shook. She was crying. Trish longed to gather her into her arms to soothe her, as she'd done so many times over the years, but this was different. She needed answers and she needed them now. Jeff needed them, for Jill's sake.

'Just tell me yes or no, Kate,' she said at last. 'So the police know what time Jill left home. It could be a matter of life and death. Please.'

Kate lifted her head up, her nose red, her cheeks streaked with tears. 'I didn't go on Monday. I couldn't face it. I hadn't practised, and Mrs Fortune always sounds so disappointed with me, as if I'm not trying hard enough, but I am, Mum, I am!'

Trish patted Kate's shoulder gently. She should have known her daughter wasn't practising often enough, *would* have known if she herself wasn't working two evenings a week, every week, now that Kate was old enough to be left alone in the house. But she'd always been such a studious girl. A bit of a swot, really. Anxious about finishing her homework ahead of time, conscientious about revising for her exams.

Maybe piano lessons were too much on top of everything else – or was there something else going on?

'So what did you do instead?'

'Just hung around in town until it was time for the bus.'

'On your own? Was Charlotte with you?'

'Charlotte? I don't go round with Charlotte anymore.'

'Since when?' The girls had been best friends all through school so far, with regular sleepovers and outings together.

Kate searched her pockets for a tissue to wipe her face. She inspected her glasses before putting them back on again. 'Since half term. Since she's been friends with Paloma, the new girl.'

Trish nodded, remembering all too well the trauma of broken friendships and changing loyalties. Kate and Charlotte had fallen out before and had always made up, but this sounded different. Maybe they were growing apart as they headed for Year 12.

'So you hung around in town on your own for an hour? Is it the first time you've skipped piano?'

The guilty look on Kate's face told its own story. 'Only once before. And that was because I had the most horrendous cramps and thought I might throw up over the keys.'

Trish let it go. She needed to call Jeff. 'I'm glad you've told me what really happened, Kate. Now you need to get back to your lesson.'

But when she stood up, Kate stayed where she was. 'So what do I say when I go back into class? They'll want to know why I got called out.'

'Say it's something private. Tell them I had some bad news, but you can't talk about it.'

'But that's lying, isn't it?'

'Please don't do this, Kate. Tell them what you want. Tell them to mind their own business. I'll see you at home.'

'Are you working late?' Behind her glasses, her eyes looked huge and accusing.

'I finish at five today. I'll see you at tea time.'

Trish phoned Lincoln as she walked back up the school drive. 'Kate missed her lesson,' she told him, in a tone she hoped would deter him from asking for details. 'You were right.'

'Shall I come over later?'

He hadn't come to the house for a couple of weeks. Hadn't spent the night with her for over two months. She'd been pleased to see him this morning, despite the reason for his visit, but tonight wasn't the ideal time to invite him round, not with Kate sounding so hostile towards him.

'Not tonight,' she said. 'We need a bit of mother and daughter time tonight.'

'Is she okay? I didn't want to land her in it, Trish, but...'

'I know, I know. She'll be fine. We're both worried about Jill. There's no news?'

'Nothing I can share with you yet. You know I would if I could. I'd better go. I've got my first proper briefing with this lot.'

She slipped her phone back in her bag and hurried to her car.

CHAPTER 23

His first team briefing, and Lincoln was nervous, unfamiliar with most of the faces upturned towards him. Rick Nevin sat near the back, arms crossed over a shirt that threatened to burst its buttons. Orla, at the front, studied the whiteboard, not making eye contact.

'Let's put together what we know.' Lincoln tapped the first photo on the board, Keiller glowering fiercely beneath bushy eyebrows. 'Ramsay Keiller, shot once outside his farm shop on Monday afternoon. He gets in his Land Rover to go after his attacker, turns off onto Hangman's Lane and pulls over into a gateway. Dies at the wheel shortly after.'

He pointed to the photo of Jill, a picture taken many years ago, her mass of fair hair a bright cloud around her face, her eyes sparkling, her smile warm.

'Jill Fortune,' he went on, 'calling at the shop for some groceries, leaves her purse on the counter, goes outside to see what's happening and is forced into the gunman's car, a Vauxhall Astra registered to this woman…'

He jabbed the only photo they'd found of Elinor, taken from her driving licence, more like a mugshot, staring straight ahead, her mouth hanging slightly open. Thin hair strained back from a pudgy face. No make-up. A sad expression in her eyes.

'Elinor Morton, sixty-five, currently absent from her house in Amesbury. We don't know who was driving her car, but…'

Nevin raised a hand. 'You're *assuming* Jill was abducted by the driver of the car, aren't you? We haven't any proof.'

'You're right, Rick,' he conceded patiently, 'but since Jill's bike and purse were left at the farm shop, and she hasn't been seen since giving a piano lesson from three to four o'clock on Monday afternoon, I'd say it's safe to *assume* there's a connection, wouldn't you? How else did her belongings get there if she didn't take them there herself?'

Nevin wiped the sweat from his upper lip. 'Still only an assumption.'

'It is, yes, but sometimes we have to put two and two together and trust we don't make five.' Lincoln paused, checking that Nevin wasn't going to argue. 'Okay, we know Keiller made a phone call to one of his suppliers round about half four. No hint of any trouble. But then at four forty-four, a man driving Elinor Morton's Astra drives out of the yard so fast he nearly collides with a passing Toyota Yaris. He then heads towards the main road. And in those fourteen minutes, he's shot Keiller in the side with a nine-millimetre handgun, overpowered Jill Fortune, forced her into his car and driven away at speed.'

A young woman sitting next to Nevin put her hand up. 'Do we know for sure that it *wasn't* Ezra Morton driving, sir? With his record, isn't he the most obvious suspect?'

'He is,' Lincoln agreed, 'but we understand he and his mother have been estranged for some time, so it's unlikely she'd lend him her car. Plus, he's stayed out of trouble since 2012. It's more likely that the car was stolen sometime on Sunday or on Monday morning, and, for whatever reason, Elinor hasn't reported it.'

'Or someone's taken it from her by force,' the young detective suggested. 'She could be dead too.'

'That's a possibility, yes.'

'And we're thinking that he put the Fortune woman in the boot?'

Lincoln nodded. 'Or she was flat out on the back seat. The gunman could have knocked her out.'

'The Astra can't have vanished into thin air, can it?' Nevin again.

'No, Rick, but if the driver's local, he'll know how to avoid cameras. He's certainly evaded all the patrols looking for him, hasn't shown up so far on traffic cams.' With any luck, Lincoln hoped, the Astra's registration would be picked up by ANPR cameras – automatic number plate recognition technology designed to spot vehicles of interest to the police.

'But we still don't know why he went after Keiller, do we?'

'No, Rick, there's no obvious motive apart from robbery. Although, as we know, nothing seems to have been stolen. He'll need to fill up with petrol some time, and that's when his number plate should get flagged by an ANPR camera.'

'Let's hope he doesn't shoot anyone else first,' said Nevin, as if Lincoln was personally responsible for the driver still being at large. 'Whoever he is.'

Bradley Owen, Jill's three o'clock pupil on Mondays, wasn't a schoolboy, as Lincoln had supposed, but was the recently retired manager of a furniture shop. As he explained over the phone, he'd always promised himself he'd learn to play the piano when he was no longer working.

'My lesson finished as usual at a few minutes to four,' he said, 'and Mrs Fortune was expecting someone after me, the little lass who's usually waiting outside when I leave. Mind you, she wasn't there this week. The schools haven't broken up yet, have they?'

He hadn't really noticed what Jill was wearing, other than a long skirt patterned with big poppies. 'Bit of a flower child, our Mrs Fortune,' he said, wryly. 'I do hope she hasn't come to any harm.'

Lincoln sat at his corner desk trying to tell himself they were getting somewhere. Because of Kate's initial dishonesty about going to Jill's, confusion over the timing had diverted them, but now they were back on track.

Orla called across to him. 'Call from your DS, boss. Your *other* DS. I'll put him through to your desk phone.'

It was surprisingly good to hear Woody's voice. Had it only been a day and a bit since Lincoln had been at Barley Lane?

'Pam's been looking at those aerial photos of Hangman's Lane,' Woody said after they'd exchanged greetings. 'There's a building at the end that she thinks we should look at.'

'But the lane only goes to the pig farm, doesn't it?' It took Lincoln a minute or two to bring up Google Maps on his laptop. 'Okay, I've got it on screen. What am I looking at?'

'See the track to the pig farm? It splits, doesn't it?'

'And runs into what looks like a bloody great hedge alongside the airfield.'

'Pam's wondering if there's a way through that thicket. Reckon it would explain how the Astra disappeared and why Ramsay was driving along there.'

'You think Ramsay was going after him?'

'Exactly. The pig farmer told us the track didn't go anywhere and we didn't question it, but supposing there's a way through after all?'

CHAPTER 24

Graham Dilke parked the car in Hangman's Lane, in the gateway where Ramsay Keiller's Land Rover had been found. He got out and followed Pam, who was intent on proving that the Astra could have evaded its pursuers by driving through an apparent dead end.

'Feels weird, the case being split between us and Park Street.' He paused to peel a vicious briar away from his shirt, where it had snatched at his shoulder. He didn't often venture into the countryside, despite having been brought up in Barbury. 'It can't be efficient.'

'Not sure the boss is any happier about it than we are, Gray, but Park Street needs our help. Let's make the best of it, show that lot they shouldn't underestimate us.'

They came to a fork in the lane. To the right, the lane continued to the farmyard, but to the left it became little more than a chalky track with a ridge of coarse grass down the middle. The track ran into a thick curtain of ivy, elder and brambles after another fifty yards.

As they approached the curtain of greenery Dilke saw it had recently been ripped apart by a vehicle driving through it, scattering vegetation to either side.

He exchanged a look with Pam. She was clearly thinking the same as he was. 'Let's check it out,' he said.

They pushed their way through the undergrowth and found themselves standing on the edge of the airfield. A few yards away, tucked into the corner, almost hidden by trees and encroaching nettles and brambles, stood a shed, its roof a rusting curve of corrugated iron.

'It's a Nissen hut,' said Dilke. 'Surprised it's survived this long.' Curious, he jogged across to it, but when he turned, he saw that Pam was holding back.

'Don't we need backup, Gray? We don't know what we're walking into.'

'Let's listen first.' He put his ear to the battered wooden door of the hut but could hear nothing. With gloves on, he gingerly turned the handle, inched the door open and stepped inside. The air smelt of canvas and earth, motor oil and rope. He reached round for a light switch. The space was illuminated by a dim bulb in a metal shade enmeshed in cobwebs.

A crumpled quilt lay on the floor and, next to it, a lidded bucket that stank of stale urine. Flies buzzed around it. 'Oh God, that smell!'

'Is it her?' From her anxious tone, he realised Pam thought he'd found a body.

'There's no one here,' he assured her. 'But someone's been kept prisoner.'

Pam stepped inside. 'That's why he wasn't picked up on camera. He drove along the lane onto the airfield and waited.'

Something caught Dilke's eye, a glint of something metallic in the shadows on the floor. He stooped down. 'It's a bracelet,' he said, holding it up to the light from the door. 'A silver bangle.'

'Mrs Fortune always wears lots of bracelets and rings, according to the description. It must be one of hers.' Pam scrabbled in her pocket for an evidence bag and he dropped the bangle in.

'Look at that.' He pointed into a corner where a piece of cloth, about the size of a tea towel, lay crumpled and soiled. 'Those could be blood stains.'

The discarded cloth was carefully slipped into another evidence bag.

He scanned the hut once more. 'No blood on the floor though, or on the quilt.'

'The light's not good enough to be sure. The CSIs need to take a proper look. We'd better call the sarge, and then get out before we contaminate it even more.'

They went back outside and he looked across to the control tower half a mile away on the other side of the airfield. A couple of light aircraft were lined up outside the only remaining hangar. The gunman could easily have hidden the Astra here, under the overhang of ivy and elder, while he dragged or carried Mrs Fortune in and out of the hut.

'He must have waited until he thought the coast was clear and then moved her,' he supposed. 'But where's he holding her captive now?'

Pam held up the evidence bags containing the silver bangle and the bloodstained cloth. 'Assuming she's still alive.'

'How's it going, Jeff?' DCI Connors parked herself on the corner of Lincoln's desk. 'I hear there's been a development. You've found where the gunman took the Fortune woman.'

Lincoln sat back from his screen. 'Yes, it looks as if he drove onto the edge of the airfield and hid her in a Nissen hut until he thought it was safe to move her.'

'A Nissen hut?' She seemed unfamiliar with the term.

'A military building, corrugated iron, a half-cylinder in cross-section. Very simple, very quick to put up in war time. Quite a few are still in use, especially round here.'

'How come it wasn't searched sooner?'

'We didn't know there was a way onto the airfield from Hangman's Lane, ma'am. It appeared to be a dead end.'

'And the blood your guys found?'

'We're getting it analysed now. Not a lot of blood, though, more like from a superficial wound.'

'And still no sign of the Astra?'

He shook his head. 'And no sign of Elinor Morton since she drove away from her house on Sunday morning.'

'Could she be behind this?'

'I doubt it. She's got mental health issues, lives in squalor with a dozen cats. If she's involved at all, it's because she's been caught up in something beyond her control.'

Connors said, 'I'm putting out an appeal to try to track her down. Carefully worded. Elinor as much a victim as Keiller. But we need to find that car and we need to find her, fast.' Arms folded, she studied the other officers busily working in the rest of the incident room. 'Getting on okay with this lot?'

Lincoln grinned. 'As long as no one nicks my chair the minute my back's turned.'

She grinned back. 'With the Met, weren't you?'

'A long time ago, yes, after Hendon.'

'Another world down here, isn't it? And not exactly multicultural. I'm a London girl, born and bred, but the way the locals look at me because I'm black...' She chuckled bitterly.

'It'll change, but it'll take time.'

Barbury's population was still predominantly white, the black and Asian residents working mostly in catering or at the hospital. Connors was the only black person in the incident room.

She pushed herself off his desk. 'Let's go public with Elinor Morton. We need to know where she is and how a gunman got hold of her car. I'll draft something for Media Relations.'

CHAPTER 25

Jill lay on her side, trying to ease her aching back. Nothing broken, but she'd hurt her neck trying to pull away from Ezra. He'd seized hold of her when she called him by name, shaken her, shouting at her to *shut up, shut up, shut the fuck up*!

And then he'd thrown her down, hard, on the concrete floor, where she was lying now, sore and frightened.

'You let my father down!' he'd yelled, spittle flying. 'You betrayed him!'

She hadn't responded. What could she say? She'd been trying to save Dan from himself, not betray him. But Ezra didn't want to hear that.

So like his father…

June 1965. Three girls at school together: Jill, Maggie, and Eva.

They live within a hundred yards of each other on the edge of Barbury, classmates at junior school, passing the eleven-plus exam together and going on to the girls-only grammar school. Now they're facing O-Levels and then the Sixth Form, having to make decisions about Life After School.

Maggie is especially brainy, clearly destined for Oxbridge to study maths or chemistry. Jill is musical, although not gifted enough to make a career out of it. She'll go to university or training college, probably, and become a history teacher, since that's her best subject. She doesn't have Maggie's drive to do something important with her life.

And Eva? Eva's a free spirit, a rebel. She's going to change the world, stop people eating meat, ban animal testing, outlaw fox hunting. Since Christmas, she's somehow got in with the Art School crowd.

'There's a party you've *got* to come to!' she tells Maggie and Jill. 'There'll be a band and it's going to be fabulous. There'll be booze and smokes and some really dishy boys, not just those drips from the boys' grammar.'

'I can't,' says Maggie. 'I've got to revise.' It's late June and, although the others have finished their O-Levels, she has one more exam to take.

'You'll come with me, won't you, Jill?' Eva is insistent, and Jill is secretly thrilled at the prospect.

The night of the party, she spends ages getting ready, only to look in the mirror and hate what she sees. No one has wavy hair these days! How can she go to a party in this boring dress, like something her mother would wear?

And why doesn't she have any make-up apart from a gloopy tube of Sheer Genius foundation that Eva dared her to nick from Woolworths?

Angry with herself, furious with Eva for expecting her to go to this stupid party, Jill dresses defiantly in a brown polo neck jumper and jeans, her white tennis shoes and her big brother's suede jacket, even though she knows she'll swelter in it. She smears Vaseline on her eyelashes and across her lips and, with a cursory brush of her thick, unruly hair, she decides she's as ready as she'll ever be.

The party is upstairs at the Art School, in one of the long, lofty studios. Jill climbs the stairs, following the sound of the music – some band playing trad jazz very badly – until she finds herself on the landing outside the studio, unsure whether to go in or to turn tail and flee back home.

'They think they're the Temperance Seven,' says a male voice behind her, 'but they sound more like the Plastered Three and a Half.'

It's a pretty pathetic joke, but it makes Jill smile. She spins round to see who's spoken. He's tall, skinny, with a shock of curly black hair. He tilts his head down, peering at her over the top of his aviator shades. 'Not a fan of theirs, are you?'

She snorts in disgust. 'Hardly. Not my sort of music.'

He sounds interested. 'What do you like, then? Beatles?' He gives her a cheeky grin. 'Cliff Richard?'

Without thinking, she reaches out and punches him on the arm. 'Don't be so rude! Nobody's a match for the Stones.'

'A girl after my own heart.' He rubs his arm theatrically. 'That hurt, by the way.'

She looks at him more closely: a sexy mouth, nice teeth, better skin than a lot of boys she knows. Is he old enough to be a student here? She can't be sure. 'You going in?'

'Why else would I be here?' He holds his hand out to her. 'You coming or are you just breathing heavy?'

'What?'

'Christ!' He snatches her hand and tugs her after him into the studio, into the laughter, the hubbub, the tinny jazz music, the cigarette smoke.

And that's how Jill meets Daniel Swann. That's how she first falls in love…

Now, she stretched her arms out carefully. She'd grazed her wrist bone, her knee was killing her and the heavy chain was digging into the flesh of her ankle. The other end of the chain was fastened to a metal ring in the wall.

No way of freeing herself. She sat up, her head swimming. When had she last eaten? She was so hungry, her stomach hurt. Had Ezra left her any water?

Her eyes slowly adjusted to the dark until she could make out a bucket in the corner, a blanket or thin quilt, just like in the first place he'd held her. How long this time? Where was she? It smelt damp and earthy, as if she was in woods somewhere. Hell, if this was Greywood Forest it could take for ever to find her.

They'd be looking for her, wouldn't they? Ramsay would've told them what had happened. He'd have described the car that ran her bike over, might even have caught the registration number. *Did* it run her bike over? She had a vague memory of looking under the car but not being able to see anything. She'd glimpsed Ramsay's worried face as he approached, but moments later, the car driver – Ezra – had hauled her up and smacked her in the jaw. Everything had gone dark.

She remembered that first phone call, nearly two months ago. Her lessons had ended for the afternoon and the house had seemed thankfully quiet. She'd been opening the windows when the phone rang and she'd picked it up, her other hand on the window hasp.

'I'm calling about Daniel Swann's book.' Abrupt, no preamble.

It had taken her a moment to work out what he meant. To her, Daniel was still Dan, and his book was still a typescript, four hundred pages of ramblings, erratically formatted and delinquently spelt. 'Daniel's book?'

'*Conspiracy To Deceive.*'

'Who is this?'

'This is his son. You still have my father's book, don't you?'

'Well, yes, but…' Dan's *son*? She'd rapidly searched her memory for a name. Something biblical… Esau? Aaron? Ezra? Ezra, that was it! How old must he be now? Several years older than Annika… He must be nearly forty.

'My father's book…'

'Yes, yes, the book.' She'd put it away in a box with the other papers Dan had asked her to look at – source material, he'd said, stuff people had sent him over the years so he could use it, evidence that he could now share with the world through the pages of his book. The questions she'd wanted to ask him: have these people given you permission to publish what they've sent you, Dan? And did *they* have permission to take what they've sent you?

While she'd waited in vain for his answers, she'd dropped the manuscript and the other material into a box and stowed it in her study, on a high shelf, out of the way. She hadn't wanted to think about it. Out of sight, out of mind.

'It's his life's work,' Ezra had insisted solemnly on the phone during that first call. 'People need to see it, to learn for themselves all that he found out. The *world* needs to see it.'

Jill had longed to cry out to him, nobody needs to see that manuscript, Ezra! It would be a tragedy if it ever saw the light of day again. Instead, she'd tried to put him off. 'It still needs editing. It needs to be proofread. And I haven't finished the index yet.'

Indeed, an index was all she'd offered to do originally. When Dan first told her, last autumn, that he'd written a book, she'd been flattered to think he'd entrust it to her before he showed it to anyone else. Excited, she'd started to read it, making a few notes to raise with him, points that needed clarifying.

But around the halfway mark, she'd noticed a sharp deterioration in the quality of the writing: ideas mooted but not developed; theories posited but no evidence offered; even his spelling and punctuation going awry.

The manuscript read like a work begun many years ago, put down and taken up again with little reference to the earlier sections, then continued in a rush, as if he'd been driven to finish it, come what may.

If Dan had thought all it needed was a good index, he'd been mistaken.

But then she'd found out he was being killed by the cancer she hadn't even known about until it was too late. The desperate urgency of his writing became clear. He'd been writing against the clock, knowing his time was running out.

Now Dan was gone, like a light turned out. A man who had been in her life, foreground and background, for the last fifty years.

She hadn't known how to grieve for him, hadn't been able to believe he was gone, not after all this time. She was still waiting for it to hit her. Still waiting…

'Do you live in Barbury?' she'd asked Ezra, that first time he'd phoned. 'Because if you do, maybe we could meet for a coffee, talk about your dad's book.'

'I don't want to *talk* about his book. I want it back. I need you to hand it over. Or are you part of the conspiracy too?'

'Conspiracy?'

'I've got your address.' His tone had been menacing. 'I know where you live.'

'Then write me that letter.' And she'd put the phone down, her heart racing.

Since then, he'd called her half a dozen times. They'd had the same conversation. He'd demand the return of the manuscript and she'd do her best to stall him. She'd always ended by hanging up as quickly as she could, but the very last time, only a few days ago, he'd phoned her straight back, furious.

'Don't you *dare* put the phone down on me! Don't you fucking dare! You don't silence me that easily!'

Why hadn't she gone to the police? Because she didn't seriously believe he was a threat. If he meant her harm, wouldn't the threats have escalated sooner? She was sure he'd get tired of asking and would leave her alone.

Or was that simply what she wanted to believe?

She'd said nothing to Annika, rarely seeing her these days, especially after she'd moved out of town. Amberstone wasn't far away, but putting more distance between them felt as if Annika was making a statement: *you've got your life, Mum, I've got mine.* They'd been so much closer before that awful Matt spoilt everything. Annika had brought him home, introduced him as someone she'd met through her voluntary work.

'And guess what, Mum, Matt's going to be working for Ramsay's son, doing his garden.'

Even though she didn't know Adam Keiller well, Annika had clearly persuaded him and his wife to take Matt on.

Matt had lots of tattoos, and wore a gold hoop through the lobe of his left ear. His hair was long, tied up in a ponytail. Despite his piratical looks, he was a charmer, or thought he was, batting his eyelashes at her, switching on a smile as if he was trying to seduce her as well as her daughter.

Instinctively, Jill hadn't trusted him, although she hated herself for being prejudiced. Okay, so he'd been in prison, but didn't he deserve a second chance?

When food disappeared from the fridge, and toiletries from the bathroom, she'd thought she was getting forgetful. But then, she'd come home one day to find Matt in her study, trying to get into her laptop, and it all made sense. He'd taken Annika's keys, let himself in and helped himself to whatever of Jill's took his fancy.

She and Annika had clashed angrily, Annika defending him, more loyal to him than to Jill.

'Adam and Jo think the world of him,' she'd protested. And Jill felt like saying, *they would!* She'd never taken to Ramsay's older son, another charmer, if more smartly dressed that Matt.

'Maybe he doesn't steal stuff from their house, Annika. Maybe he doesn't trespass in Adam's office or use Jo's computer.'

She hadn't told Annika about Ezra's phone calls because she'd say she was imagining it, or was somehow blaming her. And maybe because Jill had hoped that if she ignored the problem, it would go away. That Ezra would go away.

Now, as she tried to get more comfortable in her concrete cell, she felt the temperature dropping. The meagre bedding wouldn't keep her warm for long. Would Ezra move her yet again?

With some effort, she stood up and hobbled as far as she could before the chain on her ankle stopped her. Far enough for her to reach the bucket, but about an arm's length short of the door.

Was Ezra searching her house while she was imprisoned here? He must have her keys. They'd been in her skirt pocket when she left home on Monday, but she hadn't got them now. Oh God, was he wrecking the place, searching for the manuscript? Supposing Annika was there?

Terrible scenarios flashed up in her imagination, but she managed to dismiss them. No, no, it would be all right. Ramsay would have called the police and they'd have secured the house. They'd have Ezra's car on CCTV. They'd have seen what happened. Everyone would be looking for her.

Except they wouldn't know where to look.

Lights blazed round the edges of the door. A vehicle approached, the headlights growing brighter, raking the ceiling. The engine died. A car door slammed. Footsteps. The clatter of a chain being unpadlocked.

Ezra strode inside and dropped a bag of food and a plastic bottle of water onto the floor a few feet from her.

'Please,' she begged. 'Ezra, please!'

But he turned and left without another word, slamming and padlocking the door. He got into his car and drove away.

CHAPTER 26

FRIDAY 7 JULY 2017

DCI Claire Connors called a press conference on Friday morning, insisting that Lincoln join her. Rick Nevin eyed him resentfully, but Lincoln hadn't time to waste on smoothing his fellow inspector's ruffled feathers. As he and Connors were on their way to face the media, Woody called him on his mobile to warn him he'd be getting a call from Adam Keiller.

'He phoned here wanting to speak to you, boss,' he said. 'Wouldn't listen to anything I had to say.'

'He's got some information?'

'Reckon he just wants to have a go at someone because we haven't caught his dad's killer yet.'

'Huh! Good to know we've got his support. Any developments your end?'

'Nothing you don't know about. Except Breezy didn't show yesterday and he hasn't put in an appearance this morning either.'

'He sounded pretty rough the other day.'

'Yeah,' Woody said, 'but that was because he was hung over.'

'You've tried ringing him?'

'His phone's turned off, no landline.'

Connors turned at the door of the conference room. 'Coming, Jeff?'

He held his hand up. 'Gotta go, Woody. Keep me posted.'

The conference room was crowded and hot; the air conditioning must have packed up completely.

Connors began with a quick summary. 'On Monday afternoon, around quarter to five, seventy-one-year-old Ramsay Keiller, who had a smallholding and farm shop at Turnpike Corner, was shot and fatally wounded by a man driving this car.'

Details of the Vauxhall Astra were projected on the screen behind her and cameras flashed.

'The registered owner of this vehicle is Elinor Morton,' she continued, 'who is currently absent from her home in Amesbury. We need to trace Ms Morton urgently.'

While the DCI paused for the reporters to note the details, a young redheaded woman waved her hand in the air.

'Karen Bolitho, *Messenger*,' she announced. 'What's the connection between Mr Keiller and Elinor Morton?'

'We don't know that there *is* a connection,' Lincoln said carefully. He didn't trust anyone from *The Messenger*, and since he'd never seen Karen Bolitho before, he was even more wary than usual. 'Ms Morton's car was involved in this incident, but we are still exploring any possible connection with Mr Keiller.'

'Is Elinor a danger to the public?' Bolitho sounded more excited than fearful.

'We don't believe so,' said Connors. 'But the man seen driving her car has already shot one person, and we don't want any more fatalities. We suspect that Mrs Jill Fortune was forced into this car after Mr Keiller was shot. We have patrols out looking for it, monitoring cameras, making sure the public are aware that the driver is armed and dangerous. If a member of the public sees the car, they should call 999 immediately. They should *not* approach the driver.'

'So is Elinor in danger?'

Connors gave Bolitho a reassuring smile before delivering a noncommittal answer. 'We ask that she comes forward so we can make sure she's safe and well.'

'How's Jill Fortune involved in all this?' Bolitho persisted. 'How's she connected to Mr Keiller?'

Lincoln's reply was cautious. 'We believe Mrs Fortune was at the farm shop when Mr Keiller was shot and she's been abducted by the gunman. We have no reason to think she's come to any harm, but we need to trace this man, and Jill, as soon as possible before anyone else gets hurt.'

But *The Messenger*'s redhead wasn't finished. 'Is it true that Ramsay Keiller had been under surveillance by the security services?'

Lincoln glanced to his left, seeking help from Connors, but she was looking straight ahead.

'He worked for the Ministry of Defence, didn't he?' the redhead persisted. 'Wasn't he working on secret projects?'

Out of the corner of his eye, Lincoln saw Connors' hands clenching and unclenching on the table top. She was rattled, but why? Because the local newspaper knew something she didn't?

'Mr Keiller retired from the Civil Service a very long time ago,' he said. 'This is 2017. I don't believe anything he worked on at the MoD would have any relevance now.'

Bolitho was quick to get another question in. 'Didn't he complain to the police that his phone was being tapped?'

This was certainly news to Lincoln. 'If you have information you think may be of use to us,' he said, 'please speak to me after this briefing.'

He kept his gaze on Bolitho, wondering if she'd comply. She couldn't know how few straws there were to clutch at, that this could be one of them. But although she returned his gaze, something about the triumphant set of her mouth unsettled him. She knew something no one else knew and she wasn't keen to share it. To Lincoln's dismay, when the media briefing ended a few minutes later, she hurried away before he could catch up with her.

'What's this about a phone tap?' he asked Connors as they returned to the incident room.

She shrugged. 'No idea. Who was doing background checks on Keiller?'

'Someone from my team.' He'd asked Breeze and Dilke to find out what they could, but the only result was a lengthy history of Keiller attending protest rallies and writing letters to the newspapers – nothing about phone taps or being under surveillance by the security services. Although, how could they have uncovered that from the usual sources?

'Sounds as if you need to do a bit more digging, Jeff. Secret projects?' Connors strode into the incident room ahead of him. '*What* secret projects?'

'Keiller wasn't involved in secret projects. He was a technical draughtsman working on aircraft design. According to his son, he was pensioned off because he criticised what was going on at Porton, but that was years ago. Then he taught at the Tech.'

'The Tech?'

'It's Barbury Community College these days. Then, when the college made him redundant, he bought the smallholding that became Keiller's Yard. He's had nothing to do with the MoD for twenty years.'

'That reporter caught us out.'

'That reporter was fishing, ma'am. Anything happens to someone who works for the MoD, or used to, the press will find an angle, turn it into something sinister.'

'That woman in Cornwall.'

'Cornwall?'

'Hilda something. Nuclear campaigner.' She tutted. '*Anti*-nuclear, I mean.'

'Hilda Murrell? That was Shropshire. They found her killer, didn't they? Teenage lad who'd broken into her house. She'd surprised him and he killed her.'

Connors fixed him with a look, one eyebrow raised quizzically. 'You believe that? The kid was a fall guy. There was a lot more to that woman's death than we'll ever know.' They'd reached the whiteboard, and she paused to study it. 'How did that reporter know Keiller made a complaint about phone tapping? She can't have made it up. She must be onto something.'

Lincoln wasn't so sure. Karen Bolitho was taunting them, trying to get them to give something away. 'If he made an official complaint, it'll have been logged.'

'Sure, but how long ago did he make it?' Connors shook her head, despondent. 'Would his family know about it?'

'We'll ask the sons. We need to talk to them again, anyway, to tell them what we know.'

Orla came up behind them. 'We've had a report back on the items found in the Nissen hut, ma'am.' She held a sheet of paper out to the DCI, who scanned it quickly before passing it to Lincoln.

Connors sighed. 'So the blood on the piece of cloth isn't Keiller's.'

'No,' said Orla. 'It's being sent for further analysis to extract DNA, see if there's a match on the database. It could be the killer's or it could be Jill's. The lab needs a DNA sample from her toothbrush or something else of hers from the house.'

'At least they didn't find any more blood in the hut.' Lincoln was heartened by that. If Jill had been badly hurt, she'd have lost more blood than the small amount smeared on the rag that Dilke and Pam had found. 'The bucket in the shed, though, and the quilt. Doesn't all that suggest he *planned* to take Jill hostage?'

Connors shook her head, shrugged again, stuck for an answer. 'More like he planned to take *Keiller* hostage for some reason – and it all went wrong.'

CHAPTER 27

Towards the end of the morning, Lincoln picked up Graham Dilke from Barley Lane and drove to Barbury Electronics, where Jamie Keiller worked.

'Thought you'd be taking someone from Park Street to talk to him,' Dilke said.

'You've already met Jamie, which makes talking to him easier. And I wondered if you'd had any thoughts about what you'll do when Barley Lane closes.'

Dilke grunted. 'Dunno what I'll do. Put in for another station, I suppose, but not Park Street.' He shoved back his fringe, his toffee-coloured hair still in the boyish style he'd worn when he'd arrived at Barley Lane three years ago. 'I might apply to Swindon, or I wouldn't mind Melksham or Devizes. My mum would like me to move to Park Street so I can still live at home, but I need to get out. I need an *excuse* to get out.'

Lincoln grinned. He could understand how much Dilke's widowed mother must want to keep him close, especially since her police constable husband had been killed in the line of duty when Dilke was still at school. 'Yes, it's time she let you go.'

He turned off Southampton Road into a small industrial estate of six or seven units. Most of them looked abandoned.

'There,' said Dilke, pointing at a dreary grey prefabricated building. 'Barbury Electronics.'

Inside, too, the building needed a bit of TLC. In reception, the vinyl chairs spilled foam stuffing and the desk was battered and scuffed.

It took only a few moments for Jamie Keiller to arrive. Black T-shirt, khaki shorts that stopped mid-calf, trainers the colour of dried blood. His gaunt face, so like his father's, was expressionless, as if he expected little from them.

He led them across the foyer to a break room that smelt of coffee and microwaved curry. He opened a window, letting in the hiss of pneumatic brakes, the parp of car horns, the thrum of engines idling while the traffic lights on Southampton Road went through their laborious sequence. Diesel fumes mingled unpleasantly with the aromas of coffee and curry.

Lincoln and Dilke sat at the Formica-topped table, but Jamie stayed standing, arms folded, his skinny rump pressed against a grime-covered storage heater.

'What's the latest?' he asked. 'I've stopped checking the news.'

Lincoln told him about the morning's press conference, the mention of the security services, secret projects...

Jamie exploded. 'Secret projects? Dad didn't work on anything like that. He'd have jumped at the chance to do something exciting, but no, it was all routine stuff. Course, he wasn't supposed to talk about it because it was military, defence, classified. But it wasn't, like, *top* secret.'

'Did he ever say he thought his phone was being tapped?'

Jamie frowned at the suggestion then admitted, 'Dad was a bit of a nonconformist, not afraid to stick up for his beliefs. Like, he disagreed with what they were doing at Porton and wrote to the papers about it. Which you're not supposed to do if you're a civil servant. That's why they got rid of him. Well, got rid of his job so he'd have to leave. But I don't remember anything about his phone being...'

The break room door swung open and in flew a young woman in dreadlocks, dungarees and Doc Martens. 'Oops, sorry, guys!'

Jamie straightened up. 'Won't be long, Jazz. Okay?'

'No worries.' She backed out again, but the moment was lost. By the time the door shut behind her and Jamie slouched once more against the storage heater, his mood had changed. 'No one tapped Dad's phone,' he said emphatically. 'Why would they? He was a draughtsman.'

'But you said yourself,' Dilke argued, 'he spoke out against policies he disagreed with. He was against using animals for research, wasn't he? He didn't agree with biological warfare.'

'Yeah, but that was years ago.'

'Did he have any close friends in those days, fellow protesters?' Lincoln was thinking that a phone tap would only be worthwhile if the authorities suspected Keiller was in communication with other activists, agitators of more interest to the security services than Keiller himself.

'It was twenty years ago! I was only a kid myself, and Adam was away at uni or medical school. All I remember is that Dad was forced out of his job at the MoD when he was still only fifty.'

'I know your mum isn't around now, but is there anyone else he might have confided in?' asked Lincoln. 'Brothers, sisters...'

'There's no one else. He had a younger brother, Callum, but he died.' Jamie's face clouded and he looked towards the window. 'He was only sixteen. Went camping in Dorset with the Scouts and picked up some sort of bug, died a few weeks later, the summer of sixty-five. Dad didn't like to talk about it. I was named after him. James is my middle name. Where's this reporter got this from? The secret projects, the phone taps.'

'She's probably trying to stir things up,' Lincoln said. 'Journalists are always looking for an extra angle.'

'So it's not enough that my dad was shot by some maniac? They've got to dig up some dirt to go with it?'

'People want reasons,' said Dilke. 'They don't like stuff they can't explain.'

'We'll get him.' Lincoln wished he felt as certain as he sounded. 'We've made an appeal for any sightings of the car the gunman was driving. Someone must have seen it.'

Jamie looked doubtful. 'Have you found Mrs Fortune yet? She was friends with my mum. She used to come over to our house, her and Annika.'

'We're still looking for her. That's why it's so important to find the car that was seen outside the farm shop.'

'This is a nightmare,' said Jamie. 'A fucking bloody nightmare.'

Lincoln drove Dilke back to Barley Lane.

'Okay, Graham, so what've we learnt?'

'That Jamie must be earning a lot less than his big brother.'

'That place looked pretty rundown, didn't it?'

'And we know Keiller had a brother, Callum, who died in his teens.'

'Hardly relevant though, is it? And it doesn't explain why someone would target Keiller now.'

When Lincoln pulled up outside Barley Lane a few minutes later, he was tempted to park and go in. He was also afraid that if he did, he'd be tempted to stay. 'I'll fix up a meeting with Adam to see what more he can tell us.'

'You had the results back from the lab? The cloth we found in the hut?'

'The blood isn't Keiller's. They're looking for a match on the database and we need a DNA sample from Jill. Someone's gone to the house to pick up a toothbrush, hairbrush, whatever. Good work, you and Pam finding that Nissen hut.'

'That was Pam, spotting it on the aerial photo.' Dilke paused before he got out of the car, his hand on the door handle. 'You think Mrs Fortune's still alive?'

'We haven't found a body, have we? And the CSIs didn't find any other blood in the hut. That bucket and bedding says the gunman prepared the hut beforehand. He must've been planning to kidnap Keiller, but then Jill turned up and everything went pear-shaped.'

'But why kidnap Keiller? For money? To torture him for information?'

'Come on, Graham, what information could he have had that anyone would want now? He hadn't worked for the MoD for twenty years.'

'Officially.'

'What?'

'Breezy suggested it on Wednesday when we were talking about possible motives. He said, suppose it was all a front, and Keiller's been working for the security services all this time?'

Lincoln laughed uneasily. 'Trust Breezy to come up with something like that!'

'But he could be right, couldn't he?'

'If you'd seen how little Keiller had in his bungalow – a few books, no papers, no files, no equipment. Well, apart from his binoculars and a camera, and a little radio thing, but then he loved planes, and he was living not far from an airfield. What else would you expect? That bungalow certainly didn't look like the home of a spy.'

'Like we'd know what a spy's home looks like,' Dilke laughed. 'I'm only telling you what Breezy said.'

'Has he turned up yet?'

'Not even a text. He must feel like shit if he can't even send a text.' Dilke got out of the car. 'Not coming in, boss?'

'I'd better get back. Let me know when Breezy surfaces. I'll have to have words.'

Orla ambushed him as soon as he entered the incident room, her face grim. 'The blood on the cloth is Ezra Morton's.'

'What?'

'There wasn't much of it but enough to get a good match. So much for him and his mother being estranged! Sunday morning, Elinor must have been driving off to see him.'

'And she hasn't come home because he's taken her car – with or without her permission.' Lincoln carried on towards his desk. He'd have pulled his chair out and sat down, but the chair was missing, so he headed for the whiteboard instead. He moved the mugshot of Ezra Morton into place. The chief suspect was no longer a faceless man at the wheel of Elinor's Astra, he was her son. 'But still no sightings of the car?'

Orla shook her head. 'Nothing we can verify.'

The DCI came sailing down the room, tacking between desks. When Lincoln updated her about the shooter's identity, she responded decisively.

'We need to find him fast,' she said, banging her fist on the table. 'He's armed and dangerous. We'll have to go public, name and mugshot, last known whereabouts. Someone must know where he is, where he goes, where he might turn up.'

'Is there a risk he'll panic?' Lincoln didn't expect an answer, but he had to voice his concern. Having kept Jill alive this long, Morton might find it hard to kill her now, but there was also a chance that, having killed once, he might feel he had little to lose. If he felt trapped, Morton might react with violence.

Connors cast her gaze over the whiteboard. 'That's a risk we'll have to take.'

CHAPTER 28

Waves of nausea forced Jill to roll over and sit up. Her stomach heaved, but when she retched, she was too empty to bring anything up. If only she could move around, she could warm up, but she was trapped, tethered by a thick chain, and this concrete shelter was so cold.

Her thoughts returned to Dan, Ezra's father. How old had she been when they first got together? Fifteen, nearly sixteen?

August 1965: After meeting at the Art School dance, she and Dan spend all their free time together.

He comes to her house and they work out songs on her piano, learning from each other about what works, what doesn't. He can't read music, but he can retain notes in his head, relay to her something he's heard on the radio so she can tinker with it, use it as a jumping-off point for music of her own. She makes tapes she plays to him, music suited to his voice.

The more music she explores, the more creative she becomes, as if something's been released inside her, like she's been waiting all her life to find him. She walks on air most of the time. 'Head in the clouds, feet off the ground,' as Maggie puts it, probably because she's jealous.

The rest of the time, Jill's scared, knowing it can't last. Dan's planning to go to art school next year, after he's finished his A-Levels, with Brighton his first choice. Jill dreads him going away.

On their first proper date, they climb Lookout Hill, finding a secluded spot in the shadow of the brick signalling tower that dominates it. Sprawled beside her in the warm turf, he tells her how he's been immersed in music since he was a kid, singing in the church choir then teaching himself to play the guitar when his voice broke.

'And then I won this stupid talent contest at Butlin's. No, Jilly, don't laugh. Who wants to go to a holiday camp with their mum and dad? But it was that or nothing, so there I am in bloody Bognor, standing at the mike, pretending to be Dickie fucking Valentine.'

She can't stop giggling. 'What, like, doing an impression? Dickie Valentine's so square, Dan!'

'No! I mean, I thought about the way Dickie Valentine sings, how he looks on the telly, and I sort of *became* him. My sister's got an LP of his she plays all the time and I know all the songs. And I loathe all of them.'

'So you won a talent contest. Then what?' Jill lies on her back, gazing up at the underside of his jaw and throat, watching his Adam's apple move as he talks. She can see where he's nicked himself shaving, a wisp of cotton wool staunching the bleeding.

'Part of the prize was an intro to this talent scout, so by the time we're all back home from Butlin's I've got myself a manager.'

'A manager?' She thinks of Colonel Parker making a star of Elvis.

'Turns out he was a creepy perv, so I dumped him after a bit. He took me to a studio to have photos taken but, I dunno, there was something dodgy about him. He had a load of photos printed – even faked my signature on them, would you believe? But then Dad got cold feet about the contract and it all fizzled out. Fun while it lasted, though.'

'So now what?'

'Putting a band together with some of my mates from school.'

'A band?' She's impressed. 'Like the Beatles?'

'No, more like the Stones.'

She shakes her head. 'Sorry, Dan, no one can beat the Stones – or come anywhere close.'

'You haven't heard us yet. We're pretty good, but we need a drummer. Know any drummers?' He rolls over on top of her, pinning her down for a kiss. She loves being with him, the way he envelops her in his affection, nothing casual about it, as if he can't get enough of her.

'I don't know any drummers, Dan, but I know a keyboard player.'

'We don't need a keyboard player.'

'That's a shame,' she grins. 'I was thinking of applying.'

Instead of answering her, he rolls her over again, kisses her, squashing the breath out of her, gathering her long, thick hair into a ponytail and studying her face as if he's memorising her features.

'No girls in the band, Jilly. You should know that. No serious band's got a girl in it.'

End of discussion. She pulls away from him, sulkily tearing daisies out of the grass and throwing them aside. She never suggests it again.

During the autumn term, Dan's band takes off. They steal a drummer from Mick May and the Tournaments and play at youth clubs round Barbury and Presford, Amesbury and Downton. In December alone, Danny Swann and the Haymakers get bookings at bingo halls and church rooms, a factory canteen, even an end of term disco at Jill's school. She revels in the attention when her friends realise she's going out with the band's singer. Although she'd have been even happier if she'd been in the band.

But still, at the back of her mind, she knows their time is running out. Dan will be taking his A-Levels next summer and then leaving Barbury, while she still has another two years at school.

Now, over fifty years later, Jill fretted about the cold, the nausea, the long intervals between Ezra's visits. The drop in temperature suggested it was already evening. How much longer would he keep her captive?

If she let him have the manuscript of *Conspiracy To Deceive,* would he let her go? She'd hidden it away to protect Dan's reputation, to keep secret the record of a disintegrating mind, a genius in free fall. She'd been embarrassed on his behalf, dismayed by his wild claims about alien invasions and spacecraft from other galaxies, infuriated by his conspiracy theories about Dallas, Diana's Paris car crash, the collapse of the Twin Towers. But was it herself she was protecting? Herself and her family?

She tried to massage some circulation back into her arms and legs, but her hands were numb with cold, her fingers stiff. Had Ezra left her to die here after all?

Then a pinprick of light became a blaze as he drove up and stopped close to the door. While she listened to the laborious undoing of the padlock, she prayed he'd brought food, water, a thicker blanket.

At last he flung the door wide open and the car headlights made a bulky silhouette of him.

But he hadn't brought food or water, and most certainly not a blanket.

He'd brought a gun.

CHAPTER 29

'I have to move you. Now.' Ezra pointed the handgun at her.

'Okay, okay.' She patted the air in front of her in a bid to calm him down.

'I need to take this off you.' He picked up the chain round her ankle. As he crouched down to unfasten it from the metal loop in the wall, he dragged the chain roughly against her bare skin, making her wince with pain. When he mumbled an apology, she nearly let herself believe he didn't really mean her harm, that this could end satisfactorily with no one getting hurt.

'Where are you moving me to?'

'You'll soon find out.' He slipped the chain off her ankle and over her foot, knocking her shoe off in the process. Instead of putting her shoe back on though, he grabbed her other foot and tore that shoe off too. 'In case you try to run away.' He stood up, her shoes clutched to his chest with one hand, the gun clasped in the other. He was smiling slyly.

'What would you do if I tried to run away, Ezra? Shoot me?'

'Yeah, if I thought you were a threat. I wouldn't hesitate.'

She stared at him, her well-worn loafers held tight against his chest, his gun pointing at her once more.

'How could I be a threat to *you*? You're the one with the gun. I haven't even got a pair of shoes to put on.' She felt a terrible urge to laugh, an urge provoked by anxiety, terror that his mood had changed, that he really was dangerous.

'You're already a threat by withholding my father's book. Censorship, that's what it is. Suppression. A conspiracy to silence him.'

'What do you want his legacy to be? The beautiful songs he wrote or *Conspiracy To Deceive*?'

'His book reveals the truth. No one else knows what really happened at Boscombe Down in 1994. No one!'

'Someone else must know,' she argued. 'He wasn't there himself, was he? Someone who was there that night must have seen what happened and told him about it.'

'How do you know he wasn't there? Were *you* there?'

Jill wondered where she'd been in September 1994 when, according to Dan's book, a strange craft crashed at the airbase.

'Of course I wasn't there, but your father couldn't have been there either.' Lots of people had contacted him, he'd written, people who knew what had really gone on that night.

'If nothing happened, why did the Americans fly in and take everything away?'

'I don't know, Ezra, but they must have had their reasons.'

Everyone had lied, according to Dan's book. Everyone was still lying. He had proof that the craft was from another world, but the government, the Americans, they were all covering it up.

In Los Angeles, 1974, I was told contact would be made. And then, twenty years to the day, at Boscombe Down, contact was made. And I have the proof. So why will no one admit it? What are they afraid of?

He might as well have typed it in block capitals a foot high – if that had been possible on his old manual typewriter.

'And how come Dan was the only one who knew the truth, Ezra?' Jill asked, goading him. 'He didn't work at Boscombe Down. He couldn't have been there at the time. What made him such an expert?'

'Because he knew they were coming. They'd told him to expect them.'

'They?'

'The aliens.'

She couldn't be bothered to argue with him. She was too tired, too weak, and her ankle was sore where he'd grazed it with the chain. She looked at him, assessing him properly for the first time.

He was as tall as Dan but much bulkier, a little overweight, although it was hard to tell through all his layers of clothing: a tartan-patterned shirt, its buttons undone to reveal a black T-shirt, with a khaki jerkin over a grubby denim jacket.

His curly hair was dark brown and needed washing. His skin was sallow, but when he turned towards the light, oh, how like Dan he was in profile! The straight forehead and the long nose, the fullness of his lips, the firm, defiant chin. No, Ezra's chin was softer, fleshier, weaker.

'How well did you know him, Ezra. How well did you know your dad?'

'Well enough.'

'You live in Amesbury, don't you? With your mum?' How sad did that sound? She regretted saying it as soon as the words were out of her mouth.

'Not now, I don't. Shut up asking questions.' He waggled the gun at her. 'We've got to move. Now!'

CHAPTER 30

SATURDAY 8 JULY 2017

Adam Keiller's house was at the top of a sloping gravel drive and overlooked the river. Lincoln supposed that village life was fine if you had a car and could afford the fuel bills and the cost of getting a gardener in, but he preferred to live in a place where he could window-shop at night. A place with pubs, cafés, a bookshop.

Adam's village, two miles from Barbury, had none of these. It had a church, two chapels, a selection of expensive houses, a row of four pink prefabs built by the council after the war, and a community noticeboard.

The woman who opened the front door looked harassed, as if his arrival had interrupted something. She hurriedly introduced herself as Joanna and showed Lincoln into an enormous kitchen. It boasted the granite worktops and huge island counter he couldn't see the point of. But then, he wasn't much of a cook.

'I'll fetch my husband.' She thundered up the stairs and along the landing. An animated exchange followed. Lincoln couldn't make out the words, but the tone was heated.

Several minutes passed before Adam jogged down the stairs and strolled into the kitchen, casually dressed but still looking smart, his dark hair swept back from his forehead.

'You've identified the man who shot my father, then?'

'A man called Ezra Morton, yes. Did your father ever mention him?'

Adam shook his head. 'Never heard of him until he was all over the news this morning. And, before you ask, I've never heard of Elinor Morton either. Why's it taken you so long to identify him?'

'We had to wait for the lab results,' said Lincoln, reluctant to give too much away. 'We had to confirm he was our suspect.'

'What made him go after Dad?'

They stood either side of the island, the glossy work surface glittering in a way that made Lincoln's eyes sting.

'We don't know that Morton *did* go after him,' he said. 'The motive may have been robbery, even if he didn't get away with anything.' The preparation of the Nissen hut suggested otherwise, but Adam didn't need to know that yet.

'You've seen the newspapers? Accusing Dad of being a *spy*, for Christ's sake! Where've they got that idea from?'

'Actually,' said Lincoln, pulling out a stool from the breakfast bar and perching on it awkwardly, 'I need to ask you about that. Do you know what your dad was working on at the MoD? Any specific projects?'

'He didn't talk about his work much, wasn't supposed to. He was old-fashioned like that, honourable, obedient.'

Lincoln detected a tone of contempt. 'Nothing old-fashioned about sticking to the rules in that sort of job, surely?'

'If you say so.' Adam narrowed his eyes. 'If you think the motive was robbery, why are you asking about what Dad worked on?'

'Because I have to keep an open mind. I need to be sure that's the *only* explanation for the attack.'

Joanna thudded down the stairs, snatched the car keys from a hook inside the kitchen door and swept out. 'I'm off!' she called out as she slammed the front door.

Adam shrugged apologetically. 'She's got an event to organise. A big party. She's a one-woman band, so there's no one else to cover for her, even when this sort of thing happens.'

'This must have been a rough week for you and your family.'

'We'll get through it.'

'Your father's work…'

There was a flash of irritation. 'He drew designs for bits of military aircraft. That's all you need to know. He sat at a drawing board forty hours a week for over twenty years. Early retirement at fifty!'

'But he got another job, didn't he? At the college?'

'Until they cancelled the course. No demand, or so they said, so he was out of a job again. And then came his *wacky* idea of keeping animals and growing vegetables.' He shook his head as if despairing of his father's decision to buy Eunice Peel's smallholding.

'And he never mentioned his phone being tapped?'

'Never. Who is this Bolitho woman? Bloody *Messenger* employing adolescent fantasists to fill their columns. Where did she get this bollocks from? You want a coffee?'

The coffee tin was empty, so Adam had to search for a fresh bag. While his back was turned, Lincoln's gaze drifted to a pile of correspondence crammed untidily behind the bread bin next to where he was sitting. Several envelopes bore the angry red lettering of overdue reminders and final demands. No matter how rich you were, you could still forget to pay your bills – or run out of funds to cover them.

111

Lincoln had sat in many different kitchens in his time: as a young constable breaking bad news and as a detective questioning witnesses or suspects. He'd learnt that however smart the worktops, however plentiful the gadgets, none of it meant anything when you'd lost a close relative to murder or, indeed, were implicated in a serious crime. Cracked lino on the floor or terracotta tiles, it was all the same when you were in trouble.

Adam found the coffee at last and, a few minutes later, he'd filled a cafetière and brought it across. He glanced quickly at the offending swatch of bills behind the bread bin – guessing, no doubt, that Lincoln had spotted it too. But he said nothing.

'The reporter from *The Messenger* is probably just trawling for a story,' said Lincoln, 'but we need to be sure there's no substance in what she's saying. That's why I need to ask you about all this, even though it doesn't seem relevant.'

'You've spoken to my brother?'

'He said he was too young at the time to understand what your father was working on.'

Adam shrugged. 'If that's what he says…'

'You think Karen Bolitho's barking up the wrong tree?'

'Absolutely. Anything to sell a few more copies of her disgusting newspaper.' He put down his cup. 'How long are you going to be keeping us out of the yard?'

'Not for much longer. I'll let you know when our investigations are complete.' Lincoln took a moment to savour his coffee. 'Presumably, you'll be limited in what you can do there, what with probate and so on?'

'Christ, that place is going to be a millstone round our necks. Dad should've sold up when he had the chance.'

'Someone made him an offer?'

Adam picked up his cup again. 'Not as such, but a patient of mine was interested in it. Would've given him a good price if Dad had only taken the trouble to meet him, instead of refusing even to consider his offer.' He took a sip of his coffee. 'But he wouldn't hear of it, so the guy gave up, went back to Spain.'

'You have many foreign patients?'

'Foreign?' He laughed. 'No, no. This guy's as British as they come. Lives in Spain for various reasons.'

In Lincoln's experience, Brits moved to Spain for the good of their health or because they'd loved holidaying there so much they chose to settle there in retirement. Or they moved to Spain to evade the law. He hoped that Adam's patient fitted into one of the first two categories.

'Mum knew Jill Fortune.' Adam pulled out a stool and sat down opposite Lincoln. 'They were at school together. I've only met her a few times, but she used to bring her daughter over to our old house when Jamie was small. I think he and Annika were in the same class. And then, when my mother died, Jill used to look out for Dad, though he's always been pretty self-sufficient.'

'And they've stayed close since then?'

'What are you suggesting? That they were lovers?' The idea seemed distasteful to him.

'I'm not suggesting anything,' said Lincoln. 'I'm simply asking if they were still close. But since you raised it: *might* they have been lovers?'

'No one could replace my mother.'

'Of course not, but your father would have been only, what, in his early sixties when she died? It's not unreasonable to expect him to find companionship with another woman, eventually.'

'I'm not aware that he was involved with anyone in that way.'

'Wasn't there someone he met at U3A? Jamie told us he'd met her at the bungalow once.'

'Jamie told you that?' Adam said it as if he thought his brother had no business telling Lincoln anything.

'Heather?'

'Heather Draycott? She sent a sympathy card.' He nodded towards a pile of cards and torn envelopes on the worktop. 'She was writing a history of the airfield, asked Dad for some information, that's all.'

Might Ramsay have told Heather about the work he did for the MoD? Might he have told her about the phone taps – assuming reporter Karen Bolitho hadn't made that up?

'Do you have an address for her, or a phone number?'

Adam sighed, exasperated. 'What's my father's personal life got to do with Ezra Morton? Or are you thinking there's a jealous husband in the background employing him as a hitman?'

'Not at all.' Lincoln refused to let Adam's sarcasm rile him. 'We have to explore every angle. Morton may have threatened him or given him some sort of trouble that your dad discussed with Heather or another friend.'

Adam flipped through the condolence cards until he found the one from Heather and thrust it at Lincoln. 'Here, take it. She's put her mobile number on it, but I certainly won't be ringing her.'

Lincoln didn't need to drive past Barley Lane on his way back to Park Street, but the car somehow steered itself in that direction. Inside the station, he

113

found Pam at her desk, Woody on the phone and Dilke poring over some paperwork. No sign of DC Dennis Breeze.

'No Breezy?' He pulled his chair out and sat down, instantly comfortable.

Dilke looked up. 'I'm going round there when I knock off to see if he's okay. He's still not answering his phone.'

Pam sat back from her keyboard. 'It's a bit irresponsible of him, taking time off without letting us know if he's sick. Back here for good, boss?'

Lincoln sighed. 'Sadly no. Can one of you speak to Heather Draycott? Local, some connection with the U3A, writing a history of the airfield at Turnpike Corner. She could be the woman Jamie saw at his dad's.' He passed Pam the condolence card Adam had given him. 'The number's in there. I'm just thinking, if Morton had been harassing Keiller he may have mentioned it to her. She might be able to throw some light on these phone taps Karen Bolitho's on about, or at least tell us what Keiller worked on at the MoD.'

'Was he involved with this Heather woman?' Pam opened the card and scanned the brief message of condolence inside. 'Romantically, I mean?'

'Not sure, but go and talk to her, see what you can find out.' He stood up, reluctant to return to Park Street. Shame he couldn't take his chair with him.

Woody put the phone down. 'That was DS Cook from Park Street.'

'Orla?'

'She's been trying to get hold of you. Reckon you must've turned your phone off.'

Lincoln checked his mobile. Yes, he'd turned it off while he was talking to Adam and hadn't turned it on again. 'I'd better get back. Keep me posted.'

As he got into his car, he called Orla to find out what was up.

'Someone phoned in after the appeal,' she said. 'He saw Morton following Jill from outside her house on Monday afternoon. Jill was the target all along.'

'An Openreach engineer called us,' Orla told him as soon as he walked into the incident room. 'He saw the press conference and recognised the car. Monday afternoon, he was working on a junction box in Arundel Terrace. The Astra was parked across the road from Jill's house for at least half an hour. The driver never got out. Then, a few seconds after Jill came out of her house and cycled off, the Astra started up and drove after her.'

Lincoln was sceptical. 'How come he remembers it from five days ago, one parked car out of all the parked cars he must've seen?'

'Because it mounted the pavement and nearly knocked him off his stool as it went round the corner, so he jotted the reg down. He got the distinct impression it was following her.'

This changed everything. 'Why didn't he report it sooner, if he thought she was in danger?'

Orla shrugged. 'Thought he was imagining it, he said. Seen too many crime dramas on the telly. He'd talked himself out of it by the time he got home.'

Lincoln ran a hand through his hair. 'And he somehow missed the news about a woman from Arundel Terrace going missing?'

'It was the bike that threw him, he said. The news didn't say she was on a bike when she disappeared.'

'Christ Almighty!'

Rick Nevin ambled over. 'So does this mean Morton was targeting the Fortune woman from the word go?'

Lincoln nodded. 'Watched the house and then followed her all the way to the smallholding.'

'He'd have to be driving bloody slowly,' Orla remarked. 'It's not like she was on a racing bike.'

'Back to square one, then.' Nevin sounded almost cheerful.

Lincoln crossed to the whiteboard. 'But if he was after Jill, why didn't he shoot her there and then, when she got to Keiller's Yard? He could have caught her as she was getting off her bike. And if he missed his chance then, why not shoot her after he'd shot Keiller?'

He stared at the photo of Jill, the photo of Ezra Morton, trying to imagine a way in which these two individuals could possibly be linked, but the whiteboard stayed resolutely silent.

'We need to talk to Annika again,' he said, 'now we know it was Morton in the Astra.'

'I'll call her,' said Orla, 'to fix something up.' Her desk phone was ringing and she hurried over to answer it.

'He must want something from Jill,' Nevin said, coming up behind Lincoln. He gave off a faint odour of sweat.

'But what's a piano teacher got that Morton could possibly want? She's not rich, they're not related, we've no evidence they've ever even met before.'

'Maybe the daughter can...' Nevin broke off as Orla came darting across the room, her face grim.

'A body's been found in a house near Warminster,' she said. 'A woman in her sixties. Shot in the face.'

Lincoln's spirits plunged. 'Jill?'

'Possibly. White female in her sixties. That's all I've got so far.'

Nevin sniffed and lumbered back to his desk.

Lincoln looked across at the whiteboard. It still wasn't talking, but the old photo of Jill, the mane of bright hair, the earrings, the bangles, the smile, took on a sudden extra radiance.

CHAPTER 31

With Orla beside him, Lincoln drove fast from Park Street, out to the A303 and then west for several miles before turning off at Deptford, a hamlet far removed from its South London namesake. He had to slow down on the winding country lane that ran over, alongside and under the railway line, but after several more miles, not far from the outskirts of Warminster, he spotted Willow Lane and swung into it. After a few yards, Orla pointed to a driveway filled with emergency service vehicles.

'That must be it, boss. Willow Cottage.'

He pulled in behind the mortuary van and they got out. The cottage was long and low, built of flint and brick with a slate roof. Originally two adjoining cottages, it had evidently been knocked into one to create a living space more suited to modern expectations.

Now, though, it looked mournful, with unwashed windows and cobweb-wreathed sills. Ivy clothed its front and sides, as if steadily consuming it, and the grass in the front garden hadn't been mown for a long, long time.

They donned their coveralls – Orla rather more agile than Lincoln, slipping into her papery white jumpsuit quickly and easily. An officer from Warminster took their details and let them through the cordon. Neither was in a rush to get inside, to see Jill Fortune's ruined face.

The air indoors felt damp, despite the heat outside. The ivy clawing at the windows cast a greenish light, as if the house was underwater and the windows were portholes.

The woman's body lay in the scullery at the end of the hallway. Lincoln caught a glimpse of a hand flung out, a jacket flung open, a leg bent at an unnatural angle, a shoe adrift from its foot.

'Morning, Viv.' Orla nodded at the duty doctor, a middle-aged woman with short, straight hair dyed magenta. 'This is DI Lincoln.'

'Barley Lane?' Viv peered at him over the top of her big glasses. 'I've heard of you.'

He'd heard of Viv Caddick but never met her. He tried to see past her to where the dead woman lay, but Orla was in the way, bending down to inspect her. 'All good, I hope.'

'All good?' Viv took off her glasses and folded them up before she answered. 'Not entirely.'

He held his breath as Orla stood up again and came back to him.

'It's not her,' she said flatly. 'It's not Jill.'

His shoulders slackened with relief. He breathed out. 'Who, then?'

Viv chuckled. 'Expecting it to be the Fortune woman? I'd say this one's been lying here the best part of a week. One clean shot to the face. Fatal. No exit wound, so the round must be in her brain somewhere. It would've been very quick,' she added, as if consoling the victim's family.

'Any other injuries?'

'Can't say yet. Decomposition is well underway, as you can probably tell from the smell, so I need to get her back to the mortuary ASAP to look at her properly.'

Orla was already rooting through a handbag that sat on the scullery table. She pulled out a driving licence, holding it up for Lincoln to see. 'Guess who?'

He took the licence from her. 'Elinor Morton.' The photo was the one that adorned the whiteboard. He looked back at the woman lying on the scullery floor, although there was little resemblance between the photo, unflattering as it was, and the remains of her face.

'So now that bastard's shot his own mother?' Orla screwed her mouth up, as if she'd eaten something nasty.

'Must have shot her and taken her car,' Lincoln supposed. 'Drove to Arundel Terrace and staked out Jill's house. But we need that bullet before we can be sure it's from the same gun.'

'Was that why Elinor drove away from home on Sunday morning? He phoned her to come over here?' Orla searched the handbag's various pockets. 'Can't find her phone.'

'She's lying on it,' said Viv. 'Give me five minutes and I can move her.'

Leaving Viv to get on with her work, Orla and Lincoln began to search the rest of the downstairs rooms.

'Whose house is this?' Orla asked.

'Guy called Daniel Swann,' said one of the Warminster team, who introduced himself as Constable Dylan Wilcox. 'He was famous at one time, though I don't know what for. A bit of an eccentric, too. Just one of those names, you know, "Oh, that's Danny Swann's house."'

Lincoln and Orla looked at each other. Danny Swann, the teenage singer whose signed photographs were in a box in Elinor's filthy house.

'He made a load of money when he was younger,' Dylan continued, 'bought this place and started to do it up. But then the money must've run out. I only ever remember this place looking kind of spooky. When we were kids, we'd ride out here on our bikes and dare each other to knock on his door and ask for his autograph.' He grinned sheepishly. 'Kids, eh?'

'Swann died a few months ago, didn't he?' said Orla.

The young officer nodded. 'Easter time. Far as I know, it's just been left since then.'

'Well, someone's been living here.' Orla indicated empty beer cans and food wrappings on the coffee table in the large, dimly lit sitting room. 'Had the locks been forced?'

'No,' said Dylan. 'We got a call from the cat people. They've been trapping feral cats at the farm further up the lane. This morning, they saw some mangy-looking cats in the garden here, too. Knocked on the door, no answer, came round the back and looked in through the window. Saw that.' He jerked his head towards the scullery floor. 'Front and back doors unlocked, keys still in them.'

Lincoln took in the gloomy sitting room, the neglected hallway. Not dirty like Elinor's house, or filled with binbags or rubbish. Just desolate. Nobody home for a long time. He said, 'We need to get those beer cans checked for DNA, but I'll bet you Morton's been dossing down here. Let's look upstairs, see if there are any more surprises.'

The upper floor was brighter, with windows that looked out above the trees, but it smelt as musty as downstairs.

Orla inspected a large landscape painting of an ancient hillfort with grassy ramparts, a few cattle grazing precariously on its summit. She peered at the title scrawled in the bottom corner. 'Cley Hill?'

'Between Longleat and Warminster. UFO Central,' Dylan added with a chuckle. 'If you believe in that kind of thing.'

Her eyebrows went up. 'What, like aliens?'

'Haven't you heard of the Warminster Thing?'

She shook her head.

'There's a big mural in town,' Dylan told them, 'done to celebrate the fiftieth anniversary in 2015. Christmas 1964 it started, with weird noises, but in 1965 the town went mental, everyone out with their cameras, photographing spaceships and lights in the sky.'

'Actual spaceships?' Orla's eyes were wide.

'So they say. People thought that's why Mr Swann bought this cottage, because of the earth energies here. Not that I believe in any of that stuff. Just saying what my mum's been on about over the years.'

'Thanks for that, Dylan,' said Lincoln. 'See if they need any help downstairs while me and DS Cook look around up here.'

'Spaceships?' Orla said again as the constable clumped down the narrow, twisting stairs.

'More likely spy planes on test flights from Boscombe Down. There've always been rumours about what goes on up there. I remember newspaper stories about a flying saucer crash-landing on Salisbury Plain and being taken to Boscombe Down for investigation, but that's all they were – stories.'

'Some folk'll believe anything they read in the papers.' She opened drawers in a tall wooden chest, pulled out clothes and pill packets, cigarette papers and a bag of something that looked suspiciously like weed. 'So, what's Morton's connection to Daniel Swann?'

'Maybe he's a fan, too,' Lincoln said wryly, 'like his mother.'

'Hardly likely, is it, boss? I mean...' She stopped mid-sentence and Lincoln looked round to see her gaze fixed on a framed photograph propped up on the chest, signed *Dan Swann 1981* in the lower corner. She nodded at the photo, inviting him to take a look, so he leant in closer. 'Remind you of anyone?'

Instantly, Lincoln saw a familiar mugshot in his mind's eye, Ezra Morton in 2012, about the same age then as Daniel Swann would have been in 1981. Morton's face was plumper than Swann's, his chin weaker, but otherwise, the resemblance was undeniable.

'Swann and Morton could be father and son.' He let out a long breath. 'If we can find something here with Swann's DNA on it, then we'll know for sure, either way.'

'Hairbrush!' Orla held it aloft in triumph, wiry grey strands snagged in its bristles. 'I'll bag it.'

Lincoln left her and went into the back bedroom, which Swann must have used as a study. A wall of photographs, posters and drawings confronted him: maps of Wiltshire and Somerset, of Glastonbury overlaid with signs of the Zodiac, aerial photos of South American temple sites.

Photos of Swann were arranged roughly chronologically. He'd been photographed with Nicholas Cage, Uri Geller and – was that Bruce Springsteen or merely a lookalike? He was tall and rangy, with dark, curly hair and a lively expression. When younger, Swann had radiated charisma. More recent photos showed signs of self-neglect. His hair, beard and fingernails were untidily long. He appeared ill and unkempt, a man living on his own and out of touch. A couple of shots of him mid-speech at rallies or conventions portrayed the intense gaze of someone who has a message to deliver, come what may. Instinctively, Lincoln stepped back to distance himself from the haranguing tone.

When had the most recent photo been taken? How much more had Swann deteriorated before he died? He was curious now about Swann's music and the Barbury Blues Band. Maybe he'd be able to download a few tracks, or at least hear some of it on YouTube.

He turned towards the window. An electric typewriter sat on a desk piled high with bulging, unsealed envelopes. He picked up the top ones to see what was in them. Each was labelled in large letters: *Sightings – Cradle Hill; Sightings – Starr Hill; Hoax – Bratton; Pictogram – East Kennet; Hoax – Roswell Alien Autopsy 1947.*

A perusal of their contents revealed newspaper clippings, jotted notes, photographs – all concerning unusual phenomena, including UFO sightings and the mysterious circular patterns that appeared in cornfields overnight.

Orla was in the doorway. 'What've you got, boss?'

'Stuff about crop circles and unexplained lights in the sky. Maybe Swann was doing research for a book?'

'Not just a washed-up singer with a band, then?'

'Apparently not.' He waved his hand at the wall of photos and drawings. 'He seems to have had quite a following, even after he quit the music business.'

She came over to study the pictures more closely. 'That's Nicholas Cage. And isn't that… is that *Springsteen*? Fuck!'

'Swann looks like he wanted to save the world.' Lincoln jabbed a thumb towards a portrait of Swann as an orator, holding forth in a darkened auditorium, hands up as if he was blessing the audience, a messiah for the galaxy.

Orla turned her attention to the envelopes on the desk. '*Old Sarum - Uphill route.* What's that all about?'

'Aren't there supposed to be ancient trackways through Somerset and Wiltshire, linking places like Avebury and Stonehenge and Glastonbury?'

'Is that the same as the Michael Line? Churches dedicated to St Michael, all lining up across the country.' She dropped the envelope back on the desk. 'Old boyfriend of mine decided to walk the Michael Line once. Tried to do it one December, in Jesus sandals. He didn't get very far.'

The other two walls of the room were lined with bookshelves, their contents conveying an impression of a man who was at once beleaguered and a free spirit. The book titles were about government corruption, the inequality of the legal system, the importance of not trusting anyone in authority.

The Anarchist's Cookbook sat beside the *Whole Earth Catalog*, a few spines along from Von Daniken's books about the Bermuda Triangle. Tucked in between were various pamphlets – amateur-looking productions cautioning against using the internet, the dangers of Big Pharma, the threat of social media. There was even one on how you could be spied on through your light bulbs.

A man with a breadth of knowledge, esoteric as well as empirical, but one who trusted no one, who believed nothing he was told, who lived in fear of becoming like everybody else. How much more paranoid might he have become, how much more dangerous, if he'd used the internet.

Lincoln sat at Swann's typewriter, trying to absorb the notion that Ezra Morton might be the dead man's son. Had Swann left this house to him? Was that why he was dossing down here, why his mother had driven from Amesbury to meet him here, only to be shot when she arrived?

He let his gaze wander over the corkboard that hung on the wall beside the typewriter. Phone numbers for local cab companies. A concert poster from 2009 advertising the Plain Janes at the Guildhall, *back by popular request...* The Plain Janes? Where had he seen something else about the Plain Janes?

Orla leant over his shoulder to see what was written on the other envelopes. He was suddenly conscious of her closeness, the summery smell of her cotton shirt, something familiar about her perfume, or was it her shampoo? Sweet, a hint of coconut. He was sure it was the same as Trish's.

He stood up. 'I'd better update the DCI.'

She stepped back. 'I'll go and see how Viv's doing.'

Unable to get a strong enough mobile signal indoors, he had to go out into the garden – which seemed ironic in a place allegedly buzzing with communication networks. As he tried to get through to Park Street, he tramped farther and farther away from the house, down towards the river Wylye, which ran languidly past the bottom of the cottage garden.

At last Connors answered, letting out a gasp of relief when he told her the body wasn't Jill's. 'So who...?'

'Elinor, ma'am. Morton's mother. Looks as if he shot her as soon as she got here on Sunday. She'd still got her jacket on. He must've been lying in wait for her.'

'And then the next day, he takes her car and drives back to lie in wait for Jill.'

'Looks like it, yes. But what's he got against Jill?'

'Is it anything to do with the daughter?' Connors wondered. 'He's more *her* age than Jill's.'

Would the smart, sleek Annika get involved with a layabout like Morton? Had Morton become infatuated with her, his feelings not reciprocated? Lincoln knew of too many cases where vengeance is taken against a parent who's tried to come between a man – it was nearly always a man – and the object of his desire.

'We'll look into it.'

Back in the cottage, he found Orla sealing an evidence bag.

'Elinor's phone,' she said. 'It'll need charging before we can look at it.'

He relayed Connors' suggestion that Morton was really after Annika, not her mother.

'But where would he have met Annika?' Orla asked.

'No idea, but it's one theory, isn't it?'

Viv emerged from the scullery. 'Talk about déjà vu! I attended when the owner of the house died here in April.'

Lincoln was surprised. 'You attended? It was a suspicious death?'

'We thought it was cancer,' said Orla.

'Oh yes,' Viv agreed. 'He had cancer all right, stage four lung cancer, but he died falling down the stairs. A quicker death than he was expecting, certainly. A merciful accident.'

'Was he living here on his own?'

'Yes, with a carer coming in first thing most mornings. She was the one who found him, poor lass. He'd been there some hours by then. Probably fell down the stairs in the dark, bashed his head into the wall on the way down. I seem to remember there weren't any light bulbs in the ceiling lights, not anywhere in the house. A winding staircase in the dark? That's asking for trouble.'

'No bulbs in the ceiling lights,' said Orla as she and Lincoln got back in the car. 'Sounds familiar, doesn't it?'

'They can spy on you through your light bulbs,' he told her, with a wry smile. 'He'd got a book about it.' He thought back to the sad, squalid house in Amesbury where Elinor had lived. 'Morton must have been here before Swann died, if the light bulbs had been removed even before he fell down the stairs.' The car was stifling. He should've left the windows open a crack. 'You looked Swann up on the internet, didn't you? Any family?'

'A wife called Kitty. There was a daughter, but she died in 2000. Drug overdose.'

'We need to get in touch with this Kitty woman, then, see if she knows anything more about Morton. I'll get one of my team to track her down.'

'Or Rick could do it.' She wrenched the car door open and slid into the passenger seat. 'You know, boss, we're not *totally* incompetent at Park Street.'

CHAPTER 32

DC Pam Smyth didn't know that Ezra Morton had been watching Jill Fortune's house. No one had told her his target had been Jill, not Ramsay Keiller.

Around the same time Lincoln was at Willow Cottage, sifting through mouldering envelopes in Daniel Swann's study, Pam was arriving at Fremantle House in Spicer Street, Barbury, to interview Heather Draycott – because no one had told she no longer needed to.

Heather lived on the first floor of this newish block of "luxurious apartments for the over-55s". If not quite as luxurious as the massive photo in the foyer implied, the place was certainly smart and clean, with a spotless stairwell that smelt of new carpets and fresh paint. The flat itself wasn't huge, and Heather's choice of William Morris fabrics rather overwhelmed it, but Pam could understand why complexes like this were so popular with older people who still valued their independence but needed to downsize.

'It's a cliché, I know, but I still can't believe Ramsay's dead.' Heather passed her a chunky pottery mug of peppermint tea. 'He only emailed me the day before, full of plans for expanding the range of stock in the shop. Nothing too ambitious,' she added, her speckly blue eyes misting up behind her wire-framed glasses. 'Just some artisan breads from a local bakery and a few chutneys.'

Pam guessed she was about the same age as her own mother, mid-sixties, maybe a few years older. She wore a loose denim pinafore dress over a beige T-shirt, black leggings and clumpy Birkenstock sandals. Her face was fine-boned, but her cheeks were pale and hollow, as if she'd been unwell.

'How did you and Ramsay meet?' Pam asked, opening her notebook. 'At Keiller's Yard?'

'Oh no. I knew him long before he had the farm shop. His wife and I were at school together. I moved up to London for work after I left university, and Maggie and I lost touch. Then I saw something on Friends Reunited to say she'd died. Must've been about 2005.'

'You must have felt awful.'

'I did, especially since I'd moved back to Wiltshire by then. I got in touch with Ramsay to say how sorry I was about Maggie, and we met for coffee once or twice. Then, last year, we were at the same U3A talk about the airfields on Salisbury Plain. And, of course, Keiller's Yard is right by Turnpike Corner Aerodrome, so he knew all about it. He invited me over for supper at the bungalow. I know he missed Maggie a lot.'

'Did he ever mention Ezra Morton?'

'The man who shot him?' Heather shook her head. 'He was plagued by vandals over the last few months, as you probably know, but they were stupid teenagers, that's all. I don't recall him mentioning anyone by name. By the way, who gave you *my* name?'

'Ramsay's son mentioned you. He said his father was helping you with a book about the airfield.'

'It's only a blog, actually. Which son are we talking about? Mr Nice or Mr Nasty?' When Pam didn't answer quickly enough, Heather said, 'Jamie or Adam?'

'They both mentioned you, actually. Jamie remembered meeting you at the bungalow.'

Heather leant back in her armchair and rested her head on the pillowy back. Her grey curls grew close to her head and it occurred to Pam that maybe she'd lost her hair through chemo, and this wiry, ultra-short style was regrowth.

'Yes, I remember Jamie turning up once when I was having supper with Ramsay. He'd brought his sons over. Lovely lads. They're going to miss their grandad.' She gave a rapidly vanishing smile. 'Jamie may have leapt to the wrong conclusion. Ramsay and I weren't even friends, really. Just two people interested in the same bits of history. And naturally, we'd reminisce about Maggie, although I only knew her well when we were at the grammar school together. I sensed Ramsay was lonely in that little bungalow. Jamie's so busy with his job and running around after his boys, he couldn't get over there as often as he used to.'

'And Adam…?' Pam let the question hang.

'Oh, Adam was always trying to tell Ramsay what he should be doing with his life.' She took a sip of her tea. 'He was jealous, that's what I think. Jealous because his father had found a way of life that suited him and made him happy.'

Once more, her eyes moistened. Clutching her mug in both hands, she stared down into it. She seemed to care about Ramsay, even if they "hadn't even been friends".

'Did he ever talk about the work he did at the MoD?' asked Pam.

'Not really, although he showed me some of his drawings. Beautifully intricate diagrams of aircraft components, little works of art. When they

125

went over to computers, he learnt everything from scratch. He loved his job. That's why it was so unfair that they forced him to leave when they did.'

'So you can't think of any reason why someone would harm him?'

'None at all.' She sat up. 'That stupid girl at *The Messenger* is on a witch hunt, writing that he was working on "secret projects", trying to make out he was killed by the security services. Good God! You know what? She's trying to turn him into another Hilda Murrell.'

'Hilda Murrell? Was that the anti-nuclear campaigner who was murdered?'

'Yes. Her nephew was in the Falklands War. Told her things about the conflict, things that Margaret Thatcher wanted suppressed. Murrell's murder was pinned on some local yob. The lad was a petty thief, but he wasn't a killer.' She leant back again, her outrage evaporating as quickly as it had taken hold. 'So many unanswered questions about the Murrell case. Impossible to prove anything, of course, all this time later.'

Pam took her time finishing her tea. She put her mug down gently next to Heather's on the little table, where a book on the wartime airfields of Wessex lay, yellow Post-it notes sticking out of it, marking significant pages.

'But, Heather, Ramsay wasn't a threat to anyone, was he?' she said at last. 'Not the way Hilda Murrell might have been.'

'He abhorred what they were doing at Porton and, for a long time, he'd been trying to get them to accept responsibility for what happened with the Lyme Bay Trials.'

'The Lyme Bay…?'

'Oh, they had their inquiry and admitted procedures were a bit lax, but no one would accept that anyone suffered as a result.'

'I'm sorry,' said Pam. 'What were the Lyme Bay Trials?'

Heather seemed re-energised. 'You know Ramsay had a brother, a few years younger than him? Callum?'

'Callum? Is that the brother who died?' Graham Dilke had mentioned him after he and Lincoln had talked to Jamie.

Heather nodded. 'He went to a Scout camp down in Dorset, came back feeling ill, something he'd eaten, or so they thought. Then he developed a fever and was rushed into hospital, but too late. Ramsay always maintained it was because of the tests the MoD did in Lyme Bay, a kind of biological attack simulation. Only they used a preparation of live bacteria, including *E.coli*, spraying it into the air to see how far inland it would be spread by the prevailing winds. The Scout camp was right where these bacteria would have drifted ashore.'

Pam sat back, incredulous. 'But why did the boys go camping when the tests were going on?'

'Because they didn't know about them. *Nobody* did, except the people carrying them out. They were *secret* tests. It took years for anyone to even admit they'd taken place.'

'And Ramsay's been trying to prove these trials were responsible for Callum's death?'

'He couldn't prove anything. Back then, they didn't test Callum for a bacterial infection because no one knew he'd been exposed to anything like that. But when Ramsay found out about the trials, he was sure they were to blame.'

Pam didn't say anything, saddened that she'd known nothing of this, had been ignorant of Ramsay's crusade to implicate his former bosses in his brother's death. Was that why his job at the MoD had been done away with?

'Was he still campaigning?'

'Was he another Hilda Murrell, you mean?' Heather gave a wry smile. 'Who knows?'

They sat quietly for a minute or two, Pam casting her gaze around the flat, Heather stroking the wooden arms of her chair. A heavy lorry went past, then a double-decker bus, its scarlet roof on a level with the balcony windows.

'He loved what he was doing,' Heather said dreamily. 'Ramsay. He was content. I think he'd even stopped trying to pin Callum's death on the MoD. He knew he'd never get anywhere.'

'Did he ever say anything to you about his phone being tapped?'

Heather's hands clenched on the arms of her chair. 'No, but then I only had supper with him a few times, and we had lots of other things to talk about. Where does that Bolitho woman get her information from, or is she making it all up? If MI5 tapped his phone calls to me, all they'd have heard were angry discussions about the aerodrome being built on, the loss of all that heritage. Oh, and my grumbles about the price of supermarket vegetables.'

She stood up suddenly and took a moment to steady herself before marching across to open the French windows to the balcony. That was when Pam noticed an acoustic guitar resting against the wall, polished, beautiful.

'You play the guitar?' she asked. 'I've always wanted to learn.'

Heather left the windows open and sat down again, but her face had blossomed at the mention of the guitar.

'I learnt to play when I was a teenager,' she said. 'We all did. We all wanted to be Joan Baez or Joni Mitchell. But I haven't played it for a while, not since I was ill.'

127

'I was always a bit sporty at school. No time for music then, though I regret it now.' Pam paused before enquiring, gently, 'Are you well now?'

'Not entirely. It's under control, but it hangs over you every day. You know, when will it come back? Moving here was stupid. All the stress, everything so tiring. But I couldn't stay in my big old house any longer. Stupid to move, stupid to stay.' She picked up her mug, saw it was empty, put it down again. 'Actually, when you phoned, I thought you were going to ask me about Jill Holland.'

'Jill Holland?'

'Jill Fortune. She was Holland before she married. We were at school together too. Not best friends, though, not like me and Maggie, but we were all in the same class at the girls' grammar. When I moved back down here from Streatham, I looked for music groups, choirs, whatever, and saw Jill was a professional pianist. She'd always been the properly musical one when we were at school, so I wasn't surprised. Anyway, we got together a few years ago, without really expecting anything to come of it. We did several gigs round Amesbury, Bulford, Larkhill, the army camps on the Plain. That's where we got our name, the Plain Janes. And then we played some of the pubs round town, a couple of small festivals.'

'Just the two of you?'

'Yes, Jill on keyboards, me on guitar. And we both sang too, took it in turns, whichever voice suited the music. A bit of folk, a bit of blues. Just for fun, really. To keep us sane.' She breathed more deeply, her face softening at the memory. 'Until I was diagnosed with breast cancer in 2012 and everything stopped.'

'I'm sorry. It must be...'

'So she hasn't turned up? Jill's still missing?'

'I'm afraid so.'

'It could've been me. Someone out to get Ramsay, bursting in when I was with him, hurting me instead of her.'

Pam looked down at her notebook, not much written there after all. 'But you can't think of any reason someone would be "out to get Ramsay"?'

Heather shook her head. 'I keep thinking about Jill. I wish we'd kept in touch better the last few years, especially since I moved in here, only a stone's throw away from her house. She was so sweet, always remembering to phone me on my birthday. Oh Lord, listen to me, talking about her in the past tense already.' She pressed her fist against her lips. 'Last time she phoned, in March, we spent ages reminiscing about our schooldays, because she was in touch with Dan Swann again.'

'Dan Swann?'

'The singer. Danny Swann and the Haymakers? Oh, but you're too young to know who I'm talking about.'

'My mum may have heard of him.'

Heather's face softened again. 'Yes, I expect she has. Dan had a gorgeous gravelly voice, perfect for the blues. Jill started going out with him when she was still at school. We were all *so* jealous! Then, suddenly, he was this big pop star, off round the world.'

'So he settled abroad?'

'No, although he was in the States with his band for a while. But then he had some sort of breakdown, left the band, came home. Next thing you know, he's throwing all his money into UFO research. In some ways, he was ahead of his time, doubting everything the government said about lights in the sky over Salisbury Plain. Actually, doubting *everything* the government said about *anything*.' She smiled indulgently, as if she, too, had had a soft spot for Dan Swann. 'And then, at the end of last year sometime, he contacted her out of the blue, wanting her to look at some book he'd written, see what she thought of it. When she phoned me, she told me she really didn't know what to say to him.'

'Why ever not?'

'Because it was so...' Heather paused, searching for the right word. 'It was full of conspiracy theories. Theories he took seriously: earth had been visited by aliens and the authorities were keeping it quiet; the security services were spying on him; global forces were out to kill him because he knew the truth. Dan was clearly paranoid, she said, and his book was bonkers.' She laughed. '*Conspiracy To Deceive,* it was called, and she said it was "completely bloody bonkers"! And then, soon after that, of course, he died.'

CHAPTER 33

When Annika Fortune arrived at her mother's house on Saturday afternoon, she was stopped at the front gate by a uniformed officer who wouldn't let her in. She rang Park Street, demanding to speak to DS Orla Cook, but before she could convey her fury at being shut out, she was told that Orla and Inspector Lincoln needed to speak to her and were on their way over.

Waiting in her car, smoking nervously, she jabbed the power button on the radio, catching the end of the two o'clock news. "... body at a house near Warminster. A police spokesperson said the identity of the woman could not be released until her family had been informed. The headlines again..."

She turned the radio off and got out of the car. The detectives needed to speak to her because her mother was dead.

My mother is dead. The words marched around in her brain until they stopped making sense. She drew deeply on her cigarette, trying to calm down, but her heart only raced faster.

At the sound of a car driving past, she looked up to see Inspector Lincoln at the wheel, Orla in the passenger seat. She dropped her cigarette onto the tarmac, grinding it under her foot before rushing across the road to intercept them.

'Is it her?' she cried. 'Is it my mum?'

They told her it was another woman, not Jill. Annika felt weak with relief, but it was short-lived. Her mother was still missing.

Orla held the car door open. 'Let's get away from here,' she said, and Annika slid into the back seat. They drove her half a mile up the road to Jubilee Park, where they sat on a bench overlooking the tennis courts.

Any other Saturday, she and Roz would be away somewhere, London or Brighton, Bristol sometimes, or Poole. Roz didn't like the countryside and gravitated towards water: the Thames, the sea, harboursides and marinas.

'You can take the girl out of Australia,' Roz would say, 'but you can't take Australia out of the girl.'

That's why it felt weird to Annika to be landlocked in Barbury on a Saturday afternoon, sitting on a bench next to two detectives.

'Ezra Morton followed your mum from her house on Monday afternoon,' Orla said. There was an eye witness, she explained, and now the whole focus of their investigation had shifted. Jill had been Morton's target, not Ramsay Keiller.

Annika hadn't felt scared before, not for herself. Jill had been unlucky, wrong place, wrong time. But if Morton had been watching the house…

'What did he want with Mum?'

Orla shrugged. 'You're positive she never mentioned any concerns about a stalker, threatening phone calls, anything strange like that?'

Annika shook her head. She daren't admit she hadn't been to Arundel Terrace for weeks, hadn't spoken to her mother on the phone for at least a fortnight, or even emailed or texted her. She'd only tried phoning her on Tuesday to tell her she and Roz were starting a family.

Even if they had been in contact more frequently, Jill probably wouldn't have told her about funny phone calls or emails, not unless she thought she could blame Annika. Like that business with Matt letting himself into the house with Annika's keys and stealing stuff. Snooping round the place simply because he could. But that was months ago, and she hadn't seen him since before Christmas. Matt was water under the bridge, long gone.

'We'll need to take her mobile and her laptop,' Orla went on, 'to see if there's a history of Morton harassing her. You're sure you don't know him?' She unzipped the document wallet on her lap and pulled out a photograph. A mugshot. Morton looked ugly and dangerous. Unruly. Wild.

The way Matt had looked, Annika thought, when she'd first got involved with him, when he was still in recovery, putting his life back together after he got out of prison. She'd helped him get a job of sorts, doing a bit of gardening work for Adam and Jo Keiller. Although she wouldn't be surprised if he'd chucked it in by now. Matt was a user, in every sense.

She took a cigarette out and lit it, taking care to hold it away from her companions. 'Why would I know someone like Ezra Morton?'

Orla's eyes were flinty and bright, as if she didn't believe her. 'Could this man have been following *you*?'

'Following *me*?'

'Any strange phone calls, someone hanging around near where you work?' Orla didn't seem to want to give up.

'No, no. I…'

'He could have had a grudge against your mum because she was in the way,' Inspector Lincoln said. 'Maybe he was pursuing *you* but blamed *her* for keeping you apart.'

'No, listen, I… You're saying this is all *my* fault? If I thought someone was stalking me, do you really think I'd have kept that to myself? Do you?'

'You could be forgiven for not making the connection,' said Orla. 'See, Morton's closer to your age than your mum's. Are you absolutely sure you don't know him?'

Two women appeared on the tennis court, uncovered their racquets and tipped out lurid yellow balls from a tube. One checked the tension of the net, while the other smacked a ball into the chain link fence, a practice shot, then another and another. Annika stared at the women, mesmerised. She dropped her cigarette, half-smoked, on the concrete in front of the bench and stamped it out.

'This may not have anything to do with you, Annika,' the inspector said, in a more sympathetic tone than his colleague's, 'but we have to explore every angle to find out why Morton waited outside the house and followed Jill all the way to Keiller's Yard. And now this woman's been found dead, the press are going to be on your back, thinking it's your mum until we issue another statement. You need to prepare yourself for a lot of hurtful speculation.'

She looked round at him. He sat with his elbows on his knees, feet wide apart, hands clasped lightly together. 'What sort of speculation?'

'Armchair detectives,' he said. 'Internet sleuths. They'll all have a theory.' He straightened up, spreading his hands as if to reassure her. 'I just want you to be ready for that.'

Her heart was pounding again. 'So who is it, the dead woman? Is it anything to do with this Morton guy?'

She caught the look the detectives exchanged. They weren't sure what to tell her.

The inspector took a deep breath. 'You need to keep this to yourself for now, okay? It's Elinor Morton. Ezra's mother.'

'Oh God! If he can kill his own mother...' She bit hard on her knuckles.

The women on the tennis court started to play. The one serving reminded her of Roz, a familiar aggression about her style, the swift force behind the downward sweep of her racquet.

'Does the name Daniel Swann mean anything to you?' Orla asked.

Annika knew the name, could even recall a photo at Auntie Maggie's house. It had stood on a bookshelf to the right of the Keillers' brick fireplace, a colour photo, unlike most of the other family photos on display. Two teenage schoolgirls in their green-and-white-striped uniform dresses, a lanky, curly-haired schoolboy leaning down between them, grinning for the camera.

She'd asked Maggie about the photo once. 'That's you and Mum, isn't it? But who's that boy?'

'That's Daniel Swann, but don't mention him to your mum.'

'Why not?'

'She was madly in love with him when we were at school, but then he got famous and went away, and she never saw him again. But don't tell her I told you.'

When she heard the name Daniel now, that's who Annika always thought of: a gawky, dark-haired boy who'd broken her mother's schoolgirl heart.

'He's someone Mum used to know when they were at school,' she told the detectives. 'I think they went out together when they were teenagers. I don't know what happened to him. Why?'

'Did he ever come to the house?' the inspector asked.

They'd had few visitors after Annika's father left. Just loads of pupils. That God-awful piano playing all afternoon and into the evening. But she was sure Daniel Swann had never visited.

'No,' she said. 'I don't think so.'

'The house where Elinor Morton was shot,' he said, 'belonged to Daniel Swann.'

'You mean Daniel's in on this?'

'Hardly.' Orla was smirking at her. 'He's been dead for months.'

The Roz-like tennis player held her racquet up in the air. She'd won the first game. She pranced back to the baseline and crouched to receive her opponent's serve. Annika watched as the ball hit the top of the net, ran along it and dropped back on the server's side.

'Love fifteen!' the Roz woman crowed.

'It's just a coincidence, isn't it?' Annika tried to put the pieces together in her head, but there was already too much going on in it. 'Isn't it?'

'We don't know.' Orla lifted Ezra Morton's photo from her lap and pushed it at her as if his face would conjure up a memory or provoke a reaction. 'There could be a connection between Morton and this Daniel Swann.'

'What d'you want me to say? I don't know Ezra Morton, and Daniel Swann's just someone Mum was in love with years ago.'

Visibly disappointed, Orla put the photo away, zipped up her folder and rested her hands on it.

'We need to go back to your mum's house again,' Inspector Lincoln said gently, reassuring her as if she was a kid who needed to be spoken to with care. 'We'll collect her laptop and her mobile and then…'

'I've got her phone here.' Annika reached into her bag and, hesitating for a moment, handed it over. 'The PIN's 1983. The year I was born.' The significance of this struck her forcefully: her mother hadn't used her own birth year but Annika's. An important year for them both. 'She hasn't had any calls. She doesn't give her number out to many people.'

'Thanks for this.' Inspector Lincoln took the mobile and handed it to Orla, who fiddled around with plastic bags and labels. Annika longed to take the phone back, to hold on to it a few minutes more, but she knew that was stupid. She turned her gaze from Orla's hands to the players on the tennis court. They were changing ends. She'd lost track of the score.

She should have been relieved that the dead woman wasn't Jill, but all she felt was dread. It could only be a matter of time before they found her mother's body, and Annika wasn't in the least bit prepared for that. A chasm opened in front of her, an abyss. A world without her mother in it. Life without her. It simply wasn't possible.

They drove her back to Arundel Terrace so she could collect her car and because they wanted to pick up her mother's laptop. Finzi jumped down off the garden wall at their approach, yowling to be let in.

'Who's looking after him?' the inspector asked, bending down to rub the top of the cat's tabby head.

'He can look after himself,' Annika assured him. 'He's got a cat flap, and Helen from next door has been feeding him.' She put the key in the lock. 'Oh God,' she said, as the door swung open, 'this is the spare key.'

They both looked at her as if she was losing it. 'So?' Orla put her hand on her hip.

'I'm using the spare set of keys. Mum would've taken her own set of keys with her. Were they in her purse when you found it? Were they in the bike basket?'

'No,' said Inspector Lincoln. 'How many keys are we talking about?'

'Two, like this: a Yale for the front door, a mortice for the back. They were on a key ring I got her from the music shop. If he's got keys to the house...' Anxiety pressed down on her chest like a heavy hand.

'We can find you a locksmith,' the inspector said. 'It'd be wise to get the locks changed.'

She nodded, gripping the keys so tightly they dug into her palm.

'Now,' said Orla, 'are you sure you haven't seen anyone hanging around outside your house in Amberstone?'

'If someone was hanging around outside, or following me, I'd know about it. We live in a tiny close, only a few houses, so if anyone was acting suspiciously, I'd see them, or my girlfriend would.'

'Your girlfriend?' Orla looked up. 'Any chance your girlfriend knows him?'

'Of course not! And in case you're wondering – not that it's any of your business – I did have a boyfriend before I met Roz, but it wasn't Ezra Morton.'

'We'd like to talk to Roz,' the inspector said. 'Just in case she's seen anyone.'

Did she have to spell it out in big letters? No one had been hanging around outside the house. But it was pointless: the detectives were sure Morton was really after *her*, not her mother.

She gave him Roz's card. 'She's away at the moment, though. Back Tuesday. A work thing in London, a training course.'

He read the card. 'Rosamund Berrow. What does she do?'

'She's a social worker,' Annika said. 'She supports families in crisis.'

CHAPTER 34

It was well after four by the time Lincoln and Orla returned from Arundel Terrace.

Rick Nevin greeted them as they walked into the incident room. 'Had a phone call,' he said, nursing a can of Diet Coke. 'Chap living next door to Morton.'

'Go on.' Lincoln slid Jill's laptop and mobile onto his desk. He needed to pass them over to the tech team, but he wanted to hear what Nevin had to say first. 'Where's this?'

'Those flats at the back of the train station. Housing association. He said Morton's been there over a year. He's no bother, but he never speaks, never makes eye contact. Keeps himself to himself.'

'Don't they all?' Orla folded her arms. 'Soon as I hear that phrase, I hear trouble.'

'But then last Saturday,' Nevin went on, 'Morton asked this fella if he'd give him a lift to Warminster.'

'Cheeky,' said Orla. 'It's a forty-mile round trip.'

'Morton offered to pay him fifty quid, so he said yes. A couple of miles short of Warminster, he says to drop him off. Leaves a ten quid note on the dashboard and legs it.'

'He should've asked for the cash up front,' said Orla. 'Should've seen that coming.'

Lincoln studied the wall map until he found the likely drop-off point. 'Morton could walk to Willow Cottage from there. Anything else this bloke could tell you?'

'Morton's been working for Barbury Cleaning Company. Nights, mostly. A minibus picks him up in the evenings and off he goes in his cleaner's outfit.'

'BCC are contract cleaners,' said Orla. 'They do the hospital and some of the schools.'

'We need to search that flat, see if he's left any clues.'

'He might come back there.' Nevin swigged from his can of Diet Coke. 'Could be dangerous.'

Orla looked at Lincoln expectantly. 'Are we going over there, boss?'

*

136

He'd expected Morton's flat to be as chaotic as his mother's house, but Lincoln was surprised to find it was tidy and clean, despite its oppressive airlessness. Not that there was much in it: two dining chairs, a low table, a single divan. No easy chair, nothing decorative. There were no curtains at the windows, and the only floor covering was a large, khaki-coloured mat in the living room. No television, no radio, nothing electronic. No bulbs in the ceiling lights – just like in Elinor's Amesbury house and Swann's cottage.

'It's like a cell,' said Orla. 'He hasn't even got a fridge or a microwave. He must live on takeaways.'

Lincoln remembered his own bedsit, where he'd spent two unhappy years after Cathy was killed. He'd lived day to day, buying only what he'd need for that evening's meal. Once, he got home to find that all he had left were two eggs and a nearly empty bottle of salad cream. Another time, a tin of soup and a packet of Hula Hoops.

Orla followed him into the bedroom, gazing at the bare walls. 'I'm disappointed,' she said. 'I was expecting him to have papered it with photos of Jill Fortune.'

'Or Annika.'

'Or Annika, yeah.' She opened the door of a walk-in wardrobe – and reeled back. 'Oh fuck!'

The back wall of the wardrobe was covered with dozens of photographs and drawings, not of Jill or her daughter, but of planes and spacecraft. Many photos were blurry and amateur, but one in particular attracted Lincoln's attention. It measured roughly eight inches by ten, in black and white and, when he peered more closely, he could make out the shape not only of a strange craft but also of its pilot – slumped, apparently dead, at the controls.

Only this wasn't a man. It wasn't a woman. There was some resemblance to a human form – head, neck, shoulders – but apart from a few dark squiggles here and there, the face was as smooth and featureless as a frankfurter sausage. The photo bore a time stamp: *09:27:94 06.33* – early in the morning of 27 September 1994.

Orla inspected the pictures. 'What's that all about?'

'It must be that mystery plane that's supposed to have crashed at Boscombe Down. We were talking about it at the cottage, all the rumours about what goes on there. That happened around then, whatever it was.'

Lincoln had still been with the Met at the time, but he remembered the fuss about the incident, the newspaper stories claiming the aircraft could be an alien spaceship. The American television series *The X-Files* had just started on the BBC, so public interest about such unexplained phenomena was keen.

'So what happened to this spaceship?'

'No idea. If I believed in that sort of thing, I'd have taken more interest at the time, but I don't, so I didn't.'

She rolled her eyes. 'So people thought it was the start of an alien invasion? Mind you, the guy in the cockpit...' She shuddered. 'You can see why people made such a thing of it.'

'Because they thought the photo was genuine. But people were faking photos and films long before the days of Photoshop. Even Swann seemed to accept that a lot of these UFO sightings were hoaxes. He'd got a whole folder devoted to them, remember?'

'But where's Morton got this stuff from?'

'From Swann? If they were in touch before Swann died, Morton could have been familiarising himself with his father's greatest passion.'

'Passion? Obsession, more like.' Orla stood gazing at the wall of photos, shaking her head. 'But how does Jill Fortune figure in any of this?'

Lincoln shrugged. 'No idea. Take some photos of that wall before we go. Any other surprises in the wardrobe?'

'Like I can knock through the back and come out in Narnia?' She checked the rest of the cupboard. 'A pair of trainers and a shirt, and his cleaning company uniform.'

'What about that shelf?' Lincoln reached over her head to run his hand along the high ledge across the back wall. Unfortunately, at the same time, Orla stepped back, treading on his toes and colliding with him. Her elbow caught him in the stomach. 'Oof!'

'Sorry, boss.' She ducked out of his way. 'You shouldn't have crowded me.'

Nothing on the shelf, not even dust.

He joined her at the window, looking out towards the railway station. The train from Waterloo had arrived, its disembarking passengers pouring down into the subway and appearing on the concourse two minutes later. Taxi cabs and cars drew up to collect them, while the announcer reeled off a list of stations at which the train would be stopping on its way to Exeter St David's.

Ezra Morton must have heard these announcements day after day, night after night, but it was the mysteries of the universe that seemed to interest him more, travelling far beyond Wiltshire and the West Country. Had he sat in his wardrobe, a torch trained on those photos and drawings of strange craft, imagining what was out there? What had he made of the weird, faceless pilot in the crashed plane at Boscombe Down? What did he think his father had stumbled upon?

'Let's get back,' Lincoln said, as soon as Orla had photographed the pictures inside the wardrobe. 'See what more we can find out about him.'

Lincoln called Trish as he was leaving Park Street that evening. It was sultry, the air heavy and threatening.

'You fancy a drink?' He clamped his mobile against his ear to shut out the traffic noise.

'It's going to rain.'

'It's not raining now.'

'But it will. Can't you feel it in the air?'

'Not here, I can't.' He got into his car, noticing he was all but boxed-in by another car that couldn't find a parking space. 'Or shall I come over?'

'What, to the house?'

'Yes, to the house. To *your* house.' He checked his rear-view mirror. Would he be able to extricate himself?

'Kate's not feeling very well. She was meant to be going to Vic's today, but I've kept her home instead.'

He recalled how unenthusiastic Kate had sounded when he'd asked her about staying at her father's. She felt awkward, she'd said, especially now Vic and Gail were expecting their second child together – a baby she wasn't supposed to know about.

'Trish, we need to talk,' he said, although actually they didn't. They could go on like this indefinitely, as friends, lovers, people who only met from time to time. They could go on like this until one of them met someone else, someone willing to commit themselves to a proper relationship.

'I know,' said Trish. 'We can't go on like this. Listen, I've got to go. I'm making soup and I can't leave it. Talk to you soon.'

And she hung up. How soon would they talk, he wondered? He had to face it: he wanted more, Trish wanted more, but neither of them was brave enough to admit it. Was moving in together the solution? Could either of them give up their independence for the sake of the other? He wasn't sure of the answer and didn't feel ready to think about it.

He got out of the car to assess the distance between his rear bumper and the white Audi that had parked across him. He'd never make it. He slammed the door and headed back to his desk. Since he wasn't going anywhere, he might as well put in another hour or so.

In the ten minutes since he'd been away from his desk, his chair had vanished.

*

He was in the midst of trying to find out more about Ezra Morton when Pam phoned.

'Ramsay was campaigning against germ warfare testing,' she said.

Momentarily derailed, he had to ask her to explain.

'I met with Heather Draycott,' she went on. 'She told me Ramsay lost his brother, Callum, as a result of germ warfare tests in Dorset. They released bacteria from a ship in Lyme Bay and then measured how far inland the bacteria drifted – the so-called Lyme Bay Trials. The bacteria were supposed to be harmless, but anyone who was vulnerable, like Ramsay's brother must have been, got sick and some died. Like Callum.'

'You met with Heather Draycott? Keiller's friend?' He turned away from his screen. 'But Keiller wasn't the target. It was Jill all along. Why did you interview Heather?'

'Because you asked me to.' She sounded understandably aggrieved. 'When did we find out Ramsay wasn't the target? No one's told *me*.'

He ran a hand through his hair. He'd been so caught up in the discovery of Elinor's body, he'd forgotten to update Woody on the latest developments.

'Sorry, Pam, I should have let you know. Tell me about Ramsay's brother.'

He listened while she relayed all she'd learnt about the apparent cause of Callum Keiller's death.

'So they were *secret* tests?'

'Yes,' said Pam. 'May 1965 was when Callum and the other Scouts went camping in Dorset. The public weren't told anything about the tests. I've spent all afternoon looking into it. There was an inquiry, questions in Parliament. In Portland, there was a cluster of miscarriages. In the months after the trials, a number of babies were born with birth defects. But the MoD dismissed any connection to the testing.' She paused and sighed dramatically. 'So I was wasting my time, was I, looking for a motive for Ramsay's murder?'

'Afraid so. He wasn't the intended victim – Jill was. Still, you've probably found out what's behind Karen Bolitho's cockeyed stories.' He felt guilty. *He* was the one who'd wasted her time. He tried to lighten the mood. 'How's things at Barley Lane? Managing okay without me?'

'Just about, although something must be up with Breezy. Graham went round to the flat this afternoon and couldn't get an answer. The guy on the next floor said he hadn't seen him for days.'

'Maybe he's met someone? Someone from the wedding.'

'You think so?' Pam didn't sound as if she believed it either. 'If he'd met someone, he'd have been going on about it like he usually does.'

Although, it had been a while since Dennis Breeze had come into work bragging about his latest conquest…

'Keep trying his phone. He's got to show up sometime.'

When Pam rang off, he strolled across to the drinks machine. Dead, the lights off. He'd have kicked it if he felt that would do any good. Instead, he leant against it and looked at the whiteboard from a different angle, hoping to catch it out.

He needed to set Ramsay Keiller aside, and everything to do with him. The dead man was an innocent bystander, shot when he'd tried to stop Ezra Morton kidnapping Jill.

If Karen Bolitho at *The Messenger* wanted to hook readers by implying that Keiller was some sort of spy, then let her! She'd soon find out she was chasing red herrings – or whatever you did with red herrings…

But what did Morton want with Jill? As Orla had surmised, it was more likely that he had some sort of fixation on Annika, convincing himself that Jill was stopping them being together. He thought back to the flat near the station. A flat that resembled a cell, except for the pictures of aeroplanes and spacecraft, an interest that seemed to emulate that of Morton's father. Assuming they were right about him being Swann's son.

Whatever had prompted his assault on her in 2012, Morton and Elinor must have been reconciled for a while after he came out of prison. He'd been living with her in the Amesbury house until a couple of years ago and, when he'd phoned her at the weekend, she'd willingly driven over to Willow Cottage on the Sunday morning. She could never have imagined he would shoot her when she got there.

Lincoln's mind drifted back to the sight of her body on the scullery floor, her face pretty much destroyed. What had pushed Morton to shoot her so cruelly?

The whiteboard was as reticent as ever, even when he sneaked up on it from this angle. At least he could add another name to it now: Annika's housemate, Rosamund Berrow. He'd talk to Woody in the morning, suggest Pam go to see her on Tuesday when Roz was back from her work trip to London. Even if Annika hadn't seen anyone suspicious near their home in Amberstone, maybe Roz had.

He turned his gaze to the window overlooking the car park. The Audi blocking him in had gone. He could go home. As he left the building, it started to rain.

He'd been indoors five minutes when his mobile rang, still in the pocket of the jacket he'd discarded on his way to a generous measure of Jameson's.

He took a sip of the whiskey, savouring it before he swallowed. He retrieved his phone and checked the screen.

'Graham?'

'Just had a call from Devizes police station.' Dilke sounded unhappy. 'Breezy's been arrested.'

CHAPTER 35

Kelly Turner leant her bike against the wall and, agile as a cat, slipped in over the fence. It was pitch black until the security light snapped on at her approach. Stupid prick, he'd think it was a fox or a badger triggering it. Out here, miles from anywhere, she supposed you got all kinds of intruders – including a seventeen-year-old girl on a mission.

She stood in Adam Keiller's garden for ten minutes or more, listening for movement inside the house – voices, music, water running, anything that told her he was home, that his wife was there too, or the children. No, the children wouldn't be there. Those cute little brats would still be away at boarding school.

She caught the murmur of conversation. Too far away to make out the words. She stepped across the flower bed, ducked down and crept close against the wall until she reached a window. Carefully, carefully, she peeked over the sill and into the sitting room, which was lit only by floor lamps. Adam was slumped on the sofa, staring at the laptop on the coffee table in front of him, one hand down the front of his joggers.

She could make out the words now as they rose from the laptop: exclamations and urgings, invitations to look, to touch, to lick, to suck…

As she tried to crouch nearer, her hand brushed the edge of a flower pot balanced on the outside sill. The heavy pot thudded into the soil beside her. It didn't break, but the sound was enough to alarm him, to stop him mid-wank.

His shadow fell over the flower bed as he rushed to the window and leant out. 'What the hell?'

Kelly scrabbled away beyond his reach before standing up. 'Having fun, Mr K?'

'What are you doing here?'

'Watching you playing with yourself. Although that's not the only reason. Can I come in?'

He straightened the waistband of his joggers, pulled down his polo shirt and glanced behind him as if he expected Wifey to come in at any minute. 'Okay, okay, I'll let you in.' He began to head towards the front door.

'No worries,' said Kelly and, catlike once more, she slid over the sill to land neatly on the cream rug. 'Oh dear,' she said, noticing too late that her trainers were mucky but not even attempting to sound sorry.

'I told you not to come to the house anymore.' Adam ran his hand over his chin, which was dark with stubble.

'Not ashamed of me, are you? Embarrassed about all we got up to? Well, I'm here now, and it doesn't look as if your Jo-Jo is. So maybe you want some company?' She nodded towards the laptop on the coffee table. She had him at a disadvantage, had caught him out and he wouldn't like that. Adam was a man who liked to be in charge.

'You on your own?'

'Afraid so, Mr K. Fancied a threesome, did you? You, me and Driver?'

He shook his head, then scowled at the marks she'd left on the rug. 'What *do* you want?'

'A drink'd be nice.'

'Tea, coffee, Coke?'

'Got any vodka?'

'Vodka?' He walked towards the kitchen. 'You're not old enough to be drinking vodka.'

'I'm old enough to do your dirty work for you, though, aren't I? Old enough to spend the night with you.'

He halted in the doorway, as if he was about to turn on her, but then he kept on walking and called back over his shoulder, 'You'll have a Coke and like it.'

She followed him into the kitchen, where a couple of spotlights and the fancy plinth lights along the kickboards were on. She hadn't seen the kitchen before. She usually went straight up to the bedroom. What would a kitchen like this cost? What would a *house* like this cost?

'So, what happened? To your dad?' She took the Coke can from him, stroked the condensation from the sides then licked the metallic-tasting moisture from her fingers. 'You know that wasn't us, don't you?'

Adam looked up from pouring himself a huge glass of red wine. 'What wasn't you?'

'The shooting. That was nothing to do with me and Driver. We used an air rifle to fuck the lights but that's all. Your dad was shot with a proper gun, wasn't he?'

'I believe so.' The wine swung in the glass as he swirled it round. Didn't he want to talk about his dad? He didn't even seem sad. 'Where's Driver tonight?'

'Out with his mates.' She'd wanted to join him, but Driver'd said they shouldn't go round together for a bit in case anyone had seen them round the yard.

'He'll keep his mouth shut, will he?' Adam didn't sound worried, more like he was making fun of her and Driver. Probably thought they were as thick as shit because they didn't have money, didn't live in a fancy house with fucking spotlights in the kickboards.

'Of course. Not that you paid us much, did you? Considering.' She tipped the can up, drained the last drop of Coke.

'Has Driver put you up to this?'

'I don't need Driver to tell me what to do.'

'How much are you after?' The wine swilled round the glass again. It looked like oily blood.

'A thousand?'

His eyes kind of glinted, like he knew something she didn't. Him so clever with his degrees and his qualifications, fucking doctor, consultant, whatever. And really, when it came down to it, he was no better than the sort of people he looked down on.

'Five hundred,' he said, like it was a game.

'Eight fifty.'

'Six.'

'Seven fifty.'

'Done.'

Yeah, Kelly really felt like she'd been done. Done down. Beaten. Fucking Adam!

'Your wife know about me?' Just throwing it out there so he'd know she wasn't ashamed, wasn't afraid to brag about what he'd got her to do to him. Things Wifey didn't like doing or didn't do as well as Kelly did.

'Of course,' he said, but a tiny hesitation told her that Wifey didn't know, probably hadn't got a clue.

'Twelve fifty,' she said. 'Twelve fifty and I won't tell Jo-Jo about us.' She banged the Coke can down on the island. One of the plinth lights was on the blink, she noticed. 'Twelve fifty and I won't say a word.'

CHAPTER 36

As soon as he'd finished talking to Graham Dilke, Lincoln phoned Woody. Suki answered, annoyed that he'd woken them up.

'I know it's work, Jeff,' she grumbled, 'and you probably think it's important, but you swan off to Park Street, leaving Mike holding the fort and...'

A murmur of protest as Woody took the phone from her, yawning. 'Sorry, boss.'

'Breezy's in custody in Devizes.'

'Wha-at?'

'Something to do with some woman at that wedding he went to.'

A sharp intake of breath. 'Would explain a lot,' said Woody. 'He hasn't been himself all week.'

'Hasn't been at work for much of the week either, has he?'

'No, but I reckoned he'd got a stomach upset after the wedding. Food poisoning or something. You know what these wedding receptions are like, buffet left out on the table, uncovered, for hours on end.'

'I'll take your word for it.' When had Lincoln last been to a wedding? Too long ago to call it to mind. 'So this is the first you've heard of it?'

'Yes. What's he been charged with?'

'Not sure. I got it third-hand from Dilke, who got it second-hand from Breezy's neighbour.'

Once he knew Woody was as much in the dark as he was, Lincoln got in his car and set off towards Devizes police station. He was there within the hour and saw Breeze outside, on the steps, leather jacket folded over his arm. He didn't look as if he'd shaved for several days, or washed his hair.

Breeze caught sight of Lincoln, did a double take and started down the steps.

'Get in the car,' said Lincoln. 'You can tell me everything on the way back.'

The wedding had been his cousin Shirley's third. She'd come full circle. After marrying and divorcing a Londoner and then a Liverpudlian, she'd met up with Rod, her very first boyfriend, who'd been in her class at Barbury Fields.

146

They'd got on like a house on fire and were engaged inside a month. Trouble was, Shirley's best friend from Barbury Fields was Tracey.

'Tracey?' Lincoln glanced across at Breeze, slumped in the passenger seat.

'My ex.' Breeze fumbled some nicotine gum out of his pocket. 'And Trace and Shirl are still thick as thieves. Cuh, another few weeks and none of this would've happened.'

'Not sure I follow.' The miles ticked away as Lincoln drove down the almost empty A-road from Devizes, although he was conscious that drivers tended to take risks in the early hours on empty roads.

'Spring last year, Shirley looked Rod up on Friends Reunited – you know, the website where you can look up all your old schoolmates? Or you could. That's my point, see. Friends Reunited closed down a few weeks after that. If she'd gone looking for Rod a month or two later...'

'She wouldn't have found him and they wouldn't have got married.'

'Exactly.'

'And you wouldn't have bumped into Tracey at their wedding.'

'Exactly.'

'Bit of a shock, was it, seeing your ex-girlfriend after all this time?'

'Ex-*wife*.' Breeze looked out of the window at the dark fields, the clouds massing below the full moon.

'Sorry. Forgot you were married.'

'I don't go on about it. We were both very young at the time.'

Lincoln drove in silence for a while, suspecting that Breeze was dozing off. But he was wrong.

'Seeing her there, it all came back to me. Y'know, the way she left, selfish cow. Leaving me with rent to pay for the flat and we'd bought stuff on credit, and she just kept spending...' He snorted and sat up. 'And then she had the cheek to ask me for maintenance. Maintenance! Like I owed her something.'

'That's the way things work, Dennis.' Lincoln remembered all too clearly the painful practicalities when he and Cathy broke up. The financial impact was nothing compared to the emotional damage he'd suffered. But then, he'd been older than Breeze would have been, readier to blame himself, still in love with Cathy even if she'd stopped loving him.

'And then Tracey was there, at the wedding, in all her finery. Fucking matron of honour!' After a long pause, he declared, 'I didn't do anything wrong! I know I didn't. And if I did, I didn't mean to.'

He'd been charged with attempted sexual assault and released on bail pending further investigation. There'd be repercussions, of course, Lincoln knew: suspension from duty, limits on his movements, not to mention the mental strain of having something like that hanging over him, justified or not. But Breeze was robust, defiant. Although he didn't look very robust now, squashed up against the passenger window, his face turned away.

An orange glow in the sky showed that they'd soon be in Barbury.

'Okay, Dennis, where am I taking you?'

'Christ knows! I can't go home. Can't face it.'

No hotel would take him at this hour – it was nearly two.

Lincoln sighed. 'You can stay at my place. Get some sleep, clean yourself up. When did you last eat?'

'Yesterday sometime.'

'Where've you been the last few days? Haven't been at work, have you?'

'Went round a mate's house, but he chucked me out when he found out what had happened. He's an old friend of Tracey's, too.'

They pulled up outside the Old Vicarage. Breeze hung back as if he expected the invitation to be withdrawn at the last moment, but Lincoln beckoned him in.

'Big house,' he said, gazing around as Lincoln led him through to the kitchen. 'Nice.'

'Thanks. It's taken me long enough.' Nearly eighteen months to get the roof retiled, the floorboards replaced, the windows fixed, and there was still quite a bit to be done.

Lincoln showed him where everything was, found him towels, pyjamas – too long in the leg, but they more or less fitted everywhere else – and made up the spare bed while Breeze took a shower. While he waited to go to bed himself, he checked his mobile, seeing several missed calls and two texts from Trish:

Where are you?

Everything ok?

He texted back: *Had to go to Devizes. Will explain tomorrow.*

And then Breeze appeared in the kitchen, scrubbed and shaved.

'What do I do in the morning, boss?'

'You can't go into work. You need to get yourself a solicitor, talk to your Police Federation rep, find out all you can about what you need to do. Don't put it off.'

'I didn't do it, boss. I didn't do what she's saying I did.'

'Don't tell *me*, Dennis, tell your solicitor. Go to bed, get some rest. I'll be leaving before you're up, but you can find yourself some food, wash your clothes, whatever. Where's your car?'

Breeze grinned sheepishly. 'Crashed it Wednesday night. It's not a write-off, but one of the front wheels is buggered. I've left it at the garage.' He snorted. 'Cuh, I've fucked up big time, haven't I?'

'Yes,' said Lincoln, suddenly so tired he could've fallen asleep where he stood. 'Yes, Dennis, you certainly have.'

CHAPTER 37

SUNDAY 9 JULY 2017

Sunday morning at Park Street was surprisingly quiet. The phones rang only intermittently. Officers were off shift if they could be spared. Lincoln even found a spot in the car park without any trouble, and had a choice of spare chairs to commandeer.

He'd left the house without waking Breeze, but he made a mental note to phone him mid-morning, check he was okay. By the time he'd made up the spare bed and shown Breeze where everything was, he'd only had four hours in bed before he'd had to get up again. He just hoped he wouldn't fall asleep over his desk.

Orla came bounding through the incident room, swigging from a red metallic flask.

'Been to the gym?' he asked.

She looked down at her skinny T-shirt and tracksuit bottoms as if she'd forgotten what she was wearing. 'No, boss, I've been running.' She snapped open her flask of water and drank thirstily. 'You should try it sometime.'

She was joking, of course. He didn't have a beer belly like Rick Nevin's, but he knew he must look pretty unfit in her eyes. Right now, crawling back into bed would have been his favoured exercise move.

'I might at that,' he said, with a laugh. 'Where are we with the phone records?'

She passed him a printout. 'Keiller's and Elinor's. Still waiting for Jill's. I had a quick look, though we needn't bother with Keiller's now we know he wasn't the target.'

'Anything leap out at you?'

'Not really. Not sure why Elinor even bothered with a phone – very few calls in or out. Until Saturday night, that is, and then she gets a string of calls, late, from an unidentified number, unregistered. Most likely Morton badgering her to come over the next day.'

'Which, of course, she did. And we know how that ended.' Lincoln thought back to the sight of Elinor sprawled dead on the floor at Willow Cottage, the petite woman no match for her brawny son. Browsing through her meagre mobile phone activity, he recalled how the landline cable had been yanked out of the wall at her house in Amesbury, socket and all.

'Tried ringing the number you think is his?'

'Yes, but there's no answer.'

'There was no laptop at her house, was there?'

'No. Not sure how she got by. You have to do everything online these days – doctors, car tax, council shit, holidays.'

'Not sure Elinor went on many holidays.'

'For normal people, I mean.'

He studied the wall map of the area. 'Where's he taken Jill? He moved her from the Nissen hut, but how did he avoid any cameras picking him up? We've got dozens of uniforms out there looking for them, and yet he's managed to go to ground completely.'

'He's probably stuck to minor roads as far as he could, and then found a place where it's dead easy to hide.' She reached up and jabbed the amorphous green shape that spread across a large part of the map. 'Greywood Forest.'

'How the hell do we search eleven hundred acres of woodland?' Greywood was dotted with old bunkers and earthworks, ruined buildings and even some wartime tunnels.

'He's got to come out sometime, boss. He'll need supplies. He can't hide in the woods forever.'

Lincoln shrugged. 'I'm not so sure. Still, now we know his phone number, we can get a log of his calls, can't we?'

'I'll get onto it. See who else he's in touch with, if anyone.'

Drawn to the drinks machine, even if its output scarcely deserved to be called coffee, he put his money in and watched the thin, insipid liquid dribble down into its cardboard cup. As he waited, he rang Woody to tell him he'd taken Breeze back to the Old Vicarage last night.

'I'll text him in a bit, check he's okay,' he said. 'I still don't know exactly what happened with this Tracey woman. But whether he's guilty or not, he needs to sort himself out, talk to someone, get legal advice.'

'Any more news on Mrs Fortune?'

Lincoln gave Woody the gist of what they'd found out so far. 'We think it could be the daughter, Annika, that Morton's after. She says she's never heard of him, never seen anyone hanging around, but we need to speak to her housemate, Roz Berrow. She may have noticed something Annika's missed. Get Pam to call on her on Tuesday. I'll text you the details.'

The dribble of brown liquid stopped, and Lincoln paused to retrieve his coffee. He cursed silently because he'd forgotten to press the button for sugar. 'We're thinking he's holed up in Greywood Forest.'

Woody whistled through his teeth. 'That'll be a bugger to search.'

'We can look for the car.'

'Yeah, but if we don't even know for certain that's where he's hiding…'

'Exactly.' He carried the so-called coffee into the cloakroom and tipped it down the sink. 'We don't have the manpower to search Greywood on the off chance.'

'Graham was asking earlier, can't we ping his phone?'

'I'll get the tech team onto that. Anything to help narrow it down.' Lincoln caught sight of himself in the mirror over the sink. He looked grey and tired. He hadn't ironed his shirt properly. Actually, he hadn't ironed it at all. After so little sleep, he was surprised to see he'd put the buttons in the right buttonholes. 'It's been nearly a week, Woody, and we've got nowhere.'

He heard noises on the other end of the phone. Suki's voice in the distance, a door closing. Trish's voice. His skin prickled.

'Trish and Kate have arrived,' Woody explained. 'Sunday lunch. Ted's already here. Kate's bound to ask about Jill.'

'Tell her we're still looking.'

'She's worried about Finzi.'

'Finzi?'

'Jill's cat. She's afraid he'll have nowhere to go.'

'He's got a cat flap,' Lincoln remembered. 'And the woman next door has been feeding him. Tell Kate he'll be fine.' He paused before adding, 'Sorry, Woody, I should've let you know we'd switched the focus from Ramsay to Jill. Pam had a wasted journey yesterday, going to see that Draycott woman.'

'Reckon Pam quite enjoyed talking to her. Heather was at school with Maggie Keiller. That's how she knew Ramsay.'

'But no romance between him and Heather?'

'Doesn't sound like it.' Someone was shouting in the background. Suki, probably, annoyed that her husband was talking to his boss when they'd got guests for lunch.

'I'll let you go,' said Lincoln, and the line went dead. He imagined the Woods' house, Grimsdyke, bustling with Sunday lunch preparations: Kate tasked with keeping her young cousins occupied while the grownups talked, Trish commiserating with her father over Ramsay's death, her big sister Suki giving Woody his orders as she cooked. For just a moment, he felt envious, wishing he could be there too. But only for a moment.

'Just nipping out,' he told Orla as he lifted his jacket off the back of his chair. 'I need some proper coffee.'

'I can't believe what's happened,' Trish said to Suki. 'First we find out Ramsay's been killed, and then Jill goes missing.'

She'd offered to lay the table while her brother-in-law was strolling round the garden with her father. She paused to look out at the two men.

152

Woody and Ted got on so well. She was glad that her father had someone to talk to about Ramsay. He might not have seen his old friend in a while, but it must still have been a shock to lose him, especially in such a violent way.

She set out the place mats her mother had always used: hunting scenes, hounds chasing a terrified fox. She'd hated them then and she hated them now, but she couldn't face an argument with Suki. She began to dole out the knives and forks, the serving spoons, the water glasses.

'Don't *you* find it hard to believe, Suki?'

'Find what hard to believe? Ramsay or Mrs Fortune?' Her sister sailed out of the kitchen with a plate of bread rolls. 'What about the soup spoons?'

'Soup? We're having *soup* on a day like today?'

'It's gazpacho.'

'Since when did you start making dishes like gazpacho?'

Suki adjusted the place settings, as Trish knew she would. 'I did that Adventurous Cuisine course at the community college.'

'I'm talking about Ramsay. Why would someone shoot a man in his seventies just to rob a stupid farm shop? Imagine if it had been Dad.'

'Well, it wasn't.' Suki whisked out again to fetch something else from the kitchen.

Trish followed her. 'And I was thinking… Jill must've known Mum. They'd have been at the girls' grammar together.'

'Don't say anything to Dad.'

'Why ever not?'

'Just don't.' Suki dumped a stack of pale blue soup bowls into her sister's hands. 'He doesn't need anything else to get upset about.' Off she went again.

Trish laid a soup bowl at each place setting. Her heart was heavy with regret and apprehension.

'What's up with Kate?' Suki bustled back in, collected up the bowls again and stacked them on top of each other. 'She seems very quiet.'

Trish stared at the tower of pale blue china. What had happened to the rest of the dinner service, a wedding present to her parents over forty years ago? Were the soup bowls, seldom used, the sole survivors?

'Kate? Quiet? Is it any wonder with all this going on?'

'But she's quiet even for her.'

Trish turned away, watching her father and Woody as they came back towards the house. 'It's just her age,' she said, suddenly wishing Jeff was here too.

As if she'd read her mind, Suki said, 'I hear Jeff's enjoying himself at Park Street. Mike says he seems to be getting on well with his DS.'

'Won't be the same as working with Mike, though.'

'No, especially since it's a woman. Orla something. They seem to have hit it off.'

As if Trish needed anything else to make her feel inadequate.

The men came back indoors, both of them offering to help Suki, both getting firmly rejected.

When Woody went to see what his young sons were up to, Trish was alone with her father in the dining room.

'I'm so sorry about Ramsay, Dad.'

Ted gazed out into the garden. 'He remembered your mother.'

'He did?' A lump began to form in her throat. He so rarely mentioned her.

'Didn't know her well, but she went to their wedding. A bit before she met me, of course.'

'Of course.'

He sniffed, a signal to end the conversation or at least change the subject. 'Katy's very quiet.'

'She's worried about Jill.'

'Sure that's all it is?'

'She skived off her last piano lesson.'

He tutted. 'And now she feels guilty, as if it's her fault her teacher's gone missing.'

'And she's fallen out with her best friend or been pushed aside by someone new on the scene.' She imagined Charlotte's new buddy, Paloma: sophisticated, naturally beautiful, outgoing. Not shy and bespectacled like Kate. 'You know how it is.'

Her father nodded. 'That age, they think it's the end of the world. I remember from when I was teaching, the number of times it happened…'

'Here we are,' Suki rushed in with a big serving dish. 'Gazpacho.' She set it down triumphantly on the table.

Trish and her father exchanged a look. 'Gazpacho?' said Ted, giving the word a Spanish intonation. 'Well I never!'

Woody and the boys appeared, Davy charging in ahead of his brother. Woody's eyebrows went up when he saw the bowls and the soup spoons. 'Too hot for soup, isn't it?'

'It's gazpacho,' said Trish and Ted together as they took their places at the table.

'Where's Katy?' Ted looked about him as he poured himself some water.

'I'll go and look for her.' Trish pushed herself away from the table and hurried upstairs to find her daughter.

But Kate wasn't upstairs, or in the back garden. Trying not to panic, Trish went out through the gate and looked up and down the quiet road on which Grimsdyke stood.

Where could she be?

Then she noticed that someone was in the passenger seat of her Mini, parked at the kerbside, the window wound partway down. Kate was sitting bolt upright, staring straight ahead.

'We're starting lunch,' said Trish.

'Not hungry.'

'You didn't eat any breakfast.'

'I told you. I'm not hungry.'

'Well, at least come inside.' When Kate showed no sign of moving, Trish crouched down and leaned in through the window. 'Please, Kate. Grandpa's upset about his friend Ramsay, and he'd love to see you. It would cheer him up.'

'No, it wouldn't. And stop using emotional blackmail to make me do things I don't want to do.'

As if Kate had punched her, Trish reeled back. *Emotional blackmail?* Who on earth had she been talking to?

But she was right. And Trish was doing exactly what her own mother had done. History repeating itself.

'Just don't leave the car open.' Leaving her daughter behind, she marched back into the garden and through the patio doors, feeling bruised and shaken.

Suki was too busy fussing about serviettes and a recalcitrant pepper grinder to notice Trish's dismay, but her father saw. He gripped her hand as she sat down.

'It's a phase,' he said, too softly for Suki to hear. 'Katy will grow out of it – when she's about twenty.'

Trish had to smile. 'And you should know, the father of girls.'

'Yes,' he agreed, reaching out for a bread roll. 'I should.'

'If only I could help find Jill.' Trish picked up her spoon, although her appetite had deserted her. 'But I wouldn't know where to begin.'

'Don't be silly. You work in a library, don't you? Think of all the resources you have at your disposal. Can you pass me the butter?'

CHAPTER 38

Lincoln rang Breeze in the middle of the afternoon. He'd tried him when he nipped out to buy himself some drinkable coffee, but there'd been no answer. Now, at nearly three, he tried again.

Breeze obviously hadn't bothered to check who was calling him, because he answered with a brusque, 'Yeah?'

'Afternoon, Dennis.' The clink of glasses in the background, the zingy sounds of a fruit machine. 'You in a pub somewhere?'

'Boss? Er, yeah.'

'What is it? Hair of the dog?'

A guilty chortle. 'Something like that, yeah.'

'Found yourself anywhere else to stay?'

'Er, I thought I was okay at your place for a night or two. You want me to move out sooner?'

'Tomorrow, if you could. How about going home?' Some thumping disco music started up, clashing with the whoop-whoop of the fruit machine. 'Dennis?'

'Yeah, yeah. Only…' Breeze broke off and moved away from the speakers and the slots. 'I can't go back to the flat. I owe rent. I needed to buy myself some time, so I told the landlord I'm not well, that I'm stuck in hospital.'

Lincoln felt like telling him he'd put Breeze in hospital himself if he didn't get his act together. Instead he said, 'Another two nights and then you've got to find somewhere else.'

He saw Orla making her way to his desk as, exasperated, he hung up on Breeze.

'Seen the Sunday paper, boss?' She dropped a tabloid onto his keyboard. *SPY CLUE IN FARM SHOP SHOOTING* ran the headline. *Espionage kit spotted in death house.* 'Any ideas?'

The front page was filled with a grainy black and white photo of a pair of binoculars on top of a chest of drawers, beside a camera with a telephoto lens. He recognised them straightaway. He'd seen them himself last Tuesday in Ramsay Keiller's bedroom.

'How the hell did they get this photo?'

Orla shrugged. 'A photographer standing in the road with a long lens, I suppose.'

156

Lincoln skimmed the text. After revelations by local reporter, Karen Bolitho, the tabloid had sent someone along to investigate, and this is what they had seen: clear evidence that Ramsay Keiller was acting as a secret agent, spying on aircraft movements at Turnpike Corner Airfield.

He groaned. 'Never mind that most of the planes at Turnpike Corner these days are civilian light aircraft.'

She grinned at him. 'Don't let facts get in the way of a good story. You should warn the DCI, though. Questions will be asked about how they got so close to a crime scene.'

He cast the newspaper aside in disgust. 'I'll speak to her.'

'But it does beg the question – what was Keiller really up to? And why wasn't that camera brought back here?'

'Okay, so we should've brought it back, but we'd got his laptop and I suppose I assumed any photos would be backed up on it. Then we stopped looking into Keiller's background and I never gave the camera another thought.' Why was he justifying himself to his sergeant? He should be saving his excuses for the DCI.

'But his most recent photos would still be on the camera.'

'Yes, I realise that now, but his activities stopped being significant. This Bolitho woman's only stirring things up because she's got hold of the wrong end of the stick and wants to make a story of it.'

'Some people could get hold of the wrong end of a hoop!'

'What she's got hold of is...' He was about to tell Orla about Keiller's campaign against germ warfare tests, but he stopped himself. She'd want to know how he found out about it, and he'd have to admit he'd let Pam go and talk to Heather Draycott when – if he'd done his job properly – she'd have been told not to bother.

'And Mr Fortune's crawled out of the woodwork,' Orla went on, nodding at the newspaper. 'Page four. *Why did nobody tell me? Why haven't the police been in touch?* Dear little Annika didn't bother to tell Daddy that Mummy was missing.'

Lincoln opened the paper at page four. A head and shoulders shot of Jeremy Fortune showed someone corporate and self-satisfied, polished and buffed, his straight, grey hair cut in a style more suited to a younger man. He and Jill must have been like chalk and cheese.

'Doesn't he read the news? How did he not know she was missing?'

'He's been in Greece,' she said. 'He and the second Mrs Fortune have a holiday home there. And who could blame them? If I had that kind of money...'

157

Lincoln had never been keen on holidays in the sun. By the sea, yes, but he wasn't one for lazing on beaches. 'We need to speak to him.'

'What's he going to be able to add? He'll just want to slag off Wiltshire Police.'

'If we don't speak to him, we'll never find out, will we?'

DCI Connors appeared before Orla had a chance to reply. She was dressed for a day off, in jeans and a denim shirt maybe a size too small. 'What's this I'm hearing about the Fortune woman's husband?'

Orla showed her the newspaper article. 'Sorry, ma'am. We didn't know he didn't know. Was it *our* job to tell him?'

Connors sighed heavily and said, 'Contact Jeremy Fortune. Get him in here as soon as possible – today if you can. We need to put him in the picture and get what we can out of him. There's something here we're not being told.'

CHAPTER 39

Jill swam back up to the surface of consciousness, gasping for air. She was so cold her bones ached, and she could hardly move. How many more times would Ezra jab that needle into her arm to sedate her? As if she had the strength to try to escape him now!

Last night he'd bundled her into the boot of the car and driven here, an isolated spot on the downs, hauling her out and throwing her shoes down at her feet.

'Put them on, but if you try to run away...'

She'd wanted to laugh. After yet another night on a cold floor, she could hardly walk, let alone run. But she hadn't laughed. She hadn't dared to.

He'd pushed her ahead of him up a path through a sloping cornfield until they reached the brow of the hill. There, in the moonlight, surrounded by long grass, stood a roughly shaped concrete cube, like a squat chimney stack, with a stone step at the side. A metal lid lay across the top of the cube, secured with a padlock that Ezra had swiftly unlocked. When he cranked the lid up, Jill had seen the top rungs of a ladder.

'Climb down.'

She'd hung back, knowing what this was. 'I can't go down there.' Mouth dry, heart racing. 'Really, I can't.'

'You want me to throw you in there?' The gun had appeared again, pointing at her head.

Wanting to be shot even less than she wanted to be shut up underground, she'd taken a deep breath and clambered in, pressing back against the wall of the shaft to brace herself as she warily climbed down the ladder. She'd counted a dozen rungs before reaching the metal grating at the bottom. Ezra had climbed down after her.

Towering over her, he'd jabbed a needle into her upper arm once more. She'd leant against him as her legs began to buckle under her, and then she'd slipped away into darkness.

And here she was, hours later, throat dry, head thumping, trying to make out her new surroundings. Whitewashed walls, bulkhead lights, a concrete floor. She was on a plastic-covered mattress on a metal bedframe, the blankets rough and scratchy against her bare legs. A table was bolted to the opposite wall, with a clock and instrument dials above it, along with charts, maps, and a sign that said *ROC Larksdown.*

Jill had never been down here before, but she knew where she was: fifteen feet underground. In a bunker. Tons of concrete and soil on top of her, pressing down.

Oh God, of all the places… Larksdown, one of the redundant Royal Observer Corps posts that Dan had bought years ago. He'd written about them in his book, in the section on surviving a nuclear war – *the* nuclear war he knew was coming. He'd found out that the Ministry of Defence were selling off a number of bunkers as the Corps was being stood down. His manuscript even included the jokey piece that had caught his eye in *The Messenger* : BUY YOUR OWN COLD WAR HIDEOUT! IDEAL FOR STORING WINE OR GROWING MUSHROOMS – BUT ONLY IF CONFINED SPACES DON'T BOTHER YOU!

He'd contacted Miles and Furlong, the estate agent and, within a few weeks, two of the posts were his.

Panic seized her now, although she tried to keep it at bay with a yoga technique she used before her exercises. Breathe in through the nose, out through the mouth. Feel your pulse slow down. Breathe. And again.

Sunlight beamed down the open shaft onto the metal grating and into the room. She could escape! She could get away! But as soon as she moved, she realised Ezra had put the chain back on her ankle, tighter this time though. The cold metal dug into her flesh. Had it actually broken the skin? It felt like it.

The sound of a car engine made her pulse quicken. She heard him tramp through the long grass at the top of the shaft, and then his bulky form blotted out the sunlight as he slowly, heavily, descended the ladder.

'You're awake.' He sounded almost friendly, as if she was in a hospital bed and he was a concerned visitor. Maybe if she tried to get to know him, let him get to know her too, he'd take pity on her, let her go.

'I can't stay here, Ezra. I hate being underground like this. It frightens me.'

'You're safer here than anywhere else. It's not going to cave in.' He poured her some tea from the flask he'd brought with him.

'How can you make tea? Are you going home when you're not here with me?'

'Everything I need's in the car. I've got a little stove. A kettle down here would make too much steam.'

She took the plastic cup from him and took a sip. The tea tasted horrible, but she was so desperate for a warm drink, she gulped it down.

160

'My father was an Observer here,' she said, putting the cup down. 'I used to help him make flash cards with all the different planes on them.'

'What for?'

'Training the rest of the Observers how to recognise Russian warplanes.'

John Holland had volunteered for the Royal Observer Corps all through Jill's childhood, attending weekly meetings here in spring and summer, and in the back room of the Lamb and Flag in autumn and winter.

'They'd never spot them in time,' said Ezra, echoing Jill's objection all those years ago.

'They had very good binoculars.' Or so her father used to say.

'Binoculars won't be much good in a nuclear attack.' He sat back on the metal chair, resting one ankle on the opposite knee.

'They had all sorts of equipment that could detect a nuclear detonation,' she told him, although she'd never been convinced that a group of elderly volunteer Observers could do much to avert an enemy hell-bent on annihilation.

'A lot of it's still here.' He nodded at a large cardboard box on the floor in the corner. 'But I don't know how it all works.'

'My dad would've known.'

'Yes,' he said flatly, getting to his feet. 'So would mine.'

CHAPTER 40

'I did at least expect Annika to call me. I'm her father, for God's sake!'

Jeremy Fortune seemed too big for the interview room, even though this one at Park Street was more generously sized than any at Barley Lane. All of six foot two and heavily built, he couldn't have felt comfortable living with Jill at Arundel Terrace, a deep, narrow house so crammed with furniture it would overwhelm most people.

'She probably didn't want to worry you.' Lincoln sat back from the table, keen to placate Jill's ex-husband and get him talking. 'Tell us about Jill.'

Fortune had arrived at Heathrow from Athens late last night after a reporter from the *Sunday Express* had tracked him down at his holiday home. He looked weary, despite his light tan and expensive clothes – a linen blazer over a crisp blue shirt, cream-coloured slacks, loafers. He, too, leant away from the table, folding his arms and shifting a critical gaze from Lincoln to Orla and back again.

'Jill? What's there to tell? Piano teacher, mother of Annika. We've been divorced longer than we were married. Local girl, went to the girls' grammar school. Planned to be a teacher like her father but followed her brother into the Civil Service instead.'

'Civil Service?' Orla sounded interested. 'Which department?'

'Charles, Chas, was at the Ministry of Defence, but Jill went into the Department of Education and Science – at least, that's what it was called in those days. Never quite sure what she did there. Education policy, I think, at a lowly level.' He bared his teeth in a strange sort of smile. 'She worked with Win, my sister. That's how we met, 1980, at Win's wedding.'

Lincoln couldn't help thinking that weddings were dangerous affairs. He tried to put Breeze out of his mind, to concentrate on the man in front of him. He was about to ask another question when Orla leapt in with one of her own.

'Does the name Daniel Swann mean anything to you?'

Fortune looked puzzled. 'Dan? Why are you asking about Dan?'

'Just a name that's come up in our investigation,' said Lincoln. 'If you could tell us more about him…'

'Nothing to tell. He's dead now. A friend of Chas's from school. He got a band together, made a few records, made a lot of money. Snorted most of it up his nose.' That strange little smile again.

'How well did Jill know him?' asked Orla.

'They were teenage sweethearts, both mad about that bloody awful blues music. Middle class white kids singing black slave songs.' He shuddered. 'Then he found fame and fortune and poor old Jill got left behind. But that was aeons ago, obviously. What's Dan got to do with any of this?'

'We think someone associated with him might be involved in Jill's kidnapping,' said Lincoln, sliding Morton's mugshot onto the table. 'Ezra Morton.'

Fortune put his glasses on and peered at the photo. 'Hah! Name like Ezra, I thought he'd be black.'

'It's a name from the Bible,' said Orla sharply.

'Never seen him before, although something about him seems familiar...'

Lincoln half-expected him to ask if Morton was related to Swann, but he didn't. Instead, he pushed the photo back across the table.

'It's that pose of studied aggression, I suppose,' Fortune went on. 'They think it makes them look tough. But I don't know anyone down here these days. We've been up in Cumbria a long time now.' His gaze fell back to Morton's mugshot. 'Why in the name of God has this bastard kidnapped Jill?'

'We suspect it's Annika he wants,' said Orla. 'And he thinks Jill is standing in his way.'

He looked up, aghast. '*This* man? *This* man is after my daughter? No, no. You've got that all wrong. *This* isn't the weirdo she was involved with.'

'Weirdo?' Lincoln and Orla asked together.

'Yes, some ponytailed scrounger she met through her voluntary work. It started over a year ago now, but I know Jill didn't think much of him. Annika finished with him before Christmas.'

'What else can you tell us about him?' Lincoln asked.

'Not much. Matthew something. Matt. Sorry, the surname's gone. I'll think of it as soon as I leave here.'

'You said Annika met him through her voluntary work?'

'Her firm had some half-arsed scheme that gave staff time off to volunteer with local charities half a day a week. "Giving something back." She chose one that was supposed to help ex-offenders get rehabilitated. All very noble. Must've given the bosses a nice warm glow, but *they* weren't the ones sorting through stinking clothes and tatty bric-a-brac in the charity shop.'

'What was the charity called?'

'Christ knows! Ask Annika.'

'We will,' said Lincoln. Was the mysterious Matt the link between the Fortunes and Ezra Morton?

'Sorry, nothing more I can add.' Fortune pushed his chair back and stood up, filling the space with his powerful presence. 'What happens now?'

Lincoln stood up too. 'We continue our search for Jill. How long will you be staying in the area?'

'Until you find her.'

When Lincoln came back from showing Jeremy Fortune out of the building, he found Orla standing in front of the whiteboard, marker pen in hand.

'So, Annika works with ex-offenders. Gets mixed up with Matt.' She wrote *Matt X*, her handwriting spikier than Lincoln's. 'She dumps him at the end of last year and shacks up with Roz Berrow. Matt wants to teach her a lesson, so he gets another ex-offender, Ezra Morton, to frighten her, abduct her, whatever.' She drew an arc connecting Matt and Morton. 'But why does Morton go after *Jill*?'

'Because hurting her mother would hurt Annika more than being hurt herself? Because he made a mistake?'

She drew a thick line under Annika's photo. 'Didn't it ever occur to this stupid woman that her *weirdo* ex-boyfriend might be behind all this?'

'But why's he taken so long to get his revenge? She ended it six or seven months ago.' Lincoln was wary of jumping to conclusions, even if Orla was keen to home in on this new suspect. 'Let's get the name of that charity, his surname and an address. We need to know how he and Morton are connected. Assuming they are.'

'Oh, come on, boss!' Orla chucked the marker pen onto her desk. 'Of course they're connected! Annika does voluntary work with ex-offenders, she falls in love with an ex-offender, her mother's abducted by an ex-offender. Pretty obvious there's a connection, isn't it?'

'Likely, yes. Undeniable, no. Let's not get carried away. Got Morton's phone log yet? If he and Matt are working together, they'll be phoning each other or texting. We need Matt's phone number.'

'I'm sure Annika will know.' Orla smiled bitterly, revealing her dislike of the young woman. She rang her number, waited with her phone on speaker so they could both listen to it ringing unanswered. 'Bloody woman!'

A moment later, a text arrived on Lincoln's mobile, from a number he didn't recognise. *The name came back to me. Knew it would. Matthew Trevelyan. Cheers. Jeremy Fortune.*

*

It didn't take Orla long to find out more about him.

'Matthew Thomas Trevelyan, thirty-four,' she relayed to Lincoln. 'Originally from Warminster. Various offences. Possession with intent to supply, plus a conviction for assault. Left prison in 2013, put into a rehabilitation scheme, Triple R Barbury – release, rehab, retrain. That must be the charity Annika volunteered with.'

Lincoln added Trevelyan's mugshot to the whiteboard. The face that stared out was handsome and clean-shaven, a bright expression in his eyes. A petty criminal but one who looked personable and attractive. 'I wonder how long Matt and Annika were an item?'

'I'll try her again.' Orla called Annika. This time, the young woman answered.

She gasped when Orla explained why she was phoning. 'Matt? What's Matt got to do with this?'

'We think he and Morton know each other and could be working together,' Orla told her. 'We need Matt's phone number.'

'I'll text it to you – if I've still got it.'

'Did he ever threaten you?' asked Lincoln, leaning close to Orla's phone. 'Did he ever threaten your mum?'

'No. Although he was pissed off when I dumped him.'

'And why *did* you dump him?' Orla again.

A long pause, as if Annika was deciding how much to tell them. Then, 'He borrowed my keys, the keys to Mum's house, and let himself in when she was out. He took things like toothpaste and soap from the bathroom, food out of the fridge. But then she caught him in her study, where she keeps her laptop, and that was it. She had a right go at me, told me it had to stop, as if I knew about it.'

'You and Matt were living together at the time?' Lincoln asked.

'I had a flat off London Road and he had a place closer to town, though I don't know if he's still there. I haven't seen him for months. Why would he take it out on me *now*?'

'Maybe he's found out about Roz,' Orla suggested. 'He's jealous, doesn't like to think you've dumped him for a *woman*.'

'But that's ridiculous! I didn't meet Roz until weeks after I'd finished with him.'

Orla laughed. 'Don't they say revenge is a dish best served cold?'

'What's that supposed to mean?' Annika's anger was audible, even over the phone.

'That it's more satisfying to wait a while before you take your revenge. You wait until the other person's least expecting it.'

CHAPTER 41

Lincoln got home close to seven, a headache building behind his eyes. He wasn't sure he could face food but, with any luck, Breeze would already have eaten. Even so, the prospect of an evening in his colleague's company didn't fill him with joy.

When he got indoors, though, he found the house empty, the kitchen messy with dirty mugs, sticky takeaway cartons but – worst of all – an empty whiskey bottle that should have had several measures of Jameson's left in it.

Bloody Breeze!

Trish's voice whispered in his ear – or was it still Cathy's? *Whiskey wouldn't help that headache, now, would it?*

No, but it would take the edge off his shitty day.

He'd persuaded Annika to stay at Arundel Terrace, an officer on duty all the time, rather than return to the house she shared with Roz in Amberstone – at least until Roz was back from London.

Then he and Orla had called at the only address Annika had for Matt Trevelyan, a flat in a converted Victorian house close to the ring road and the railway line. No answer. The woman downstairs told them he hadn't been around all week. Nice lad, always happy to chat.

'You wouldn't know he was there half the time,' she'd said with a fond smile. 'But he's definitely not there now. He went off with his rucksack last weekend.'

'What sort of car does he drive?'

She shook her head. 'Couldn't tell you. If he's got a car, he must park it somewhere else. You can see for yourself, there's nowhere to park in this street.'

Now, back at home, hugging a mug of coffee, Lincoln sat alone on his verandah, staring out over the garden, noting with relief that the windows of Fountains all looked shut. No lights on, all quiet.

He should switch off, stop going over the case in his head, but that was impossible. He'd wanted to talk it over with DCI Connors now they knew about Trevelyan and suspected that Morton wasn't acting alone, but Connors, off duty anyway, had gone home while he and Orla were out, and she wasn't answering her phone.

'Trevelyan's like a puppet master,' Orla had said before they left the incident room. 'He's wound Morton up and let him go. Pulled his strings, I mean.'

Lincoln didn't feel as certain as she did. A collaboration between the two ex-convicts was a theory, but that's all it was, no evidence to back it up. 'But what's he told Morton to make him pursue Jill like this?'

She'd shrugged. 'We know Morton's got mental health issues. He's probably suggestible, easily led. Trevelyan's manipulating him.'

'He manipulated Morton into shooting his own mother?'

Orla didn't seem to be in any doubt. 'He's found Morton's weak spot, turned him against her, convinced him that Elinor's out to get him, that she's the enemy. That's how men like Trevelyan get control over people.'

Lincoln didn't share her certainty. Too many questions, he decided now, sipping his coffee and savouring his solitude. Were the two men holed up together? Was it a coincidence that Trevelyan left his flat the day before Morton killed Elinor, two days before he shot Ramsay and took Jill captive? How had he persuaded Morton to follow and abduct a woman who meant nothing to him?

Was there enough evidence to justify searching Trevelyan's flat? Connors wouldn't think so and, if Lincoln was honest with himself, he didn't think so either. But could he persuade her to apply for a warrant for his phone records? Then they could find out when he and Morton had last been in contact.

But that would all have to wait until tomorrow.

In need of company, if only at a distance, he rang Trish. He half-expected her still to be at her sister's, but she answered straightaway, sounding as pleased to hear his voice as he was to hear hers.

'Enjoy your lunch?'

'It was good to see Dad,' she said. 'But Suki drives me up the wall. I can never do anything right in her eyes. You were working all day?'

'More or less. It's a tricky case.'

'No news of Jill? No, don't say anything. I know you can't tell me.'

'I can tell you there's no news, but that's about all I *can* tell you.'

'I keep seeing pictures on the news. All those officers drafted in to help look for her. And in this heat, too. I wish I could help somehow. If there's anything you need looking up, local newspapers, stuff like that, you only have to ask.'

'Actually, there is something, *someone*, you could help me with.'

'Who?'

'There was a singer called Danny Swann in the sixties, played venues round Barbury. Danny Swann and the Haymakers. They morphed into the

Barbury Blues Band, but then he went off the rails and got into studying crop circles, UFOs, that kind of thing. He lived near Warminster and…'

'He died a few months ago, didn't he? There was something about him in the *Western Daily Press*, a very short obituary.'

'He was an old flame of Jill Fortune's.'

'Really? Wow! And you want me to find out more about him?'

'You think you could?'

'I'm a librarian, aren't I? And in charge of the Local Studies collection.' She sounded as if she was flexing her biceps as she said it. 'I'll see what I can find.'

'Thanks. How's things with you?'

'Don't ask! Kate sat in the car for two hours instead of coming in to lunch.'

'Worried about Jill?'

'She won't say, but I'm sure that's part of it.'

He listened while she related her concerns about her daughter: a rift with best friend Charlotte; guilt about skipping her piano lesson and lying about it.

'And I thought she'd be excited about going to stay with her dad after she breaks up,' Trish went on, 'but she even seems miserable about that now.'

He didn't dare tell her what Kate had confided in him about feeling awkward staying with Vic and his wife, especially now there was a baby on the way.

'Give her time,' he said. 'It's a lot to process.'

'So… Danny Swann. What's he got to do with any of this?'

'I can't really say. We're following a lead that probably doesn't go anywhere, but he could be relevant.'

'Even though he's dead?'

'Even dead rock stars have their uses. I'll be grateful for anything you can find, but it's been a while since the Haymakers were headlining at the ABC Bingo Hall.' He heard the slam of his front door and turned to go back inside. 'I'd better go. Breezy's home.'

'Breezy?'

'Didn't Woody tell you? I'm putting him up for a couple of nights till he's sorted himself out.' Although it would take a lot longer than that to get Breeze into any kind of shape.

'You see what happens when you jump ship and run off to Park Street!' There was a smile in her voice now.

'I wasn't given a choice.'

'I'll look up this Swann guy. I'll let you know what I find.' And she rang off.

Lincoln went into the hall. Breeze was trying to climb the stairs, but his legs weren't co-operating. He'd put his right foot on a stair, bring his left foot up to join it, then put the right foot back down on the stair below.

'New dance routine, Dennis?'

'Think I've had a bit too much to drink.'

'Get to bed. Drink lots of water. I'll look in on you later.'

'Yes, Mum.' Crawling up on his hands and knees, Breeze reached the landing and staggered into the spare room.

Lincoln made himself more coffee, but it was a poor substitute for the Jameson's he'd been hoping to drink. Ah well, this time tomorrow, he'd have the house to himself again.

CHAPTER 42

Ezra left Jill on her own for the rest of Sunday. At least, she guessed it was Sunday, although the days were running into each other. How long since Ezra had turned up at Keiller's Yard? Nearly a week ago, that afternoon when she'd set off to see Ramsay because Kate Amos hadn't turned up for her lesson.

Jill felt dirty and smelly after wearing the same clothes for a week, unable to wash, hair lank and greasy, breath sour. Her ankle felt sore where Ezra had yanked the chain against it and broken the skin. Might the wound become infected?

She longed for a bath, for something to eat, for a long sleep in her own bed. Would she ever go home? She mustn't give up hope.

As the light dimmed towards evening, her dread of the dark crept up on her once more. How often had Dan come down here? She should have told him he'd bought her father's old post. He'd have marvelled at the coincidence. The sadness of that lost opportunity weighed heavily upon her.

As night fell, though, fear assailed her along with the sadness. She was alone down here, chained to a bed that was bolted to the floor. Suppose someone – a farm worker, a rambler – noticed the hatch cover was open? Would they climb in? Or would they close the hatch without checking if anyone was down here? How long could she survive without fresh air? Two days? Three? How long were Observers expected to stay down here in the event of a nuclear attack, with hatch battened down and air vents closed to protect them from radioactive fallout?

Hadn't it depressed her father, preparing himself – at least in theory – for such an eventuality? The prospect of nuclear war had certainly terrified Jill as a teenager after reading the manuals he brought home and hearing him talking about the procedures in such a matter-of-fact way. She'd kept her fears to herself, but Chas had had no such qualms.

'Honestly, Dad, do you think the Soviets are having to rely on elderly war veterans to man their underground monitoring posts?' His tone was sneering. 'Can you see the Russians scrambling squads of *pensioners* when the tocsin sounds?'

Their father hadn't responded, and Chas had given up trying to rile him.

How she missed them both! Alone like this, with nothing to do but remember, you could so easily lose your mind, punish yourself with negative thoughts until you didn't care about anything anymore.

Oh come on, Jilly, pull yourself together! Oh, to see Dan again, to hold him, to be held by him. How ridiculous to be kept captive by his son, the son of that nondescript little Ellie.

May 1966: Ellie is one of those silly girls hanging around Dan and his band.

'She's just some skinny little scrubber,' he says when Jill asks him about the girl who waits outside his house, tearing leaves off the privet hedge and shredding them onto the pavement. 'Ignore her and she'll go away.'

Ellie is about fourteen but looks more like twelve. She's a couple of years younger than Jill, with long, mousy hair parted in the middle, a school blouse done up to the neck with no tie, and a maroon pleated skirt pulled up higher than she'd have been allowed to wear it in class. White ankle socks and scuffed lace-ups.

'What does she want?'

Dan grins lasciviously at her question. 'What d'you think?' Her name's Elinor Morton, he says, and she goes to the girls' secondary modern on the Down. 'So she's not very bright.'

'And yet she's in love with *you*.' Jill squeezes his arm tighter against her. 'She can't be totally stupid.'

'Dunno about *love*. All she's after is a good fuck with somebody famous.'

She hates him talking this way, but she knows that's how boys talk, especially among themselves. Chas is every bit as bad, although he never uses such coarse language within earshot of their parents.

'Famous?' she scoffs. 'You? Hah! That Ellie girl's going to get into trouble if she's not careful.'

Jill hasn't gone all the way with Dan yet. When they do make love properly, she wants them to be in a big bed at a grand hotel. A four-poster perhaps, with breakfast brought to them on a silver tray.

That's how she imagines it, anyway. Dan isn't a virgin, and that's okay because she wants her lover to be more experienced, to know what to do. Nothing can happen while she's living at home though, and he'll be leaving for college in the autumn. Supposing he meets someone else in Brighton?

'You can't expect Dan to be celibate,' Eva declares when Jill shares her anxieties. 'Even if he goes out with you when he comes home, you can't expect him to bottle it up all term.'

'Okay,' says Jill, 'just as long as he comes back to me in the holidays.'

'Vacations,' Maggie corrects her. 'You have vacs at university, not holidays.'

'He's not going to university, he's going to art college.'

'Same difference.'

Dan and Jill make love for the first time one night that September. No crisp cotton sheets, no slow, erotic undressing. Jill loses her virginity in a hurry in the back of his mate's Minivan, a spider wrench digging into her shoulder, her feet colliding with the spare tyre. She leaves spots of blood on the dog blanket Dan has spread out on the van's ribbed floor. She wishes their last night together could have been more romantic.

Two days later, he leaves for Brighton, promising to write to her as soon as he gets settled. Only he doesn't.

Dan's been at Brighton less than two months when the band's cover version of a Muddy Waters number scrapes into the Top Forty. When he comes home at Christmas, he goes to the pub with Chas and some other mates from school.

'He's dropping out of college so he can go on the road with the band,' Chas reports back. 'They're changing their name to the Barbury Blues Band. Oh, and he's got a new girlfriend.'

In the wake of the break-up, Jill's friends shore her up. With Maggie's encouragement, she gets stuck into her A-Level studies and, during the Easter holidays, she hitchhikes across France with Eva.

It'll be a long time before she sees Dan Swann again.

Hard to believe now that the elfin Ellie gave birth to Ezra some forty years ago. Jill would never have expected Dan to get caught out, be made to take responsibility for their son. Maybe he really did love Ellie, although he mentioned her only a couple of times in his book, and then only as the founder of his first fan club.

He didn't mention Ezra once in the whole of the four-hundred-page manuscript.

Jill wanted to sleep now, to escape the terror of being down here on her own, but sleep wouldn't come. Suppose Ezra didn't come back? Suppose he got arrested but wouldn't tell the police where he'd been? No one would know where she was.

And now her ankle was throbbing under the chain, the skin hot to the touch. She could rip a piece off her skirt to wrap around her ankle and pad the wound, but her skirt was so dirty now, she might make things worse.

She sat on the clammy, plastic-covered mattress, leant her head back against the cold, whitewashed walls and tried not to panic.

CHAPTER 43

MONDAY 10 JULY 2017

Adam Keiller stepped out of the en suite, wrapping his bathrobe tightly round him only moments before he heard the jaunty sounds of a Skype call coming through. He swept his laptop up off the bed and carried it across to the dressing table.

Pete Doubleday. Trust him to be an early riser! Look at him! Bullet-shaped head closely shaved, pink shirt crisply tailored, collar turned up, a big bottle of mineral water close at hand. His face was tanned, eyebrows plucked, small teeth regular and unnaturally white.

Adam didn't like him much, but he didn't need to. Doubleday had had knee trouble painful enough to bring him back to England in April for a consultation at Baddesley Grange, although he'd wanted it kept hush-hush. He'd even insisted on being registered under a different name – Peter Smith.

'Just so my ex can't track me down,' he'd explained with a wry smile. 'You know how it is. If she knows I'm back in the country, she'll be after me – or her lawyers will.'

Doubleday seemed to have taken to Adam, trusting him to operate on his problematic knee – an operation that was now scheduled for the first week of September.

'How's it going, Doc?'

Adam cleared his throat and hurriedly smoothed down his still-damp hair. 'Fine, fine. How's the knee?'

'Fucking sore. Gave out on me again yesterday on the golf course. Any chance of bringing my op forward?'

Adam ran rapidly through the schedule he kept in his head. No gaps for the next six weeks at least. It wasn't just the operation, it was the rehabilitation afterwards, the oversight needed to ensure the replacement knee was working as it should.

The only solution was to bump some other clients' procedures back a bit, tell them an emergency had forced the delay.

'I'll see what I can do,' he promised. 'Shouldn't be a problem.'

He discreetly appraised the room he could see on screen behind Doubleday, a room as clinically plain as the treatment suites at Baddesley Grange. The walls were tiled, and the marble floor stretched away through an archway towards huge windows. Spain in the summer.

How did his own house compare? Adam checked the inset image at the top of his screen, noting with relief that only the cream-coloured walls of the bedroom were visible, the back of the door, the pale wood of the wardrobe.

'And that other matter, Doc? Where are we vis-à-vis the purchase of that bit of land?'

Adam's spirits dipped. 'It's tricky. Probate's going to take a while to sort out.'

'Yeah, yeah. Hey, I shouldn't be troubling you with things like this, should I? You'll be wanting to concentrate on grieving for your poor old dad. By the way, how come that all went sideways? Kids getting a bit over-enthusiastic?'

'Some maniac with a gun who came to rob the shop.'

'An armed robbery? Your poor dad! And after all he'd gone through with those little vandals!' He gave a crooked grin. 'And those kids'll keep quiet?'

'Actually...' Adam leant closer to the screen and dropped his voice so there was no chance of Joanna overhearing. 'They want a bit more money now it's all blown up.'

'What're you saying?' The screen flickered briefly and Doubleday's face distorted as his mouth froze in a snarl before the unstable link was restored. 'How much are those kids asking for?'

'Fifteen hundred would cover it.'

'Fucking hell, that's greedy! And these are teenagers?'

Adam nodded, afraid his request might be refused.

'I'll sort it,' said Doubleday. 'And find me a date for my op, soon as possible, yeah?'

'Yes, if I can...'

But the screen had already gone blank, the connection cut.

CHAPTER 44

Once her usual Monday morning tasks were out of the way, Trish retreated to her office in the library and started to look for information about Daniel Swann. She enjoyed tracing the history of places, but she really relished the detective work involved in researching people. Especially when she was doing it for someone else, someone like Jeff. Would she be helping him find Jill? Deep down, she feared the worst. She wasn't stupid. The man who'd shot Ramsay Keiller had probably shot Jill, too. They just hadn't found her body yet.

Where did Daniel Swann feature in Jill's life? Teenage sweethearts, Jeff had said, but Jill was sixty-eight now, so how could Swann still be relevant?

Trish scoured the internet to find out more, but the only girl mentioned in the numerous articles about his early career was Ellie. She'd launched a fan club for him and his band, Danny and the Haymakers, as a fourteen-year-old schoolgirl. Danny became Dan, the Haymakers became the Barbury Blues Band, and Ellie seemed to disappear from the scene.

A theme of many articles was Swann's growing dependence on drugs and booze, which he blamed on the crazy routine of touring.

Drugs to keep you going, drugs to slow you down so you could sleep. Instruments and massive amps to lug in and out of the van. No money for proper hotels, so we'd sleep in the van, more often than not. Madness!

If there had been a woman in his life in those days, apart from the casual relationships typical of the time, she wasn't mentioned. He'd experimented with LSD when the band toured the States, but a bad trip left him in a stupor for days. He preferred not to talk about it in interviews, but that didn't stop other band members and fellow musicians lamenting the change in his personality and its effect on the quality of his song writing – although Swann seemed to think his music had been improved: *The doors of perception were opened. I went through them and never looked back.*

Sacked from the band in 1975 after walking out of a recording session, Swann fell into...

'Are you busy?' Trish's assistant, Bryony, put her head round the office door.

'What's up?'

'Steve Quilter's here again, about that Abbey thing.'

'Trust him to turn up when I'm in the middle of something!'

Steve Quilter, assistant curator at the museum, waited impatiently on the landing, still annoyed, no doubt, that their last meeting had been curtailed by Jeff barging in to ask her about Kate. He was putting together an ambitious exhibition about Barbury Abbey, scheduled for display in the library in October. She guessed he was particularly anxious to get it right because he hoped to be appointed curator. Everything he did was a way of proving himself capable of promotion.

'The exhibits have got to be in place by half term,' he said. 'I need your input as soon as possible. How about a brainstorming session around the content.'

'What, now? I'm dealing with an enquiry. Tomorrow sometime?'

He pursed his lips, then, defeated, yanked open his big diary to check his availability. 'Ten-thirty, here?'

'Fine, yes, okay.' She began to turn away, impatient to get back to her research into Daniel Swann.

'Jill Fortune's sitting on some manuscripts we were expecting to publish.'

She turned back. 'I'm sorry?'

'Jill was doing the index for Marie's book about Moses Thatcher, and for my Abbey book.'

'There's not a lot anyone can do about that now, is there?' How could he be whingeing about his bloody manuscript when Jill was missing, possibly dead?

'Yes, but it's the only printed copy I've got, with my original illustrations. I wouldn't want to have to print it all out again.'

She sighed, exasperated. 'I'm sorry, Steve, I've got to go.' And she hurried back into the library before he could stop her.

CHAPTER 45

DCI Claire Connors marched into the incident room and pointed a finger at Lincoln, Orla and DI Rick Nevin in turn. 'My office,' she snapped. 'Now.'

Lincoln glanced across at Orla, who glanced across at Nevin. Neither seemed to know what this was about, but they got up and dutifully followed Connors. He trailed after them.

The previous day's *Mail on Sunday* was spread out on top of her keyboard, open at the blurry photo of Ramsay Keiller's binoculars and camera in the bedroom of his bungalow.

She nodded at the newspaper. 'Care to explain how a bloody national tabloid got this photo?'

'The scene was cordoned off straightaway,' Lincoln said, 'but with a long lens, a photographer…'

'Why's Keiller's camera still there?' she demanded, cutting him off. 'Why wasn't it picked up along with his laptop and phone?'

'It was overlooked during the first search, ma'am,' he admitted, 'and I take responsibility for that. But then the focus shifted from Keiller to Jill Fortune, so we didn't go back.'

'This story's down to Karen Bolitho from *The Messenger*,' Orla put in. 'She's got a bug up her arse about Keiller being a spy. She probably took this photo herself to try and get a national paper to notice her.'

'It's a distraction we don't need.' Connors plucked the newspaper from her keyboard and flung it to the far side of her desk, where the pages slid away from each other and cascaded onto the floor. Lincoln and Orla didn't move, but Nevin took a step back.

'I'll get one of my team to collect the camera,' Lincoln said. 'Keiller's phone and laptop must still be with the tech team, but since he's neither a suspect nor the intended victim, do we still need to check them out?'

'Just get that camera picked up.' Connors' tone was grim. 'I don't want this coming back and taking a savage bite out of my rear end.'

'Do we need to speak to Bolitho, ma'am?' Orla asked. 'See if she's holding on to anything we should know about?'

Connors shrugged. 'I'd like to find out how she knew Keiller's camera was there. Is someone talking to the press who shouldn't be?'

'Must be one of the uniforms,' Nevin suggested. 'Unless it's someone from Barley Lane.'

Lincoln shook his head emphatically. The only members of his team who'd visited the crime scene were himself, Woody and Pam. And he could be sure neither of them was to blame. 'Definitely no one from Barley Lane.'

'Talk to Bolitho,' said Connors, 'but don't let her think she's onto anything important. Like I said, this is a distraction, and that's the last thing we want.'

'While you're here, ma'am...' Lincoln noted the flash of irritation in her eyes, but he carried on. 'We need to get hold of Matt Trevelyan's phone records.'

'Matt Trevelyan?'

Orla leapt in. 'We think he's using Morton to get back at Annika.'

'And what will the phone records tell you?' Connors looked unimpressed.

'The extent of his contact with Morton.' Lincoln quickly filled her in on what they knew about Trevelyan and Annika, his likely friendship with Morton and his possible manipulation of him.

'A pretty tenuous link, Jeff.'

'Okay, ma'am, but getting his phone records could be the best way to find out, one way or the other.'

'I'll think about it.' The way she said it, he wasn't optimistic.

Back at their desks, the three detectives didn't speak to each other for a good ten minutes. Then Orla said, 'Okay, so who's talking to Bolitho? You want me to see her, boss?'

She was addressing Lincoln, but Nevin looked up too. He must surely resent Lincoln being in charge.

'Yes, have a quiet word,' said Lincoln. 'Find out if she's got anything else up her sleeve.'

Orla snorted. 'She's not gonna tell me *that*, is she? She's a journalist.'

'And you're an investigator.'

Impasse. Nevin kept his head down.

Lincoln grabbed his jacket and keys. 'I'll speak to Bolitho myself,' he said, desperate to get outside. 'See you later.'

He didn't know if Karen Bolitho would be at her desk or if she even had a desk. If she did have a desk, he'd bet his life she'd got a chair to go with it.

He phoned her from the street outside the offices of *The Messenger*, a scruffy sixties building squeezed in between two much larger Georgian ones.

'There's a coffee shop round the corner,' she told him. 'Or are you here to accompany me to the police station?'

A few minutes later they were sitting opposite each other in the window of the Kasbah Coffee House. As he watched her stirring her flat white, he realised she was older than he'd first thought, closer to thirty than twenty. And she wasn't a natural redhead, darker roots showing where her short wavy hair was casually parted.

'Is this official, this chat, or off the record?' She tapped the spoon against the rim of her cup.

'Unofficial. At this stage, anyway. Depends what you can tell me about Ramsay Keiller.'

She chuckled. 'You should read the article in the *Mail on Sunday*. It's all there.'

'All that's there are unanswered questions about why a retired civil servant owned a pair of binoculars and a camera with a telephoto lens.'

'And an airband scanner.' She met his gaze. 'Yeah, I saw that through the window too, only I couldn't get close enough to photograph it. So don't tell me Keiller was a twitcher or whatever they call those plonkers who go chasing after weird birds.'

'He was interested in aircraft. If you'd done your research, you'd know that he took photos at air shows, perfectly permissible photos, and posted them on the internet. What kind of spy does that?'

'One who's hiding in plain sight?' Karen sat back, a smug look on her face. But then her expression dissolved into something softer, more sad than smug. 'Listen, I can't help it if my editor wanted to go with the spy angle.'

'You didn't have a say?'

'I was taking photos of the outside of his bungalow and – lucky or what? – I spotted that fancy lens and the binoculars sitting there. So I photographed them through the window and my editor liked what he saw. It was up to him to use what he wanted, give it the headline he did. And then he's calling some guy he knows at the *Mail on Sunday* and...' She gave a careless shrug.

Lincoln didn't believe her. He tore open another sachet of sugar and shook it into his coffee. 'So none of it's your fault?'

She frowned at his hands as he tipped yet more sugar into his cup. 'You know sugar's bad for you, don't you?'

He stirred his coffee defiantly. 'So I've heard. Who told you Keiller thought his phone was being tapped?'

'He told me himself.'

'Really? When did you talk to him?'

'The middle of May.'

'Why did you approach him?'

Karen jabbed the tabletop with her index finger. '*He* came to *me*. You know he had a younger brother?'

'Callum, yes. He died in his teens.'

'Callum died because he went camping with the Scouts and the government sprayed him with poison.'

'A neat summing up of the Lyme Bay Trials!' Lincoln laughed bitterly. 'But wanting answers about tests that could've killed his brother didn't make him a traitor or a spy.'

She snorted. 'Maybe the government thought it did.'

He sat back, his gaze drifting to the window and the street outside. Keiller had wanted answers about poorly regulated tests over fifty years ago. Did that make him a threat to national security?

'How did he think *The Messenger* could help?'

'Hoped we could put pressure on the MoD,' she said. 'But there was nothing we could do. No documentation, nothing in the public domain that said there was testing the weekend of the Scout camp.' She took a sip of her coffee and carefully lowered her cup. 'Look, the spying thing started out as a bit of a joke, okay? I took those photos, I showed my editor, and straight off he saw an angle: Ramsay Keiller's an old guy who used to work for the MoD and now somebody's shot him. It seemed like a good story.'

'So are you going to cover the *real* story? About Keiller's belief that his brother died because of germ warfare testing?'

Karen shook her head. 'What's the point? There's no proof. *If* he had any, Christ knows what he did with it. To be honest, now Keiller's not around who cares?'

His sons might care, thought Lincoln. And wasn't it important to hold the government to account? But she was right, without the documents to prove it, how could she proceed? He couldn't remember seeing any papers lying around in Keiller's bungalow, although, since his laptop was in the farm shop office, maybe that's where he kept all his paperwork, business *and* personal, locked away in the safe.

But none of that was relevant now.

One question still remained. 'So, what about the so-called phone taps?'

Karen stirred the milky froth at the bottom of her cup. 'I didn't make it up,' she said defensively. 'When he told me his phone had been tapped, I thought it sounded pretty far-fetched, but he was adamant. He told me he wrote to the MoD in December 2010, demanding answers about the Lyme Bay Trials, and not long after, he started to hear clicking on the line. He supposed they wanted to know who else he was talking to about it.'

'And when was this?'

'He first suspected some sort of phone tap around Christmas 2010. It stopped the following summer, August 2011.' She pushed her cup aside and reached down for her bag.

'So now you've nothing scandalous to write about.'

She sighed heavily. 'My editor wants me to dig up some weirdo pop star who died at Easter. Not literally dig up,' she added more brightly, 'but you know what I mean.'

CHAPTER 46

Lincoln left the Kasbah Coffee House and headed for Barley Lane with his car windows wound down. The sky was the colour of porridge, but it was still hot.

His conversation with Karen Bolitho had revealed more than he'd expected. She'd taken the photos of Keiller's bungalow herself, not been sent them by some enterprising police officer. Although *The Messenger* had fabricated the story that Keiller might be a spy, and the *Mail on Sunday* had run with it, the man had genuinely been afraid that the security services were monitoring his phone calls seven years ago. Assuming Bolitho could be believed. But none of that helped the search for Ezra Morton. None of that helped to find Jill.

'So we're no further forward.' Pam stood in front of the whiteboard, arms folded.

As he leant back in his chair, Lincoln let himself bask in the familiar atmosphere of Barley Lane. The building might not have air conditioning, but he could open the windows to let a cool draught waft over him.

'We don't think Ezra Morton's acting alone,' he said. 'Jill's daughter, Annika, was involved with an ex-con called Matt Trevelyan. I'll send a description and his mugshot over to you. He could be using Morton to get back at her by harming Jill.'

Dilke frowned uncertainly. 'What makes you think Trevelyan's behind it all?'

'He's got motive. He used to let himself into Jill's house, help himself to food and anything else that took his fancy. He got caught out when Jill came home unexpectedly and found him there. Annika dumped him, probably because Jill told her to. Trevelyan and Morton were in the same prison at the same time, so it's likely they've stayed in touch.'

'Bit of an assumption, isn't it, boss?' Now it was Pam who seemed uncertain. 'And where's Trevelyan now?'

'No idea. He left his flat the day before Morton shot his mother.'

'You think Trevelyan put him up to that, too?'

'Not sure he needed to, Graham. Morton's relationship with his mother was volatile. That's why he was jailed in 2012, for attacking her. He's troubled and unstable and Trevelyan's taken advantage of that. If we could only get hold of his phone records.'

He stood up and headed for the kettle. On top of the filing cabinet-cum-drinks station sat his coffee mug, reassuringly unused since he'd left for Park Street, although it needed a proper wash, not just the usual quick rinse under the tap.

'Morton's troubled how?' asked Pam when he came back from scouring his mug.

'When Morton came out of prison, he lived in a caravan in the front garden of his mother's house for a little while. Wouldn't go indoors even to use the bathroom.'

She winced. 'I don't want to think about the consequences of that!'

'Then he and Elinor fell out again and he left home, got a job and a place of his own here in town. The Saturday before the incident at Keiller's Yard, he phoned her, got her to go to a house near Warminster, Willow Cottage, where he was dossing down. Soon as she got there, he shot her in the face.' Lincoln strode across to make his coffee. 'He may not have intended to kill Keiller, but there's no way the death of his mother was accidental.'

'What's the significance of Willow Cottage?' Dilke asked. 'Why doss down there?'

'The house belongs to the man we think is his father. Daniel Swann.'

Pam gasped. 'Daniel Swann? The singer?'

'You've heard of him?'

'Yes, Heather mentioned him.'

'Heather?' Lincoln couldn't think who she meant.

'Heather Draycott, Ramsay's friend. The woman Jamie said he saw at the bungalow, remember? I interviewed her when the focus was still on Ramsay.'

'Ah, yes.' He made his coffee, stirring in two teaspoons of sugar, stopping himself as he was about to add a third. 'Did Heather know Swann?'

'Years ago, yes. She said how jealous she and her friends were when Jill started going out with him at school. He was in a band with some classmates...'

'Danny Swann and the Haymakers.'

'That's right,' said Pam in surprise. 'How did you know? A bit before your time, weren't they, boss?'

'A *lot* before my time. Swann's name keeps cropping up, that's all. Jill's teenage sweetheart and, possibly, Morton's father.'

'Wow!' She looked across at the whiteboard, and Lincoln was suddenly aware of how much was missing from it, compared to its counterpart at Park

Street. How could he expect his team to contribute to the investigation when they had access to only part of the information surrounding it?

The sooner he was back here at Barley Lane, the better.

'Okay, Pam, so what else did Heather tell you about Swann?'

'Dan's band took off and he went to the States, then he had a bit of a breakdown and left. When he came back, he was into all sorts of weird stuff – UFOs and conspiracy theories. He sent Jill a manuscript...' She broke off as Woody came in.

'Park Street too quiet for you, boss?' Woody was grinning broadly.

Lincoln lifted his mug. 'I needed a proper cup of coffee.'

'Still no sign of Jill?'

'Nope. Most likely, Morton's hiding her somewhere in Greywood Forest, but it's too big an area to search blind, especially since he's armed and dangerous. We can't get parties of civilian volunteers involved, and it's impossible to cover the ground until we can narrow down where he might be. We're waiting for him to make a move and get caught on camera.'

When Woody heard the theory about Matt Trevelyan, he seemed doubtful too. 'How's Trevelyan got Morton to kill for him?'

'Maybe Trevelyan's brainwashed him or promised him some sort of reward.'

'But wouldn't Trevelyan want to be the one to hurt Annika or her mum? Why get someone else to do your dirty work when it's something as personal as your girlfriend finishing with you?'

Lincoln couldn't answer that. 'As for the idea that Keiller was a spy – Karen Bolitho blames her editor.'

Woody chuckled. 'Reckon these journalists are more trouble than they're worth.'

With reluctance, Lincoln pushed himself out of his chair and stood up. Time to go back. 'While I think about it, Woody, can someone go to Keiller's bungalow and pick up his camera?'

CHAPTER 47

Ezra climbed down the ladder and dumped his rucksack on the floor. He'd brought Jill some water and half a dozen energy bars.

She stretched her leg out on the bed and showed him her ankle. The skin around the cut was puffy and – as far as she could see in this light – inflamed where he'd grazed it with the chain.

'Look,' she said, 'it's infected. It's gone septic.'

He unlocked the first aid tin that was screwed to the wall. When he took out some cotton wool and a bottle of TCP, she recoiled in horror.

'You can't put that stuff on my leg! It must be nearly as old as I am!'

Squatting down, he took hold of her foot and, with surprising gentleness, bathed her ankle. 'It's not old,' he reassured her. 'We refreshed it all last year.'

'We?'

'Me and Dad. He wanted to be sure we were ready.'

She didn't need to ask him for what Dan had wanted to be ready: *Conspiracy To Deceive* revealed his fear of invasion by the Russians, the Chinese – or by aliens from another planet, another galaxy. How poignant was the image of father and son preparing to take on the enemy together!

After the initial agony of the antiseptic entering the wound, she began to feel a little better. But she was still a prisoner, now with the chain around her other ankle.

She drank thirstily while Ezra watched, then ripped the wrapper from one of the energy bars.

'Where do you go to get these?' she asked. If he was going into shops, why had no one spotted him? Why had no one recognised the car? Ramsay would have been sure to give a good description of him.

'It's all in the boot. I've got enough for days.'

So he was going no farther than the stand of trees on the edge of the field, where he'd parked on Friday night. He must be sleeping in the car too and, by the smell of him, he hadn't taken a shower any more recently than she had.

'You may be able to hold out for days, Ezra, but I'm not sure I can. I need proper food. I need a bath. What is it you want from me? I'll hand over the manuscript. I've told you already that you can have it, if only you'll let me go.'

'I can't,' he said, snatching the water bottle from her hand. 'It's got too complicated.'

'Seems easy enough to me. You let me go. You turn yourself in or...' She shrugged.

'Like I said, it's got too complicated.' And without another word, he lumbered to his feet and went back up the ladder, huffing and puffing as he climbed.

Jill felt abandoned. Wary of him as she was, she would have preferred him to have stayed so she didn't feel so alone down here in the failing light. The hospital smell of the TCP comforted her a little, although her ankle ached. She lay back, still hungry and cold, the thin, scratchy blankets providing little warmth. Would she ever get out of here? If only she could rewind the last seven days, the last few months.

February 1983: Dan phones her, out of the blue, invites her out and she goes along for old times' sake.

'I got your number off your brother,' he explains as they find a corner table in the Monk and Abbot. 'In case you were wondering.'

She'll give Chas a piece of her mind next time she sees him. What made him think meeting Dan was a good idea? Had he forgotten how brutally Dan had finished with her? Didn't he remember how upset she'd been for months afterwards? Without the support of Maggie and Eva, she might have had a breakdown.

She and Dan share a packet of crisps. They haven't set eyes on each other for years and now they're sitting in a pub drinking beer and, like a couple of teenagers, they're dipping into the same packet of ready salted crisps.

The years have not been kind to the baby-faced singer of the Haymakers, the good-looking front man of the Barbury Blues Band. Jill is thirty-four, married to Jerry for a year but already wishing she'd stayed single. Dan is thirty-six but looks closer to forty. She steals glances at him, saddened by his gaunt face, his receding hairline, the weariness emanating from him.

He's been in the States, in London, in rehab. She's determined not to remind him of how casually he discarded her all those years ago. He'd been little more than a kid, seduced by the promise of fame and fortune, with a future that didn't include his schoolgirl sweetheart. Still, she'll never forgive him completely.

When she'd answered the phone earlier that day, the sound of his voice – still rich, if a little huskier – had thrilled her as much as it had when she was a teenager.

'I need someone to talk to,' he'd said. 'Someone to have a beer with. And it'd be good to see you again, Jilly.'

So now they sit over their drinks, reminiscing, and the years magically dissolve.

'I've got a son,' he tells her, a little sheepishly. 'Ezra John. He's five, nearly six. His mum and me aren't married, don't live together. Can't even remember sleeping with her, but I must have.' He grins.

Dan was always so scathing about 'family men' that Jill's surprised to hear he's acknowledging this little boy. He and his bandmates lived – and loved – so recklessly, there must have been many accidental pregnancies they never even knew about.

'Are you close to his mum?' Why does she feel jealous after all this time? Why does she still care?

'Not so's you'd notice. I help her out with money, that's all, and she tells me what he gets up to. Funny little kid,' he adds, wistfully. 'In a world of his own half the time.'

Quarter to ten, and Dan nods towards the clock over the bar. 'Won't Hubby wonder where you've got to?' Ash from his cigarette tumbles into his lap.

'Why should he?' She raises her glass and finishes off her Barbury Ale. She's told Jerry she's meeting Maggie, who's married to Ramsay Keiller, a civil servant working at Boscombe Down. The Keillers already have a son and have been trying for another baby for a while. 'Jerry and I trust each other.'

'Of course you do.' He brushes ash from the thigh of his skin-tight jeans. Her gaze settles there for a brief moment. He's lost weight, is unhealthily thin. She wants to wrap him up and take him home, rescue him from whatever he's doing to himself.

'Where are you staying, Dan?'

'The Full Moon.' He drains his glass. 'Not exactly the Black Swan, but it's all I can afford these days and the bar doesn't close till eleven. You could come back for a nightcap.'

They hurry through frosty streets to the Full Moon and go straight up to his room, not even pausing at the bar. The room's cold, the curtains thin, and the streetlamps outside the window bathe the bed in a light the colour of barley sugar.

He pulls her close, his hands cradling her face. He kisses her hungrily, his energy taking her by surprise. She's as eager as he is, not acknowledging until he's frantically undressing her how much she's missed him, has longed to see him again, has yearned for this to happen.

It's over all too soon, and they lie side by side, his arm flung across her, his face against her shoulder.

'I need to get home.' She makes no effort to move.

'Tell him you missed the bus.'

'I'm driving. I'll think of something.'

Abruptly, Dan sits up on the edge of the bed with his back to her, leaning forward to pull his shorts back on. In the sickly orange light, she can see how little flesh covers his bones. He needs someone to look after him, someone to protect him.

'Don't let anyone see you on the way out.' He stands to tug his jeans up. 'I've only paid the single rate and I don't want them charging me for a double.'

Stunned, Jill slides off the bed, her skin suddenly icy cold, then she scrabbles round on the floor, gathering up the clothes he'd stripped from her so wildly an hour ago. She pulls on her T-shirt and jeans, shoves her bare feet into her boots, stuffs her socks into her shoulder bag and grabs her coat.

She flees from his room, the cheap hotel, ashamed and smarting. They aren't star-crossed lovers rekindling their romance after years apart: he's used his charm on her, guessing she'd be an easy lay.

And he'd been right.

Jerry doesn't ask why she's back so late. He's fallen asleep in the armchair with a glass of wine, waking as she returns, groggily unaware of the time.

Three days later, she finds the socks she shoved into her bag during her hurried departure from the hotel bedroom.

Three months later, she discovers she's pregnant.

CHAPTER 48

'Is your phone off, boss?' Orla pounced on Lincoln as soon as he got back to Park Street. 'I've been trying to get hold of you.'

He pulled his phone out of his pocket. He'd turned it off while he was speaking to Karen Bolitho.

'Getting forgetful in my old age.' He made a show of switching it on. 'Has something come up?'

'Gamekeeper in Greywood Forest called it in.' She bounded across to the wall map next to the whiteboard. 'He saw a black saloon parked near a disused army building on Friday. Here, in the north east corner of Fir Plantation.' She jabbed the map. 'Noticed it because not many cars drive up there, not even on the metalled road through the forest. Didn't think anything of it at the time, but this morning he went inside and found empty water bottles, blankets, a pillow, a slop bucket.'

'Same set-up as in the Nissen hut on the airfield.'

'Exactly. And some keys.'

'Keys?'

'Door keys, on a key ring. There's a medallion on the key ring, with an emoji on it, like somebody frowning.' She pointed to a photo on the whiteboard. 'The gamekeeper sent that over.'

Lincoln studied the photo of the medallion for only a moment before unpinning it and turning it ninety degrees. 'It's not an emoji,' he said, re-pinning it. 'It's the symbol for the bass clef. Must be Jill's. Don't you remember Annika telling us she'd bought her mum a key ring from the music shop?'

Orla pouted. 'Did she? If you say so. The CSIs are going up there to see what else they can find.'

'So where's Morton taken Jill now?' He was heartened by the news that as recently as Friday, the missing woman was apparently being held captive. If he'd kept her alive this long, was it too much to hope that Morton wouldn't kill her now?

Orla was studying the wall map again. 'He must have driven on through Greywood Forest. He could've come out at Speldon Magna or carried on even farther west. Wherever he's going, he's got to hit a main road sometime, find himself some petrol, provisions, whatever, and that's when he'll be spotted.'

'How about pinging his phone?'

She shook her head. 'He must've turned it off or dumped the SIM, because the tech team got nothing.'

'So how's he keeping in touch with Trevelyan?'

'Assuming he is.' DCI Connors' voice took him by surprise. He hadn't heard her come in.

'Ma'am?'

She approached the whiteboard, her hands in her trouser pockets. 'Orla and I were discussing your theory while you were out, Jeff, and it all seems pretty shaky to me.'

He glanced across at Orla. *His* theory? 'Er, we were working on the assumption...'

'A spurned lover using his prison buddy to kidnap his girlfriend's mother? Why not kidnap her himself? If he really wants to hurt Annika, why isn't Jill already dead? Why would this Trevelyan character trust someone as unstable as Morton to keep his shit together? What's in it for Morton?'

All the questions Lincoln was already asking himself, questions he'd tried to push to one side.

'Morton's a loner,' Connors went on. 'He's not a collaborator. Read what his work colleagues are saying about him on social media. They hardly knew him. He never spoke more than was absolutely necessary. Kept himself to himself. And these are people who've worked with him for a while. Okay, so maybe he and Trevelyan were in jail together, but did they actually *know* each other? How can you be so sure that Trevelyan's involved?' She stepped back, turning to Lincoln for an answer.

'Well, it seemed logical...'

She cut across him. 'You're clutching at straws, Jeff. First Keiller's the target, then it's Jill. First Morton's behind it all, then it's Trevelyan. It doesn't look good, Jeff. In fact, it looks bloody chaotic.'

She spun away and marched back to her office, leaving him and Orla looking at each other. Orla was the first to look away.

He slunk back to his desk. Connors had challenged the assumptions he and Orla had made, and quite rightly. It was her job to make sure they didn't go chasing down blind alleys. But now he doubted himself. He was quietly angry that Orla had made him look stupid when, to start with, it was he who'd challenged *her* assumptions about Trevelyan's role in all this.

Behind his desk, there was a noticeable absence of a chair. For a full minute, he stared at the place where the chair should be. If he didn't get out of the building, he'd smash something.

'I'm off out for some fresh air,' he told the room at large. 'I'll be five minutes.'

He walked around the block. By that time in the afternoon, the air out of doors wasn't much fresher than the air inside, but he could see trees and sky, could walk past people going about their business, oblivious to the search for Jill Fortune.

That was all he needed, simply to get away, give himself a mental kicking for losing heart and letting doubt creep in. He'd allowed Karen Bolitho and her stupid spy story to distract him, and he'd let Orla's theory about Trevelyan run away with him. Now he had to make up for lost time, get back on track. And he had to find Jill Fortune before it was too late.

CHAPTER 49

While Lincoln was enjoying five minutes away from the oppressive atmosphere of the incident room, Pam was arriving at Keiller's Yard. She was saddened to see how empty the place looked after just a week. Blue and white tape still cordoned it off, but there were no longer any uniforms keeping guard. The display crates that were usually outside the farm shop had been removed, and the shop sign was turned to CLOSED.

Eunice Peel emerged from one of the outhouses, a bucket of chicken feed weighing her arm down.

'No one's allowed in,' she snapped, shielding her eyes with her other hand. 'Oh, it's you. Thought you lot had finished.'

'I just need to pick something up from the bungalow. How're you coping?'

Eunice dumped the heavy bucket down. 'It's too much for one,' she said, 'and there's my mother to look after too.'

How much longer would she be able to stay here? How long might probate take? When her grandfather had died in February, Pam and her mother had been warned that probate could take months, maybe even a year, depending on the complexities of his estate.

'You'll want the keys,' said Eunice, and led her into the shop.

Shut up during a very hot week, it smelt of stale food and something fermenting. Inevitably, Pam recalled the many times she'd stopped off here on a cycle ride to pick up a cold drink or some fruit, have a chat with Ramsay, pet the animals in the paddock and inwardly celebrate the survival of such a rustic place so close to the town.

'I salvaged a lot of the fruit and veg,' Eunice went on, handing her the door key, 'anything I could make use of. Can't bring myself to go into his office, though. I've unplugged the phone because I couldn't stand the ringing.'

The bungalow, like the shop, smelt fusty. Here, too, food had been left to go off: some pears overripening in a fruit basket; a pint of milk solidifying in the fridge; cooked meat acquiring a greenish tinge.

The camera sat on a shelf in Ramsay's bedroom. Pam couldn't resist taking a peek in his wardrobe, where jackets and trousers hung neatly and a trace of aftershave lingered. She'd been fond of him and the senselessness of his murder saddened her. She wished she'd known more about his campaign over Callum's death, could have talked to him about it. Now, though, it was a campaign that would come to an end.

She stole a last look out of the window, towards Turnpike Corner Airfield. A light aircraft was lazily sliding through the cloudless sky, sunlight glinting on its fuselage. How Ramsay must have loved sitting here watching the planes, especially when there'd been more military activity to watch.

She handed the key back to Eunice, who was feeding the donkeys, stroking each heavy head in turn.

'Thank you,' she said, taking her leave, but the diminutive Eunice didn't even bother to look round.

Back at Barley Lane, Pam popped the memory card out of the camera and slotted it into her laptop. Sixteen images, the earliest from the end of May, the last from the weekend before Ramsay's death.

The first few were of a helicopter landing and taking off from the airfield. The most recent, taken the day before he died, was a shot of one of the donkeys in the paddock. In the middle were five shots, taken on the night of 28 June, of two figures in hoodies. Ramsay must have lain in wait for them, his camera and long lens at the ready.

She recognised the vandals' anonymous shapes from the segment of CCTV footage that had caught them before they damaged the security cameras, but these photos were different: in the tenth and eleventh photos, the young hooligans were looking towards the camera, their faces clearly visible.

One of them was a young boy with light brown skin, thick black eyebrows, glasses. The other one was a girl.

CHAPTER 50

When he got back from his stroll around the block, Lincoln was relieved to learn from Orla that Connors, albeit grudgingly, had agreed to get a warrant for Matt Trevelyan's phone records.

'But she's not a happy bunny,' Orla warned him. 'You'd better hope it's worth it, boss. The other bit of good news? We've had the autopsy report for Elinor Morton. Shot at point blank range, nine mill. As we expected, the bullet's a match for the one that killed Keiller.'

He took the report from her and skimmed through it. Elinor was described as being in poor health, undernourished and anaemic. The round that killed her had entered her face below her left eye and lodged in her brain. Death would have been instantaneous. There were no defensive wounds, although it would appear that she had suffered minor injuries in the past: a broken wrist, the other arm broken in two places at different times, a fractured clavicle.

'Evidence of abuse by Morton over the years?' Orla inclined her head towards the report. 'He's a big bloke and didn't that neighbour of hers say Elinor was scared of him?'

'Yes, though given the trip hazards in that house of hers, she could've broken various bones falling over her bin bags. But then again...'

'And those are only the injuries that show up on X-rays. What else did he do to her over the years?'

'What do we know about her? Who was looking into her background?'

'Rick couldn't find much. He concentrated on Swann's family, but he didn't get very far with that either. Swann's daughter, Poppy, died from an accidental overdose in 2000, something iffy she took at a music festival. And his wife, Kitty, killed herself a year later. No trace of any other family.'

'And until we get the DNA results, we can only suppose that Morton's his son. Talking of results, anything from Ballistics yet?' Might there be an open case file on a bullet that had been fired from the same gun previously, or was that too much to hope for?

'Yes and no. Yes, we got the results, and no, there isn't a match.' She paused. 'Are you okay, boss?'

'Fine, fine.'

'You've got problems with your Barley Lane team? Dennis Breeze? In custody at Devizes?'

Lincoln wondered how she'd found out, but guessed the grapevine had carried the news all the way from Devizes. 'He was in custody, yes, but he's back in Barbury now, going through the appropriate procedures.'

Or so he hoped. When he'd left the house this morning, Breeze was still getting himself out of bed and into the shower, moaning about how much his head hurt and how he really should go back to bed for another hour or two.

Rick Nevin ambled over on the pretext of checking there was enough paper in the printer. 'Got a bit of a rep, hasn't he, your Dennis?'

'*My* Dennis?'

'He was knocking around with one of the WPCs here a few years ago. She always used to say he was a bit of a slob.'

'Since when did being a slob become a punishable offence, Rick?'

'Didn't say it was. Just saying he's got a bit of a rep.' Nevin plodded back to his desk.

'Let's concentrate on the job in hand,' said Lincoln. 'Then we might get somewhere.'

CHAPTER 51

Kelly saw Matt coming across the beer garden towards her, weaving in and out of the tables, an uncapped bottle of San Miguel in each hand. It was nearly seven and the garden was filling up with drinkers who preferred to be outside in the late sunshine, not cooped up in the bar. She hadn't seen him for two or three weeks, but he must've guessed she'd be at the Poacher's on a Monday night.

He dumped the bottles on the table beside her empty Coke can. 'Wanna tell me what happened with the old guy?' He sat astride the wooden bench opposite her.

'The old guy? At the farm shop?' She reached for one of the bottles, but he grabbed it first.

'No,' he said, handing her the other bottle. 'This one's yours.'

'For fuck's sake!' She rolled her eyes. 'What difference does it make? They're both San Miguel.'

'So, what happened?'

'That wasn't us. Me and Driver did what you asked us to do, that's all. The old guy was shot with a proper gun, not a fucking air rifle.'

'Sure? Because if either one of you thought you'd get clever...' He shook his head slowly, solemnly, as if he was warning her.

'I told you. That was nothing to do with us!'

Matt suddenly grinned and tapped his bottle against hers. 'I'm messing with you, Kel. I know it wasn't you.'

'Bastard! I hate it when people wind me up. Do it once, they don't do it again.' She took a swig of beer straight from the bottle. She wasn't eighteen yet, but the place was too busy for the bar staff to notice. And she looked eighteen, didn't she, with her make-up on?

She'd met Matt some months back. He'd caught her and Dev Driver red-handed with their spray cans in the station car park, when he was hanging out with a mate who lived nearby.

'Wanna earn some money?' he'd asked, and she'd thought he meant for sex. She'd have been up for it, but Driver would've jumped on his bike and cycled away as fast as he could. But no, Matt was offering them a job. An *assignment.* 'There's this little farm,' he'd said, 'where this old guy lives. I want you to scare the bollocks off him.'

Funny thing was, she knew the little farm he was talking about. She'd had a holiday job there last summer, cash in hand. Didn't see much of the old guy, but she'd met his son Jamie. He was the one showing them what to do. And then she'd met his big brother, Adam, who she'd gone on seeing for quite a while.

Although it was never said, she was sure it was Adam who'd put Matt up to it. Paying him to pay her and Driver to vandalise the farm.

She'd wanted to shoot at the chickens, or let the donkeys out of their paddock, but Driver wouldn't have it. 'You can't,' he'd said. 'That's cruel. It's not their fault.'

Driver was soft, or maybe it was his religion. He didn't eat meat either, or fish.

'Where's Driver?' Matt was asking, looking round the beer garden. 'Should've bought him a beer too.'

'He doesn't drink. You should know that by now. He's inside, playing pool with his mates.'

'Driver plays pool?' He pretended to be shocked at the idea, then leant back, still grinning at her, and she couldn't help comparing him to Adam. Matt looked better dressed in a scruffy T-shirt and frayed jeans than Adam did in a smart polo shirt and chinos. And Matt was fit, like he worked out. He was far, far sexier, with those long eyelashes and arching eyebrows.

'He's fucking good, too.' She took another swig of beer. She should've had something to eat. The beer was making her head spin.

Some raucous students at the next table were toasting each other and taking selfies. End of term, she supposed, exams done, holidays ahead. A life she'd wanted but could never have, not with the way the world worked. As she turned back, dazzled by the flash of the students' phone cameras, she felt so off-balance, she nearly tipped off the bench.

Matt reached out a steadying hand. 'You okay, Kel? Thought you were gonna pass out just then.'

'Fine. Hungry, that's all.'

'You want something from the bar? They've got peanuts, crisps...' He stood up, pulling a five-pound note out of his pocket, ready to buy her something.

'Don't leave me. I feel a bit sick.' She stretched herself out along the length of the bench. She was scared she'd throw up in front of all these people, in front of Matt.

'I need to get you home, then.' He came over to her side of the table, his arms going round her to help her sit up. 'Upsy-daisy.'

'What about Driver?'

'Never mind about Driver. He'll find his own way home. Come on, I'll give you a lift.'

CHAPTER 52

When Lincoln got back to the Old Vicarage that evening, he found Dennis Breeze lolling on the sofa, reading *Guns and Ammo* magazine. He'd made himself successive cups of tea without bothering to wash up the dirty crockery, and an empty takeaway pizza tray sat open on the kitchen table, smeared with lurid red sauce.

'Come on, you're not a teenager, Dennis.' He shoved Breeze's trainer-clad feet off the cushions. 'Aren't you meant to be staying somewhere else tonight?'

Breeze cast the magazine aside and started to clear up, as if he'd only just noticed all the dirty cups and packaging around him. 'I've tried to get hold of my sister, but she's not answering. Course, she's a mate of Tracey's, too.'

'You think Tracey's told her not to help you?' Lincoln picked up a couple of the mugs, the faster to clear them off the coffee table. The prospect of another twenty-four hours of Breeze's company filled him with dismay.

'More than likely. No one'll want to hear *my* side of the story.'

'Which is?' Lincoln had deliberately avoided asking for Breeze's account of the incident that had got him arrested, but now seemed as good a time as any to find out what had happened. 'You want to sit outside, have a drink, tell me all about it?'

Breeze looked momentarily stunned, as if this was the last thing he'd been expecting.

'Er, about your whiskey…'

'I bought some more,' said Lincoln. 'Come on.'

The wedding had been fine, Breeze told him.

'Went without a hitch, you might say,' he added with a chuckle.

Things started to go wrong after the ceremony. The photographer didn't want the usual line-up, preferring informal photos that showed bride, groom and guests having a good time.

'So, straight after we got outside the church, the champagne came out and the gin, and everyone was getting a bit merry. Including me, okay? No food in sight, so I'm drinking on an empty stomach. And Shirley's getting everyone to gather round for the photos and before I know it, there's Tracey with her toy boy and...'

'Toy boy?'

'Harry. He's at least ten years younger than her. Looks a bit of a tosser, to be honest. And she said something to him about me. I could tell by the way she was looking across at me, and he comes out with some dickhead comment and...' Breeze broke off to take a sip of his whiskey. 'So I steered clear of her all through the reception, which wasn't easy because she seemed to be everywhere. And afterwards there was an open bar, you know, all the drinks paid for, so of course everyone's going up for more. Well, you can imagine...'

A wedding party where guests could drink as much as they liked for free? Lincoln could imagine it all too well.

'Must've been midnight, one o'clock,' Breeze went on, 'and people were starting to call it a night and go up to their rooms, the ones that were staying overnight. And it was all kind of running down and the staff were turning lights off, you know, to encourage guests to go. And I was pretty pissed, mixing my drinks...'

'Never a good idea.'

'... and I'd got my room key in my pocket, but you know those key card things, there's no number on the actual card and I'd lost the little wallet doodah they gave me when I checked in. I couldn't for the life of me remember my room number. I could find the room, though. Or thought I could. Two doors past the lift. So I get out the lift and go along the corridor, first door, second door. Key card doesn't work. So I must have put it in the wrong way, yeah? So I try it every which way. No go.'

Silently urging Breeze to cut to the chase, Lincoln sipped his drink, staring out across his garden to the back of Fountains, the house rising quietly and in darkness at the top of its sloping lawns.

'So I'm just thinking I'll go down to reception, ask them why the card won't work, and the door opens and it's Tracey. And she thinks I've come to her room on purpose, and I'm not in the mood to explain that I've made a mistake, and she doesn't give me a chance anyway, just slams the door in my face.'

'Nice welcome.'

'Exactly.'

'And then I think, maybe it's the right room but on the wrong *floor*, so I knock on her door to ask her what floor this is, and she thinks I'm just trying to get into her room, and she yanks the door open and gives me a mouthful and shoves me in the chest and…' He put his head down, wagging it as if he really didn't understand what he'd done that night.

Lincoln put his glass down on the floor of the verandah. 'What happened next? Can you remember anything?'

'I *think*,' Breeze replied, with heavy emphasis, 'I *think* I went back along the corridor and got back in the lift. I *think* I went up to the next floor and found my room, exactly where I thought it was…'

'Only on a different floor.'

'On a different floor, yeah. The key card worked, I went inside, lay down on the bed and passed out. Didn't even take my shoes off.'

'But that's not what Tracey says happened?' Lincoln knew there must be more to the story. Much more.

Breeze lifted his glass to his lips, sipped, sipped again. 'Tracey says I shoved my way into her room, pushed her onto the bed and tried to screw her. I mean, seriously? In the state I was in?'

Neither of them spoke for a few minutes. Tux appeared, curious about why they were out on the verandah at feeding time. Sensing Breeze might be a soft touch, the cat rose up on its hind legs and delicately placed its forepaws on his knee.

'No good asking me, mate,' Breeze said. 'I don't even know what you eat.'

'Anything, but he can wait a bit longer.' Lincoln gently pushed Tux down. 'You're absolutely sure you didn't go into Tracey's room?'

Breeze pushed his hand through his hair, which wasn't slicked back like it usually was. 'Can't remember. Mind's a blank. I went up in the lift and into my own room, fell on the bed. But did I actually go into Trace's room first? No idea.' He drained his glass, sat back. 'Haven't got a leg to stand on, have I?'

'It's your word against hers. No possible witnesses? Anyone in the rooms either side of hers?'

'Shirley's daughter, Carly. Her room was somewhere along that corridor, but if she'd seen or heard anything, she'd have come forward, wouldn't she?'

'What about CCTV? The hotel could confirm what time you went along the corridor to your room.'

'Their system was down that night, some sort of fault. Cuh, just my luck.'

'What evidence does Tracey have that this happened the way she says it did? She must think she's got a strong case.'

Breeze shrugged. 'Her outfit got torn. Says I did it. Necklace got broken. That was my fault, too. But see, I've got no recollection of that, no recollection at all. And as for getting close enough to *do* anything to her…'

'How soon did she report it? They'd have examined her, surely, to recover any forensic evidence? If you say you didn't even get that close to her.' Lincoln tried not to think about the indignities Tracey and Breeze might have been put through in the process of establishing the truth of what happened that night – whether or not any bodily fluids had actually been exchanged.

'She didn't go to the police until Tuesday evening. I think that tosser, Harry, talked her into it.'

'What did you say when you were interviewed at Devizes?'

'Told them what I've told you, that I don't remember. But wouldn't you think I'd remember *something* if I'd forced my way into my ex's hotel room and attacked her?'

Lincoln thought back to a case they'd dealt with only a few months earlier when a young woman claimed a guest had tried to rape her at the country club where she worked. The claim had turned out to be false, but not before she'd convinced everyone she was telling the truth.

What motive did Tracey have for making this up? If she had no proof, how did she think she'd be able to make a case, especially against a police officer?

'Except, there was lipstick on my shirt,' Breeze volunteered unhappily, 'and I've got these scratches on my neck where she had to fight me off.' He reached for the bottle, but Lincoln snatched it away. 'I mean,' Breeze went on, anxious and confused, 'how else did I get those scratches, eh?'

Lincoln was half-listening to a song by the Barbury Blues Band – penned by Dan Swann, and far better than he was expecting – when his phone rang.

'Hi,' said Trish, 'are you busy?'

'I was about to look in the fridge to see if Breezy's left me anything to eat. He seems to have snacked on most of what was in there.'

'He's gone now?'

'Not quite.' Indeed, he could hear Breeze banging about upstairs.

'When's he leaving?'

'Not soon enough. Good to hear your voice.' He said it before he could stop himself.

'Really? Call me more often, then.'

'Come on, Trish, I'm doing my best. This case…' He shut the fridge door and sat at the kitchen table. This kitchen, this house, were way too big for one person. Or even two. 'We haven't made much headway, that's all.'

'Still no sign of Jill?'

'Yes and no. I'm sorry, but…'

'I know. You can't talk about it. Want to know what I've found out about Daniel Swann?'

He'd forgotten all about asking her. 'Of course. Any luck?'

'There's lots on the internet, but I also checked the local newspapers.'

'What did you find out?' He was on his feet again, keen to hear what she had to say.

'An interesting guy. Teenage pop star, destined for great things and then he crashed. Metaphorically, I mean. He had a bad experience taking LSD and never properly recovered.'

Nothing Lincoln didn't already know. 'That's it?'

'There's lots more, but I'm not sure what's relevant. Jill doesn't get a mention, only some kid called Ellie who ran his fan club.'

'Ellie?' Ellie short for Elinor, as in Elinor Morton, he thought. That box of Danny Swann photos in a cupboard in the Amesbury house. That body on the floor at Willow Cottage, arm flung out, face destroyed. He swallowed hard. 'Go on.'

'Swann disappeared from the news for years. We're talking pre-internet, so if it wasn't in the newspapers, it didn't happen. Then he turned up at the Stonehenge Free Festival in 1984, urging everyone to read James Lovelock's *Gaia,* warning about the damage we're doing to the environment. Swann was ahead of his time on that, really. But then, the following year, everything changed.'

'Everything?'

'The direction he took. No Free Festival in 1985 because the authorities tried to stop it taking place, but the Peace Convoy headed to Stonehenge anyway, or tried to, until the police and the MoD ambushed it. Which resulted in the Battle of the Beanfield.'

'The travellers *were* trespassing, Trish.'

'Yes, but the police didn't have to beat up women and children!'

He'd had too long a day to get into an argument about that now. 'Swann was there? At the Battle of the Beanfield?'

'Yes. And he claimed it was a turning point for him. It made him more concerned about civil liberties and government interference than the environment.'

Lincoln had been a young Worcestershire teenager in the mid-eighties, but he could still recall his outrage over the handling of the Miners' Strike. The Battle of the Beanfield in June 1985 hadn't impinged on him in the same way – fewer headlines in the papers, less coverage on the television news –

but the principles were the same: the Thatcher government apparently setting out to suppress people and steal their freedoms, and using the police to do it.

'Where did Swann's money come from? Was he working?'

A pause while Trish checked her notes. 'The Barbury Blues Band sacked him. He was living off the royalties from his songs. After the Battle of the Beanfield, he went to live in a commune in Glastonbury for a bit.'

'He bought a house near Warminster a few years ago, didn't he? Any information about that?'

'1993, that was. Willow Cottage. I found a photo. It looks pretty.'

It must have been, thought Lincoln, before Swann let it go to rack and ruin. 'Anything else?'

'He was passionate about UFOs and crop circles, but he was also paranoid about a nuclear war. He started giving interviews about the need to learn survival skills. In 1995 he actually bought an underground bunker at Hunter's Ridge, across the A36 from Lookout Hill. There are pictures in the *Barbury Bugle* of him climbing out of it.'

'A bunker? You can *buy* an underground bunker?' A prickle of excitement ran over his scalp and down his back. Would Ezra Morton know about the bunker his father bought? Would he have access to it?

'The MoD sold them off after the Royal Observer Corps was disbanded,' Trish explained. 'Some people bought them for storage or for the hell of it. But Swann said he'd bought his so he'd be safe when the bomb dropped.'

Lincoln called Claire Connors as soon as he got off the phone to Trish.

'I think I know where Morton's keeping Jill prisoner, ma'am,' he said without preamble. 'Daniel Swann bought an underground shelter near Lookout Hill, ex-Ministry of Defence. I think he's holding her there. A hiding place well out of the way, one he can easily defend.'

Before ringing the DCI, he'd searched the internet and found section diagrams of a typical underground ROC post. In essence, each one was a concrete box with an air shaft. Primitive, but capable of sheltering two people for weeks at a time. Swann – or Morton – could have laid up provisions, water, batteries, a generator, whatever was needed to outlast an anticipated attack.

Connors tutted, sounding wary. 'The way you describe this hole in the ground, Jeff, we'd have to wait for him to come out. Anyone climbing down after him is going to get shot, aren't they? And if he's got Jill down there with him, an attack on this place would put her at even greater risk. We need to check it out before we go in there. But we can do nothing until it's light. You say you've got a grid reference?'

CHAPTER 53

Early next morning, when it was still barely light, DCI Connors addressed Lincoln, Orla, Nevin and the rest of her team.

'We believe Ezra Morton is holding Jill prisoner at Hunter's Ridge,' she told them, 'but we need to reconnoitre the site before we take any action. A drone is the safest answer. What's more, with the pressure on our budgets, sending a drone up over the bunker is the *only* answer.'

'A drone?' Nevin scrunched his face up in disbelief. 'How's a drone going to help? Have we even used them before?'

'Of course we have,' she retorted, indignant, 'or I wouldn't be suggesting it. It's new technology, admittedly – new to *us*, at least, this year – but we've got volunteer pilots willing to support us wherever an operation calls for aerial surveillance.'

Lincoln agreed with her. A drone flying quietly over the disused ROC post could send back images of the bunker and its surroundings without alerting anyone inside – unlike a helicopter.

'How soon can we get that organised, ma'am?' he asked.

'Already in hand, Jeff. We should be able to see what the terrain's like, access, egress. Work out a strategy for flushing him out without the Fortune woman getting hurt.'

'Assuming she's there,' Nevin muttered.

'Did you say something, Rick?' Connors cocked her head on one side, the better to catch his words.

'I said, then we'll know if he's there, ma'am.'

She fixed him with a caustic look before quickly moving on. 'Jeff, I think you've done some research on the layout of these bunkers. What can you tell us?'

Two hours later, Lincoln was sitting in a car across the A36 from Lookout Hill, watching images fed back from a drone hovering, almost soundlessly, over Hunter's Ridge. Following his instructions, the drone pilot was checking out the disused ROC post where Lincoln was sure Ezra Morton was keeping Jill prisoner.

The drone climbed over a sloping field of wheat until a grassy paddock, about twenty feet by ten, came into view on the brow of the hill. In the centre of the paddock, a grey stone block stood out: the top of the access shaft to the bunker sunk deep beneath the soil.

Lincoln held his breath as the drone hovered over the top of the shaft and zoomed in on it, but he already knew what it would tell him: he'd got it wrong. No one could have walked through that wheat in the last few days without leaving a trace. No one could have crossed that paddock to the access shaft without treading a visible path through the long grass. The metal plate covering the top of the shaft looked rusted in place, as if it hadn't been lifted for years.

'I'm sorry, ma'am,' he reported to Connors as soon as he got back to Park Street. 'It was a waste of time.'

She shrugged. 'Less of a waste than getting Armed Response up there on the strength of your hunch. And, talking of hunches, any sightings of Matt Trevelyan yet?'

'Not yet.'

'Remind me why you think he's involved.'

He could have told her it was Orla's idea and that he, too, had his doubts, but that would be disloyal. 'His connection with the Fortunes,' he said. 'Morton doesn't have a beef with Jill and Annika but Trevelyan does. Jill made Annika dump him. He's got a grudge against both of them.'

'Trevelyan may have a grudge, Jeff, but where's your proof? Let's concentrate on finding Morton, shall we? He's the one we *know* is a killer.'

'Did you ask for the report on Daniel Swann's death? I've printed it off.' Nevin made it sound like he'd been sent dirty photos.

'Thanks.' Lincoln took it from him, though he wasn't sure what it would tell him that he didn't already know.

As Viv Caddick had said when they'd met at Willow Cottage – with Elinor Morton's body sprawled only a few feet from them – Swann's death had initially been defined as suspicious, even though he was suffering from stage four lung cancer and had evidently fallen down the stairs.

According to the police report, his carer, Mrs Jennifer Judge, had found him lying on the half-landing of his twisting staircase when she arrived at the cottage early on Saturday 15 April, Easter Saturday. He'd been dead for some hours.

The official conclusion was that he'd lost his footing on the stairs in the dark the previous night, colliding with the banister rail as he fell. He'd then bounced back against the opposite wall, banging his head hard enough to fracture his skull. There was no evidence of anyone else being involved.

How could they be sure of that? Swann, weakened by his illness, would have put up little resistance if someone had tried to push him down the stairs. Had Morton killed his father as cold-bloodedly as he'd killed his mother three months later?

What hope for Jill? Assuming she wasn't already dead.

The carer, Mrs Judge, had made the official identification. Next of kin? Unknown. For a man who'd attracted such a following in his lifetime, it was ironic that, in death, Swann was very much alone.

As Lincoln finished reading the report, Orla appeared, polishing off a bowl of salad from the deli around the corner. 'Tough luck with the bunker, boss,' she said. 'It seemed such a logical place for Morton to lie low.'

'That's what I thought, but I was wrong.'

'There must be other bunkers,' Nevin commented. 'They were dotted all over the place once upon a time.'

'Yes, but Daniel Swann bought the one at Hunter's Ridge.' Lincoln crossed to the whiteboard to add another name to it. 'Jennifer Judge. Swann's carer. She was the one who found him.'

'And she could help us how?' Orla dropped her empty salad pot into the bin.

'Let's go and find out.'

Mrs Judge's neat chalet bungalow sat in a hilly residential road on the edge of Warminster. She was watering her front lawn when Lincoln and Orla arrived, but gave them a friendly wave in greeting before turning the tap off and letting the hose drop onto the path.

They sat on rattan chairs in the conservatory, the doors open on a small but immaculate back garden.

'You were a carer for Daniel Swann for how long?' asked Lincoln.

In her fifties, with a bouncy hairstyle and subtle make-up, she seemed eager to talk. 'Six months, give or take,' she said, 'from last October until – well, until he died. Are you here about him or about... the other thing, the woman that was killed at his house?'

'Both,' said Orla. 'Did you ever see this man at the cottage?' She produced the mugshot of Morton, but Jennifer had to go off in search of her glasses before she could look at it. When she returned, she took the photo and stared at it.

'That's his son, isn't it?' she said, handing it back. 'He's the one who did that shooting, isn't he? Even though he's not called Swann, he *is* the son, isn't he? Same features, a bit fuller in the face than Daniel, but I can see the resemblance now. Did he kill the woman too?'

'We're trying to find out more about his relationship with Daniel,' said Lincoln, sidestepping her question. 'Did you ever see him at the cottage?'

'No, but I know he came over from time to time. He worked nights, Daniel said, so he'd drive over in the afternoons, stay for an hour or two. Daniel got in touch with him after he was diagnosed and asked him to visit. Making up for lost time, or trying to. So the woman that was murdered...'

'Ezra would *drive* over?' Orla interrupted. 'So he had his own car?'

'He had Daniel's car, a lovely Jaguar, but it was a bit of an old banger. Sat outside the house in all weathers for ages. Ezra might as well have it, he said.' She took her glasses off and shook her head sadly. 'All this time, there's me thinking he was called Ezra Swann. I saw that photo when you put out your appeal, and I never made the connection. But now I can see the likeness. So that woman...'

'Did you sense there was any tension between Daniel and Ezra?' Lincoln asked.

'No, quite the opposite. Daniel said it put his mind at rest, having someone to carry on his work.'

'His work?'

'All his research into other worlds, outer space, that kind of thing. I'm more of a sceptic myself, but Daniel believed in it. There was a moment in his life, he said, when everything was revealed to him.' She smiled indulgently at the memory. 'You see those people standing on street corners with their boards out, don't you, those evangelists, and if you challenge anything they say, they'll never give you a straight answer, they're so firm in their beliefs. It's *you* that hasn't seen the light, not them. And that's how Daniel was. He'd experienced his revelation, he said, when he'd been let into a secret that he wanted to share with the world. I suppose if you've witnessed something that nobody else has...' She ended with a shrug.

'Was that what Daniel told you? That he'd *witnessed* something?' Lincoln thought of the envelopes of press cuttings in his study at Willow Cottage, the photos and drawings stuck on the wall inside Ezra's wardrobe, spacecraft and aliens from other galaxies, the image – real or faked? – of the non-human pilot, dead at the controls of his craft.

She leant forward to confide in them. 'He told me that someone from another world landed near here back in the nineties, as he knew they would. But it was all covered up. Anyone who saw what happened was silenced. And the authorities were *still* covering it up.' She sat back and said, with a laugh, 'He told me he had proof, hidden away in the cottage, but that's like those relics the pilgrims used to put in churches years ago, the thigh bone of Saint

This or Saint That. Only the poor saint must have had seven legs, the number of thigh bones he had!'

'Did Daniel ever mention Elinor Morton?' asked Orla, unsmiling.

'Is Elinor Ezra's mum? I've been thinking Ezra's mum was Kitty, but she couldn't have been, not if he's forty. Kitty wouldn't have been old enough.'

'Kitty?' Lincoln didn't recognise the name.

'Swann's wife,' Orla put in. 'A lot younger than him. She killed herself.'

'That's right,' Jennifer said. 'All very sad. They'd lost their daughter, Poppy, the year before. Someone slipped her some pills at a pop festival. Kitty blamed herself, Daniel said, couldn't live with the guilt.' She paused to tuck a strand of hair behind her ear. 'All that money and fame, and for what? The poor man lost everything.'

If Swann had money, why hadn't he spent some of it on Willow Cottage?

'Did he leave a will?' Orla asked.

'I suppose so, although he told me he'd given most of his money away. Anything left over was going to some organisation that researches UFOs.'

'And nothing for Ezra?'

She shrugged. 'He didn't say. Maybe Ezra gets the house? I know he had keys to it.'

Lincoln glanced across at Orla. Did any of this help the investigation? Viv Caddick hadn't suspected anyone else of involvement in Swann's death, and she'd seen enough crime scenes to know what to look out for. Morton may have murdered his mother, but he sounded close to his father, a keen disciple. He was hardly likely to want him dead.

'Did Daniel have many other visitors?' he asked.

Jennifer shook her head. 'If he did, they didn't come when I was there. I don't think he wanted people to see him the way he'd got. He had a whole gallery of photos up in his study. And what a handsome man he was when he was younger! And right up until he lost his daughter, he was still quite a looker. But after she died, he stopped caring, and then he must have lost Kitty. You could see it in the photos, the way he went downhill.'

Lincoln recalled the pictures of Daniel delivering a speech a few years ago, his curly hair long and tangled, his fingernails dirty and in need of a trim. The effect of grief on a man.

'Did he go many places after he was diagnosed?' he asked.

'No. He'd go out in the garden, go down to the river, sit in the sunshine, even when it was cold. But most of the time, he was working at his typewriter, tap tap tap. Thank God I never had to use one of those. But you see, he wouldn't have a computer or even a smart phone. The security services would be able to bug him, he said, film him in secret, send images to the government, MI5, the CIA, whatever. I'm not saying he was paranoid, but…' She shook her head sadly.

'What was he writing?' asked Orla.

'Oh, he didn't say, and I didn't like to ask, but I think it was his life story. He finished it around Christmas time, and then it disappeared. He must have sent it to a publisher or a printer or something. I never saw it again.'

Lincoln and Orla drove back to Park Street. 'Just to be sure,' he said, 'let's find out where Morton was the night his father died. If he was working, there should be a record of where he was and when.'

'Swann slipped on the stairs. No one else was involved.'

'Yes, I know, I know. But for my own peace of mind…'

They drove for quite a while without speaking, until a car passed them, an elderly souped-up Mini, belching fumes, and he recalled what Jennifer had told them. 'Swann's car, what happened to it? Morton needed a lift to the cottage the night before he shot his mother, so what did he do with the Jaguar?'

'And that's relevant how?'

'God knows. It's a loose end, that's all.'

'We need more loose ends?' She turned her head to watch the Wiltshire countryside go by. 'That incident at Boscombe Down. What's this proof that Swann said he had?'

'No idea. I can't see how he'd have got hold of it, anyway. He never worked at Boscombe Down. That incident in 1994 was most likely an experimental spy plane that crashed during testing. It was hushed up because the MoD and the Americans didn't want the Russians to find out about it.'

'Okay, boss, so now what?'

'Let's get back, see if there've been any developments.'

CHAPTER 54

Later that afternoon, Graham Dilke took a call from Dennis Breeze.

'Can you meet me somewhere, Gray? I've gotta talk to someone – someone who isn't the boss.'

When Dilke arrived at the Full Moon, Breeze looked as if he'd been sitting there all day, occupying a corner table with a pint glass in front of him and several empties besides.

'I'm not supposed to talk to you,' Dilke told him, shunting some of the empty glasses out of the way to make room for his own half pint of lemonade.

'Cuh, some drinking buddy *you* are!'

'I've got to be back at work in half an hour. I can't sit here all afternoon like you can.'

Breeze drained his glass, wiped his mouth with the back of his hand and told Dilke what had happened after his cousin's wedding. 'I've been set up, Gray,' he said when he'd finished his account. 'I know I have. She's set me up. Tracey.'

'How? If she really wanted to set you up, she wouldn't have waited so long before going to the police, would she? She'd have made sure there was proper evidence.' He watched Breeze's face, thinking how unwell he looked, his eyes puffy and bloodshot, his hair a mess, his skin grey.

Breeze leant towards him and dropped his voice. 'I keep getting these flashbacks. I can see Tracey's face, but then there's someone else as well. Another woman.' He put his head in his hands. 'If only I could remember! It's all such a muddle, Gray. My mind's in a mess.'

'Maybe if you laid off the drink a bit...'

'Christ, don't *you* start!' He picked up his pint glass and banged it down again on the table top. 'You're as bad as the boss.'

Dilke picked up his lemonade and sipped it, trying to imagine Breeze years ago. He and Tracey were probably married by the time he was Dilke's age. Married and divorced. Had neither of them moved on in all the years since?

'Was there anyone else there?' he asked. 'You said the CCTV wasn't working, but there could've been other guests hanging around who might have seen what happened. Where was Tracey's toy boy when all this was going on?'

'I don't bloody know! Nothing was *going on*, and if it was, I wasn't there. Don't *you* believe me either?'

Dilke sighed. 'Didn't our colleagues at Devizes question anyone?'

'No idea. They weren't gonna work their way through the guest list, were they?'

'No, but they'd be able to find out who else was staying on the same floor as Tracey that night, ask them if they heard anything.'

'There was nothing to hear. I keep telling you.'

'Someone might've heard you and Tracey arguing, and then heard you going away again. But that's for Devizes to follow up.' Dilke glanced at his watch. 'I've got to get back.' He quickly finished his lemonade. 'Take care of yourself.'

As he hurried back to Barley Lane, he knew he'd let Breeze down. He hadn't listened to him properly, had been sceptical from the start. And now he'd left him to his own devices without offering even a sliver of moral support.

As he turned into Spicer Street, he saw two men ahead of him, scruffily dressed, one in his thirties with a ponytail and lots of tattoos, the other in his twenties, shaven-headed and even more heavily tattooed. They stood, heads close together, backs turned, and Dilke guessed a drug deal was going down. He took his phone out, ready to call for backup, but then the man with the ponytail spotted him.

While his companion melted into one of the many alleyways along Spicer Street, Ponytail sprinted away. Or tried to. Seconds later, he tripped on a loose paving slab and went flying.

Dilke caught up with him and stood over him, trapping him against the wall. His face was familiar. That mugshot Lincoln had sent over yesterday, of the man thought to be manipulating Ezra Morton in his pursuit of Jill Fortune.

'Matthew Trevelyan?'

Next thing he knew, Dilke was sprawled on the ground and Trevelyan was haring off into the distance.

CHAPTER 55

Lincoln and Orla had been back at Park Street an hour or so when Dilke phoned to report his run-in with Matt Trevelyan.

'Some sort of drug deal was going down in Spicer Street,' he told Lincoln. 'I went after him, but he floored me and ran off.'

'Assaulting a police officer? That's grounds for an arrest warrant. You okay?'

'A bit bruised but nothing broken.'

When Lincoln passed the news on to Orla, she was jubilant.

'We've got an excuse to get him in here, boss. Then we can find out what he knows about Morton.'

Lincoln's mobile rang – Pam Smyth. He drifted back to his own desk to take her call.

'I went to see Roz Berrow, Annika's housemate,' she said, 'but she hasn't noticed anyone hanging around, no funny phone calls. I showed her the mugshots of Morton and Trevelyan, but she didn't recognise either of them.'

'Thanks for checking anyway.'

'And I picked up Ramsay's camera. He'd actually managed to photograph the vandals. In a couple of shots, you can see their faces. One's a lad, sixteen, seventeen, possibly Asian. The other's a girl the same age. I've sent you the photos.'

'Thanks. Good work.' He didn't like to tell her that the vandalism at Keiller's Yard wouldn't be investigated further, irrelevant as it was to Keiller's death.

He found the photos in his inbox and gave them only a cursory glance. The smallholding's security lights had illuminated two teenagers: one, a youth with thick, dark hair and glasses; the other, a young girl, her heart-shaped face shadowed by her hood, her mouth open in a delighted laugh as the boy took aim with an air rifle.

He consulted the whiteboard, hoping it had come up with a few answers while his back was turned, but he was disappointed.

'So, let's recap,' he said to Orla. 'What did we learn from Jennifer Judge?'

'We found out that Swann had given most of his money away and had given his old Jaguar to Morton to drive. His wife and daughter are both dead. He was writing a book. He didn't have any visitors apart from Morton.

He may have left the cottage to him. And he was a lonely old saddo when he died.'

'What about his songs?'

Arms folded, visibly bored with this game, Orla pouted. 'What about them?'

'He was living off the royalties. Who benefits from them now he's dead?'

'His estate, I suppose.'

'His music's pretty good, actually. I downloaded a few tracks.' Lincoln had preferred the earlier, sad songs to the later, catchier ones. Plaintive, yearning, informed by the influences of classical music as well as classic blues, the songs he'd liked best had an almost feminine sensibility, clashing nicely with Swann's husky, masculine voice.

'I didn't see a guitar or a keyboard at the cottage,' said Orla. 'Did you, boss? He was a musician, a songwriter. What musician doesn't have an instrument or two lying around? Even if it's only propped against the wardrobe gathering dust.'

'Maybe he gave up on music when he gave up on himself. It must be hard to stay in touch with what's going on these days, especially if you haven't got a computer.'

'I didn't even see a CD player.'

'Or a record player.' Lincoln thought of Jill's vinyl collection filling shelves on three walls of her dining room, *Dan's Swannsong 1974* still sitting on her turntable.

'Gets us no nearer finding Jill and Morton.'

Lincoln pushed himself away from the whiteboard. 'I was so sure about the old ROC post at Hunter's Ridge.'

She grinned sarcastically 'Maybe Swann bought more than one bunker.' She unfolded her arms, went briskly back to her desk. 'You think he really was writing his life story?'

'More likely some polemic about saving the planet.'

'Like I said, a sad and lonely old sod.' She nodded at the clock. 'I'm off, if that's okay. See you in the morning.'

Alone in his corner of the incident room, Lincoln felt the case of Jill's disappearance running away from him, out of reach. If Trevelyan was ultimately responsible for Morton's actions, what had prompted him to have Jill kidnapped that day? Annika had finished with him over six months ago, so what made him take his revenge last Monday?

And why had Morton shot Elinor the day before? Was Trevelyan behind that murder too? Was it his way of testing how far Morton would obey him?

Weariness weighed him down. He couldn't face an evening with Breeze or, worse, an evening clearing up after him.

He drove to Trish's house. She wouldn't be expecting him, but even if she turned him away, he'd have seen her, would have made the effort to go to the house instead of talking himself out of it.

The lights were on in the hall and the front room. He rang the doorbell.

'I've been waiting for you to call me,' she said, leading the way down the hall to the kitchen.

'It's been a long day.'

'That bunker I told you about – any good?'

'Afraid not.' Taking his jacket off and slipping it over the back of the chair, he slumped down at the kitchen table. 'No one's been there for a while.'

'Sorry. Wild goose chase.'

'More like a gentle drone flight.'

She peered at him, begging for elucidation, but when he didn't offer any, she sat down opposite him. 'I'm cooking supper. You want to stay? There's more than enough.'

'Haven't got much appetite. I couldn't face going home and finding Breeze there, surrounded by beer cans.'

'So you're not here because you craved my company, then?'

'I didn't put that very well, did I?'

A quick, forgiving smile. 'I thought you were getting rid of your house guest from hell.' She stood up again, darting across to the hob to check the pasta.

'I'll give him an ultimatum.' He sounded firmer than he felt. He hadn't the stamina for an argument with Breeze. 'How's Kate?'

'Oh, you know...' She shrugged. 'She's a teenager. Up one minute, down the next.'

He stared at his hands on the table top. 'Why don't we move in together?'

Had he asked her out loud, or only thought of asking her? When he looked up and saw her startled face, he knew he'd said it loud and clear. She turned back to the hob, lifted up a few shells of pasta with a draining spoon to test if they were cooked, switched the burner off, carried the pan across to the sink and tipped the pasta into a colander.

He watched her, mesmerised. Maybe he *hadn't* said it out loud. Maybe he'd imagined the stunned look on her face. When she'd given the colander a hearty shake, she transferred the pasta to a bowl, sprinkled some grated cheese on top and slid it into the oven. She made it look so easy. Only then did she turn round and give him her answer.

'Jeff, you know why we can't.'

'Do I?'

'We'd only argue. We get on okay when we don't see much of each other, but it wouldn't work if we were living under the same roof.'

'It worked when I stayed here with you last year. It worked when you stayed with me after you came back from Essex.'

'After I *escaped* from Essex, you mean.' She'd taken a temporary job at a library on the coast, working with an assistant who wasn't all he was cracked up to be. She was lucky to get away with nothing more than a broken wrist. 'I can't uproot Kate again. She hated staying with Suki and Mike while I was in Essex. She's got her exams next year and I can't risk screwing things up for her.'

Well, at least he'd asked. She needed to put her daughter's happiness before her own or his. He understood that, but it still hurt. And they *did* get on when they were under the same roof. Maybe she found it easier to pretend they didn't.

Or was he missing something? How long had Cathy been seeing Andy Nightingale before Lincoln realised their marriage was doomed? Was there someone else in Trish's life now? What about that bloke – Steve something – she was talking to at the library when he went to ask her about Kate missing her lesson?

'Staying for pasta?' She held an empty bowl up, ready to put it warming if he accepted her invitation.

He shoved his chair back, crossed the kitchen and hugged her. She tensed in his embrace and then relaxed, putting her arms around him, the bowl still in her hand.

'I'm sorry,' he whispered into her hair. 'This case is just so… I'm out of my depth at Park Street, I know I am, like they're all waiting for me to fail.'

Gently, she pushed him away. 'Don't be daft. You're there because they need you.'

He took the bowl out of her hand and put it down on the counter. 'Thanks for the offer, but I do need to get home and sort Breezy out. Don't give up on me, Trish. Don't give up on us.' He grabbed his jacket. 'I'll call you tomorrow, let you know if there's any news. And thanks for finding out stuff about Daniel Swann.'

'I listened to some of his music,' she said, following him out into the hall. 'I like the upbeat ones the best. The bluesy ones are too sad.'

CHAPTER 56

Maureen Turner rang her daughter's number for the tenth time since getting back from Southampton at lunchtime and finding the flat empty. Her call went to voicemail every time, so she'd given up bothering to leave Kelly a message. Most likely, she'd be round a mate's house or hanging out at the Half Moon Centre.

Maureen dreaded getting a phone call telling her Kelly had been caught shoplifting. She'd done a bit of that herself when she was at school, but in those days, who didn't? Little chance of getting caught then, but now, what with CCTV and all that…

Kelly's room was in a mess as usual. Funny, Maureen had been Little Miss Tidy Drawers when she was the same age. Prissy Pants, her brother had called her. Better than living in a pigsty like he did – and like Kelly was doing now.

Something was chiming, a light flickering. For God's sake! She'd left her tablet switched on, chucked down there on the dressing table in among spilt make-up and sticky patches of slopped Coke. She'd begged Maureen to buy her that tablet, and now she was treating it like…

A WhatsApp message was waiting to be read. She tapped the icon. Message from Dev Driver, sent this morning. *Where the fuck r u? Shitting myself here. Pick up!!!!!!!*

She felt the first shivers of real unease. Joined at the hip, those two, even though Kelly had been suspended from Barbury Fields and then stopped going to school altogether, whereas Dev was staying on to finish his A-Levels. Kelly could do so much more with her life if she put her mind to it.

Maureen rang him. 'Dev, it's Mrs Turner, Kelly's mum. Is she with you?'

'I saw her yesterday after school.'

'She was all right, was she?'

'Think so. Why?'

'She's not come home, that's all. Dev, have you got any idea where…'

'Sorry, Mrs Turner, I don't know,' and he hung up.

If Dev didn't know where Kelly was, nobody did. She picked the tablet up and, noting the low battery warning, turned it off.

Once more, she rang her daughter's number.

CHAPTER 57

Lincoln couldn't quite dispel his suspicions about Daniel Swann's death and needed to confirm, for his own peace of mind, that Ezra Morton wasn't responsible. On Wednesday morning, he and Orla drove over to Morton's workplace, Barbury Cleaning Company.

If Jamie Keiller's place of work had looked scruffy and rundown, Barbury Cleaning's premises were even worse. Approached across a potholed car park, the entrance was flanked by smeary plate glass windows.

'Dirty glass, sticky handles. Not a good ad for a cleaning company.' Orla wiped her hand on her jeans after she'd opened the door and stepped inside.

The personnel department was a young woman who didn't look as if she'd been out of school more than a few weeks.

'We need to know if Ezra Morton was working over Easter,' said Lincoln. 'Good Friday was April fourteenth,' he added when it was clear she had no idea when Easter had fallen this year.

With a heavy sigh, she hauled out a ring binder from under her desk and, licking her thumb every few pages, turned the sheets over until she found the rota for the Easter weekend. To answer his question, she turned the binder round and let him see for himself: Morton was on cleaning duty at the hospital from the Friday to the Sunday, with Monday off – a shift that included the crucial hours between Swann's estimated time of death and the discovery of his body.

'Any chance he could falsify these records?' Orla asked.

The girl shook her head. 'These are the hours he was scheduled to work. We'd have had complaints if he hadn't turned up. It would've been marked on the sheet so we'd know to dock his pay.' She let Orla photograph the worksheets before taking the ring binder back. 'I was wondering when you'd come round, after I saw what Ezra's supposed to have done.'

Orla slipped her mobile into her pocket. 'Are you surprised by any of this?'

'He's a bit weird, but I'd never have thought he'd do anything like what you're saying he's done. Didn't think he had it in him. Mind, he never says much, so how would I know?'

'Was he close to anyone here?'

'You're joking!' Her laugh was cold. 'Most of the time, he acted like he was from another planet.'

'If those records are accurate,' Lincoln said as they headed back to the station, 'there's no way he could have killed Swann.'

Orla tutted, exasperated. 'You really think Swann's death *wasn't* an accident? Come on, boss, Viv Caddick was happy to call it an accident, so why are you going looking for a murder?'

'I'm not. I simply wanted to rule out the possibility. And now I have done.'

They entered the incident room to see Rick Nevin putting the phone down and looking worried, the most animated Lincoln had seen him.

'A young girl's gone missing,' he announced, sweat glistening in his eyebrows. 'Her mother's just reported it. Seventeen-year-old. Mate of hers was with her at the Poacher's Pocket Monday evening, they got separated and no one's seen her since.'

Orla frowned. 'Why's her mother only just got round to reporting it? She's been missing over twenty-four hours.'

'She's been away, working. Only got back yesterday. Thought the kid would turn up.'

Lincoln studied the details of the missing girl. Kelly Turner, seventeen, living with her mother, Maureen Turner, at Farmfield Close on Barbury Down.

'I'll get my team to follow it up,' he said, 'at least to start with. Barley Lane's closer to the Down anyway. Have we got a picture of the girl?'

'Her mother's sending one over.'

'Get it circulated as soon as you get it.' As if they needed anything else to be dealing with right now.

And then the phone on Orla's desk rang and she picked it up.

'When? Where?' She kept her eyes on Lincoln's face as she listened, her frown deepening. 'And the pathologist's been called? Okay. We'll be there ASAP.' She put the phone down. 'A body's been found in an empty house in Gas Lane. Young girl. Looks as if she OD'd.'

'Kelly Turner?'

'Could be.'

'I'll call my DS.'

She looked put out. 'I'm your DS.'

He hadn't got time for this. 'My DS at Barley Lane, Mike Woods. We've got enough to deal with here right now, Orla. Woody can report back and we'll take it from there.' He headed for his desk before either Orla or Nevin could object to his proposal.

While he waited for the pathologist to finish his initial examination, Woody stood outside, in the cramped yard of the derelict house in Gas Lane. The building had evidently become a refuge for kids taking drugs. One of those kids had anonymously raised the alarm after finding the girl's body in what remained of the downstairs bathroom, head against the bath panel, feet against the lavatory pedestal. A horrible place to die.

Ken Burges called him back inside. 'A classic picture,' he said wearily. 'Accidental heroin overdose, self-administered.' He indicated the ligature pulled tight around the girl's left arm, needle jammed into the crook of her elbow. 'No track marks to suggest she was a regular user, so this was probably her first time with the needle and she misjudged it. I'd say she's been here at least twenty-four hours but more like thirty-six.' Job done, he got ready to leave. 'You said a girl had gone missing? Could this be her?'

'Reckon it is, yes. Her mum described a bird tattoo on her ankle and, well...' Woody nodded at the inky image of an unidentifiable bird, wings outstretched, just visible in the mottled skin of the girl's lower leg. 'Someone's got to break the news to her.'

Ken grimaced. 'Rather you than me.'

When he arrived at Farmfield Close fifteen minutes later, Woody was surprised to see a redheaded reporter outside the block of flats where the Turners lived. She had a photographer with her. How had she found out so quickly that Kelly Turner was missing?

He pushed his way past the two women and took the uncarpeted stairs, two at a time, to reach the door of number fourteen. He knocked, standing back with his ID held up to the spy hole. After much unlocking and unbolting, the door opened and Maureen Turner stood there.

She must have read the concern in his face because, even before he'd said a word, she'd slumped against the wall, sobbing.

CHAPTER 58

By Wednesday morning Jill's ankle felt as if it was on fire, the skin hot to the touch. The antiseptic had done nothing to reduce the inflammation, and she was sure the wound must be infected.

All the time she'd been underground here, she'd tried to keep her mind occupied by rehearsing piano music in her head, progressing through the current examination pieces from the simplest grade to the most challenging. When she'd done that, she hummed what she could of Bach's Goldberg variations, flexing her arms and her hands in rhythm, a surprisingly efficient way to warm herself up.

Then she'd worked her way through her lists of pupils, this year, last year, the year before, but when she could remember a face but not a name, or a first name but not a surname, she became irritable with frustration, berating herself for her forgetfulness – just as her father had done in the months before his dementia was eventually diagnosed. His memory had always been so good, he could reel off whole classes of battleship or steam engine, cricketers in Test match teams, Olympic gold medallists, Derby winners and their jockeys.

She'd always dreaded reaching her eighties and losing her mind as he had done. Now, it looked as if she'd be lucky to reach sixty-nine. And all because of bloody Daniel Swann!

She'd had nothing to do with Dan after that foolish encounter at the Full Moon in 1983, when he'd screwed her and sent her packing as if he'd picked her up off the street or she'd been one of his groupies.

Jerry had never suspected anything, even when she'd told him, a few months later, that she was pregnant. He was thrilled – more thrilled than she was, really – and made a fuss of her right up until Annika was born. How soon after that had he fallen in love with someone else? Had he ever suspected that Annika wasn't his?

Jill took no interest in Dan's music, his escapades with the band, his rise and spectacular fall. Anything she found out, she learnt from Chas, who followed his schoolfriend's activities with a kind of amused interest, passing on a few snippets even though she didn't want to hear them.

And then Dan had called her as she was finishing her teaching for the day.

August 1999: Dan phones, telling her he's in town and wants to meet her for dinner at his hotel.

'Dinner? Where? If you're staying in some seedy pub again...'

'The Black Swan. A proper hotel this time, Jilly.'

She's heard from Chas that Dan is living off the royalties from songs he wrote in the seventies. If he can afford the Black Swan, he must really be doing okay.

He looks healthier than the last time they met, though something's missing, that spark of mischief he used to have, that energy. *We're both older,* she tells herself. *He's probably thinking the same about me.*

She can't quite relax at the table, as if she's dining with a work colleague, having to be on her best behaviour, no shared memories, no intimacy. All very civilised, until Dan berates the waiter for the poor choice of vegetarian meals and insists his complaint is relayed to the chef.

'It's because I care about the planet,' he tells Jill. 'This isn't the only galaxy, the only universe – I *know* that for a *fact* – but people need to have their eyes opened about what we're doing to our world.'

When they settle down in the lounge for coffee, he leans close to confide in her that the government is controlling everything, but no one realises it. It's censoring the media, indoctrinating children through the National Curriculum, monitoring people through their electronic devices.

'And this Y2K business,' he continues, 'this so-called threat to all our IT systems. You really think every computer will grind to a halt on the first of January 2000? Do they *really* expect us to believe no computer in existence can cope with the change from 1999 to the year 2000? That's just bullshit. You know what's really going on? They're forcing us to buy new PCs, pay billions to companies in Silicon Valley to fix a fault that doesn't even exist.'

'But Dan, surely they wouldn't...'

'And when they install these new machines, you know what they're *really* doing? The intelligence services are actually, secretly, infiltrating your system, putting spyware into it, getting access to computers they couldn't get at before. Not just office PCs but home PCs too. The CIA's told them to. This country's in America's pocket. We're like the fifty-second state of the USA.'

'Oh, Dan...'

'Then, with the spyware installed, they can harvest all your data. It's Big Brother, *1984*. There'll be no privacy, none at all. They'll know everything about you that there is to know.' He drinks more of his coffee, puts his cup down. 'I'm seriously considering ditching my PC. It's the only way to stop them spying on me. They know I know, you see. They know I've seen through them. That's the gift I was given, way back in 1974. My Damascene moment, the great truth revealed.'

'The great truth of what?' Something he'd experienced during his infamous acid trip in LA, when the doors of perception were opened to him?

'What's really Out There.' He throws his arms open as if to embrace the firmament. 'I was taken up into the heavens and told to wait twenty years and they would come down and show themselves to us, here on Earth. I waited and they came. As good as their word.' He pitches forward again, whispering in her ear. 'But now I have to convince the rest of the world.'

She waits for him to laugh, to tell her he's just kidding, but he doesn't. He's deadly serious. She longs to get away.

After coffee, he orders brandy, and then he calls a cab for her. She's relieved that he hasn't invited her up to his room this time, but a mite disappointed that he doesn't even suggest it. Does he no longer find her attractive?

Dan gives her a brief hug as they part, and they thank each other for a lovely evening.

So many years have passed since they were teenage sweethearts sitting at her piano together, or lying in the warm grass on Lookout Hill. But that's not why she feels so wretched as she travels home in the taxi. The Dan Swann she used to know is gone.

Not once, all evening, did he ask her about her life, her marriage, her daughter, her music. All the time he was talking, he rarely made eye contact. Even when he looked *at* her, he was really looking *through* her.

She's lost him forever. Next time he calls – if there's ever a next time – she'll tell him she's too busy to see him.

Chas comes over to her house the following weekend.

'Heard from Dan lately?' she asks him, trying to sound casual.

'We met for a drink when he was in town last week,' says Chas. 'Christ, he's got some crackpot ideas! He hasn't been the same since he dropped acid with that girl he picked up in Copenhagen.'

'It was LA, wasn't it? And that was years ago.'

'Wherever it was, he hasn't been the same since. Dan and I have been mates since school, and I love him to bits, but he's gone so far round the bend, one of these days he's going to meet himself coming back.'

Now, both Dan and Chas were gone. Too late, Jill had found out that, much as Chas had derided Dan's beliefs all those years ago, it was merely for show. Despite Dan's ridiculous claims, his conspiracy theories, his allegations of government corruption and manipulation, Chas had been slowly, steadily, gathering evidence to help Dan make his case – culminating in *Conspiracy To Deceive*. Chas, her subversive, cynical, civil servant brother, had been one of Dan's most important sources.

Did Ezra know any of this? Jill flexed her foot. The ankle was stiffening, the skin becoming shiny and taut. Did he really believe she was part of some conspiracy of silence?

She winced as pain shot up her leg and into her groin. Would she ever get out of here? She hadn't cried in a long, long time, but pain and fear took her to the brink of breaking down. But then she stopped herself, breathing deeply, telling herself Ezra would see sense and come back for her, take her once more up into daylight.

CHAPTER 59

'I've got Matt Trevelyan's phone records here.' Orla waved a printout over her head. 'And Morton's. You want me to go through them, boss, or will you?'

Lincoln wished, not for the first time, that he was back at Barley Lane, where Graham Dilke would have dived on the phone records as soon as they arrived.

'I'll leave that to you,' he told her. 'We need to see when they were phoning each other and if they were phoning Annika or Jill. You know which numbers to look for.' His phone rang. Woody.

'Kelly Turner,' said Woody grimly, 'the girl from Farmfield Close who went missing. She's the kid found dead in Gas Lane. Accidental overdose, Ken reckons, but obviously he can't confirm it until after the autopsy.'

'Was she an addict?'

'Her mother didn't even know she took drugs. But mums are often the last to find out, aren't they?'

'Any other family?'

'The dad hasn't been around for a long time, but there's an older sister living in Downton. Mrs Turner runs training courses in customer care. She's often away a couple of days and nights at a time.'

'Nothing more we need do, then.'

'No, unless you want me to speak to the sister, see if she knows anything?'

Lincoln wished he could say yes, but with resources under pressure, and no suspicion that anyone else was involved in Kelly's death, he had to say no. 'As long as her mother knows she can come back to us if she's got any questions.'

'Yes, I told her that. Someone from *The Messenger* was outside when I got to the flat.'

'Karen Bolitho? Redhead?'

'That's her. How did she find out so fast? Reckon she must have a contact in the control room.'

Lincoln didn't like to think a call handler was leaking information to a journalist, but how else had Bolitho found out so quickly?

'Thanks, Woody. I'll let the DCI know you've dealt with it.'

A few minutes later, his phone rang. Woody again.

'Pam says she's seen Kelly Turner before, boss. She was one of Keiller's vandals.'

Lincoln stood in front of the whiteboard, staring at the column of photos relating to Keiller's Yard – Ramsay, Adam and Jamie Keiller, and the hooded vandals caught by the CCTV cameras before they damaged them. Thanks to Woody, he now had a name and address for both those youngsters: Devesh Driver, eighteen, from Abbot's Path; and Kelly Turner, seventeen, of Farmfield Close. For Kelly, they also had a place and approximate date of death: 7 Gas Lane, July tenth or eleventh.

'I'm not sure what we're dealing with,' he told DCI Connors after he'd tracked her down by the drinks machine. 'One of the kids who vandalised Ramsay Keiller's smallholding has been found dead.' He told her what little he knew about the girl and waited for her reaction.

Connors retrieved her cup of hot chocolate – it smelt so sickly, Lincoln had to fight the urge to gag – and led him back to her office.

'She's a teenager,' she said. 'Sounds as if she runs wild, has fun harassing an old guy on an isolated property, not much chance of getting caught. She takes risks, she does drugs, she stops out when her mum's away overnight and she overdoses. Sadly, it fits the profile, yes?' She sipped her hot chocolate, made a face, set the cup aside. 'What about the other kid? Got an ID for him yet?'

'Devesh Driver. He and Kelly have been mates for about a year, in the same class at Barbury Fields – when Kelly wasn't excluded.'

'I can't see how this is connected, Jeff. Not another of your straws, is it?'

'Straws, ma'am?'

'To clutch at.' She fixed him with a look that was not unkind but wasn't indulgent either. 'We need results. Interviewing a schoolboy about his mate's accidental overdose isn't going to get us anywhere nearer finding Jill Fortune, is it?'

She was right, he was clutching at straws.

But then, when he got back to his desk, the phone was ringing, and it was Woody.

'I've had Mrs Turner on the phone,' he said. 'Something about Kelly's death doesn't add up.'

'They let you out then?' Woody pulled away from Park Street nick ten minutes later, taking Lincoln to Farmfield Close on the sprawling Barbury Down estate.

'I didn't go into details.' Indeed, Lincoln had grabbed his jacket and phone and hurried out of the incident room, telling Orla only that he had to speak to a witness. Which wasn't strictly true, but he couldn't face explaining and having her, too, denigrating his suspicions about Kelly's death.

Maureen Turner looked about forty, slim and neat in a plain, dark suit. The flat she'd shared with Kelly was simply furnished, few ornaments, even fewer photographs, two big sofas, a large television.

'I went to identify her,' she said, sitting on one of the sofas with her knees clamped together, 'and I looked at her arms. You could see where the needle went in. When she was seven, seven or eight, she fell off the slide at the park, broke her wrist. It mended okay, but it never had the flexibility it had before.'

Lincoln glanced across at Woody, wondering where this was going.

'It was her right wrist she broke,' she went on, 'but it didn't interfere with her school work because she was left-handed anyway. Still, after she broke her wrist, it was always a bit stiff and that hand was always a bit weak.' She looked at Lincoln, looked at Woody. 'You don't know what I'm getting at, do you?'

Then Woody nodded slowly. 'She couldn't have injected into her left arm because her right hand wasn't strong enough. That's what you're saying, isn't it?'

She nodded. 'Someone must've stuck that needle in her arm, yes. If she was going to inject herself...' She broke off to take a deep breath before carrying on. 'If she was going to inject herself, she'd have put the needle in her *right* arm, not her left.'

Lincoln sat forward on the edge of the sofa. 'You told DS Woods that Kelly went around with a boy she knew from school, Devesh Driver.'

'Dev, yes. They've been friends for ages.'

'Might they have taken drugs together?'

Maureen shook her head, adamant. 'Dev's mum and dad are strict. He'd never dare. And I never knew Kelly to take drugs, not after Sarah nearly died. That's her sister. She got in with a rough crowd when she was about Kelly's age. Took Ecstasy at a party, went into cardiac arrest. I've never been so scared in all my life, sitting in that hospital room, praying for her to make it. Kelly never forgot what we went through, how easily these things can go wrong. Sarah's on holiday, in Tunisia. She's coming back as soon as she can get a flight.'

As they took their leave, Maureen caught Lincoln gently by the sleeve. 'Please find out who did this to my little girl. She was no angel, I know that, but she deserves better than this.'

The Drivers lived on Abbot's Path, a more salubrious address than the Turners' flat in Farmfield Close. Their house, modern and detached, was elaborately furnished but comfortable, although Devesh, perched on the edge of the bright red sofa, didn't look at all comfortable. With his parents waiting in the next room, he was chewing his lower lip and repeatedly tapping the arm of his glasses as if he feared they were slipping off.

'How did you find out about Kelly?' Lincoln asked.

'I knew she didn't come home Monday night. Her mum phoned me. And when it said on the news a teenage girl had been found dead...'

'Did Kelly take drugs?'

He shook his head, as adamant as the girl's mother had been. 'She didn't want to end up like her sister nearly did. She could've died, her sister, taking pills without knowing what was in them.'

'When did you see Kelly last?' Woody had his notebook ready.

'Monday, we went to the Poacher's. The Poacher's Pocket. I don't drink. I go there to play pool.'

'Did Kelly drink?'

'Sometimes. She looked eighteen. No one ever stopped her. She bought a Coke when we got there.'

'So she was in the bar while you were playing pool?'

'No, she went out into the beer garden. Said it was too hot inside.'

'What time was this?'

'About six forty-five. Eight o'clock, I went out to tell her I was going home, but she was gone. Normally, she'd have come in to tell me she was leaving.'

Dev didn't look the kind of lad to carry out the acts of vandalism Keiller's Yard had suffered, but evidently he was. In his mind's eye, Lincoln saw one of the photos from Keiller's camera: a hooded youth aiming an air rifle at one of the outbuildings; a hooded girl by his side, laughing while she egged him on.

'Would Kelly have stayed there drinking on her own?' Woody asked. 'Might she have met up with another mate? Your age, you want to have some company when you go to the pub for a drink, don't you?'

'She made friends easily,' he said, 'but there wasn't anyone special.'

'We know about Keiller's Yard,' said Lincoln.

'Wh-what about Keiller's Yard?'

'We know you and Kelly vandalised it a number of times over the last few months.'

'Reckon you did quite a lot of damage,' Woody put in. 'Fence panels having to be replaced, security lights broken, security cameras smashed. Not to mention the effect on Mr Keiller.'

The boy's brown cheeks paled, as if dusted with ash. He shuffled backwards a few inches on the sofa. 'We didn't mean to hurt anybody. It was just a bit of fun. Kelly wanted to shoot at the animals, but I wouldn't let her.' He dipped his head. 'What happened to the old man, that wasn't our fault, honestly.'

'Why him?' Woody asked. 'Why did you keep on at him for so long? You *terrorised* him. Like you said, he was an old man, living on his own. Why did you target him the way you did?'

'It was Kel's idea. Once she got an idea in her head, you couldn't stop her.'

'No one put you up to it?' Lincoln took out the photos Ramsay Keiller had taken of Dev and Kelly, the ones where you could see their faces.

'No.' His denial lacked conviction.

'You did this for a bit of fun?'

'Yeah.' Dev swallowed hard, tapping his glasses back in place. 'Though it stopped being fun after a bit.'

CHAPTER 60

'Kelly Turner couldn't have injected herself.' Lincoln laid the scene photos out on DCI Connors' desk. 'She was left-handed, and her right hand would probably have been too weak to put that ligature on and stick the needle in.'

'And yet, there she is.' Connors pulled the photos towards her, scanned them quickly and then shunted them back towards him. 'Nothing's ever simple with you, is it, Jeff?' She sighed impatiently. 'What do you think happened, then?'

'She was drinking in the pub garden, then went off without telling her mate she was leaving. I think she left with someone who later gave her a fatal dose of heroin and set it up to look like an accidental overdose. Not knowing she was left-handed.' He paused. 'I want a second autopsy.'

'Are you sure that's justified?'

'Can we justify ignoring the possibility that her death is linked to what happened at Keiller's Yard?' He was winging it, but it troubled him that the girl's death had taken place so soon after the death of the man she'd terrorised.

'You're suggesting Keiller's sons had something to do with this?' She tapped the scene photos. 'That it's some sort of revenge killing?' Her tone was dismissive.

'I'm suggesting there are unanswered questions, ma'am. In the light of what we now know, Kelly's death looks more like a murder than an accident. If we don't explore how she was killed, we may never find out who killed her. Or why.'

He stood his ground, waiting for her response.

After a long minute, she made up her mind. 'Okay. But what are you expecting to find?'

He shrugged. 'Rohypnol, GHB, something slipped into her drink. Whoever was with Kelly was able to get her away from the pub, take her to the house in Gas Lane and inject her with heroin. We need that second autopsy as soon as possible.'

He'd been back at his desk for only a few minutes when Connors phoned him.

'The autopsy's arranged for tomorrow morning at nine,' she said. 'You'd better hope they find something more than heroin in her system.'

*

Orla was sitting with her head in her hands, the phone records of Ezra Morton and Matt Trevelyan spread out in front of her.

'No calls between Morton and Trevelyan,' she said. 'How did they keep in touch?'

Lincoln leaned over her desk to see the records for himself. 'You've identified most of these numbers, at least. But no calls to Annika or Jill?'

She shook her head.

'Maybe we've been wrong about Trevelyan being involved,' he said. 'We wouldn't even know about him if Jeremy Fortune hadn't given us his name. There's nothing else that points to him, is there?'

She sighed crossly and gathered up the sheets of phone numbers. 'What did the DCI want to see you about?'

'*I* wanted to see *her*. A second autopsy on the Turner kid. I think someone picked her up at the pub on Monday night and then murdered her, setting it up to look like she overdosed.' He told Orla what Mrs Turner had said about Kelly being left-handed, unlikely to be able to inject herself using her right hand. 'And she'd never shot up before. No evidence of using needles.'

'So we've got yet another murder on our hands?' She shook her head, despairing. 'Are you some kind of murder magnet, boss?'

He wasn't sure how to take that. 'I just don't want to make assumptions, especially when a victim like Kelly Turner is connected to an ongoing case. Her death could be a coincidence, but maybe it isn't.' He held his hand out for the phone records. 'So who *has* Trevelyan been in touch with?'

'A lot of these numbers are already dead – burner phones, probably. Your DC Dilke saw him buying or selling, didn't he? These calls could be setting up drug deals, meets, whatever.'

'And you've rung them all?'

'Quite a few more to go. Morton, on the other hand, doesn't seem to have used his phone more than a few times since he bought it in April. Mostly calls to his workplace, apart from calling his mother that Saturday night when he wanted her to go to Willow Cottage.'

'I'll leave you to it.'

He switched his screen on, listening to Orla making calls as he waited for his laptop to come to life.

'Hello?' She'd got through to another of the numbers Trevelyan had phoned. She kept her gaze on Lincoln's face as she listened. Then she hung up. 'I reached the voicemail of Devesh Driver,' she said with a cold smile. 'What's the betting one of these other numbers Trevelyan called is Kelly Turner's?'

CHAPTER 61

It was late when Lincoln got back to the Old Vicarage. All the lights were on downstairs, Radio Two was blaring in the kitchen and Breeze seemed to be preparing a meal.

'Hope you're hungry, boss,' he said, sawing a doorstep off a white loaf.

Three other doorsteps were already piled up on the breadboard, and slices of cheese and a couple of eggs sat in a bowl Lincoln normally put Tux's food in. Butter was melting in the big frying pan that he rarely used – too much faff – and two plates were warming on the rack.

Breeze was beaming. 'Thought I'd cook us supper.'

Lincoln wasn't *that* hungry, or hadn't been until his nostrils caught the aroma of burning butter. Ten minutes later, he and Breeze were sitting at the table, stuffing themselves with fried cheese sandwiches, not a vegetable in sight.

'How's the case going?' Breeze asked.

'Which one? The vanishing piano teacher? The pop star turned ufologist who fell down the stairs? The staged drug overdose?'

'Sounds like you've got your work cut out.' Breeze dabbed his buttery lips with a square of kitchen towel. 'Cuh, I wish I hadn't got myself suspended!'

'So do I.'

Breeze shook a dollop of HP sauce over his sandwich. 'So, what's the latest?'

'The bloke we thought was behind Jill's kidnapping probably wasn't, but he's been in touch with the kids who've been vandalising Keiller's Yard. One of those kids was found dead this morning.'

'Fuck! And the other one? The other kid?'

'Gone AWOL.'

One of the numbers on the list had indeed belonged to Kelly Turner. After Orla had reached Dev Driver's voicemail – a cocky little message at odds with the solemn young man Lincoln and Woody had interviewed earlier – they'd gone back to the Drivers' house to speak to him again.

'He's not here,' said his father, coming to the door ahead of his short, stout wife. 'He went out after you left.'

'Devesh is upset about his friend,' Mrs Driver chipped in. 'Not a good influence, that girl. A little wild if you ask me, but Devesh is very loyal to his friends.'

Woody had given her his card as they left.

'The kid'll be back,' said Breeze now, carrying his plate to the sink. 'Where's he gonna go?'

Lincoln stifled a belch and picked up his own plate. 'Could be afraid he'll be next.'

'You're thinking it's something to do with Keiller's Yard?'

'I don't believe in coincidences. And yes, I know they happen, but this feels… off.' He put the kettle on, trying not to notice how much washing-up Breeze's cooking had generated. 'You seem very chipper.'

'My car's fixed. I can collect it tomorrow. And it won't cost as much as I thought it would.'

'Won't the insurance cover it?'

'Didn't want to lose my no claims bonus.' Breeze watched as Lincoln made coffee. 'Funny, the way it's turned out.'

'What, you moving in with me?'

A sheepish grin. 'The case, I mean. Us thinking Keiller was the target because of his work for the MoD.'

'It's what the woman from *The Messenger* tried to make us believe, but we always thought it was a bungled robbery – until we found out Jill Fortune was the intended target all along.'

A shrug. 'When I found out about all the stuff he'd protested about…'

'Ramsay Keiller was a campaigner, but you can't work for the MoD and publicly criticise it.'

'Made me wonder if he'd carried on working for the government, kind of undercover, and then they had to get rid of him.'

'You've been reading too many thrillers, Dennis. Spies in Barbury? You think he was a double agent?' Lincoln recalled the theory Breeze had shared with Dilke days ago, that the smallholding, the farm shop, were just a front.

'You've only got to read the newspapers,' Breeze retorted. 'There's all sorts going on we don't know about.'

'Don't believe all you read in the papers, Dennis. Yes, you could be right, but there's no evidence that Ramsay Keiller was still working for the government – or *against* it.'

'You think those kids were put up to it, the vandalising?'

Lincoln nodded. 'They were targeting Keiller's Yard for weeks, months. Kids usually get fed up after a bit and move on, but these two kept at it.'

'You're thinking someone wanted to push Keiller into selling up?'

'Well, when you consider the value of that smallholding, where it is, the last remaining stretch of potential development land that side of Barbury...' And hadn't Adam Keiller said a patient of his had expressed an interest in the property? The man had gone back to Spain when Ramsay wouldn't even consider meeting him to discuss a sale.

'Especially now the airfield's quieter. But, like you said, boss, no evidence of someone putting them up to it.' They stared into their drinks without speaking for a while, then Breezy tried, 'Is it okay if I bring my car back here tomorrow?'

'I was joking about you moving in with me.'

'I know, I know, but just until I sort things out with my landlord.'

'Okay,' said Lincoln, too weary to argue. 'But the sooner you sort yourself out, Dennis, the better.'

CHAPTER 62

Ezra had scarcely reached the foot of the access shaft before Jill was telling him to get some help.

'I need to see a doctor,' she said. 'That cut on my leg has gone septic.'

'You're fine.' He dumped his knapsack of provisions on the floor at the end of the bed. 'I cleaned it up with TCP.'

'That wasn't enough. It's gone bad. I could die if it's not looked at.' It occurred to her that he might really want her to die. Had she been kidding herself all this time, telling herself if he wanted her dead he'd have killed her already?

He snorted. 'Suppose we were in the middle of a nuclear attack? You'd have to put up with it then.'

'If we were really in the middle of a nuclear attack, we'd both have other things to worry about. But right now, my leg is infected and I need antibiotics.'

He lumbered across to the first aid box to fetch the TCP and cotton wool. He took them out carefully, as if he was a medical professional doing everything by the book, unhurried. He brought them across to the bed and reached for her foot. She could tell from the startled look on his face that he knew she was right. That wound needed attention.

'I'll bathe it again,' he said, 'and I'll bandage it up. I know what to do. I work in a hospital.'

'You're a doctor?' She was shocked.

'Not exactly. But I know what to do.'

Once more, she submitted herself to his care. She had no choice. No one else could help her while she was stuck down here.

But as she leant back against the wall, her foot in his lap, his hands diligently winding the crêpe bandage around her ankle, she noticed a glint of metal beside him. He'd put his keys down on the bed while he tended to her. Her hand crept towards them until it was covering them. Surreptitiously, she pulled them under a corner of the blanket.

While he bent his head over her ankle, she eyed the rucksack, his flask poking out of the top. Could she reach it? She leant back a little. Yes, she could.

As he fastened the bandage with some tape, she grabbed hold of the flask, pulled it out of the rucksack and brought it down hard on the back of his head. Flung forward over her ankle, he crashed to the floor.

He lay completely still, but she daren't waste time waiting to see if she'd knocked him out. She searched his keyring for what looked like the right key. Crawling over his prostrate form, she reached the wall where the other end of the chain was padlocked into a big metal ring. Her hands shook as she forced the key into the padlock and turned it. The chain dropped away. If only her other leg wasn't throbbing like an extra heartbeat! Now, where had he put her shoes?

Jill had no idea what she'd do when she got to the top of the access shaft. It was now night time, and the bunker was some distance from the nearest road, across a cornfield, but she had to risk it. Anything to get away!

Cramming her feet into her shoes, she limped across to the ladder. She climbed slowly, hauling herself up, her bad leg dragging. One rung, then the next. Two more rungs, then the next.

'Bitch!' His hand went round her bad ankle, crushing the bones, squeezing the swollen, angry flesh. 'Bitch!'

Ezra hauled on her leg so hard, she couldn't hold on. She fell backwards, snagging her clothes and grazing her arms on the rough sides of the shaft. Catching her at the bottom, he stood her upright, turned her round and hit her hard across the face. She saw stars, dots, flashes of light. Blood flooded her mouth. She was slipping away, trying to hold on but slipping away, down, down, even farther down than she already was.

She reached out to touch his face a split second before she lost consciousness.

CHAPTER 63

Thursday morning brought a lull in the heat, a freshening of the air. Clouds were building up, but as Lincoln arrived at Park Street, he hoped rain wasn't on the way. Wet weather would hamper the search for Jill.

The latest issue of *The Messenger* lay across his keyboard and after he'd hunted down a chair to sit on, he read the front page.

Music teacher Jill Fortune has now been missing for eleven days, but police are no nearer finding her and Ezra Morton, the man suspected of abducting her. In a dramatic development this week, the woman found shot dead at a house near Warminster has been named as Amesbury pensioner Elinor Morton, believed to be Morton's mother. Mrs Fortune, sister of disgraced Ministry of Defence supremo Charles Holland, is sixty-eight.

He chucked the newspaper onto his desk. 'Disgraced Ministry of Defence supremo? What's that all about?'

'Since it's in *The Messenger*,' said Orla, 'they've most likely made it up. You'll notice it's by Karen Bolitho, arch-fantasist. And that's Rick's copy, by the way, boss. I've never bought a single issue of that arse-wipe in my life.'

'No, but you look at it online. We all do.'

'My nan buys it to see who's died that she knows, and then it goes in the cat's litter tray.'

'Do we know anything about Charles Holland?'

Her eyebrows went up. 'Do we need to?' She turned her laptop off. 'I've got to take some personal time, boss. I'll be back this afternoon.' And she was gone before he could say anything.

He headed for the whiteboard, hoping it would tell him something new, but it was as tight-lipped as ever. When he turned round, DCI Connors was standing behind him.

'DCS Youngman isn't too happy about the front page of *The Messenger*,' she said. 'We need to make some progress on finding the Fortune woman. Ezra Morton can't have vanished into thin air.'

'As you know, ma'am, we've got patrols looking out for him. We're confident he's no longer in Greywood Forest, but the Astra hasn't been spotted since Friday.' He indicated the corner of Fir Plantation where the gamekeeper had noticed the car parked near a disused army shelter.

'He can't have driven far from there or the car would've been picked up by a camera at a filling station – unless that bloody Astra's got a bottomless petrol tank. Have we identified any other areas of woodland we *do* have a hope of searching?' Connors stepped closer to the wall map, jabbing at Greywood Forest, sliding her fingertip in various directions as she sought other possible hideouts.

'We could search each area in turn,' he suggested, 'working outwards from the forest, but that'll take a lot more personnel.'

'Better than sitting on our arses waiting for him to show himself, isn't it?' She shook her head at him. 'I expected you to be more proactive than this, Jeff.'

The rebuke stunned him. He could tell her he'd be more proactive if his chair didn't keep disappearing, if he felt he had Rick Nevin's support, if Orla was less prickly, if he had his usual team around him – all of which would sound like petty excuses.

'This case is a tricky one,' he said instead. 'It's impossible to guess what Morton wants out of this, why he's kidnapped Jill, why he shot his mother. He's obsessed with Swann's belief in UFOs and aliens, and we know Jill and Swann were sweethearts when they were at school. But we've no reason to think she was in touch with him before he died.'

'You can worry about Morton's motive *after* you've caught him. Come on, Jeff, I want results. We *need* results.' And she stomped back to her office.

Lincoln stared at the wall map. He'd been wrong about the bunker at Hunter's Ridge, even if he'd been right about Morton having a hideout in Greywood Forest. Swann may have purchased that bunker – Trish had found the newspaper photo to prove it – but flying the drone over it had shown that it hadn't been visited in a long time.

What had Orla said a couple of days ago, a remark he'd dismissed at the time as sarcasm? *Maybe Swann bought more than one bunker.*

Perhaps she'd been closer to the truth that she'd realised.

He picked up the phone and rang Trish, impatient for her to answer. Without even a greeting he asked, 'That newspaper article you found, about Swann buying the Observer Corps post at Hunter's Ridge. Can you remember which estate agent was handling the sale?'

She laughed. 'And a good morning to you, too, Inspector Lincoln. Is it urgent? Because I'm in the middle of…'

'Yes, it's urgent.'

'Give me five minutes and I'll call you back.'

She was as good as her word and, five minutes later, told him, 'Miles and Furlong – and yes, they really were called that.'

'Were?'

'Went out of business in 1997. Sorry.'

Woody rang shortly after. 'I'm off to the hospital,' he said. 'Ken Burges phoned to say he's doing a second PM on Kelly Turner, though the results may take a couple of days.'

'Let me know how it goes. Listen, I need to talk to Keiller's sons, make sure they didn't decide to pay Kelly back for what she did to their dad. Can you spare Graham or Pam for an hour or so?'

Lincoln picked Pam up outside Barley Lane and drove her to the scruffy industrial estate where Barbury Electronics was situated.

'Is Jamie expecting us?' she asked as they waited in the lobby. Since Lincoln had been here with Dilke, a panel had dropped off the front of the reception desk and was now propped against the wall.

'No, it's a surprise visit.'

Shock rather than surprise filled Jamie Keiller's face when he came out to see who'd asked for him. Without a word, he led them into the airless room where he'd spoken to Lincoln and Dilke the previous Friday. Someone's burger breakfast still stained the air, and Pam asked if they could have a window open.

She and Lincoln sat at the table while Jamie banged on the window frame with the flat of his hand. At last the window lurched open, and the sound and smell of traffic rushed in.

When he sat down again, Jamie was confronted by a photo of Kelly Turner – not as a hooded vandal or a murder victim in a squalid empty house, but as a cheekily smiling schoolgirl, the photo that would be used by the media, thanks to her mother.

'Do you recognise her?' Pam asked, her tone genial.

Jamie shook his head as if he wasn't entirely sure. 'Is it someone I know?'

'That's what we're asking *you*.' She slid two more photos out of her folder: Kelly and Dev at Keiller's Yard one night in June. 'Do you recognise this place?'

The sight of his father's smallholding didn't seem to surprise him, or the presence there of the schoolgirl. He began to rock almost imperceptibly in his seat.

'Your dad took those photos,' she went on, 'after the CCTV cameras were vandalised by these youngsters.'

Jamie ran his hand down the back of his head and squeezed the back of his neck, his eyes fixed on the photos. The rocking continued.

'This young girl was found dead yesterday morning,' said Lincoln. 'She'd been murdered.'

Only then did Jamie look up, searching Lincoln's face, then Pam's. 'Kelly's dead?'

Lincoln's pulse raced. They hadn't told him the girl's name.

'I'm afraid she is,' said Pam as if she hadn't noticed Jamie's stumble.

'But she... are you sure?'

'How do you know her?' Lincoln asked.

'She worked for Dad last year. Extra pair of hands harvesting the veg.'

'Do you think your father recognised her when he photographed her vandalising the place?'

'He never said. And he didn't have much to do with the kids he brought in to help. He let them get on with it most of the time.'

'So who told them what to do?' Pam asked.

'Me, on their first day. It wasn't complicated to explain. We're only talking three or four weeks in the summer, four or five kids doing a bit of work for cash.' He stared again at the photos. 'So it was *Kelly* terrorising Dad? I'd never have thought...' He shook his head, bewildered.

'Were you involved with Kelly?' Pam sat back, her hands in her lap, waiting calmly for his response.

'*Involved* with her? No! She was sixteen then, just a kid! It was Adam who...'

Lincoln felt another quickening of his pulse. He waited for Jamie to finish what he'd started to say or to correct himself, but when he didn't continue, Pam asked, very delicately, 'So your brother was involved with Kelly?'

Through the open window came the wheeze and squeal of pneumatic brakes, the gritty air of summer traffic. At last, Jamie said, 'I don't know what happened exactly. Adam came to see Dad one evening last summer – another try at getting him to sell up, probably – and Kelly was there, helping with the picking. Adam said something to her and she got a bit flirty with him. I didn't think anything more about it, but then...' He reached for the photos his father had taken. 'I went over to Adam's house one evening a few weeks later and Kelly was just leaving on her bike. Joanna and the kids were away, so it was obvious what was going on.'

'Did your brother know you'd seen her at his house?' asked Pam. 'Did you say anything to him about it?'

Jamie's gaze was fixed on the photos. 'I didn't want him to know I'd seen her. None of my business.'

Had Jamie been saving it up for later, intimate knowledge with which to shame his older brother should the need arise? Lincoln sensed that the relationship between them, if not toxic, wasn't exactly loving.

'And I may have got it all wrong, of course,' the young man went on. 'For all I knew, she was there to see the guy who did the garden.'

'And who was that?' Pam took the photos as Jamie let them drop from his fingers.

'Guy called Trevelyan, Matt Trevelyan. A friend of Annika Fortune's.'

Lincoln drove Pam back to Barley Lane. 'What d'you think?' he asked her. 'Is he telling the truth?'

'Not sure. Landing his brother in it, though – that seemed like a genuine slip-up.'

'And he didn't need to tell us about Trevelyan.'

'Didn't you dismiss the idea that Trevelyan was behind Jill's kidnapping?'

'Yes,' Lincoln agreed, 'because there was no record that he'd ever phoned Morton. But he'd phoned Kelly and Dev Driver a number of times. Now, did he meet Kelly at Adam's house, or did he know her already? What was their relationship? He's twice her age.'

'She must like older men.'

'We need to talk to Trevelyan.'

'Because you think he was behind the vandalism?'

'Because he could be Kelly's killer.'

CHAPTER 64

As it turned out, Lincoln didn't have to go looking for Matt Trevelyan. As he was driving back to Park Street, he got a call from Woody telling him Trevelyan had been arrested at lunchtime following an altercation outside a kebab shop in Finisterre Street.

'What happened?'

'Couple of kids jumped him as he was queuing for a doner kebab. One of them pulled a knife.'

'Anyone hurt?'

'Trevelyan head-butted one of the kids as a patrol car happened to be passing, the car stopped and the fight was broken up. The kid with the knife got away, but Trevelyan and the other kid were taken into custody.'

'Get Pam to tell you what we found out from talking to Jamie Keiller. I need to make sure Trevelyan isn't released until I've had a word with him.'

Orla was back from wherever she'd had to go earlier and joined him in the interview room. Matt Trevelyan and his brief sat across the table from them. The room was stuffy, the air solid with heat.

Trevelyan's dark hair was tied back in a ponytail, although wisps of it had come adrift since the incident in Finisterre Street and he hadn't had a chance to retie it – or hadn't bothered to. A large gold ring pierced his left earlobe and tattoos darkened his neck and arms. His eyes were bright, the lashes long, and his wide, thin-lipped mouth was cocked in a grin.

'Tell us what happened in Finisterre Street, Matthew.' Orla sat back, inviting him to explain.

'I got mugged for my dinner money. Kids these days, eh?' A sidelong glance at his solicitor, a smart, youngish chap who'd brought the cloying scent of his aftershave into the room.

Orla didn't smile. 'A witness said the youths involved had bought some pills off you not long before they jumped you.'

Trevelyan reared back in his seat, appalled at the suggestion. 'An unreliable witness, then. You find any pills on me? You didn't, did you? So where's your proof? Can I go now?'

'Not yet.' Lincoln took his time opening his folder and finding what he wanted. 'How do you know Kelly Turner?' He scooted the girl's photo across to him.

'Who says I do?'

'Your phone records,' said Orla. 'Lots of calls to and from her mobile since the beginning of May.'

'My phone records?' He looked more earnestly at his brief, who kept his eyes down, studying his immaculately manicured hands folded calmly on his document wallet.

'Why were you phoning Kelly Turner?' Lincoln pushed the photo a little closer to him.

'We're mates, me and Kelly.' He tried for a disarming grin.

Orla scoffed. 'Mates? She's half your age. Or she was.'

The grin disappeared. He shifted in his seat. 'I was sorry to hear what happened to her. She was a nice kid.'

'How did you meet her?'

'Can't remember now. It was a while ago. One of those kids that hangs around, y'know? Wanting you to notice them.'

'And you certainly noticed Kelly, didn't you?' Lincoln took her photo back, looked into the dead girl's face. 'More's the pity.'

'Used to see her around, that's all. Her and that mate of hers, the Indian kid. Driver.'

'Devesh Driver?'

'Is that his name? She always called him Driver. Thought it was a nickname.'

Orla's turn now to pull out a photo, the mugshot of Ezra Morton. 'Do you know this man?'

He peered at the photo, pushed it back to her. 'He's been on the news, yeah? Guy with the gun at the farm shop?'

'The guy who's kidnapped your ex's mother,' she snapped back. 'You were involved with Annika Fortune, weren't you? Until you broke into her mother's house and...'

'I didn't *break in*, I had keys.' Trevelyan stopped short, sniffed, explained. 'Look, I'm a nosey bastard and I wanted to see where Annie used to live, where her mum lives. I've never lived anywhere like that, never actually lived in a proper house, only flats, only rooms, y'know? She's clever, her mum, all these books she's got, and she helps other people write books. And she writes music. I found that out from looking around her house. An interesting woman, I'm telling you. Annie never told me any of that.'

'Ezra Morton.' Orla drummed her fingertips on his mugshot. 'How well do you know him?'

'I don't, not really. Met him at one or two Triple R meetings. You know, the rehab and retraining thing. Didn't take to him. He kept on about how his dad was famous and he had some important message for the world, something he'd been entrusted with, the only human being to know the truth.' He held up his hands as if he too was receiving some sort of divine communication. 'Okay, so I found out his dad *was* famous, but that was *years* ago. Nobody'd know who he was now, but to hear Ezra go on about him...' He let his hands drop again. 'You'd think Ezra was the Son of God!'

'Do you know why he kidnapped Mrs Fortune?' Orla asked.

'No idea' He slumped in his seat, rubbing the thighs of his jeans impatiently. 'Can I go now?'

'You can go when we're done.' Lincoln stared into Trevelyan's eyes until the young man looked away. 'Did Ezra ever mention a hideout, a refuge? Somewhere he could lie low?'

'A hideout?' Trevelyan laughed bitterly. 'He's got a fucking Cold War bunker kitted out for when the bomb drops, hasn't he? His famous dad bought it way back when. Fucking Boy Scout! Always be prepared!'

They had to let Trevelyan walk. He wasn't pressing charges against the youth who'd attacked him, and neither he nor his assailant had any evidence on them that the assault was linked to an earlier drug deal. No evidence, no chance of prosecution. Both of them were back on the streets before the shops shut.

'Did *you* know Jill wrote music?' Orla asked as they made their way back to their desks.

Lincoln shook his head. 'She plays the piano, she's a music lover, and I think she's one of the Plain Janes – I saw a poster – but I don't know that she's composed anything.'

'You think she read Swann's life story, that stupid book his carer was telling us about. *Tap tap tap.*' In an exaggerated fashion, she mimicked Jennifer Judge mimicking Daniel Swann typing.

'Jill and Swann hadn't been in contact for years, had they? Or Annika didn't seem to think so.'

They sat and looked at each other across their desks. 'You believe him, boss?' Orla asked at last. 'That he had nothing to do with Jill's abduction?'

'I didn't expect to, but I do.'

'So where does that leave us?'

He sighed wearily. 'Back where we started. Some good news, though... I spoke to Jamie Keiller this morning. Adam was involved with Kelly.'

'Adam?' Her jaw dropped. 'Then we need to speak to him, don't we?'

From the bottom of its curving, tree-lined drive, Baddesley Grange looked like a medieval manor house. Only after they parked the car and crunched over the gravel to its plate glass entrance doors could Lincoln read the decorative brick plaque above the porch: *A.D.1987.* Not quite as old as all that, then.

He'd phoned ahead so Adam Keiller was expecting them. They were shown into a tastefully bland anteroom and sat, looking out of the window, while they waited for him.

'Everything okay?' Lincoln asked Orla, sensing even more tension about her than usual.

'What?'

'Are you feeling okay?'

'Why, don't I look okay?' She put a hand up to her cheek.

'You look fine, I just wondered if...'

The door swung open and Adam marched in, smartly casual in chinos and polo shirt, a sheaf of papers under one arm. He sat down, the chair emitting a quiet squeal that punctured his show of importance.

'As you can see, I'm ridiculously busy,' he said, dropping the paperwork on the low table in front of him. 'If we can keep this short.'

Orla pulled out the photo of Kelly, the smiley schoolgirl shot. 'Do you recognise this girl?'

He pinched his lower lip between finger and thumb. 'I don't think so... No, wait, was she one of the kids helping Dad out?' He must have sensed complete denial would be unwise.

'She was, yes. Have you seen her since last summer?'

'Have I...' He sat back. 'Er, yes, I think I may have seen her around.'

'And where *around* do you think you might have seen her more recently?'

He wiped sweat from his upper lip, pretending to scratch an itch. 'I don't know, I... Her face is certainly familiar, but... Has she been in the news?'

'Yes,' said Lincoln. 'She was found dead yesterday. Drug overdose.'

Adam frowned. 'Terrible,' he said. 'What a waste. She was a lovely girl. Not that I... er... She looks a lovely girl.'

Out came the photos Ramsay Keiller had taken, but with Dev Driver's face pixellated.

'She was one of the teenagers attacking your father's smallholding.' Orla slapped the photos down on the coffee table, making Adam flinch. 'Kelly Turner. Seventeen.'

He stared into Kelly's laughing face. 'Where did you get these?'

'Your father took them.'

'Did Kelly ever come to your house?' asked Lincoln.

'To my...'

'We believe Kelly visited your house at least once. Do you remember that?'

Adam's face showed him thinking fast, a man dancing on ice without skates. 'I don't recall that.'

'Maybe your wife would remember. We can go and ask her.' Orla reached for the photos, but Adam got to them first and picked them up.

'No, don't do that. Okay, look... Kelly had a bit of a thing about me.' He smiled sheepishly. 'She was a troubled young lady. She kept turning up at the house. I had to tell her to stay away. Which she did.'

'And Matt Trevelyan?' Lincoln was about to show him a photo, but he didn't need to.

'Matt helps out in the garden from time to time. Under my wife's supervision, of course.' His laugh had little warmth in it. 'That was thanks to Annika. She put him in touch with us when she was... helping him. He'd been in prison, but you probably know that, don't you?'

'We do.'

He let the photos drop back onto the coffee table. 'Was Kelly's death... was it an accident? She didn't... she didn't take her own life, did she?'

'Possibly,' said Orla. 'Her death is being treated as suspicious at this stage.'

Lincoln leant forward, elbows on knees. 'Do you know why Kelly and her friend vandalised your father's smallholding?' He saw panic flicker in Adam's eyes.

'I assume for fun. There's not much for kids to do round Barbury in the evenings.'

'Why Keiller's Yard, though, Adam?' Lincoln asked. His face was so close to Adam's, he could smell something cheesy on the man's breath and the sharp citrus scent of whatever he'd used to wash his hands. 'Why carry on vandalising the place for so long? Seems to me it was a campaign of violence deliberately directed against your father. Personal.'

'I don't know what you want me to say.'

'We want you to tell us what you know about these two kids targeting your father's property.'

'I'm sorry. There's nothing more I can say. Now, if that's all, I've got patients to see.' He waved a hand at the stack of papers on the coffee table.

'If we find out you know more about all this than you're telling us now...' Lincoln sat back, preparing to stand up.

'Did you have sex with Kelly Turner?' A rapid-fire question from Orla, who showed no signs of leaving.

It hit its target. Adam went pale.

'Well,' she persisted, 'did you? It's a simple enough question.'

He slumped back in his seat. His patients would have to wait a little longer. He took a big breath in. Let it out. 'Yes,' he admitted. 'Yes. Once or twice.'

'Once? Or twice?' She wasn't going to let it go.

'Twice. And I've regretted it ever since.'

'When was the last time you had sex with her?'

'That's none of your business. I'm sorry I let myself be drawn into it, but Kelly was seventeen, nearly eighteen. Not a child and not a patient. I've done nothing wrong, legally or ethically.'

Lincoln sensed they'd get nothing more out of him. He'd be calling for his solicitor next, claiming harassment.

'We'll leave it there, then, Adam. But if you do think of anything else that might help our investigation into Kelly's death...' He laid his card on top of the pile of patient records. 'Thank you.'

'Why did we stop?' Orla was fuming as they crunched away down the drive to the car.

'We weren't interviewing him under caution. He agreed to talk to us, but I think he'd reached his limit. He's not stupid, Orla. He must've known he'd incriminate himself if he told us much more. But well done! You got him to admit he and Kelly had a relationship.'

'Don't patronise me! I'm not one of your fucking DCs.' And she stomped ahead to the car, her rude show of defiance spoilt by having to wait for him to unlock it.

CHAPTER 65

That evening, Devesh Driver walked around town for a couple of hours, tormenting himself by revisiting places he and Kelly usually hung out. He didn't speak to anyone. It was Kelly who'd impulsively get chatting to strangers, barging into their conversations, admiring their outfits, their hair, their make-up, while he stood off to one side.

He kept looking at his phone as he walked, scrolling through pictures of them together, of places he'd photographed when she'd been with him.

What was the last photo she'd posted? Wherever she went, even if it was only Greggs or Subway, she posted a selfie, usually pulling a stupid face.

Her account on Instagram was still live, her last pictures still there for him to scroll through. There they were, a selfie she took of him and her, waiting at the bar at the Poacher's, ordering Cokes, ten to seven on Monday night.

'Too fucking hot in here, man,' she'd said. 'I'm roasting.'

His last memory of her was her skipping out of the door into the beer garden, twiddling her fingers at him without looking round, her phone jammed into the back pocket of her denim skirt. She'd tagged the Poacher's in her Insta post, and he tapped on the tag, opening a whole screen of recent shots of the pub and its garden, groups of kids his age, randomly snapping each other, euphoric at the end of term.

Including a shot of Kelly, sitting at a table with a Coke can in front of her, and a bottle of beer. And there was someone with her: that creepy prick, Matt Trevelyan.

CHAPTER 66

'Is there someone outside? I can hear noises, Annie. Can't you?'

Annika looked up from the magazine she was pretending to read – she really couldn't concentrate on anything, she was so anxious – and saw Roz opening the front room window and leaning out into the night. She flung the magazine aside and went over to look. Might Matt really be stalking her? She'd dismissed the idea when Inspector Lincoln and Orla had suggested it, but they'd got her worried. For all his charm, Matt Trevelyan was a clever, duplicitous man, outwardly honest but secretly scheming. Supposing he really had set Ezra Morton on her mother? What a disgusting way to pay her back for dumping him! Or was he still angry because Jill had caught him out?

'There *is* someone outside. I can see them.' Roz sounded more thrilled than scared as she strode to the front door and wrenched it open. 'Show yourself! I know you're there!'

The security lights popped on, revealing a wiry young man in jeans and a fawn jacket, blinking like a frightened rabbit.

'What d'ya want, fella?' Roz put her hands on her hips and glowered at him. 'Is this who I think it is, Annie?'

'No, it's not Matt. I don't know who this is.' Annika's heart raced as she imagined a scenario unfolding in front of her: Matt gets a strange man to entice her and Roz out onto the front path, where Matt – or the strange man – shoots them down.

He held his hands up in a gesture of submission. 'I need to speak to Annika,' he said. 'Please.'

Roz wouldn't let him over the threshold. 'You can speak to her from there.' She stood, arms folded, feet apart, seemingly filling the door frame.

'Mrs Fortune has my m-manuscript,' he stammered. 'She was doing the index. She's got the illustrations, too, and I n-need to get them back. It's for an exhibition,' he added, trying to give more weight to his plea. 'At the library.'

'I don't care if the exhibition's at the fucking National Gallery,' said Roz. 'You do know her mum's missing, don't you? What kinda crass bastard puts his book ahead of a woman's *life*?'

The man cringed. 'I'm sorry, but it's something I've been working on for years. Absolutely years.'

Roz shook her head at him. 'We coulda called the cops on you. We thought you were a stalker.'

He looked round desperately. 'I'm not a stalker, I promise you.' He took a wary step forward. 'My name's Steve Quilter, and I'm an historian.'

Quilter drove Annika and Roz to Arundel Terrace.

'But stay in the car,' said Roz when they got there.

After a brief exchange with the officer stationed outside the house, Annika led Roz up to Jill's study. Ranged along a shelf were several piles of typescript, one of which was *Barbury Abbey: an exploration of its mystical origins* by Stephen P Quilter. She flipped through it, noting that Jill had already begun to mark it up, certain words and phrases highlighted in fluorescent pink or green ink for inclusion in the index.

'What's all this?' Roz thumbed through another typescript, also marked up in pink and lime green. 'Who's Moses Thatcher, the farmer bard? And why would anyone want to write a two-hundred-page book about him?'

'Mum reads stuff through for people, local history mostly, and does an index if they want.'

While Annika searched for an empty box file in which to transport Quilter's precious manuscript and drawings, Roz poked around on the other shelves.

'What's in this box?' Taller than Annika, she could easily reach the top shelf that Annika couldn't. She brought down a cardboard box and opened it gleefully. '*Conspiracy To Deceive?*' Glee turned to disgust as she flipped through the typescript. 'Looks like it's all about little green men, and who *really* shot President Kennedy. Huh! Who believes in all that crap these days?'

'You'd be surprised!' Annika glanced across to see what Roz had found. Her heart seemed to skip a beat. The title page bore a name she knew: Daniel Swann.

Her mother had been in touch with Dan? A date was pencilled at the top of the title page: *December 10th 2016*, with a scribbled note beneath it: *Jilly – thanks for offering to read this. Always value your opinion. D xx*

'Grab that box, Roz. We need to take it home.'

CHAPTER 67

'Did you think I'd let you get away?'

Jill opened her eyes – only her left eye, since her right eye was swollen shut – to see Ezra sitting across the bunker from her, drinking from his flask and chomping greedily on an energy bar.

'I can't stay down here much longer, Ezra. And what about my family? They must be worried sick.'

He chuckled, spraying sugar-coated peanut crumbs towards her. 'They won't give a fuck about you. Why aren't they here if they care about you?'

She ached all over, unable to distinguish one pain from another. And now he was piling on emotional pain, too. 'Do you love your mum, Ezra? Think of what Ellie's going through, worrying about you. Why don't you make this right? Let me go, then give yourself up.'

'My mum's not going through anything. Not anymore.' He took a swig of tea, emptying the plastic cup and screwing it back onto the flask. 'My mum's dead.'

'I'm sorry. I didn't know.' She shivered. She'd lost a bargaining chip.

'And she wouldn't have cared what I did, anyway. Stupid woman.'

'You loved your dad, though, didn't you? Would your dad be proud of you, causing all this pain to someone he... To someone he loved?' Saying it aloud, the words sounded strange, but it was true, Dan had loved her. Jill was his *first* love, he'd always said, and he was certainly hers.

'Why were you there?' He stood up, towering over her.

'Where? Why was I where?'

'At his house.'

'Which house?' She was losing the thread, unable to work out what he meant. She had a dim recollection of the house where Dan had lived with his parents, a well-meaning couple bewildered by their ambitious and rebellious son. But they'd liked Jill, with her teacher father, her clever brother of whom Dan spoke so highly.

'The house where he died.'

She caught her breath. 'I never went there.' She wanted him to stop. Memories of Willow Cottage reared up, unbidden, in her head. Those last hours with Dan. Those last moments.

'Yes, you did. I know you did.'

'Ezra, I was helping your dad with his book. You know that. He sent it to me, but there were things in it I had to ask him about. That's why I was there, so I could ask him.'

'But then you stole it. You stole his book so no one would ever know what he'd found out. He knew something that could change the world, but you stole his book so no one could find out the truth.'

She didn't want to talk about Dan's bloody book. A book no one would have published. A book he should never have written. She tried to turn the conversation away from Willow Cottage and his father's last hours.

'What happened to your mum, Ezra? When did you lose her?'

'The day before I came after you.'

'I'm sorry. I didn't realise. You must have been so upset.'

'No, I was glad. One more obstacle removed, one more doubter eliminated. For weeks she'd been trying to turn me against my father. She'd sent me these nasty little letters, telling me how crazy he was, how I needed to get out of his house. She wanted me to go back to live with her. She was evil, my mother. A monster trying to poison my mind with her foulness. How could I carry on my father's work living in that vile place, with her always there, telling me I'm not right in the head? So I killed her.'

Shock sent a shudder through Jill's body. 'You killed her?'

'The day before I rid the world of her, she sent me a letter telling me I wasn't even his son. Making out that Daniel Swann wasn't really my father.'

'But you look so like him,' Jill said, although she wondered how much she'd convinced herself of this because it made her feel safer with him. 'Of course you're his son!'

He looked at her, as if not really seeing her. 'I got her to come to Dad's house so she could see everything for herself – his writings, the photos, all the evidence people had sent him to help him in his quest. But as soon as she walked in, she told me I had no right to be there. She wasn't interested in all he'd achieved. She didn't want to share him with the rest of the world. She *screamed* at me that I wasn't good enough to be his son.'

Jill sat, still as stone. She longed for the oblivion of being drugged by him, something she usually dreaded.

'And once I'd killed her,' he went on, 'I knew I had to kill you next. So the day after, I drove to your house and waited for you.'

A kind of blankness overcame her, as if she was no longer in her body. He'd planned to kill her all along. All her attempts at winning him over, bargaining with him… All in vain.

'But why kill *me*, Ezra? Why?'

'Because I know you were there the day he died. I saw you before you drove away. I found him on the stairs, lying where you'd left him. You thought you'd got away with it, didn't you? Thought you'd silenced him without having to pay the price.'

'Ezra, no, you've got it wrong! Listen...'

He turned away, rummaging in his bag for the syringe. Was this how he'd killed Ellie, shooting her full of drugs that knocked her out forever? It would've been a quiet, painless death. But how could he do that to the woman who'd brought him up?

He held the syringe up to the dim beam of the bulkhead light. In a Pavlovian reflex a taste like marzipan filled her mouth as she recalled all the other times he'd driven the needle into her arm, lowering her into a deep, uneasy sleep.

An idea came to her. Her heart beat faster. She held her breath.

As he grabbed her arm to inject her as usual, Jill rounded on him, grabbed the syringe and jabbed it into his neck. Hand shaking, thumb slipping, she pushed the plunger down before he could tug the needle out again.

For a moment he stared at her, then he roared, tearing the syringe from his neck and hurling it across the bunker. He blinked slowly a few times, before sinking down, unconscious, where he sat.

She shuffled across the bed until she could reach his pockets and search them for his keys. She recognised the padlock key, freed herself, sat back wondering how she could escape before he came round. She found her shoes under his chair and put them on, although her left foot was so swollen, she had to squeeze it into the shoe.

Limping, she crossed to shut the air inlet, then pulled the blankets from the bed. What else could she make use of? What else could she carry up the ladder? A flashlight sat on the shelf, and she grabbed it, slinging the strap round her neck. It banged against her breastbone as she climbed up, every movement sending pain through her neck or her leg, her back or her shoulders. Every rung she climbed, she feared her strength would give out, but somehow, somehow...

Driven as much by willpower as by physical strength, she dragged herself over the rim of the access hatch, tumbling into the grass when her bad leg buckled under her. She lay there for a minute or two, dew soaking through her clothes. But she was out. Out in the fresh night air.

Terrified lest Ezra come after her, she closed the heavy metal hatch cover and slid the bar across to fasten it. Now, even when the sedative wore off and he climbed the ladder after her, he wouldn't be able to get out.

The flashlight illuminated the air vent protruding from the grassy mound on top of the bunker. It looked a bit like a green-painted beehive, with downward-sloping louvres. She took hold of the blankets and draped them over it, trying to anchor them in place by tucking the edges up under the louvres, although she couldn't really see what she was doing and was too weak to fix them properly.

Then, using the flashlight to seek a path ahead of her, she hobbled into the cornfield and made her way slowly, painfully, away.

CHAPTER 68

FRIDAY 14 JULY 2017

Lincoln was still in bed when his mobile rang next morning. He groped for it under his pillow, tried to read the screen with bleary eyes.

'Annika?'

'I think I know where Mum is. There's an underground bunker on the downs at…'

'I know. We've been there. It hasn't been used in years.'

'No, listen! We've found this book Daniel Swann wrote. Mum was reading it through for him. He says he was getting the bunker ready last summer.'

His head felt woolly. He peered at the clock. A minute after six. 'Are you sure he meant last summer?'

'Yes, 2016. He says he paid several visits to Larksdown to make sure it…'

'Larksdown?' He sat up, his head suddenly clear. 'Are you sure?'

She and Roz had been up all night going through *Conspiracy To Deceive*, Annika told him. It was rubbish, laughable, she didn't understand how her mother could work on something as crazy as that, but the bit about buying two underground bunkers jumped out at her.

'He bought one at Hunter's Ridge,' she went on, 'but it was damp, so he only used the one at Larksdown. That's the village where Mum used to live. My grandfather taught at the school there.'

'I'll get onto my boss,' he said. 'I need to let her know what you've found. This is a real breakthrough.'

'You mean you're not going to go there straightaway?' She sounded surprised. Surely she understood the dangers of descending on the bunker unprepared!

'Let me call her now,' he said, 'and we can get things moving.'

As soon as Annika had rung off he phoned Connors, but she wasn't picking up. He tried Orla but had to leave a message. He didn't even bother to try Rick Nevin.

After a quick shower and shave, he manoeuvred his way past Breeze's hastily repaired car – now parked askew on his drive – and drove to Park Street, arriving soon after seven. The incident room was quiet, filled with an eerie, metallic light, as if rain threatened.

He tried Connors' phone again, tried Orla's, but still couldn't reach either of them. So much for being proactive!

Then Connors walked in, and he relayed what Annika had told him and showed her the location of ROC Larksdown.

'A similar set-up to Hunter's Ridge,' he said. 'Can we get a drone up there?'

She frowned at him. 'Look out the window.'

He looked. The strange silvery light had darkened and rain was starting to fall. Heavily.

'It's not a good idea to fly drones in the rain,' Connors told him.

Bugger! He stared out dolefully. 'We've got to do something!'

'Yes, we've got to wait. And then as soon as the rain clears up...'

CHAPTER 69

'He's got to talk to his boss.' Annika chucked her mobile onto the table, fuming.

'Doesn't he realise your mum's life is at stake?' Roz grabbed her car keys. 'Come on! I'm not gonna sit on my butt all day while your precious Inspector Lincoln waits for his boss to give him permission to do his job!'

Roz drove fast towards Larksdown village with Annika navigating. In little more than thirty minutes, they were parked on the steep lane that climbed the down. Heavy rain was falling and the tree tops swayed in the gathering wind.

Annika enlarged the aerial view on her phone. 'The bunker must be up there, on the far side of that cornfield, beyond that stand of trees.' Much as she wanted to try to reach the bunker, she was dreading what they'd find. Her mother dead, perhaps? Or they'd find nothing at all. But Roz was pressing on, despite the rain.

They trudged up through the field of ripening corn towards the stand of trees. It was like swimming to shore against a strong current, that feeling of getting no nearer however hard you struck out for dry land. The rain fell in huge drops, quickly soaking through their clothes.

At last they reached the trees, a few yards from an enclosure out of which rose an incongruous structure like a chimney stack. Annika was about to set off towards it when Roz yelled, 'Over there!' and pointed to their right, where a black car stood, partly hidden in the trees. 'There's something on the ground over there!'

Annika turned towards the car, wading then galloping through the corn when she realised someone was lying beside the car, someone in clothes she recognised.

'Mum!' She rushed to where Jill lay, dropping to her knees beside her. 'Mum?'

Roz stood over them, rain coursing down her face. 'We need to get her to the hospital, Annie. Fast.'

When Lincoln saw DCI Connors striding towards his desk, he guessed, hoped, she'd authorised the use of a drone to fly over ROC Larksdown. But she was bringing even better news.

'Jill Fortune is on her way to Presford General,' she told him. 'She was found in a field somewhere west of Greywood Forest. I don't have any details yet, but she's in reasonable shape, considering what she's been through. We'll keep it quiet to avoid the media piling in, but we'll need to make a statement later this morning. Get over to the hospital ASAP, and take Orla with you.'

Except Orla still hadn't arrived, still wasn't answering her phone. Lincoln drove to Barley Lane and collected Pam before she'd even had time to turn on her laptop. They headed for Presford General.

A doctor explained that Jill was on a drip because she was dehydrated and hadn't eaten properly for days. 'Another hour or more in the cold and rain and she'd have died from hypothermia,' she said. 'But luckily, she was found in time. She's also got a nasty cut on her leg, so we're treating her with antibiotics. From what little she's been able to tell us, she's been injected with some sort of sedative every night, but that shouldn't have any lasting effects. She needs to rest, though.'

'We have to speak to her as soon as possible,' Lincoln said. 'We need to catch this man before he hurts anyone else. Did she tell you how she got away from him?'

The doctor shook her head. 'All her daughter could tell us was that they found her lying by a locked car.'

'Her daughter?' Lincoln looked round to see Annika and a large, sun-tanned woman sitting farther along the corridor.

'That's Roz,' said Pam, and set off towards them.

'We couldn't wait for you,' Roz told Lincoln before he could say anything. 'We had to rescue her. Could've been risky, I guess, a crazy guy with a gun. But we needed to do something.'

'We found her by his car,' Annika said more quietly. 'The black Astra you were looking for. It was locked, so she couldn't get in out of the cold. She'd been there on the ground all night without a coat or anything. She was barely conscious.'

'Could she tell you anything about what happened?' asked Pam.

Annika shook her head. 'She wasn't making any sense. Something about the air.'

'Grateful to get some fresh air at last,' Roz supposed. 'Cooped up underground, she must've felt like she was buried alive.'

Pam sat down beside her. 'How did you know where to look for her?'

'Went through that loony book of Daniel Swann's,' Roz said ruefully. 'Pages spread out on the floor, going through it all night looking for clues. I spotted a drawing of an underground bunker and it kinda made sense to hide Jill somewhere like that.'

'And then he says about kitting out the bunker at Larksdown,' Annika butted in, 'and that's when I phoned you.' She looked up at Lincoln. 'Only you couldn't do anything right away. And *we* could.'

'That must be the manuscript Heather mentioned,' Pam told him as they headed for Jill's room. 'Ramsay's friend. I started to tell you about it, but then the sarge arrived and I didn't get to finish telling you.'

'You should have told me again. I probably thought it was something to do with Ramsay, not Jill.'

'Heather was Jill's friend as much as she was Ramsay's. I think Heather was a little in love with Dan Swann too, when they were at school.'

The doctor would allow them only five minutes, although Lincoln knew that wouldn't be anything like long enough. Jill was sitting up in bed, one leg swathed in a bandage from ankle to knee. The skin around her right eye was swollen and purple, and there were cuts and scratches on her face and streaks of blood on her chin. Her hair was lank and matted, unwashed for nearly two weeks. He supposed she'd be cleaned up after she was rested and rehydrated.

He sat beside her while Pam stood. 'It's good to know you're going to be okay, Jill,' he said. 'Can you tell us what happened?'

'Didn't Ramsay tell you?' Her voice was little more than a hoarse croak. 'He must have seen it all.'

Christ, she didn't know Ramsay was dead! He must have been shot *after* Morton overpowered her outside the farm shop. Lincoln caught Pam's eye and she said, gently, giving nothing away, 'We need to hear it from *you*, Jill. And we need to know where Ezra Morton is now.'

Jill sighed heavily and shut her eyes. 'He must still be in the bunker. I locked the hatch cover behind me. Can I see Annika? Is she there?'

They went back out to the waiting area to tell Annika that her mother was asking for her. 'But she doesn't know about Ramsay,' Lincoln warned her.

Roz hung back, 'I'll leave them alone.'

'Did you get as far as the bunker?' Lincoln asked her as Annika hurried to her mother's bedside.

'No. We were heading for it, but then I saw the car under the trees, a body next to it. Jesus, if we hadn't gone up there when we did…' She left Lincoln to imagine the dire consequences if she and Annika had waited for him and his colleagues to get their act together.

'You did well,' he said. He'd spare her the lecture about taking risks. He was a fine one to talk.

He drove Pam back to Barley Lane, updating Connors on the way.

'Jill somehow managed to escape from the bunker,' he told the DCI. 'Morton must still be down there – she locked him in.'

At least now, with Jill safe in hospital, the armed response team could try to apprehend Morton, even if that meant chucking tear gas down into the bunker to incapacitate him.

'I'll get that organised,' Connors promised, and rang off.

Woody was on the phone when they arrived at Barley Lane but hung up when he saw Lincoln and Pam walk in. 'Our friend Devesh was picked up last night,' he said. 'That was his mum on the phone. His dad's gone off to Park Street to collect him.'

'Picked up? What for?'

'Caught spray painting the garden wall of the Keillers' house.'

'Ramsay's bungalow?' Pam was shocked.

'No,' said Woody. 'Adam Keiller's house.'

'Why there?' Lincoln wondered. 'What's he got against Adam?'

Dilke looked up, interested. 'Did he spray words or just his tag?'

Woody grinned. 'He'd started on a word with a big letter K. Mrs Driver doesn't believe any of it, of course. Her little Devesh can do no wrong.'

'I'd better get over there,' said Lincoln. 'Any results from the second autopsy on Kelly?'

Woody shook his head. 'Ken warned me it could take a few days. I'll let you know when there's any news.'

Mr Driver was sitting in reception at Park Street when Lincoln arrived. 'They won't let me see him,' he said. 'They won't let me see my son.'

'I'll find out what's going on. But first, did you know Devesh and Kelly had been vandalising the buildings at Keiller's Yard?'

'Vandalising? Devesh? No! No!' He shook his head emphatically until he realised Lincoln was telling him the truth. 'It's that girl,' he said angrily. 'She's wild. No wonder…' He stopped himself. 'Her mother should have kept a better eye on her.'

Orla joined him in the interview room, out of breath and looking harassed, as if she'd only just arrived.

Lincoln asked Devesh what he'd been doing at Adam Keiller's house. 'You'd started to spray the front garden wall when you were spotted. A letter K,' he added, glancing at the photo he'd been given. 'Was that a K for Kelly?'

'It was a K for Killer. Kelly's dead because of him. Because of him and Matt Trevelyan.'

Orla leant in. 'Matt Trevelyan? What's Matt Trevelyan got to do with any of this?'

'If they hadn't taken my phone off me, I could've shown you.' He hung his head, his thick, shiny fringe falling forward and casting a shadow over his face.

Lincoln noticed something was different about him. 'You're not wearing your glasses, Devesh. Do you need them?'

'They fell off when I was being put in the police car, and someone trod on them.'

'Got a spare pair?'

He shook his head. 'I'm fine.' More urgently, he said, 'Matt was with Kelly at the pub on Monday night. They were drinking beer together. I know because someone on the next table took a photo, posted it on Instagram, tagged the Poacher's. If I had my phone, I could show you. It was Matt who took her off somewhere.'

'If Matt Trevelyan's to blame, why did you target Mr Keiller's house?'

'Because it all comes down to him, doesn't it? Mr Keiller wanted to scare his dad into selling up and moving out, and he got Matt to tell us what to do.'

'So you were partly right, boss.' Orla pulled her chair out and flopped down, switching on her screen and uncapping her water flask.

'I was?'

'Matt Trevelyan was behind the vandalism, even if he didn't have anything to do with Keiller's shooting. And Adam Keiller was pulling his strings.'

He couldn't be bothered to remind her that *she* was the one who'd thought Trevelyan was behind everything Ezra Morton had done. Instead he said, 'Adam told me last week that one of his patients wanted to buy the smallholding. Some bloke based in Spain. While I was talking to him, I noticed a lot of unpaid bills sitting on the kitchen counter. He may have stood to gain a nice, unofficial commission if he could persuade his dad to sell up.'

She sat back from her screen. 'So Adam asks Matt to find a couple of kids to make his dad's life a misery for a few weeks...'

'Except that one of those kids is Kelly, a girl he's already been involved with...'

'But only once or twice.' Her tone was ironic.

'So what went wrong?' He gazed across at the whiteboard, pleased that they could now update it.

'Maybe her death was nothing to do with any of this. When do we get the results of the second autopsy?'

'They'll go to my sergeant first. My *other* sergeant,' he added quickly, catching her eye before she could take offence. 'Devesh Driver clearly thinks Matt's to blame, acting on Adam's orders. Not sure how we're going to prove that though, even if the tox results show Kelly was sedated before she was shot full of heroin.'

'Matt must've driven her away from the pub. Maybe look for his car, get forensics to go over it?'

He was about to say *Good thinking*, but he stopped himself lest she think he was patronising her again. 'You're right,' he said instead. 'Does the Poacher's Pocket have CCTV?'

CHAPTER 70

What should she be feeling? Relief, regret, remorse? Jill leant back against her pillows and tried to make sense of the last few hours. After she'd bolted the hatch cover on the Larksdown bunker, she'd limped through the cornfield to where Ezra had left the car. To her dismay, it was locked. Miserable, exhausted, she'd collapsed beside it, curling up where she lay, trying to keep warm. She could have gone back to the bunker to retrieve one of the blankets she'd draped over the air vent, but she hadn't the energy.

For hours, she'd lain beside the car, certain she was drifting into death – until a woman started tapping her cheek and shouting at her to wake up, calling her name over and over again, rubbing her arms, her hands, her shoulders.

Blue lights in the distance, paramedics surrounding her. Losing sight of the woman but hearing Annika's voice fading in and out as Jill herself faded in and out.

The woman tapping her cheek had been Roz, she knew now. She must thank her when she could.

Have I killed him? Have I killed Ezra? How long since she'd covered up the air vents and staggered away through the field? Had she killed Dan's only son? How could she do that? He was sick, not evil. Another death on her conscience.

Annika came in, looking pale and drawn. She sat down beside the bed.

'I need to tell you something, Mum,' she said gently. 'It's about Ramsay.'

CHAPTER 71

Lincoln updated the DCI as soon as he and Orla got back to Park Street.

'Adam Keiller was behind the vandalism at his father's smallholding,' he said as she poured herself a tall glass of diet lemonade. 'He got Trevelyan to find a couple of teenagers to terrorise Ramsay into selling up.'

'Except that Ramsay didn't scare that easily.' Connors sipped from her glass. 'You sound very sure. You've got proof?'

'Devesh Driver's made a statement. Trevelyan approached Kelly when he saw her spray painting somewhere in town, and she brought Devesh in on it.'

'What Trevelyan didn't know,' Orla put in, 'was that Adam had been Kelly's lover since last summer.'

Connors grinned. '*O what a tangled web we weave*! And Kelly's death? Know what happened yet?'

'Devesh found some photos on Instagram. Her and Trevelyan having a beer together in the pub garden. We're hoping there's CCTV footage showing them leaving together. Any news on Jill?'

'She'll be fine once she's had a day or two in hospital. But Ezra Morton hasn't been so lucky. When Armed Response got into the bunker, they found him at the foot of the shaft, badly hurt. Looks as if he fell down the ladder trying to get out.'

'No shoot-out, then?' Orla sounded disappointed.

'No, thank God.' Connors set her glass aside. 'The Astra's been brought in. Packed with protein bars, tins of beans, bottled water, packets of noodles – survival foods. Plus a camping stove and a trenching tool.'

Orla rolled her eyes. 'For fuck's sake!'

'The CSIs will check the car over for forensic evidence, see if it can be linked to the two shootings and Jill's abduction. One thing that sounds a bit ominous…' The DCI picked up her glass again and drained it. 'At some point, Morton had covered up the air vents above ground and then shut off the air vents down in the bunker too. Makes me think he was trying to kill himself, and Jill. Thank God she got away from him in time!' She banged her glass down. 'Let's nail Trevelyan for Kelly's murder if we can. I'll bet that was down to Adam Keiller too.'

*

264

The Poacher's Pocket was starting to get busy with workers enjoying a Friday evening drink in the beer garden, a group of lads playing pool, a raucous quiz show on the screen above the bar.

The manager grudgingly let Lincoln and Orla sit in his cluttered office while they skimmed through his CCTV footage of the pub car park on Monday evening. They saw Kelly arrive on foot with Devesh and watched her leave without him forty minutes later, her phone jammed in her back pocket. She was stumbling across the car park, supported by a man with a ponytail: Matt Trevelyan. He helped her into the passenger seat of a pearly grey Ford Fiesta and drove her away.

Lincoln was exhilarated by the way the pieces were slotting together. 'If we can place that Fiesta in Gas Lane later that night…'

'There must be cameras round there. And we've got the car reg now.'

'Let's go over there now, take a look.' They hurried back to their car.

'What, now?'

'The sooner we can get the proof we need to arrest him…'

'Yeah, but I…'

'Is there a problem?' He looked round at her.

'Just… Sorry, boss, I've got to be somewhere.' She checked her watch. 'Like, in a few minutes.'

'We're in the middle of something here, Orla. You can't just duck out when you feel like it.'

They drove in silence until Lincoln pulled over and stopped the car. 'Well, do you have to be somewhere else or not?'

She muttered a hurried thanks, scrambled out of the car and rushed away in the general direction of the town centre.

Woody met him at the end of Gas Lane, at the junction with the main road. Blue and white tape still fluttered outside the house where Kelly's body had been found, but no one was guarding it now.

Flowers and teddy bears had been left on the pavement outside, some plaster lovehearts, plastic doves. A foil balloon, tied to the lamp post, bobbed around on the pavement like a demented pink pigeon.

'No one from Park Street willing to slum it down here, then?' Woody had a wry grin on his face.

'Something like that.'

'Not many cameras around here. I had a look myself on Wednesday.'

'Let's broaden the search, then.'

They walked back to the main road and, separately, tramped up and down, looking for security cameras that might have picked up Trevelyan's

Fiesta on Monday night. However, the only ones they spotted were trained on shop doorways, not on passing traffic.

When they returned to the car, disheartened, an older man in a shell suit and trainers, his laces trailing, was waiting for them. His head was bald, but he'd cultivated an impressive handlebar moustache.

'You police?' He tottered towards them.

They showed him their IDs, asked him how they could help.

'Name's Jim. Live over there.' He pointed to a house on the end of the terrace, diagonally opposite the empty one. 'I've been taking notes.' He produced a dog-eared notebook from his pants pocket. 'Fed up with those kids using that house as a drug den.'

Lincoln held his hand out for the notebook. It was warm from Jim's body heat. He skimmed through the first few pages: dates and times, precisely to the minute; brief descriptions of visitors to the empty house. He'd bestowed nicknames on some of the regulars and, lo and behold, he'd recorded the registration numbers of cars, motorbikes and scooters that had parked outside.

'And photos,' Jim added, pulling an iPhone from his other pants pocket. 'I've been taking photos. It's not just the druggies, y'know. Tarts use it, too. Christ, I've seen some sights!'

CHAPTER 72

Graham Dilke was about to leave Barley Lane that evening when his mobile rang. It was Dennis Breeze.

'What d'you want, Breezy?'

'Wondered if you could do me a favour.'

'I've heard that one before. Usually involves something iffy. And you know you're not supposed to be contacting me, or any of us, while you're suspended.'

'I got this phone call from my niece, Carly. Well, she's my cousin Shirley's girl, so maybe she's some sort of cousin, not my niece exactly but... She's family, okay? Calls me Uncle Den.'

'And?'

'Says she knows what happened at the hotel, only she doesn't want to fall out with her mum, who's siding with Tracey.'

'What am I supposed to do about it?'

'Go and talk to her. Find out what she saw that night.'

'I can't do that! Aren't the Devizes lot...'

'Unofficially, I mean. Please, Gray.'

'I can't go to Devizes. There's too much going on here.'

'Carly's not in Devizes. She lives here in Barbury. Got a pen? I'll give you her number.'

Dilke met Carly that evening at the Full Moon, a poky little pub in one of Barbury's many back streets. He knew from Breeze that she was about twenty-five, but she looked years younger, blonde and petite, doll-like.

They sat at a very small table, Dilke with a half of shandy, Carly with a big glass of red wine and a KitKat.

'Thing is, I can't go to the police,' she told him. 'Mum'd be furious and so would Rod.'

'Rod?'

'My stepdad. My latest stepdad,' she added with a groan. 'It's all a bit complicated. He's going into business with Tracey's partner, Harry, so if I upset Tracey by saying something...' She unwrapped the KitKat, carefully peeling the silver paper open and even more carefully separating each of the four fingers of biscuit. 'Want one?' She pushed the chocolate bar towards him and he helped himself to a finger.

'Okay, Carly, so what happened at the hotel? This is all unofficial, off the record.'

She tucked her hair behind her ears and leant forward over her glass. 'Tracey got off with this guy at the wedding reception. He liked things a bit rough, and her dress got torn. She told Harry she'd caught it on a door handle in the Ladies, but when they got home on the Monday, he saw she'd broken her necklace too, one he'd given her, and she told him Uncle Den did it.'

'How do you know all this?'

'Tracey sent Mum a message on WhatsApp, and I saw it. Mum doesn't know I saw it, though. Like I said, it's complicated. But that's not all of it.'

Dilke gulped down some of his shandy. It tasted like half ginger beer, half pee. 'Go on.'

'He was really drunk, Uncle Den was. I mean, *really* drunk. I went up to my room about midnight, and while I was looking for my key card, I could see him coming along the corridor from the lift, lurching from one wall to the other, like he was on board a ship in a storm.' She popped a finger of KitKat into her mouth. 'He tried his key card, but it didn't work. Of course it wouldn't, the numpty was putting his card in Tracey's door! She comes out, gives him what for and off he goes. A few minutes later, he's back, knocks on her door, and she's yelling at him, telling him to eff off, slams the door in his face again. I went into my room after that. My head was splitting and everything was going round. All I wanted to do was lie down.'

'So you don't actually know what happened?' Dilke was annoyed that he'd been led here on false pretences.

She glared at him. 'I do, *actually,* if you'd only let me finish.'

'Sorry. Go on.' He picked up his glass, smelt the vile smell, put it down again.

'A bit later, I was about to get into bed when I heard this big row going on in the corridor. I looked out and there were these two girls – nothing to do with Mum's wedding, on a hen night or something – and they were fighting. I mean, *really* fighting, claws out, threatening each other with their stilettos.'

She offered him another piece of KitKat, and he took it, if only to get rid of the taste of the shandy.

'And I'm standing there,' she went on, 'keeping well out of it, and who comes lumbering along the corridor like the Incredible Hulk but Uncle Den. Straight into the middle of it.'

Dilke could imagine the scene. Breezy, pissed out of his brain, charging into the fray without a second thought. 'And you saw all that?'

'Through the crack in the door. Yeah, I know, coward or what?' She folded the empty silver paper into a neat triangle and tucked it under her beer mat. 'You know what he did?'

Dilke shook his head dumbly, unable even to guess.

'He charged in, put his arms round one of the girls from behind and pulled her away from the other one. Stood her against the wall and told her to calm down. Of course, she didn't. She turned on him instead, scratched his face, all down his neck. Tried to bite him. Think that's when he knew he was outgunned!' She laughed. 'Poor Uncle Den. Desperately trying to find his room but getting caught up in a cat fight. If he hadn't been so pissed, he'd have kept well out of it, like I did.'

'Any idea who those girls were? What rooms they were in?'

'The one who went for him was called Cilla. They had rooms a couple of doors along from mine, seventeen and eighteen.' She paused and looked anxiously at him. 'What're you going to do? If Mum finds out I was looking through her WhatsApp messages…'

'I'll keep you out of it.' He wasn't sure how, but at least he had enough information to follow it up, or for Devizes to follow it up if he or Lincoln passed the information on.

'Sure?' She sounded conflicted, loyalties divided between her mother and stepfather, and her Uncle Den.

Dilke couldn't offer her any more reassurances. He'd do his best, but he was a mere DC. Who was going to take any notice of anything he said?

CHAPTER 73

SATURDAY 15 JULY 2017

Saturday morning, nearly two weeks since Ezra Morton had shot his mother at Dan Swann's cottage. Had he slept in the house that night, with her body on the scullery floor? How long had he been hiding out there before calling and asking her to drive to Willow Cottage to meet him? What had Elinor done to anger him so much that he'd brutally taken her life as soon as she arrived?

Lincoln stood in front of the whiteboard at Park Street, coffee in hand – a strong Americano he'd bought from the shop around the corner – and tried to make sense of what he'd learnt in the last few hours. Morton's father had written a book, *Conspiracy To Deceive,* and entrusted it to Jill. A book he'd thought would change the world. Did Morton kidnap her simply to get it back? Why not barge his way into her house in Arundel Terrace and force her to hand it over? And what was so important about the bloody book, anyway?

Even if Matt Trevelyan had had nothing to do with Morton's campaign against Jill, he'd be facing murder charges when they tracked him down. The toxicology results had been waiting for Lincoln when he arrived this morning: as he'd suspected, Kelly had been slipped Rohypnol, the so-called date rape drug, in the hours before her death.

On the whiteboard were the photos Devesh Driver had found on Instagram. Kelly and Trevelyan on Monday evening, drinking beer at the Poacher's Pocket – a beer that Trevelyan could easily have spiked so she'd have been unable to put up a fight when he shot her full of heroin.

And there, too, was the photo taken by Gas Lane resident Jim, showing the back view of Kelly and a man with a ponytail. The man had a small rucksack over his shoulder: small, but big enough to carry all he needed to set the scene for the young girl's accidental overdose.

The bastard. What kind of a threat would Kelly have been to him?

Or had she been a threat to Adam Keiller?

Lincoln's mobile rang. Graham Dilke.

'Morning, boss. Have you got five minutes?'

Dilke looked around him curiously as Lincoln led the way through the incident room, which was relatively quiet, only a few officers on duty so far.

'Smart,' he said. 'Newer laptops than ours, nicer desks.'

'But not enough chairs. What's up, Graham?'

Dilke perched himself on Orla's desk. 'I know what happened with Breezy. His cousin's daughter got in touch.'

Lincoln's eyebrows went up. 'With you?'

'With Breezy.'

'And Breezy reached out to you? He's not supposed to contact his colleagues. You know that, don't you?'

'He's staying at your house, isn't he? Is *that* allowed?'

Lincoln sighed. 'Almost certainly not, but… Go on. What did this girl tell you? Has she got a name?'

'Carly. She's his cousin Shirley's daughter. She said that Tracey, Breezy's ex, copped off with someone at the wedding reception but didn't want her partner, Harry, to find out. When Harry saw her dress was torn and her necklace was broken, she told him Breezy had done it.'

'And Harry believed her?'

'Sounds like it. Tracey's friends and Breezy's relatives all closed ranks. Even after Tracey messaged Shirley to tell her what really happened.'

'Good bit of family solidarity there!'

'Harry's going into business with Shirley's new husband, but if he and Tracey split up, he'll probably take his money out and leave Shirley's husband in the shit.'

'So Shirley puts her husband's business interests ahead of her cousin's career, reputation, pension,' Lincoln fumed quietly. 'But Breezy had those scratches on his neck, lipstick on his shirt. That's why he thought he must be guilty, even if he didn't remember anything. How do you explain that?'

'He broke up a couple of girls having a fight in the corridor outside Tracey's room. Carly saw it all. One of them, a girl called Cilla, turned on him. He was so drunk, most of what happened must've been a blur.'

'Why didn't Carly tell the police any of this when he was arrested?'

'Scared to break ranks. Her mum would never forgive her.'

Lincoln groaned. 'Families, eh?' He stood up and went back to the whiteboard. 'You need to speak to our colleagues at Devizes, let them track down this Cilla girl. Even if they can't establish exactly what happened, with everyone too drunk to remember clearly, it undermines Tracey's version of events.'

'I thought maybe you could have a word with Devizes. I'm only a DC and…'

'You can do it, Graham. Give them a ring, tell them what you've told me.'

'But what if they won't listen?'

'Make them listen. You can do it.'

'Okay.' Dilke joined him at the whiteboard. 'The sarge said you'd identified Matt Trevelyan's car.'

'Identified it, yes. Found it, no. But the old boy we talked to yesterday had chapter and verse on Trevelyan's movements the night Kelly died. *Grey Fiesta drove up, 19:41. Ponytail got out with young lady who looked asleep on her feet. Ponytail left, 21:00.* And photos! We couldn't have asked for a better witness.'

Dilke poked a scribbled note on the edge of the board. '*Old Jag.* What's that all about?'

'Daniel Swann gave Morton his Jaguar, a bit of an old banger according to the carer. But he had to get a lift to Willow Cottage the weekend he shot his mother, and after that, of course, he had *her* car. I keep wondering what happened to the Jag.'

'Maybe it wouldn't start, or had a flat tyre so he couldn't drive it. It's probably still parked near his flat.'

Such a simple explanation. Lincoln glared at the whiteboard, angry with himself for not thinking of the most obvious answer. He added three words to the scribbled note: *Check near flat.*

'Any news from the hospital?'

'Jill's recovering,' Lincoln told him. 'Should be out later today or tomorrow. Morton hasn't regained consciousness. More than likely, he never will.'

'He must've thought the end of the world was coming, underground bunker, survival rations, a gun. Where did he get the gun from?'

Lincoln shrugged. 'No idea. Could've been Swann's, picked up when he was abroad. It was a different world in the seventies.'

Dilke still hovered. 'I've been thinking about Melksham. When Barley Lane closes. Or anywhere else but here. I need to move away a bit.'

'Good idea, Graham. Spread your wings before you get settled.' Lincoln thought of Breeze, who'd been at Barley Lane a long time and had never moved far from Barbury. Dilke had his whole career ahead of him, a chance to branch out, see other places.

'Okay, boss, I'll call Devizes, tell them about Breezy. I'll let you know what they say.'

Karen Bolitho ambushed Lincoln when he slipped out for coffee later that morning.

'Any news on Ezra Morton?'

'Still in hospital.' Lincoln kept walking, his eyes on the street ahead, hoping she'd take the hint and leave him alone.

'Hear about Adam Keiller?' She had to jog to keep pace with him.

'What about him?'

'Some kid sprayed graffiti all over the walls of his house.'

'A slight exaggeration.' One big letter on the wall beside his entrance gates. How did Bolitho know about that?

'Doesn't it bother you, Inspector Lincoln, that it was Jill Fortune's *daughter* who rescued her, not the police?'

'It bothers me that you write stories for *The Messenger* that don't bear much resemblance to the truth.' He halted as he thought of something. 'What do you know about Charles Holland? You called him a disgraced Ministry of Defence supremo. What did you mean?'

'I did some research on Jill Fortune. Her brother was Charles Holford Holland. Google him. He was suspected of leaking classified documents a few years back and forced to resign from his post. No one knew if he was working for the Russians or for CND. He could even have been leaking stuff to Ramsay Keiller. That would make sense, wouldn't it? Ramsay wanting answers about those germ warfare tests and Holland being in a position to get them.'

'Not another of your flights of fancy, is it?'

'I'm putting two and two together.'

'That's not journalism, Karen, that's speculation.' He set off again towards the coffee shop.

'Kelly Turner. You had a suspect in custody and then you let him go. Sounds a bit careless.'

How did she know they'd brought Trevelyan in but couldn't hold him? Could *Orla* be the source of these leaks? Surely not! *Nevin*?

Lincoln turned to face her. 'Whoever you're getting this from, they're feeding you garbage.'

'Garbage?' She pushed her dyed red fringe back from her forehead. 'If it's garbage, it's bloody good garbage.'

'Come on, Karen, who's tipping you off?'

'I never betray my sources.'

But she didn't have to. Out of the corner of his eye, Lincoln saw someone sneaking out of the fire exit and looking across towards them. He recognised the tall, thin woman as a member of the call handling team in the control room.

The panic in Bolitho's eyes told him all he needed to know. The women had a pre-arranged rendezvous but the journalist hadn't been able to resist the chance to hassle him for information when she'd spotted him leaving the building.

'You've landed your mate right in it,' he told her. 'She'll probably lose her job over this.' He nodded at Bolitho's informant, wanting her to know he'd spotted her and knew what she'd been up to. He had the satisfaction of seeing her scuttle back indoors.

Orla had arrived by the time he returned with his coffee. 'I dropped by the hospital,' she said. 'Jill's being discharged this afternoon.'

'She's going home?'

'No, to her friend Heather's flat in Fremantle House.'

Jill might want longer to recover before talking to the police, but Lincoln needed to find out what had happened to her since that fateful afternoon when she'd cycled up to Keiller's Yard.

Heather Draycott let them into her flat, clearly unhappy that they were questioning her friend so soon after her release from hospital.

'Can you imagine what she's been through?' she asked as she showed them into a smart but over-decorated living room. 'And she's terribly upset about Ramsay.'

Jill sat sideways on the sofa with her leg up, and didn't even attempt to stand when Lincoln and Orla came in. Her grey hair, freshly washed, reached to her shoulders in an unruly cascade. She was wearing a cheesecloth shirt and flower-print skirt that Annika must have fetched from Arundel Terrace.

'You don't waste any time, do you?' She set aside the *Wiltshire Life* magazine she'd been reading.

'The sooner we talk to you, the better,' said Lincoln.

While Heather made tea and coffee, Jill told them all she could remember.

'I saw this black Astra outside the house as I was leaving that Monday, but I didn't think anything of it. I was talking to Ramsay in the farm shop and this big bloke comes in. It was Ezra Morton, but I didn't realise that at the time. He said he'd trashed my bike and I fell for it. I went outside to see what he'd done and he knocked me out. He took me somewhere near the airfield, I think, to start with. He kept sedating me, moving me somewhere else after a few days, and then into the bunker. I lost all track of time.'

'Do you know *why* he kidnapped you?'

She shook her head, her hair rustling against the sofa cushions. Then she said, 'Well, yes, I do. He'd been phoning me over the last few weeks, pestering me for a book I was working on, by an old friend of mine, Daniel Swann, who also happens to be Ezra's father. I'd been stalling because, quite frankly, it's not a very good book. Dan wasn't well when he was writing it. It's full of some very odd ideas.'

'Is that the book Annika read to find out where the bunker was?' Orla asked.

'Annika's read it?' Jill looked shocked.

'She was looking for clues that could help us find you.'

Jill was quiet for a moment, staring at the cover of the magazine. 'I was so sure Ramsay would have told you what happened. I couldn't understand why you hadn't come after me.' She took a deep breath. 'You know Ezra killed his mother?'

'Yes,' said Orla. 'Did he tell you why?'

'She tried to turn him against Dan. Kept sending him letters, notes, warning him not to stay in the cottage, telling him he wasn't worthy to be his son. He couldn't take any more and something snapped. So he shot her.' Another deep breath. 'But why did he shoot Ramsay? Because he tried to stop Ezra taking me?'

Lincoln nodded. 'He may not have meant to kill him. Most likely, the gun went off accidentally when Ezra grabbed you and Ramsay was in the way.'

Sadness filled her eyes. 'Ezra believed Dan had found the secret of the universe. *Dan* believed he'd found the secret of the universe. All because of some stupid plane crash at Boscombe Down years ago. He claimed to have proof that it was an alien spaceship.'

'Proof?' Orla leaned closer. 'What sort of proof?'

'I have no idea. Whatever it was, it seemed to change his whole outlook on the world. He couldn't have seen this strange craft for himself, so someone must have sent him something. He had such a following. People were always sending him photos, stories, their own memories of weird things they'd experienced, all to put into his famous book.' She leant her head back, shut her eyes for a moment, opened them again. 'Is Ezra going to pull through?'

When Lincoln and Orla got back, Rick Nevin – in weekend gear of an over-large Hawaiian shirt and droopy tracksuit bottoms – told them PC Dylan Wilcox from Warminster had called to say there'd been a break-in at Willow Cottage and he thought they should know.

'Anything taken?' Lincoln asked, although it would be hard to tell, given the general clutter in Swann's house.

Nevin shrugged. 'Comprehensively turned over,' he said. 'Someone searching for something.'

Lincoln picked up his keys again and turned to Orla. 'Let's go over there.'

'To Willow Cottage?' She hung back. 'Aren't Warminster taking care of it?'

'I want another look at it, see if we missed something earlier.' He made no attempt to hide his irritation. 'I'll go on my own if there's somewhere else you'd rather be.'

She sighed and then, with obvious reluctance, followed Lincoln out to the car.

PC Dylan Wilcox met them on the front path of Willow Cottage. Chipboard covered the glass door panel that must have been smashed to gain entry. The house felt clammy with damp, cold despite the outside temperature.

'Anyone see anything unusual?' As soon as he'd said it, Lincoln realised the question was pretty stupid. The cottage wasn't overlooked and was obscured on all sides by overgrown trees and shrubbery.

'Actually, yes. I checked with the neighbours. Guy down the lane's got a security camera. Clocked a car going by late last night, a grey or silver Fiesta he didn't recognise.'

Lincoln and Orla exchanged looks. Matt Trevelyan.

'I'll be out front when you're done.' The young police officer tramped back outside.

Orla surveyed the untidy living room. 'Wonder what Trevelyan was looking for?'

Lincoln shrugged. 'There's nothing of real value here, but he must have thought there was. Didn't he say Morton boasted to him about his famous father? He may have laid it on a bit thick to impress him.'

She spread her arms dramatically. 'Just think, boss! In this rundown cottage outside Warminster, we could stumble on the secret of the universe!'

'Unless Trevelyan has beaten us to it.'

Upstairs in Swann's study, drawers had been pulled out, the envelopes of newspaper clippings emptied, the bookshelves ransacked.

An open box file caught Lincoln's eye. It contained some manila folders full of papers with CONFIDENTIAL printed in red block capitals in the headers and footers. The folders themselves bore the distinctive crest of the Ministry of Defence.

Immediately, he thought back to what Karen Bolitho had told him. Jill's brother had been suspected of passing classified MoD documents to an unknown contact. Could that contact have been Daniel Swann?

'What's Swann doing with these?' He showed Orla what he'd found. They dated from 1994 and were reports of sightings of unidentified flying objects, or unidentified aerial phenomena, mostly over Wiltshire.

'UFOs?' She flipped through one of the reports. 'This is just about lights in the sky over Salisbury Plain. Okay, boss, so what's so *X-Files* about that?'

'Look at the date. August 1994. Not long before the so-called alien spaceship crash that Swann and Morton were obsessed with. If Swann really did believe that a flying saucer and its pilot arrived at Boscombe Down that September, a report like this would add weight to his theory. This is exactly the sort of thing Jill was talking about, Swann's followers sending him material to back up his theories.'

'But what was Trevelyan after?'

'Something he thought he could sell, I imagine. Something that might make him some money.' Lincoln put the folders back in the box file, snapped it shut and tucked it under his arm. 'Better take this with us.'

He followed Orla back along the landing but couldn't help pausing at the top of the stairs, thinking about Swann slipping down them, crashing into the banister and slamming back against the wall – with fatal consequences. Had he been climbing up the stairs or going down? How had he hit the banister with such force if he'd simply lost his footing?

Did he fall or was he pushed?

'Who else might have been here when Swann died?'

Orla halted at the foot of the stairs and frowned up at him. 'We know it wasn't Morton, he was working. You're seriously still thinking Swann was murdered? Viv Caddick didn't think his death was suspicious, and she's attended dozens of murder scenes. If Viv can accept it was an accident, boss, why can't you?'

'I don't like things I can't explain.'

Her frown became a grin. 'Isn't that what all this is about, the unexplained?'

'Come on, let's get back. We need to track Trevelyan down before he does any more damage.'

CHAPTER 74

'Does Jerry know you're out of hospital?' Heather put a cup of coffee down on the table where Jill could reach it.

'I haven't told him. Annika might have done, although she cares for her father about as little as I do. He didn't hang around for long once he knew I'd been rescued.'

'That's a bit unfair, isn't it? He came back from Greece as soon as he heard you were missing.'

Jill sniffed. 'Only because he wanted to make the right impression, not because he was concerned.' She didn't want to think about her ex-husband. Didn't want him and his gormless second wife to come and visit her, to gloat over her misfortune. He'd known Ramsay slightly but not enough to mourn his loss. 'I hate sitting around all day like this. Sorry, Heather, I don't mean to sound ungrateful. It's very good of you to let me stay here.'

'Why don't you buy one of these apartments? There are still some available. You could easily afford one if you sold your house.'

'I don't want to sell my house. God, you're as bad as Annika.'

Heather drifted across to the window with its silly little Juliet balcony. 'The only drawback is the limited parking.'

'There's limited parking in Arundel Terrace, but that's no longer a problem. I got rid of the car.'

Heather turned back. 'But how will you get anywhere without a car?'

'I'm sure I'll manage.' She drank some of her coffee. She didn't want to talk about the car and why she'd sold it. 'I'll be out of your way tomorrow.'

She saw the look of dismay on her old friend's face. Was she lonely here in her beautiful flat? Then she reminded herself that Heather had been very ill, had faced dying. Unable to return to the detached house she'd bought years ago, she'd had to downsize. Jill, in contrast, was lucky still to be living in the same house where she'd raised Annika and nursed her mother.

'Annika's read that awful book of Dan's,' she said, more brightly.

'I know,' said Heather. 'She was trying to find out where that Morton man might have taken you.'

'*That Morton man* was Dan's son. You remember Ellie Morton?'

'The dopey girl who ran his fan club? Funny little thing, greasy hair, spots. She was at the secondary modern, wasn't she?' Heather came and sat down again. 'Whatever did Dan see in *her*?'

'She was easy. That's all those boys cared about in those days.' Jill braced herself before making her confession. 'I blocked the air vents into the bunker. With blankets. I shut the air vents inside, and I covered up the air vents above ground. I wanted Ezra to die.'

Heather tensed beside her. 'You tried to kill him?'

'Yes. I shut him in down there, locked him in. He couldn't possibly have come after me. But I wanted him to die. He's Dan's son and he's sick, but I wanted to kill him. I feel like a monster.'

'You can't blame yourself, Jill. He put you through hell. You were starving, thirsty, desperate to get away. You weren't thinking straight. You weren't yourself.' Heather got up and collected Jill's empty cup. She gave her shoulder a gentle squeeze as she passed her. 'You came through it, Jill, that's the important thing. *You* survived.'

CHAPTER 75

Martha had been a PCSO for only a few weeks. Now she was patrolling the market place with a more experienced colleague. Half past three and the stallholders were beginning to pack up. Vans were parked ready to be filled with rolled-up awnings and unsold produce. Cauliflower stalks and onion skins littered the ground near the fruit and vegetable stall. Martha nearly slipped on some squashed grapes.

'Steady,' said her colleague. 'We don't want to lose you that soon.'

A young man with a ponytail was leaning against one of the Victorian statues that rose, hardly noticed, on the edge of the marketplace. A deal seemed to be going down with a boy who looked no older than thirteen, stood astride his bicycle and holding out his hand. At the kerb, on double yellow lines, sat a Ford Fiesta, dirty and dented. She recognised the index number that had been circulated earlier in the day.

'Wanted vehicle,' she hissed, nudging her colleague. 'That's Matthew Trevelyan, the guy they want for that girl's murder.'

'Keep your eye on him. Don't let him know you've seen him.' Her colleague turned away to use her radio.

Martha did as she was told. Was this what a murderer looked like in the flesh?

The boy said something to provoke an angry response from Trevelyan, who grabbed the front of the kid's T-shirt and pulled him roughly towards him.

Instinctively, Martha stepped forward. Trevelyan swung round, shoving the boy away, ready to make a dash for it. His escape was foiled by the fallen bicycle, which tangled itself in his legs and brought him down with a crash at the stone feet of the Victorian worthy. Winded, with a young and bulky PCSO bearing down on him, he must have known that resistance was futile.

Using reasonable force, Martha sat on his legs until a patrol car swept into the marketplace. Minutes later, Trevelyan was under arrest. The young boy had already fled, leaving his bike behind, its wheels spinning.

'Here we go again.' Matt Trevelyan slumped back in his chair, a grin on his face. Since his last appearance across the interview desk from Lincoln and

Orla, he'd been caught on camera drinking with a teenage girl and, soon after, helping her into an empty house where she was later found dead.

Lincoln put before him one of the photos Devesh Driver had found on Instagram.

'Recognise anyone in this photo, Matthew?'

Trevelyan leant close to the photo as if he couldn't see it properly otherwise. 'Is that me?' He sounded amused. 'Yeah, that's me, isn't it? And that's Kelly. I ran into her there, Monday. She was there with Driver.' He peered closer. 'Can't see him in the photo though.'

'He was inside,' Orla said, 'playing pool. Kelly left without telling him. Which was out of character.'

He sat up. 'If you say so. I don't remember Kel as being especially reliable, I'm afraid. Just as likely to go off with someone without telling him.'

'Go off with someone like you?'

That soppy grin again. Lincoln wanted to smack it off his face.

'Like me,' Trevelyan agreed, 'or someone like me.' Trying to make them think Kelly might have left the pub with another man who looked a lot like him, leaving him in the clear.

With a flourish, Orla produced another photo: a man with a ponytail steering Kelly along the pavement of Gas Lane at nearly quarter to eight on Monday night.

'This man looks a lot like you, doesn't he, Matthew? And look, he drives a Ford Fiesta that's registered to you. Or is it a car that merely looks a lot like yours?'

The grin slipped. He might have prepared himself for the Instagram photo of the beer garden, but he hadn't realised he'd been photographed by Gas Lane's moustachioed and self-appointed Neighbourhood Watch.

As he looked at the photos, Lincoln saw something that had escaped him before. In the beer garden, Kelly's phone was stuffed in the back pocket of her skimpy denim skirt, but by the time she was stumbling towards the house where she'd died, her back pocket was empty. No pockets in her T-shirt, no other visible pockets in her skirt. When her body'd been found, her phone was missing.

The Fiesta had yet to be searched, but he wouldn't mind betting her phone was lying in it somewhere.

'Is that you, Matthew?' Orla jabbed the photo. 'Is that you leading Kelly to an empty house where you pumped her full of heroin, then tried to make her death look accidental?'

His gaze scanned the walls behind his interrogators, as if he was looking for escape – or inspiration.

'She wasn't feeling too good,' he said. 'She wanted me to leave her somewhere to sleep it off before she went home to her mum. I knew that house was empty. Thought it was somewhere she could, y'know, chill for a bit.'

'Her mum wasn't home,' Lincoln said, 'and Kelly knew it. Why wasn't she feeling too good? Was it because of the drugs you'd slipped into her beer?'

'No comment.'

Lincoln backed off, took a minute or two to shuffle the papers in his folder. He pulled out Trevelyan's phone records, key numbers highlighted by Orla when she'd worked through the list. He scanned the pages for a minute or two more, reminding himself what her various markings signified.

'Twentieth of April. The first of numerous calls to Kelly's mobile. May, June, calls to Kelly and Devesh at least once a week. Can you see that?' He laid the list down in front of Trevelyan, who gave it only a cursory glance.

'So what?'

'The vandalism at Keiller's Yard began at the end of April and continued pretty regularly through May and June.' Lincoln took the list back. 'Interestingly, every time you call Kelly, you receive a call shortly beforehand. From *this* number.' He turned the list round again so Trevelyan could read it. 'See, there's a pattern. A call to you from this number and then, very soon afterwards, *you* call Kelly or Devesh. Can you see a pattern emerging?'

Trevelyan sat back. He didn't want to see any stupid pattern emerging. 'Meaning?'

'Do you recognise the number that's calling you?' Lincoln pointed to it with his pen.

'Not offhand, no.'

'It's Adam Keiller's number. Adam calls you, you call Kelly, she and Devesh go up to Keiller's Yard and spray some paint around or take pot shots at the windows with an air rifle, or they smash a few fence panels. Is that just a coincidence?'

Trevelyan was beginning to look distinctly uncomfortable, but at the same time, Lincoln realised Orla hadn't finished her work on the phone records. Some of the numbers remained unidentified, unmarked, as if she hadn't got as far as checking them.

He also noticed that the last call from Adam was on 27 June. How had he contacted Trevelyan during the last week to tell him he wanted Kelly out of the way? A ripple of uncertainty ran through him.

'Whose idea was it to kill Kelly?' Orla asked. 'Yours or Adam's?'

'No comment.'

She didn't let that answer stop her. 'Because you did kill her, didn't you, Matthew? A kid you recruited to vandalise the smallholding, who did as you asked, who trusted you. Trusted you to look after her on Monday night when she felt like shit. Would you have hurt her if you hadn't been told to?'

'No one tells me what to do! I do what I like!'

'Then you'll have to take full responsibility for her murder, won't you?' Lincoln took the phone records back and slipped them into his folder.

Out in the corridor, with Trevelyan heading back to his cell, Orla banged her fist against the wall.

'Bastards!' she hissed. 'Him and Keiller both.'

'He can't go on denying it. There's too much evidence against him. I was hoping he'd spread the blame, land Keiller in it. I'm hoping we'll find Kelly's phone in Trevelyan's car. She had it with her when she left the pub, but not when she got to Gas Lane.'

'Have the CSIs gone over the car yet?'

'They'll go over it first thing tomorrow morning. Go home and get some rest.'

'Why, do I look like I need it?'

He turned away. He couldn't seem to get it right. 'Go home. We'll have lots to do tomorrow.'

CHAPTER 76

Saturday night, and the Keillers had friends round for drinks, friends of Joanna's and clients for whom she organised events, people Adam didn't much care for. After a few drinks, he'd like them better.

'Is that someone's phone?' one of the friends asked. Straining his ears, Adam recognised the sound of a Skype call coming through on his laptop. He excused himself and hurried into the study.

'How's it going, Doc?' Pete Doubleday's usual greeting, except tonight it sounded sarcastic.

'Fine, fine. I should be able to book you in for your op the week after next. A couple of calls to make before I can confirm it, but it's looking good.'

'Not looking so good on the other front, though, is it? Although you've got rid of half your problem.'

'Half my...'

'Only one kid to worry about now instead of two. And she was the greedy one, wasn't she?'

'Yes, but...'

'They've arrested someone, I hear. Charged him with murder. Not going to point the finger your way, is he?'

Adam's guts turned to soup. Murder? Was this something else Doubleday was going to hold over him: *Look what I did for you, Doc. Now you owe me.*

'Listen, Pete,' he managed to say, 'I've got people here. I'll confirm your op on Monday when I'm back at my desk. How does the twenty-fourth of July sound?'

A chuckle from faraway Spain. 'Sounds a bit optimistic, the way things are going for you, but I'll put it in my diary.' And the call ended.

Adam sat staring at the blank screen for several minutes. He'd assumed Kelly's death was a timely accident. But *murder*? If it wasn't Doubleday's doing, then who was responsible?

Come on, man, think of the dodgy people she mixed with. She took drugs, hung about in pubs, and her mother never seemed to be around. The kid was a prick-tease. Sooner or later, she'd have been caught out.

He wiped his face. He was sweating profusely and urgently needed a shit. He rushed upstairs to the en suite and, ignoring Joanna's irritated summons, locked himself in there until his bowels were empty and his heart had stopped racing.

CHAPTER 77

When he got back to the Old Vicarage that evening, Lincoln was relieved to find Breeze was out. He must have gone on foot or called a cab, because his red Peugeot 207 was still on the drive, parked awkwardly, close to the path to the back garden. The damaged wheel had been replaced, but the car badly needed a paint job.

The house felt warm, full of the comforting smell of warm fabric, scents from the garden drifting in when he opened the doors to the verandah. He poured himself a drink, noting with relief that if Breeze had dipped into the Jameson's, he'd only taken a single measure or two.

Drink in hand, he phoned Trish. She took so long to answer he was on the point of hanging up.

'Sorry,' she said, sounding breathless. 'Kate's got some friends over – wonder of wonders – and we're making some snacks together.'

'She's patched things up with Charlotte?'

She dropped her voice to a whisper. 'Fingers crossed. I got her to invite Paloma over, too.' At a more normal volume, she said, 'And isn't it wonderful that Jill's okay? We were all so worried about her. What about this awful Morton man?'

'Still waiting to see if he pulls through, but it's not looking good. You were doing some research on Daniel Swann, weren't you? Was Morton mentioned anywhere?'

'No, only Ellie Morton, who ran the fan club. I'm sorry I told you the wrong Observer Corps post.'

'You weren't to know. We got there in the end.' He was running out of easy things to say to her. More than anything, he wanted to be there with her, not trading banalities over the phone while she was distracted by her daughter's friends. 'When this is over,' he said, praying that it soon would be, 'let's go away somewhere. A long weekend. Not far, just… away. What d'you think?'

'That would be… Oh Lord, I think they've let the popcorn burn! Gotta go.' And she hung up.

He felt better simply for having spoken to her, even if he hadn't said much of what he wanted to say. Would they ever work things out between them?

Much later, a cab pulled up outside and Breeze came bowling in, a bit merry but still coherent.

'Gray came up trumps.' He flung himself down on the sofa opposite Lincoln. 'Devizes are going to speak to a couple of girls who were at the hotel. Not friends of Shirley's or Tracey's. I broke up a fight,' he told Lincoln with some pride. 'No memory of it at all. I was beginning to believe I really had tried it on with Tracey.'

'Great, but that'll all take time. You can't stay here until it's resolved, Dennis. It could take weeks.'

'That's okay. I took my landlord out for a drink tonight. Explained the situation and got a stay of execution. I'll be moving back next week. He's not a bad bloke, all things considered.'

Lincoln wondered how Breeze would handle the fallout when his ex-wife was shown up as a liar. Would Cousin Shirley be filled with remorse for doubting him, or would he be branded forever as a troublemaker?

Tux was waiting to be let out as Lincoln crossed the hall to go up to bed, and he opened the door, watching the little black and white cat disappear into the night, probably heading for the old hen house that had become its hideout.

The last thing Lincoln heard before he fell asleep was Breeze blundering around in his bathroom, not long after midnight. Thank God he'd soon be moving out!

CHAPTER 78

SUNDAY 16 JULY 2017

Sunday morning, but there'd be no lie-in for Lincoln. He was up early and at his desk by seven-thirty, keen to wrap up the Kelly Turner murder case.

Maybe he'd never know why Ezra Morton had killed his mother and kidnapped Jill. If Morton didn't recover from his fall in the bunker, there'd be no chance to question him.

Recalling his unsatisfactory exchange with Karen Bolitho yesterday, he searched the internet for information on Jill's brother, Charles Holford Holland. Two years older than Jill, a grammar school boy who'd gone to Cambridge, he'd become a senior civil servant at the Ministry of Defence, based in Whitehall.

However, his glittering career ended in the summer of 2011, when he was accused of leaking classified material and had been forced to resign from his post.

Three weeks later, he'd committed suicide.

Was it him leaking those documents to Daniel Swann? Lincoln thought back to the reports they'd found in the study at Willow Cottage, with CONFIDENTIAL in red block capitals. They'd been mostly about UFOs, but what else had come across Holland's desk and been passed on?

Had Jill known what her brother was up to?

Karen Bolitho had told him Keiller first heard strange noises on his phone line at the end of 2010, and the suspected phone tapping ceased in August 2011 – around the time that Charles Holland hanged himself in Savernake Forest.

That familiar shiver ran down Lincoln's back. Holland, Swann, Keiller: top civil servant, conspiracy theorist, campaigner. Had Holland passed Swann classified information about the incident at Boscombe Down in September 1994? Had he been helping Keiller pursue his case against the MoD over his brother's death in 1965?

And the one common factor between them? Jill Fortune.

By the end of the morning, Trevelyan's Ford Fiesta had been searched and examined for forensic evidence linking it to Kelly Turner. Her mobile phone was found under the front passenger seat, where it must have fallen when she was bundled, stupefied, into the car.

It didn't take Orla long to guess the PIN – 2000, the year the girl was born – and she was soon skimming through the dozens of photos Kelly had taken.

'How many times did Keiller say he'd screwed her?' Her question sounded rhetorical.

'I'm betting it was more than once or twice,' said Lincoln.

'Kelly photographed them in bed together at least *twenty* times since last summer. Usually when he's asleep. Let him try to wriggle out of that one!'

Lincoln shared her disgust, but he had to remind her of what Adam himself had said: Kelly had been sixteen or seventeen. He'd been stupid to risk his marriage and his reputation, but he'd done nothing illegal or unethical, and the sex was evidently consensual.

'Let's get him in here,' he said, 'see what he's got to say for himself now Trevelyan's in a cell.'

Sitting across the interview desk from Lincoln and Orla, Adam Keiller looked ruffled, as if he'd dressed in a hurry. Even though he wasn't under arrest, he'd taken the precaution of bringing his solicitor with him. The man sat next to him wearing an expensive suit, signet ring glinting, cufflinks catching the light as he toyed with his Mont Blanc fountain pen.

'Thank you for coming in to talk to us,' Lincoln began. 'We simply need to ask you a few more questions in relation to Kelly Turner.' He laid a photo on the desk, a selfie from her phone, her face in mischievous close-up.

Adam flinched slightly. Maybe he could guess what was coming. 'It was terrible, what happened to her, yes.'

'When we spoke to you on…' Lincoln paused to check when he and Orla had called on him at Baddesley Grange. 'Thursday, wasn't it? You said you'd had sex with Kelly – and I quote – *twice, and I've regretted it ever since.* Now, if you'll look at these photos, Adam, I think you'll agree it looks as if you and Kelly had sex on many more than two occasions.'

Shock silenced Adam. He'd evidently had no idea she'd taken photos of them in bed together.

'What are you accusing Mr Keiller of, exactly?' the solicitor asked. 'This relationship was demonstrably consensual.'

'Clearly, it was. But as you've already told us, Adam, you regretted it. You're a married man with children, a good reputation in your field. Naturally, you regret your relationship with a teenage tearaway like Kelly. Makes me wonder if you regretted it enough to do away with her when she threatened to tell your wife. Regretted it enough to pay your gardener,

Matthew Trevelyan, to inject her with heroin and make her death look accidental. Because that would be conspiracy to commit murder.'

'Murder?' Adam spluttered. 'That's utterly ridiculous!'

Lincoln paused again. 'We know that Matthew Trevelyan instructed Kelly and her friend Devesh to vandalise your father's smallholding repeatedly, from April to the end of June. Why did he do that? Did he have a grudge against your father?'

'Of course he didn't. He didn't even know my father.'

'So why...' Orla spread her hands, begging for an explanation.

Adam was stuck for an answer. His solicitor laid down his fountain pen on his pad of yellow paper and folded his hands.

Lincoln took a moment to scan the phone records in his folder before continuing.

'Between the end of April and the end of June, Adam, you made several phone calls to Matthew Trevelyan – quite short calls, not long enough for a proper conversation. In every case, your call to him would be followed by him calling Kelly or Devesh. Soon after that, your father's smallholding would suffer another act of vandalism, as captured on CCTV. A chain of events, starting with your phone call to Matthew. Can you explain that?'

'Matt did some gardening for us. I was... er... calling to ask if he could come over to do some gardening.'

'And if we asked Mrs Keiller, would she be able to corroborate that?'

'Leave my wife out of this!'

Had a nerve been touched? Was Joanna the key to getting him to confess? Lincoln sat back and waited. And waited.

'Okay, yes, yes.' Adam pressed his hands, palms down, on the table, as if to show how steady they were, or, indeed, to steady himself. 'I wanted Dad to give up the farm. He was too old to be carting sacks of poultry feed around, mending fences. I was worried about him. But as for getting kids to vandalise the place...'

'You told me someone in Spain was interested in making an offer on the land,' said Lincoln, 'but that your father wouldn't even meet with him. Must've been frustrating for you, embarrassing, even, because the potential buyer was a patient of yours, wasn't he?'

Adam cleared his throat, swallowed. 'Yes, that's right. But that was a while ago, and it was all very... vague. Mr Doubleday was simply enquiring...'

Lincoln sat up. 'Pete Doubleday?'

'You know him?'

'You could say that, yes.' Pete Doubleday had owned Cartway Farm, on the far side of Barbury. He'd hidden high-performance stolen cars there, and overseen a criminal empire inherited from his father. He'd be in prison now if he hadn't fled to Spain. Trust Doubleday to want to buy a stake in Barbury, stick his finger back in the pie! How the hell had he slipped back into the country without being picked up? Although, knowing the sort of company he kept, he wouldn't find it hard to get hold of a fake passport, travel under a false name, arrive back in the UK undetected.

'Keiller's Yard would fetch a lot now, though, wouldn't it, Adam?' Orla said. 'Nice piece of land, right on the outskirts of town, not far from the main route to the A303. Desirable, as the estate agents say.'

He nodded, but pointed out that it was all academic. 'There'll be probate to sort out,' he said. 'It'll take months, years maybe.'

She gave him a wry smile. 'Shame your dad died when he did. It would've been so much easier if you'd waited for him to make up his own mind to call it a day.'

'What are you saying?' The blood shot up into his cheeks and his eyes shone. 'I've come in here of my own volition to try and clear this up, and you're saying I *killed* him?'

'We're suggesting,' said Lincoln, 'that when your father wouldn't even consider selling up, you decided he needed some persuasion, so you arranged for a couple of kids to vandalise the place, to make life difficult for him until he gave in.'

Adam's shoulders sagged. 'Okay, okay. Yes.'

Lincoln felt a rush of relief. 'Do you admit using Matthew Trevelyan to pay Kelly and Devesh to cause criminal damage at Keiller's Yard?'

'Yes.'

'You admit that you had an ongoing sexual relationship with Kelly?'

Adam sat up again. 'A relationship that *was* wholly consensual.'

Lincoln shrugged. 'An affair, then.'

'Yes, an affair.'

'Did your wife know about it?'

Adam pitched forward over the desk. 'Of course she didn't know about it! Why else would I...'

'Why else would you what?' Lincoln waited.

'Kelly was blackmailing me. She threatened to tell my wife about... our affair.'

'That's a compelling motive for murder,' said Lincoln.

'I know. I know. But I swear on my children's lives, I *didn't* have Kelly killed.'

*

291

'Liar, liar,' Orla sang quietly as they went back along the corridor to the incident room. 'Liar, liar, pants on fire!'

'We've got him for conspiracy to commit criminal damage. That's a start, isn't it?'

Back at his desk, Lincoln pulled Trevelyan's phone records out of his folder. 'Did you finish going through these numbers?'

'Yeah, I think so.'

'Just that some of them aren't ticked off or identified.'

'Give it here.' She held her hand out for the printout and flounced back to her desk. 'Sorry, boss, I thought I'd been through them all.'

'I want to make sure we haven't missed anything.'

Head down, she pored over the list. 'Okay, I confess! I missed one or two towards the end. I'll check them now.'

CHAPTER 79

'I need to go home some time.' Jill watched Heather loading the dishwasher after a light Sunday lunch, wishing she could do more to help. 'But I can't face a barrage of photographers and reporters.'

Heather laughed. 'Hark at you! Fame at last.'

'A bit late for that, isn't it?' Jill hobbled back into the living room.

'Better late than never.'

'I don't want to be famous for being a victim.'

They sat in silence for a while, both pretending to read, until Heather said, 'At least Dan's book was good for something in the end. If he hadn't written about the bunker at Larksdown, Annika wouldn't have known where to find you.'

'If Dan hadn't written that bloody book, I wouldn't have been stuck underground for the best part of a week.'

'Was that the only reason Ezra kidnapped you? To get Dan's book back?'

'Of course it was! I'd been stalling him for weeks on the phone. I never thought he'd take it that far. But of course, I was part of the global conspiracy to silence the great Daniel Swann.'

'That poor boy – so deluded about his father.'

'That *poor boy* is a forty-year-old thug, Heather. He shot his mother, he beat me up, he killed Ramsay.' Jill pushed herself up off the sofa and limped across to an armchair closer to her friend. 'And you know the only reason I went up to see Ramsay that afternoon? To try and help him.'

'Help who? Ramsay?'

Jill nodded. 'When Dan sent me his manuscript, he sent a whole load of other stuff with it – his source material, he called it. I didn't bother to look at half of it, but that afternoon, I was tidying my study and I found a report about the germ warfare tests in Dorset...'

Heather leant towards her eagerly. 'The Lyme Bay Trials?'

'Yes. Dates and times, locations, the combinations of bacteria used. It was all there.'

Heather sat back. 'But Ramsay already had that information.'

'Yes, but he didn't have the letter I found with the report.'

Jill relived her excitement when she'd opened the report to find a typed letter stapled to it. Dated March 1995 and addressed to a senior official at the

MoD, it was from a counterpart at Porton Down, confirming that biological warfare testing off the Dorset coast had taken place in April and May 1965:

Please be aware that the official listing of these tests does not include serial number 28, which took place on May 9th, one week after the tests were scheduled to be completed. You may wish not to disclose this information in light of the case being pursued by Mr Ramsay Keiller.

She would never know for sure, but she guessed this was one of the many reports Chas passed on to Dan over the years, trying to do the right thing but actually fuelling Dan's paranoia about official cover-ups, government conspiracies, establishment deceptions.

Heather peered at her. 'A letter?'

'Yes, from somebody at Porton. Confirming what Ramsay had always believed. That a test had taken place on Sunday May ninth, the weekend Callum and his Scout troop were camping down there. The air along the Dorset coast would've been full of bacteria that could have been the cause of his illness.'

'Ramsay was told the tests stopped on May second.'

'Exactly! The MoD lied. That letter would've been the ammunition Ramsay needed to pursue his case against them. He wasn't looking for compensation, Heather, just vindication. For fifty years, he'd wanted answers about his brother's death, and there it was.'

'Probably.'

'What?'

'No one will ever know for sure that's why Callum died, will they? The doctors didn't know he'd been exposed to those bacteria, did they? They didn't consider it as a cause while he was alive, or look for it after he died. Ramsay could never have proved it, even with that letter.'

Deflated, Jill knew that Heather, the ever-logical Heather, was right. Whatever his intentions in revealing the truth, Chas had been misunderstood and discredited. And she blamed Dan for much of that, encouraging her brother to jeopardise his career, to risk everything so the great Dan Swann could make a point.

But then, Chas had idolised Dan ever since they'd been at school together. Maybe he'd been as much in love with Dan as she had, in his own way. Thank God he hadn't lived to see what Dan had become!

But what had happened to the report and the letter? She remembered putting them on the counter in the farm shop. Ramsay had been about to read the letter when Ezra stormed in and told her he'd run over her bike. And she'd believed him, rushed outside, Ramsay following. Leaving the report on the counter.

She doubted if it would still be there.

'Do you want some music on?' Heather was fiddling with the CD player by her chair.

'No, not now. Which reminds me. Why did you send me that LP, *Dan's Swannsong?*'

'Oh, well, I'd had that album for years, since it first came out in 1974. I thought you'd like to have it.'

'Don't lie to me, Heather. I know you too well.'

Heather's face fell. 'I wanted you to know the truth about Dan, about his music. As soon as I heard that album, I knew the melodies were familiar, and the words. Those were *your* songs, weren't they? *Your* words, more or less. A record by Dan Swann and nothing on the sleeve or the label to say Jill Holland had written the songs. He'd stolen your music and passed it off as his own. Then, of course, after America, he crashed and burned, and it didn't seem to matter anymore.' She looked across at her. 'And you really didn't know?'

Jill shook her head. 'We worked on a lot of stuff together when we were still at school, but I didn't know he'd kept anything of mine. Once I moved to London, I stopped listening to music, apart from classical stuff on the radio, a few jazz concerts.' She smoothed out the wrinkles in her skirt. 'Why didn't you tell me about it at the time?'

'We weren't really friends by 1974, were we? I was still smarting from you going off to France with Eva after Dan chucked you.'

'For God's sake, Heather, that was Easter 1967! And you're still upset because I went to France with Eva?'

A little colour flared in Heather's pale cheeks. 'You had no idea, any of you. Clever Maggie. And you, looking so gorgeous, with your music and your brainy brother. And Eva, always off to her pop concerts and poetry readings and charity walks and her amateur dramatics. And then there was plain old me. No good at anything much, never allowed to go anywhere, do anything exciting.'

'Your dad was so strict, wasn't he? I didn't really like going to your house. I was scared of him.'

'You and me both.'

'You haven't answered my question. Why did you send me the *Swannsong* album?'

Heather ran her hand over her short, curly hair, the texture so different since chemo. 'Because when you phoned me on my birthday, you said you were reading Dan's manuscript. You were laughing at how crazy it was, but you sounded ready to forgive him for all he'd put you through. And that didn't seem right. I thought you should know the truth: that for the last fifty years, Dan lived off the profits of music that *you* composed, lyrics that *you* wrote.'

'Oh Heather...!'

'The music he wrote later? Everyone said it changed after that bad trip, blaming his breakdown, but the truth is much simpler, Jill. Up until that bad trip, most of the music he recorded was written by *you*.'

Jill's heart felt like a lump of stone in her chest, pressing down so heavily she could hardly breathe.

Heather had sent her the album before Easter, special delivery, and Jill had played it over and over again, hardly able to believe what she was hearing. Her own music flowing beneath Dan's embellishments. Heard her own words, more or less unchanged .

On Good Friday, she'd driven over to Willow Cottage, ostensibly with a list of points to raise with Dan about his manuscript.

He'd been tired, weakened by all the prescribed medication, unable to eat properly, unable to sleep. They'd sat in his study, surrounded by a gallery of photos of him throughout the years: Danny, the winsome teenage songster; Dan, the leader of the Haymakers and the singer with the Barbury Blues Band; Daniel the evangelist, the would-be messiah, saviour of the world.

He'd listened half-heartedly as she queried various details in his book. He'd kept saying, 'Do what you think best. You know I trust your judgement, Jilly.'

Something had clattered downstairs. His carer only came in the mornings, so who...

'Is there someone else here?'

'Oh, that's Ezra. My son. Ellie's son.'

'I didn't know you were still in touch with him.'

'I reached out to him when I got sick,' Dan had said. 'Someone needs to carry on my work.' He'd waved a feeble hand around the room, as if all the papers, the books, the pictures amounted to more than one deluded man's vanity project.

She'd loved Dan so much when they were teenagers. She'd felt a part of him, as if they were meant to be together for ever. Then he'd left Barbury, left her behind for good, and that was the natural way of things. But she'd never dreamt he'd steal the music she'd written, pass it off as his own, without even mentioning her.

No girls in the band, Jilly. You should know that.

'I've got your *Swannsong* album. My name isn't on the record anywhere.'

'Come on, Jilly, you know how it is.'

'Have you still got the originals, Dan? All those manuscript books, all those tapes I made?'

'Tapes *we* made. We worked on a lot of those songs together.'

'But mostly they were mine. And you stole them.'

She'd stood up and started to rake through the various boxes on his shelves. With every vain search, she'd grown angrier, throwing the boxes on the floor, upending them, spilling the contents everywhere.

And then she'd found it: a battered cardboard box of cassette tapes and the grey-covered manuscript books full of music she'd composed when she was still a stupid, naïve, lovelorn teenager. She'd hauled the box down off the shelf and carried it out onto the landing while he struggled to stand up.

'I'm taking this back, Dan, since it's mine.' She'd gone down the stairs and left the box in the hall. She had no idea what she'd do with the tapes and music. It was enough just to take everything back, to recover a lost chapter of her teenage years and pore over it when she was safely at home.

'What about my book?' He'd reached the study doorway, holding onto the door frame to steady himself as he called down to her.

She'd gone back up, pushing past him into the study to gather up his precious manuscript, her notes and her bag. 'If I need to ask you about any other changes, I'll write to you.'

'No, don't do that! You can't trust the post. They open my letters to see who I'm in communication with. Come back and see me instead.' He'd reached out to her, to slow her down, to stop her rushing out of his house for ever.

'I can't, Dan. I need to leave.'

He'd gone ahead of her along the landing, halting at the top of the stairs. 'Please stay, Jilly, just a little longer. I want to explain.'

'Too late for that, Dan. I'm going home now, and I won't be coming back.'

How did it happen? How did he fall? She'd gone over it in her head so many times in the months since, she could no longer be sure. Had he tried to stop her leaving one more time? Had she barged into him as she reached the top stair, her arms full of papers, unable to grab him when he lost his balance?

She could only remember him falling, milliseconds seeming like minutes, the pleading look in his eyes as he fell, and she could do nothing to save him.

She'd crept down the stairs to where he lay on the little half-landing, scrunched up, still. Checked his pulse. It slowed, slowed, slowed, stopped.

Down in the hall, she'd gathered up her box of music, his manuscript, her notes, and hurried out to her car, chucking everything into the boot. Only as she was reversing out of the overgrown driveway did she see an unkempt, bulky man watching her from the side of the house.

Ezra.

The following week, she'd sold her car. As if that would solve anything.

'None of that matters any more, though, does it, Heather?' she said now, getting to her feet and limping back to the spare room to pack her things. 'None of that matters any more.'

CHAPTER 80

'Guess who?' Orla had her phone on speaker, so Lincoln could hear the dialling tone. It cut out and voicemail kicked in.

You have reached the voicemail of Barbury Event Management.

Please leave your message...

'Barbury Event Management?' Lincoln looked at her, puzzled.

'One of the numbers I hadn't checked. I looked up Barbury Event Management and, guess what? Director and manager and sole employee – Joanna Keiller.'

'Adam's wife?'

'Why is she phoning Trevelyan late at night?' Orla grinned. 'To ask him to come over and do the garden? Phoning to tell him the lawn's looking a bit shaggy?'

'When did she phone him last?'

'The night before Kelly went to the Poacher's Pocket.'

'The night before Kelly died.'

'Maybe Adam's telling the truth,' she said. 'He wasn't the one who had Kelly killed.'

Lincoln found DCI Connors at the drinks machine, waiting in vain for it to dispense a cup of hot chocolate.

'There's a coffee shop around the corner, ma'am,' he said. 'It's open until four.'

He updated her as they walked, relieved that yet another piece of the puzzle had slipped into place: Joanna Keiller had ordered Kelly's murder.

Connors stopped walking. 'She was jealous of a silly teenager having a fling with her husband?'

'Possibly, but Kelly was blackmailing him and, given the state of that family's finances... Cheaper for Joanna to go behind her husband's back, pay Trevelyan to get rid of the girl, make it look like an accident. That way, Adam would have no idea his wife had any part in it.'

Connors shook her head. 'The stupidity of some people!' She carried on walking. 'Still no idea why Morton kidnapped Jill?'

'To get Swann's manuscript back from her. He was sure she was part of the conspiracy to suppress his father's views. From what Annika's told me after reading most of it, Swann shifted from being a left-wing environmentalist to being a right-wing extremist, seeing global conspiracies everywhere he looked. Unfortunately, Jill's brother may, inadvertently, have helped him get that way.'

Once more, Connors stopped dead. 'What's Jill's brother got to do with any of this?'

'He worked for the Ministry of Defence. He was leaking documents to somebody, exposing government cover-ups. I daresay, if we delved a bit deeper, we'd discover it was Swann he was leaking them to.'

'Except we're not going to delve a bit deeper, are we, Jeff?'

'No,' he agreed, resignedly. 'We're not. And, talking of leaks...' He told her how he'd caught one of the control room team slipping out through the fire door to meet Karen Bolitho.

'Aha! That would explain the resignation that was on my desk this morning.'

In the coffee shop, they sat in the window, the afternoon winding down, energy dissipating.

'DS Cook came to see me this morning, Jeff.' She stirred her hot chocolate, which she'd made even more sickly with the addition of three marshmallows.

'Oh?'

'Things aren't too happy on the home front, I understand.'

He hadn't given Orla's home front much thought. She'd disclosed so little of her personal life, he'd dismissed any curiosity he might have had when he first met her.

'I guessed something was up,' he said. 'She seemed a bit... distracted.'

'A controlling partner, but you haven't heard that from me. She's a very private person.'

'So?'

'She'll be taking some personal time. Which means you'll have a lot of paperwork to deal with on your own, preparing these cases for court.'

His spirits sagged. He couldn't see himself back at Barley Lane any time soon.

'Of course,' Connors added, popping a pastel pink marshmallow into her mouth, 'you may find Barley Lane a more conducive workplace. Lord knows when we're going to get the air con fixed at Park Street, but it's going to involve a lot of disruption. So, if you want to go back to Barley Lane...'

His spirits soared again. 'If that's okay with you, ma'am.'

'I'm sure Rick Nevin can hold the fort here while Orla takes some time off.' She stirred her drink and licked the spoon. 'Mmm, this is really good! Much better than the shit that comes out of *our* machine.'

Back in the incident room, Orla was going through the rest of the items recovered from Trevelyan's Ford Fiesta.

'What's that?' Lincoln nodded at a dented tin, the size of a lunch box, that sat on her desk.

'No idea, boss. I was about to take a look inside, but I was afraid it could be month-old fishpaste sandwiches.'

With gloves on, she lifted it out of its plastic evidence bag. A scuffed label on the lid read: *Bosc Down 26 09 94*, and she looked up at him enquiringly. 'Boscombe Down?'

'The night the so-called space ship crashed there.' Despite his scepticism, Lincoln felt his heart beating faster.

'You think we should wear masks? Oh, what the hell!' And Orla eased the lid off the tin.

Instinctively, he stepped back, thoughts of contamination, toxic spores and radioactive material whizzing through his brain. Too late for a risk assessment.

She tipped the contents of the tin onto her desk. 'What the...'

A wrinkly white balloon lay there, black squiggles still visible on its crumpled surface. The smell of perished rubber rose from it and Lincoln could imagine what it must have looked like when it was inflated: the featureless face of the pilot of the crashed spacecraft.

'Remember the photo pinned up in Morton's wardrobe?' he said. 'Supposedly taken by someone the day after the crash. I think we know how they faked that shot.'

'But what's this doing in Trevelyan's car?'

'This must be the huge secret Swann was going to reveal to the world – evidence of life elsewhere in the universe.' He picked up the shrivelled balloon and dropped it again. Trevelyan had told them how Morton had boasted that his father had an important message to deliver to the world. Swann had been entrusted with something important – and Trevelyan must have hoped to make money out of it.

'*This* is the huge secret?' Orla poked the crumpled balloon. '*This* is what Trevelyan stole from Willow Cottage?'

Lincoln nodded. 'Not sure it was worth it.' And to think Ramsay Keiller lost his life because of this, and Jill Fortune had nearly lost hers.

Orla picked up the bedraggled balloon and folded it back into its tin. She snapped the lid shut before looking up at him. 'You've heard I'm taking some time off?'

'The DCI mentioned it. I sensed something was up, but...'

'Have I been a pain in the arse? Be honest.'

'Sometimes, yes. But the rest of the time, you've been good to work with.'

'So have you, boss,' she told him with a grin, 'Though you're not a patch on Rick Nevin!'

Breeze was in the back garden when Lincoln got home – not gardening, but sitting on the bench with his feet up. The evening was warm, the air full of insects, the scent of cut grass wafting from somewhere.

'I could be back at work in a couple of weeks,' Breeze told him, casting aside his *Mail on Sunday*. 'And I'll be out of your hair tomorrow.'

Lincoln cheered inwardly on both counts, then embarked on relating the events of the day.

'So Morton thought his dad had preserved a piece of an alien?' Breeze rocked with laughter. 'You think Swann knew it was faked?'

'We'll never know. And that's something else – Swann wasn't Morton's dad.'

The DNA results had come through as he and Orla were packing up for the day. Ezra Morton definitely wasn't Daniel Swann's son. Elinor may have thought he was, or else she brought him up to believe he was. Swann had taken responsibility for him, accepting him as his own flesh and blood, but despite a striking resemblance, the two men were quite unrelated.

'Will Morton ever wake up, d'you think?' Breeze asked.

Lincoln answered with a shrug. How could he know? Morton had climbed that ladder in the dark, not knowing the hatch cover was closed. He'd rammed his head into metal instead of open air. If he came out of his coma, he'd never fully recover. Better not to wake up.

On the far side of midnight, as he was drifting off to sleep, Lincoln was roused by a loud crash, glass breaking, a roar. He stumbled out of bed and across to the window. Down on the drive, steadily being consumed by fire, was Breeze's car. Breeze had been woken too, so both men raced downstairs, Lincoln dialling 999 on the way.

They stood on the front doorstep, watching as the Peugeot blazed. A sudden gust of wind carried a wisp of burning material across to the old hen house, which caught light in an instant, tinder dry in the summer's heat.

The hen house that had become Tux's nightly hideout.

CHAPTER 81

'Cuh, a fucking petrol bomb.' Breeze sat at the kitchen table with his head in his hands. 'Bet that was down to one of Tracey's boys.'

Lincoln poured himself more coffee, more tea for Breeze. 'What makes you say that?'

'Now Tracey knows I'm in the clear, Toy Boy's probably dumped her and she's sent one of her lads after me.'

'She'd be pretty stupid to pull a stunt like that.'

'The story of our marriage. She was pretty, I was stupid!'

'The fire investigator said they'd recovered most of the bottle that was used. Could lift some prints, maybe?' Though the man hadn't been very hopeful.

'I'm sorry about your cat.' Breeze sounded genuinely remorseful. 'He was a nice little chap.'

Lincoln picked his mug up and carried it to the sink. 'Well, let's hope it was quick.'

'That old shed went up like a rocket!'

'It did indeed.' At least only the hen house had caught fire and not the Old Vicarage itself. Tux's food dish sat, unwashed, on the kitchen floor.

'I can still move out today,' Breeze said. 'I'll have to wait till they've finished checking the car over, and then they'll have to take it away, but as soon as they've done that…'

The incident room at Park Street was busy when Lincoln arrived. There'd been some sort of major incident on the A303, so the phones were ringing constantly, voices raised, printers churning out reams of paper. Without thinking, he looked round for Orla, but of course, she was already off duty, taking some personal time. He felt unexpectedly disappointed that she wasn't around.

DCI Connors summoned him to her office.

'Joanna Keiller was arrested last night,' she said. 'We shouldn't have any problem making a case against her for conspiracy to murder. Trevelyan has indicated his willingness to tell all.'

'If Joanna and Adam are in custody, what happens to their kids?'

'Social Services can worry about that.' In a softer tone, she said, 'I'm sorry to hear about the attack on your house. You think it was personal?'

'Yes and no, ma'am. DC Breeze's car was sitting on my drive and became a bit of a target.'

'Much damage?'

'His car and a shed.' He didn't mention the cat. He couldn't bear to think about what Tux had gone through, much less talk about it.

'We're taking Barley Lane off the market,' Connors told him, 'at least for the time being.'

'Why's that, ma'am?' He tried not to show his relief.

'Parts of this building won't be fit to work in while they fix the air con, so we may have to relocate personnel from here to Barley Lane for a while. For now, though, you'd better get yourself ready to move back. I expect your team will be pleased.'

CHAPTER 82

Jill lifted the lid of the piano and ran her hands over the keys. She was so glad to be home. Yesterday evening, when Annika had phoned to check how she was, she'd begged her to come and pick her up first thing in the morning.

'Don't you want to stay longer with Heather?'

'If I stay here any longer,' Jill had replied, keeping her voice low, 'I may end up saying or doing something I'll regret.'

And now here she was, back at Arundel Terrace, relieved to be home at last.

'Roz and I want to start a family.' Annika said it in a rush, as if she'd been steeling herself to break the news. She stood framed in the doorway, braced for her mother's response.

Jill limped over to her. 'Are you sure? You and Roz haven't known each other five minutes.' She couldn't bear to think about the logistics.

'I'll be thirty-four next birthday, Mum. We don't want to wait any longer. And yes, I'm sure.'

Jill reached out and stroked her daughter's hair: straight and smooth, so unlike her father's wild, dark curls. All she wanted was for Annika to be happy. 'Then I'm pleased for you. And thank you for rescuing me – again!'

A few cards and letters had arrived, wishing her well. Once she got her laptop back from the police, she'd probably be inundated with emails too. She opened the first card, with a Ruskin Spear painting of a cat on the front. *From Trish and Kate. Glad to know you're okay.*

Closing the card, she saw there was a message on the back: *Not sure if you know, but my mother was Eva, your friend from school. I would love to hear your memories of her. Trish Whittington.*

Trish was Eva's daughter? Then Kate was Eva's granddaughter! Jill felt as if someone had put an arm around her and given her a hug. The years fell away. It would be all right.

'Where's that cat?' she called out, hobbling towards the kitchen to show Annika the card. 'Where's my lovely Finzi?'

CHAPTER 83

Eunice Peel finished sweeping the yard in front of the farm shop and put her broom away. She'd go into Ramsay's office today, turn things on again and have a bit of a clear-up. She couldn't keep putting it off.

Even though it was still closed, she'd been looking after the shop, getting rid of out-of-date stock, giving everything a good clean and letting some fresh air in. But the office, she hadn't touched.

She plugged the phone in again and surveyed the desk, the order book still sitting there from the Monday when Ramsay was shot, the diary still open at 3 July. Better check what animal feed was needed, then contact the suppliers, tell them it would soon be business as usual again. She wished now that she'd let Ramsay teach her how to use a computer, but she'd always shrugged him off. She regretted that now, but she'd manage, somehow. Maybe she could get someone in.

She noticed an A4 envelope that he must have left on the counter, with some sort of official report poking out the top of it. It was years old, with a letter attached, but the print was too small for her to read without her glasses. Best put it all through the shredder, add it to the rest of the animal bedding.

When the shredder stopped, she heard the outer door opening.

'We're closed!' she shouted.

Jamie Keiller stood in the entrance, the spit of his father in so many ways.

'Hello, Eunice. Just came to see how you were getting on.'

'Well enough. Could do with some help, though. This place is too much for one. There's some boxes need moving, and the fence in the chicken run needs fixing. You can help me with that. You know where everything is, don't you?'

But Jamie didn't budge. 'When were you going to tell us about the arrangement you made with Dad?'

She sniffed. He must have been to the solicitor to ask about Ramsay's estate. He'd have got a shock, she guessed.

'Your dad wanted to buy this place years ago,' she said, 'but I didn't want to sell. And I still don't. I grew up here and this is where I'll be when I drop. So we agreed he could rent it off me in return for letting me stay here and work. I'd go spare if I had to spend all day looking after Mum. He put his money into setting up the farm shop, but the land and the bungalow are still mine.' She started for the door, keen to get outside. 'Thought he'd have told you at the time.'

'He never said. We always thought Keiller's Yard was all his.'

'He didn't want the hassle. Happy to be my tenant. Of course,' she said, striding ahead of him down the path to the chicken run, 'you could take over from him if you wanted. It's tough work, but you'd be out in the fresh air, working with animals, and you've helped him out before. And you know about computers, don't you, which would be a plus. And look, it's already got your name over the door.'

She didn't turn around to see Jamie's face, but she could imagine he was at least thinking about it.

CHAPTER 84

Lincoln took a detour past the railway station on his way back to Barley Lane that afternoon, and drove to the block of flats where Ezra Morton lived. Sure enough, as Dilke had suggested, there at the kerb was a dark red Jaguar car, twenty years old, the offside front tyre flat as a pancake. A parking penalty notice was stuck to the windscreen. Another twenty-four hours and the Jag would have been towed away.

He parked and walked back to it. Too much to hope that it might be unlocked. Whipping his gloves out, he tried the front passenger door. It creaked open.

He crouched down to take a look inside. From the smelly detritus of used takeaway trays and paper cups in the footwell, he salvaged a bundle of letters in a Greggs paper bag, their envelopes roughly torn, addressed to Morton at his flat.

He stood up, resting the letters on the roof of the car. The first letter was sent on 20 April, and the most recent was postmarked 29 June. They were all from Elinor and were little more than messages that grew increasingly angry:

You got no right to be in his house!
He doesn't belong to you!
You never knew him like I did!
You got no right to read his book!
Get out of his house!
He's not your father!

Had Elinor been jealous of her son's closeness to the man he believed was his father? Had she tried to drive them apart even after Swann was dead?

Lincoln could imagine Morton receiving the last of these letters on the Saturday morning and deciding to have it out with her. He couldn't drive himself to Willow Cottage because of the flat tyre, but he got a lift there, then waited for her to answer his summons.

The reclusive Elinor set out on a rare outing from Amesbury next morning, perhaps as intent as he was on resolving the situation. Hoping to persuade him to stay away from Swann's cottage and move back in with her.

But as soon as she got there, he'd shot her. No one was going to take his father away from him ever again. Next day, he'd kidnapped Jill to hold her until he got Dan's book back. And then he'd kill her, too. Or that was the plan.

Lincoln dropped the letters into an evidence bag and headed back to Barley Lane, another piece of the puzzle slipping into place.

CHAPTER 85

'It's ages since we've done this.' Trish stretched out on the sun lounger and gazed contentedly down the garden of the Old Vicarage. She sipped her chilled cider and watched Kate and her new friend Paloma as, chatting and giggling, they strolled slowly around the flower beds.

On impulse, Lincoln had phoned Trish as he left Barley Lane that afternoon, inviting her over for supper.

'Oh, but we've got Paloma here,' she'd said. 'She's staying overnight.'

'Bring her over too.'

Now, he and Trish were relaxing while the girls explored the garden and checked their phones.

'I've found out what's been bugging Kate,' she said, 'and why she doesn't want to go to her dad's to stay.'

He braced himself. Had Trish found out about the baby that Vic and his wife were expecting? 'Oh?'

'Gail's son keeps winding her up. He's a bit older than her and probably doesn't realise how awkward it makes her feel. She hates being teased.'

'That's it?'

'Oh, and Gail's pregnant again. Not sure when it's due. Kate's starting to feel outnumbered!' She sat up. 'So she might go and stay with Paloma for a few days instead. Funny, I imagined Paloma quite differently, but she and Kate are so alike they could be sisters.'

Lincoln kept quiet. Suki and Trish were about as unalike as sisters could be.

'So I was thinking,' she went on, 'we could go away somewhere, couldn't we? You and me. Just for a few days. Talk things through, work out where we go from here.'

'That sounds ominous. Make or break, d'you mean?'

She leant closer, looking at him intently. 'Do *you* want us to break up?'

'Of course not, but the way you said it…'

'Then let's have a few days away. On our own. Soon. Get to know each other all over again. We've been drifting, haven't we? Not wanting to commit ourselves. Maybe now's the time to change that.'

He sighed. 'Listen, Trish, when the old hen house caught fire, don't tell Kate, but Tux…'

'Hang on, who's that chatting to the girls?'

Lincoln looked down the garden. A fair-haired man was standing on the other side of the hedge that divided the Old Vicarage garden from Fountains, and he seemed to be passing something to Kate.

'I don't know who lives in that house,' he said, 'except they've got bloody awful taste in music.'

He got up and marched down the garden, but before he could get near enough to speak to him, the Fountains man was walking back up to his house. As Kate turned round, Lincoln saw what was in her arms: a small black and white cat. Tux.

'That man said he found Tux hiding in his shed this morning,' Kate told him. 'He must have got shut in overnight.' She smoothed the top of the little cat's head. 'Oh, Tux, how have you managed to singe your whiskers?'

ACKNOWLEDGEMENTS

Thank you to members of Frome Writers' Collective for their support, especially through Silver Crow Books. Thank you, too, to readers who've taken the trouble to get in touch to tell me how much they've enjoyed the books, and to the book groups who've invited me along to talk to them. Special thanks to Richard Pike, who's championed DI Jeff Lincoln in his part of the country, as well as offering encouragement in the early stages of this book.

Barbury is largely based on Salisbury, with inevitable alterations. My fictional Turnpike Corner Aerodrome may bear some resemblance to the very real Old Sarum Airfield, but there the similarity ends. However, I'd like to mention Trish Thomas, who was passionate about the campaign to protect Old Sarum Airfield from redevelopment. She was thrilled to learn this book featured an airfield on the edge of the town, not far from where she lived, and we planned to meet up. Sadly, Trish died suddenly in June 2023, so we never got to meet in person. Still, I'll always be grateful for the memories we shared and for her enthusiastic approach to life.

Last but not least, thanks to my husband for his support, as ever, and to friends and family who have always been there for me.

ABOUT SILVER CROW BOOKS

Silver Crow Books, the imprint of Frome Writers' Collective (FWC), offers authors a collaborative approach to independent publishing.

FWC members submitting manuscripts receive a helpful appraisal and report service provided by experienced readers. Where manuscripts meet the agreed criteria, authors have access to publishing guidance and have the opportunity to see their titles promoted through FWC.

Launched in 2016, Silver Crow Books has a growing list of titles, and its authors have taken part in a wide range of literary events and festivals.

Find out more about Silver Crow Books at www.silvercrowbooks.co.uk

THE DI JEFF LINCOLN SERIES (IN ORDER)

THE PRICE OF SILENCE

When popular businesswoman Holly Macleod is found strangled in public toilets on the outskirts of Barbury, DI Jeff Lincoln assumes she's fallen victim to a violent Peeping Tom. But as he sifts through the details of her life, he uncovers one mystery after another. A car abandoned at the crime scene belongs to Leo Goldsmith, a family man from London with no apparent connection to Holly or to Barbury — and now he's disappeared.

Lincoln and his team must find out who Holly really was and why she came to this Wiltshire market town. Was Leo Goldsmith an innocent witness to her murder — or her killer? Lincoln soon starts to suspect that the attack on Holly that dark October night was anything but random — but who would want her dead?

The Price of Silence is the first book in the DI Jeff Lincoln series.

WHAT READERS SAY:

"What a complex plot, but very well thought out! Even though there is a large cast of characters, each was well-defined with their own balance of attractive and repelling sides, something that's not easy to achieve. Lincoln himself is very sympathetic – a 'good copper' who persists – but one who is all too human. I really liked the way the plot unpeeled, suitably messy as real life tends to be. And just when you think you've cracked it, the author throws something else in. Recommended."

"Great quality & a fantastic read."

A SAINTLY GRAVE DISTURBED

When archaeologists Beth Tarrant and Josh Good excavate a ruined chapel at Barbury Abbey, they don't expect to uncover a modern mystery too...

Finding the tomb of a medieval abbot would mean a lot to Beth. Fifty years ago, her grandfather was forced to abandon his own search for the tomb, but nobody knows why. Can Beth finish what he started?

As one incident after another threatens to sabotage the dig, Detective Inspector Jeff Lincoln is called in. When a bungled burglary at the museum turns into murder, he finds a shocking link to a case he's already investigating.

A Saintly Grave Disturbed is the second book in the DI Jeff Lincoln series.

WHAT READERS SAY:

"This book really grabs the reader's attention from the very beginning and continues to pull you in the whole way through. Perfectly paced with believable, engaging characters, an exciting storyline and lots of clues dotted throughout."

"Flawlessly written."

"If there's one thing I love, it's a book that you can read in one sitting… the book is so brilliant that I was late for a meeting because I became so engrossed in the story!"

THE SHAME OF INNOCENCE

Stage-struck teenager Emma Sherman is found dead on a Wiltshire golf course — no witnesses, no suspects. Detective Inspector Jeff Lincoln gets little help from Emma's neurotic mother, but he's sure she knows something. When explicit photos of Emma are found hidden in an abandoned summer house, Lincoln's sure they hold clues to her murder. But who was the photographer, and why doesn't Lincoln's boss want him to find out?

Days later, another teenage girl is brutally murdered, her body dumped in a country lane. The disappearance of a third teenage girl makes Lincoln realise he's facing a more dangerous enemy than he first imagined.

The Shame of Innocence is the third book in the DI Jeff Lincoln series.

WHAT READERS SAY:

"Keeps you entertained and curious right to the end."

"I was hooked from start to finish. A definitive 5* from me."

"Fast paced, with several threads of the story woven together to a clever conclusion. Gritty, and hard reading at times, but I promise you won't be able to put this book down."

THE PROMISE OF SALVATION

When little Yazmin Fletcher's bones are discovered in Wiltshire woodland twenty years after her disappearance, DI Jeff Lincoln promises Sonia, her mother, that he'll find out what happened to her. His efforts are hampered by his new boss, though, who'd rather he investigated an incident at the country club.

But then local aristocrat Hugh Buckthorn dies, apparently in a bizarre sex game, although Lincoln suspects murder — and he's soon proved right. Once a headline-grabbing playboy, Buckthorn had become a respected art historian, returning to the family seat of Greywood Hall with plans to restore its fortunes. But who wanted him dead?

Searching for Buckthorn's killer, Lincoln and his team at Barley Lane uncover a trail of fraud and deception going back decades. And then Sonia decides to take the law into her own hands...

This is the fourth book in the series featuring DI Jeff Lincoln

WHAT READERS SAY:

"What an amazing story. This is the first book I've read by this talented author and will be reading more. DI Lincoln is so well written he becomes real. There is such a strong plot with so many dodgy people ...who to believe?? It's gripping and very hard to put down. Loved it."

"The complex plot – with an additional mystery elsewhere – heads up several blind alleys and has the reader occasionally yelling 'No! Not that!' before it all becomes beautifully resolved. A very enjoyable read."

Milton Keynes UK
Ingram Content Group UK Ltd.
UKHW010405191023
430902UK00004B/34